STARGAZER

STARGAZER

Michaeal Jan Friedman

SCIENCE
FICTION

GAUNTLET Copyright © 2002 by Paramount Pictures. All Rights Reserved.
    Printing History: Pocket Books paperback May 2002

PROGENITOR Copyright © 2002 by Paramount Pictures. All Rights Reserved.
    Printing History: Pocket Books paperback May 2002

First SFBC Science Fiction Printing: May 2002

Published by arrangement with:
Pocket Books
A division of
Simon & Schuster, Inc.
1230 Avenue of the Americas
New York, New York 10020

ISBN: 0-7394-2617-6

Visit our website at *http://www.sfbc.com*
Visit Pocket Books's website at *http://www.simonsays.com/startrek/*
Visit STAR TREK's official website at *http://www.startrek.com*

Printed in the United States of America.

CONTENTS

GAUNTLET

Chapter One

Captain's personal log, supplemental.

We have arrived at Starbase 32, where Commander Gilaad Ben Zoma and I are to attend a convocation of starship captains and their executive officers. While such gatherings have rarely taken place before, our newly minted Admiral McAteer seems intent on closely coordinating the activities of all ships in his sector.

Ben Zoma thinks the entire meeting will be a waste of time—particularly the cocktail party the admiral is hosting this evening. I, on the other hand, am looking forward to the opportunity to rub elbows with my fellow captains.

No doubt there is a great deal I can learn from them . . . considering I have officially been on the job less than a week now.

JEAN-LUC PICARD, captain of the Federation starship *Stargazer*, surveyed the imposing dome-shaped room that opened before him. It was filled with a sea of crimson uniforms and gold-barred sleeves, along with several matching crimson-draped tables bearing pale bowls of Andorian punch and piles of dark brown finger sandwiches.

Glancing at his first officer, Picard said, "I don't think I've ever seen so many command officers in one place."

Ben Zoma, a man with dark good looks and a mischievous glint in his eye, smiled at the remark. "One well-placed photon torpedo and you'd wipe out half the fleet."

"Perhaps not *half,* Number One."

"Close enough," Ben Zoma insisted.

"Think of it as a unique opportunity," Picard told him. He regarded a knot of a half-dozen men and women gathered around the nearest punch bowl. "A chance to pick the brains of those more experienced at this than you or I."

Ben Zoma, like Picard, had been promoted only recently. Before being named first officer of the *Stargazer,* he had served as the vessel's chief of security.

"Follow me," the captain said, meaning to take his own advice.

Joining the group by the punch bowl, he smiled at the glances that came his way. Then, as he helped himself to some punch, he listened in on the conversation.

"Of course," said a man with red hair that had begun graying at the temples, "I had never done anything like that before. But the circumstances seemed to call for it."

A large-boned woman with dark features nodded. "I've been in that situation myself."

A second woman grunted. She didn't look like the type who smiled much, despite the youthful scattering of freckles on her face. "I think we all have," she said soberly.

"I hate to interrupt," Picard chimed in, "but what are we talking about exactly? An encounter with a hostile force? A brush with some undiscovered phenomenon?"

He sounded more gung ho than he had intended. But then, he was *feeling* rather gung ho.

That is, until the others looked at him as if he had placed his hindquarters in the punch bowl. There was an awkward silence for what seemed a long time. Then one of the officers, the man with the red hair, offered a response.

"I was talking," he said, "about putting my dog to sleep."

Picard felt his cheeks grow hot. "Yes. Yes, of course you were. How silly of me to assume otherwise."

No one replied. They just stood there, looking at him. Finally, he took the hint.

"If you'll excuse me . . ." he said rather lamely.

When no one objected to his doing so, Picard separated himself from the group and strolled to the other side of the room. Ben Zoma walked beside him, a look of bemusement on his face.

"Gilaad," Picard said to his first officer, "is it my imagination or was I just snubbed?"

Ben Zoma looked back at the group they had just left. "I'd like to tell you that it's your imagination, Jean-Luc, but I don't think I can do that."

"What I said was admittedly a bit inappropriate, given the tenor of the conversation. But it wasn't deserving of that kind of response. Someone else might even have laughed at it."

Ben Zoma nodded. "True enough."

"Then why did they react that way?" Picard asked. He looked down at his newly replicated dress uniform. "Did I put my trousers on backward this evening?"

"Your trousers are fine," his friend said. "I have a feeling it has more to do with the age of the person inside them. You *are* the greenest apple ever to take command of a Starfleet vessel."

Picard couldn't argue the point. "So I am."

At the tender age of twenty-eight, he was the youngest captain yet in the history of the fleet. Even younger than the legendary James T. Kirk, and that was saying something.

"And it's not just your age," Ben Zoma said, ticking off the strikes against the captain on his fingers. "You've never had the experience of serving as first officer. You would never have gotten your commission so quickly if Captain Ruhalter hadn't been killed in the course of a battle with hostile aliens. And—because an inexperienced whippersnapper like you couldn't *possibly* have gotten a captaincy on merit—it was probably a political appointment."

Picard grunted. "Thank you, Number One. I was beginning to actually feel capable of commanding a starship for a moment there, but you have managed to completely disabuse me of that notion."

"My pleasure," his friend told him archly. "What's a first officer for if not to deflate his captain's ego from time to time?"

"Indeed," Picard said thinly, sharing in the joke at his own expense.

He looked around the domed room again and noticed a few sidelong glances being cast in his direction. They didn't exactly look like expressions of admiration.

Perhaps Ben Zoma was right, the captain reflected. Perhaps his colleagues were looking at him differently because of his age and relative inexperience.

But if the looks on their faces were any indication, he wasn't just an object of curiosity. He was an object of disdain.

It hurt Picard to think so—even more than he would have guessed. After all, they had no firsthand observations to go on. They could only know what they had heard.

Yet these were starship captains and first officers—men and women who represented the finest the Federation had to offer. Picard would have expected them to be more welcoming of a fledgling colleague, more sensitive to his situation.

Apparently, he would have been wrong in that regard.

As was often the case, Ben Zoma seemed to read his thoughts. "All in all, not the friendliest-looking group I've ever seen."

"Nor I," Picard said. "I get the feeling I'm running a gauntlet."

"If you are, it's undeserved. You've earned your command, Jean-Luc." He jerked his head to include the other captains in the room. "Maybe more so than *they* have."

Picard didn't want to appear to feel sorry for himself, even if it was just in front of Ben Zoma. However, his colleagues' doubts weren't all that was bothering him. If they were, he could have taken the situation in stride.

Unfortunately, the glances they sent his way underlined a much more troublesome and insidious fact: the captain harbored some doubts *himself.*

Weeks earlier, when Admiral Mehdi called him into his office, he had expected the admiral to lay into him—to chew him out for the chances he had taken against the Nuyyad. Instead, Mehdi had ordained him Captain Ruhalter's successor.

Picard had been too stunned at the time to question the admiral's judgment. He had been too excited by the challenge to consider the wisdom of such a move.

But was he *qualified* to be a captain?

He had seized the reins in an emergency and brought his crew out of it alive, no question about it. But did he have the ability to command a starship over the long haul? Was he a long-distance runner . . . or just a sprinter?

"You're not saying anything," Ben Zoma pointed out. "Should I send for a doctor?"

The captain chuckled. "No, I don't think that will be necessary." He caught sight of a waiter with a tray of food. "Perhaps an hors d'oeuvre will brighten up the evening for me. I've always been partial to pigs in blankets."

His first officer looked skeptical. "Really?"

Picard smiled at him. "No. But they'll do in a pinch."

He had already embarked on an intercept course with the waiter when he felt a hand on his arm. Turning, he saw a tall fellow with a seamed face and a crew cut the color of sand.

Like Picard, he wore a captain's uniform. "Pardon me," the fellow said. "You're Jean-Luc Picard, aren't you?"

Picard nodded. "I am."

The man extended his hand. "My name's Greenbriar. Denton Greenbriar."

Picard recognized the name. Anyone would have. "The captain of the *Cochise,* isn't it?"

Greenbriar grinned, deepening the lines in his face. "I see my reputation's preceded me."

In fact, it had. Denton Greenbriar was perhaps the most decorated commanding officer in Starfleet.

Picard pulled Ben Zoma over. "Captain Greenbriar, Gilaad Ben Zoma—my executive officer."

The two shook hands. "A pleasure to meet you," Greenbriar said. He turned back to Picard. "And a pleasure to meet *you,* sir. I've heard good things about you."

"You have?" Picard responded, unable to keep from sounding surprised. Embarrassed, he smiled. "Sorry, Captain. It's just that I feel like a bit of an oddity here."

"Why's that?" asked Greenbriar. "Just because you're the youngest man ever to command a starship?"

"Well," said Picard, "yes."

"People are often not what they seem, Jean-Luc." Greenbriar took in the other men and women in the room with a glance. "Looks to me like our colleagues here have forgotten that."

"I appreciate the vote of confidence," Picard told him.

Greenbriar shrugged his broad shoulders. "Admiral Mehdi is a sharp cookie. Always has been. If he has confidence in you, I'm certain it's well deserved."

"It is," Ben Zoma agreed.

Picard felt his cheeks turn hot. He cleared his throat and said, "I'm not sure what I find more uncomfortable—the cold shoulder or the company of flatterers."

Greenbriar laughed. "That's the last bit of flattery you'll get from *me*, Captain. I promise."

And with that, he left to refill his glass.

Ben Zoma turned to Picard. "That was refreshing."

"Unfortunately," the captain replied, "it's not likely to happen again this evening."

"What do you say we find something else to do?"

Picard frowned. It was a tempting suggestion. He said as much. "Nonetheless," he continued, "I feel obliged to stick it out here a while longer."

"Your duty as a captain?" Ben Zoma asked.

Picard nodded. "Something like that, yes."

So they stayed. But, as he had predicted, no one else came near them the rest of the evening.

Not even Admiral McAteer. In fact, Picard couldn't find the man the entire evening.

Chapter Two

CARTER GREYHORSE, CHIEF MEDICAL OFFICER on the *Stargazer,* watched Gerda Asmund advance on him in her tight-fitting black garb. The navigation officer's left hand extended toward him while her right remained close to her chest, her slender fingers curled into nasty-looking claws.

"Kave'ragh!" she snarled suddenly, and her beautiful features contorted into a mask of primal aggression.

Then her right hand lashed out like an angry viper, her knuckles a blur as they headed for the center of his face. Greyhorse flinched, certain that Gerda had finally miscalculated and was about to deal him a devastating, perhaps even lethal blow. But as always, her attack fell short of its target by an inch.

Looking past Gerda's knuckles into her merciless, ice-blue eyes, Greyhorse swallowed. He didn't want to contemplate the force with which she would have driven her flattened fist into his mouth. Enough, surely, to cave in his front teeth. Enough to make him choke and sputter on his own blood.

But she had exercised restraint and pulled her punch. After all, it wasn't a battle in which they were engaged, or even a sparring session. It was just a lesson.

"Kave'ragh?" he repeated, doing his best not to completely mangle the Klingon pronunciation.

"Kave'ragh," Gerda repeated, having no trouble with the pronunciation. But then, she had been speaking the Klingon tongue from a rather early age.

The navigator stayed where she was for a moment, allowing Greyhorse to study her posture. Then she took a slow step back and retracted her fist, as if reloading a medieval crossbow.

"Now you," Gerda told him.

Greyhorse bent his knees and drew his hands into the proper position. Then he curled his fingers under at the first knuckle, exactly as she had taught him.

Gerda's eyes narrowed, but she didn't criticize him. It was a good sign. During their first few lessons, she had done nothing *but* criticize him—his balance, his coordination, even his desire to improve.

To be sure, Greyhorse wasn't the most athletic individual and never had been. When the other kids had chosen sides to play parisses squares, he had invariably been the last to be picked.

But he was big. And strong. Gerda seemed to know how to tap the power he possessed but had never made use of.

"Kave'ragh!" he bellowed, trying his best to duplicate his teacher's effort.

She spoiled his attack with an open-handed blow to the side of his wrist. It sent his fist wide of her face, where it couldn't do any harm. But at least he didn't stumble, as he had in their first few sessions. Maintaining his balance, he pulled back and reloaded.

"Kave'ragh!" he snapped again, determined to get past Gerda's defenses.

This time she hit the inside of his wrist and redirected the force of his attack upward, leaving the right side of his body woefully unguarded. Before he could move to cover the deficiency, Gerda drove her knuckles into his ribs.

Hard.

The pain made him recoil and cry out. Seeing this, Gerda shot him a look of disdain.

"Next time," she told him, "you'll do better."

He would too. And not because she had nearly cracked a rib with her counterattack. He would do better because he bitterly hated the idea of disappointing her.

The first time they had fought, in one of the *Stargazer*'s corridors, he had surprised her by getting in a lucky punch, and she had gazed at him with admiration in her eyes. It was to resurrect that moment that he endured this kind of punishment.

He didn't do it in order to become an expert in Klingon martial arts—he had no aspirations in that regard. He came to the gym three times a week and suffered contusions and bone bruises for one reason only: to force Gerda to see him as an equal. To see him as a warrior.

And eventually, if he was very diligent and very fortunate, to see him as a lover.

With this in mind, Greyhorse again assumed the basic position. Knees bent, he reminded himself. One hand forward, one hand back. Knuckles extended, so.

More important, he focused his mind. He saw himself driving his fist into his opponent's face, once, twice, and again, so quickly that his blows couldn't be parried. And he ignored the fact that it was Gerda's face he was pounding.

"Kave'ragh!" growled the doctor, a man who had never growled at anything in his life.

This time Greyhorse's attack was more effective. Gerda was unable to knock it off-line. In fact, it was only by moving her head at the last moment that she avoided injury.

He was grateful that she had. He didn't want to hurt her. He only wanted to prove to her that he could.

It was an irony he found difficult to accept—that he could only hope to win Gerda's love by demonstrating an ability to maim her. But then, the woman had been raised in a culture that made aggression a virtue. She had, to say the least, an *unusual* point of view.

Again, Greyhorse roared, *"Kave'ragh!"* and moved to strike her. Again, Gerda was unable to deflect his blow. And again, she managed to dodge anyway.

Getting closer, he told himself. She knew it, too. He could see it in her gaze, hard and implacable, demanding everything of him and giving away nothing.

Not even hope.

Yet Gerda knew how much he wanted her. She *had* to. He had blurted it out that day in the corridor.

She hadn't acknowledged it since, of course, and Greyhorse hadn't brought it up again. All they did was show up at their appointed time in the gym, teacher and pupil, master and enslaved.

"Kave'ragh!" he cried out.

Then he put everything into one last punch—too much, as it turned out, because he leaned too far forward and Gerda took painful advantage of the fact.

She didn't just elude Greyhorse's attack. She sidekicked him in the belly, knocking the wind out of him and doubling him over. Then she hit him in the back of his head with the point of her elbow, driving him to his knees.

Stunned, gasping for breath and dripping sweat, he remained on all fours for what seemed like a long time. Finally, he found the strength to drag himself to his feet.

Gerda was waiting for him with her arms folded across her chest, a lock of yellow hair dangling and a thin sheen of perspiration on her face. He had expected to find disapproval in her expression, maybe even disgust at the clumsiness he had exhibited.

But what he saw was a hint of the look she had given him in the corridor. A hint of *admiration*.

It made Greyhorse forget how Gerda had bludgeoned him, though his throat still burned and his ribs still throbbed and there was a distinctly metallic taste of blood in his mouth. In fact, it made him eager for more.

"Tomorrow?" she asked.

He nodded, inviting waves of vertigo even with that modest gesture. "I'll be here."

Gerda tilted her head slightly, as if to appraise him better. She remained that way for a moment, piercing his soul with her eyes. Then she turned her back on him, pulled a towel off the rack on the wall, and left the gym.

Greyhorse watched her go. She moved with animal grace, each muscle working in perfect harmony with all the others. When the doors hissed closed behind her, he felt as if he had lost a part of himself.

How he loved her.

Chief Weapons Officer Vigo looked at his friend Charlie Kochman, contemplating the experience they had just shared. Then he broke out in a broad, toothy grin.

"You like it?" Kochman asked.

"I like it a great deal," Vigo told him.

"Thought you would."

Vigo considered the wooden sharash'di game board that sat between them, with its skillfully carved terrain and its clever simulations of various natural features. It was really quite a work of art—the kind the ship's lounge seldom saw.

But the game itself . . . it was like nothing he had ever played before, either on his homeworld of Pandril or anywhere else. And he couldn't wait to play it again.

"And you say you picked this up on Beta Nopterix?" he asked.

"Uh-huh. From an Yridian. He wanted to sell me the game, so he taught me how to play. Interesting, eh?"

Vigo nodded. "Quite interesting."

Kochman, who was one of the ship's navigators, smiled back at him. "And guess what, buddy? It's yours."

Vigo didn't understand. "Mine?"

"That's right. It's a birthday gift."

The weapons officer held up his large blue hands. "I can't accept it. We don't celebrate our birth anniversaries on Pandril."

"But we celebrate them on Earth," Kochman reminded him. "And as my friend, I can't imagine that you'd deprive me of the opportunity to celebrate *yours.*"

When he put it that way, it was hard for Vigo to turn him down. "I don't know what to say," he said.

"Say thank you," his friend advised.

Vigo looked down at the board, then flashed another expression of delight. "Thank you, Charlie. Thank you very much."

Idun Asmund, the *Stargazer*'s primary helm officer, was almost finished with her dinner when she saw Pug Joseph approaching her with a tray of food.

As Joseph got closer, steam from his meal wafting in front of him, he seemed to notice that Idun's plate was already empty. "Aw, geez," the baby-faced, sandy-haired security officer said, making no effort to conceal his disappointment.

She looked up at him. "Lieutenant?"

"It's all right," he told her stoically. "I guess we can talk some other time."

There wasn't anything that demanded Idun's attention at the moment. "What was it you wished to talk about?"

Joseph set his tray down and pulled out a chair opposite the helm officer's. Then he looked around to make sure no one in the mess hall was listening too closely.

"Actually," he said, leaning forward, "I wanted to talk to you about your voice."

Idun wasn't sure what she had expected the security officer to ask, but that wasn't it. "My voice?"

Joseph nodded enthusiastically. "You've got a way of making people listen when you speak. Your sister has it too. I want them to listen to *me* that way."

"In my experience," Idun said, "people *do* listen when you speak. You're widely liked, Mr. Joseph."

"Liked," he conceded. "But not respected. And a security chief has to be respected."

Security *chief?* Now Idun was *really* confused.

She knew that Lieutenant Ang was leaving the *Stargazer* to accept a second officer's post on the *Sutherland*. However, she hadn't heard that Joseph would be succeeding him as security chief.

And now that she knew, she thought it a rash choice. Although Joseph was one of the more senior officers in the security section, he had never exhibited any particular affinity for command.

What's more, he seemed to be aware of his deficit—but to be fair, he was trying to address it, if in an unusual way.

"So you've been named our new security chief," she concluded.

Joseph blushed and shook his head. "Not permanently, mind you. It's only a temporary assignment until the captain can find a replacement for Lieutenant Ang."

Idun felt better about that. It wasn't that she didn't like Joseph or trust him implicitly, or that she would have hesitated for a moment to give him her back in a firefight.

It was only his ability to lead that the helm officer questioned. Nothing else.

"I see," she said.

"Anyway," he plunged on, "about your voice . . . do you have any tricks you might be able to share with me? Or . . . I don't know, suggestions?"

Idun thought about it. "I don't think so," she said at last. "I don't use any tricks. I just *speak.*"

Again, Joseph seemed disappointed. "Right. I just thought you might . . ." He shrugged. "Never mind. Thanks anyway."

"You're welcome," she said. But she wished that she could have been of more help.

* * *

Phigus Simenon was a Gnalish, a lizardlike being from a world called Gnala, who stood as high as the shoulders of most human males. He was also the *Stargazer*'s chief engineering officer.

Usually, Simenon could be found in the engineering section, scrabbling over the controls of a sleek, dark console. At the moment, however, he was in his quarters, studying the image of an old friend and former colleague on his computer monitor.

"Hans Werber," he observed with his customary sibilance.

The man who had been the *Stargazer*'s weapons chief nodded. "Good to see you again, Phigus."

"Where are you?" Simenon asked.

Werber smiled beneath his walrus mustache, his blue eyes dancing. "New Zealand. Not a bad place, actually. If you've got to be in a penal colony, you might as well be in *this* one."

"And they give you the run of the place?"

Werber shrugged. "I'm wearing an electronic anklet. It's not as if I can go very far."

"I see," said Simenon.

"How's Picard?"

"Well enough. He's at a meeting at the moment. Captains and second officers from all over the sector."

"Really. That's unusual."

Simenon nodded. "Very."

Werber swatted suddenly at his balding head, then inspected his palm and brushed his hands together. "Damned insects. You forget how annoying they can be when you're on a starship."

"I'll take your word for it."

"You know," said Werber, "I was wrong about Picard. I had him pegged as the vindictive type. But you know what he did?"

"What?" Simenon asked.

"He came to my cell at Starfleet Command and told me he'd put in a word on my behalf with the judge advocate general. He said that I put our differences aside and helped him."

"You mean *after* you entered his room in the dead of night and tried to stun him with a phaser beam."

Werber chuckled at the irony, his eyes crinkling at the corners. "Yeah. *After.* But the thing is Picard forgave me. He let bygones be bygones. Which, I'll bet, is why I'm doing short time here in New Zealand instead of life on some high-security asteroid."

"You're probably right," Simenon told him.

"Anyway," Werber said, "I thought I'd let you know where I am. You know, so we can talk from time to time. No friend like an old friend, I always say."

"I'd be happy to correspond with you," the Gnalish replied. "More than happy. That is, if I still considered myself your friend."

The man's brows met over the bridge of his nose. "What?"

"When you betrayed Picard, you betrayed me too," Simenon said. "I went charging into his office, accusing him of incarcerating you for no good reason. Then he told me about your little mutiny."

"But Picard's *forgiven* me for that," Werber reminded him.

"He may have," Simenon snapped, "but *I* haven't. Good-bye, Hans. Enjoy New Zealand."

And with that, he cut the comm link.

Old friend indeed, the Gnalish thought feeling a single deep pang of remorse. Then, glad that it was almost time for his shift, he made his way to engineering.

Chapter Three

AS JEAN-LUC PICARD WALKED into the dimly lit briefing room, he had an entirely different attitude than the one with which he had gone to bed the night before.

Having slept on the problem, he had woken up certain that there was only one course of action open to him. Despite the disdain he saw in the faces of his fellow captains, despite their obvious disapproval, he would do his best to earn their respect.

He would comport himself with dignity. He would do what was asked of him quickly and efficiently, deploying every resource at his disposal. In short, he would be the best captain he could be.

But if he came up short in that regard, he wouldn't fret over the outcome or let it distract him. He would simply accept the situation and move on.

He had a job to do, and a rather important job at that. If it bothered people that he had been chosen to do it, it was *their* problem—not *his*.

Scanning the room, Picard found himself searching the shadows for a friendly face. Captain Greenbriar's was the only one that might have fit that description, but Greenbriar didn't seem to have arrived yet.

Looks like I'm on my own, Picard thought.

He didn't even have Ben Zoma for company. His friend had transported down to the base forty-five minutes earlier for a separate first officers' briefing.

Picking out the nearest unoccupied chair, Picard deposited himself in it. He found himself shoulder to shoulder with a rail-thin Vulcan, who turned to glance at him with narrowed eyes.

Picard smiled as cordially as he could. "Good morning."

The Vulcan didn't say anything in reply. He just inclined his head in the smallest gesture possible, then returned his attention to the unmanned podium at the front of the room.

Somehow, Picard reflected, being snubbed by a Vulcan didn't seem as objectionable as being snubbed by someone else. Maybe it was because they were so reserved to begin with.

Someday, he told himself, *I would like to get to know a Vulcan better. Get inside his head, as it were.*

Putting the thought aside, he looked around some more. The stream of captains passing through the open doorway was rapidly increasing in volume. No doubt, they were nearing the time when the briefing was scheduled to begin.

Greenbriar was among the last to walk in. He took a seat on the other side of the room, between an Andorian and a heavy-tusked Vobilite.

A moment later, a stocky man in an admiral's uniform blew into the room, stopped behind the podium, and turned on a light that illuminated his face. He had lively eyes, a ruddy complexion, and a receding shock of pale-yellow hair.

"Good to see you all," he said in a deep, resonant voice that required no microphone. "For those of you who haven't run into me yet, I'm Admiral McAteer. I considered attending the cocktail party last night, but I decided you'd have a better time without the boss looking over your shoulders."

A ripple of laughter made its way through the gathering.

Picard thought it strange that McAteer hadn't attended his own event. On the other hand, he was relieved to know he wasn't the only one who had been unable to find the man.

McAteer appeared to sober a bit. "I know you're not used to meeting this way. Until now, you've all been pretty much on your own, operating independently except in the rare instance where two or three of you might need to coordinate your efforts."

The rare instance indeed, Picard mused.

"I'm afraid," said the admiral, "that such an approach is no longer viable. The galaxy is too big and our responsibilities too great for any of you to continue operating in a vacuum—no pun intended."

Again, there was a ripple of laughter.

"From now on," McAteer told them, "we're going to get together like this periodically. That way, we can approach our workload in an organized and logical manner."

Picard sampled his colleagues' reactions. The Vulcan beside him was nodding his head in quiet agreement, but many of the other captains seemed less than enthusiastic.

Ruhalter, Picard's predecessor, would have come down firmly in the latter group. Picard had no doubt of that. Ruhalter was a man who had preferred to respond instinctively, avoiding meetings and planning sessions as much as possible.

If the same topic was being discussed in the first officers' briefing, Ben Zoma would be resisting it as well. Picard had no doubt of that either.

Nor could he help agreeing with his predecessor and his exec.

Captains had always been chosen for their ability to act on their own. It was the strength of the fleet, indeed one of the principles on which it had been built, and it didn't seem wise to inhibit it.

On the other hand, McAteer was the man Starfleet had put in charge of this sector. If he thought it was time for something new, Picard would at least try to keep an open mind about it.

The admiral looked out over his audience. "I've made up a list of missions that we need to tackle. The first one—and the most critical—is the capture of the pirate known as the White Wolf."

McAteer's announcement fell like a stone into the midst of the assembled captains. In the ripples of silence that followed, Picard saw his colleagues exchanging glances.

He had no trouble understanding why.

"For the last two years," McAteer said, "the White Wolf and his crew have raided Federation cargo ships left and right. And every time we've sent a Starfleet vessel after him, he's managed to elude us by hiding in one of the odd features of Beta Barritus—which, as you'll note, is rather a unique system by anyone's reckoning."

As he finished his sentence, he manipulated the controls before him and created a hologram to one side of the podium. It was a computerized representation of the Beta Barritus system—a sun surrounded by a thick layer of gases and who knew what else.

But then, Beta Barritus was a Lazarus star—one that had burned out and somehow resurrected itself. It couldn't help but present an unusual set of problems to anyone seeking to plumb its depths.

Which was why the White Wolf, a man reputedly named for the color of his hair as well as his resourcefulness, had picked Beta Barritus as his favorite hiding place.

"Until this point in time," the admiral told the assembled captains, "the apprehension of the White Wolf has been a low priority for us. That changes as of this moment."

Picard wondered why that might be. McAteer didn't take long to satisfy his curiosity.

"His latest attack on a defenseless transport vessel took place less than a week ago. It netted him a cargo of exotic flora from Elekiwi Prime." The admiral scowled. "I think you all know how difficult it is to extract anything from that world—and how valuable such cargo can be to our research people at Starfleet Medical."

Picard nodded. Elekiwi Prime was a dying world, increasingly beleaguered by volcanic eruptions and resulting clouds of carbon dioxide. A team of scientists had risked their lives to obtain the flora samples in question, knowing that plant life wouldn't survive conditions on the planet much longer.

"Someone has to go after the White Wolf and attempt to recover the cargo," McAteer said, his voice steely with resolve. "But even if recovery is no longer possible, I want to end the menace of this pirate once and for all."

He had barely finished his sentence when half a dozen hands went up. *Volunteers,* Picard thought. No doubt they included the captains who had been thwarted by the White Wolf in the past. If he were one of them, he too would have wished to settle the score.

Picard studied the hologram of the White Wolf's hiding place. Beta Barritus appeared to be a complex system indeed. It presented the kind of obstacles Picard had heard about, even read about, but had never personally encountered.

If the captains who had hunted the White Wolf were any judges, the man was impossible to find, much less apprehend. And if his colleagues wanted the assignment that badly, he would do his best not to stand in their way.

"I appreciate your eagerness," McAteer told them. "I understand how important it is to you to bring the White Wolf to justice. But I think we need a new approach to the problem."

A new approach? Picard repeated inwardly. He wondered what the admiral had in mind.

He was still wondering when McAteer turned to him and smiled like a fox noticing an unguarded henhouse. "Captain Picard," he said, "I'm giving *you* this job."

Picard turned red in the face. *Me?* he thought.

Apparently, he wasn't the only one inclined to question McAteer's choice, if the stares and the muttered comments that followed were any indication. Obviously, his fellow captains were wondering why McAteer might tap a man who had been a mere second officer a month earlier over a wide assortment of seasoned veterans.

The White Wolf had beaten the best the fleet had to offer. How was a green apple going to do what those other captains couldn't?

Picard would have liked to hear what the admiral had to say in that regard. But McAteer wasn't offering any explanations at the moment. He was just standing there, staring at his youngest captain as if awaiting the man's response.

Picard gave the only one he could. "I hope to prove myself worthy of your confidence."

The admiral nodded. "I've no doubt of it."

Then he went on to dole out the other assignments. In each case, he discussed the difficulties of the mission and what Starfleet stood to gain by it. But Picard barely heard him. He was still trying to figure out what he had done to deserve the White Wolf.

Mollie Katz had served as a Starfleet transporter operator for more than thirty years, first on a series of space-spanning starships named *Phoenix* and *Exeter* and *Yorktown,* and now here at Starbase 32. In the course of her long career, she had met with more than her share of unusual transports.

But never anything like this.

The customized gray-and-white containment suit and matching helmet had been Katz's first clue. The second had been the ghostly visage visible through the helmet's transparent faceplate.

But even as the figure stepped up onto the transporter platform, Katz hadn't imagined the challenges with which she would be presented— challenges she was even now trying to meet as she made careful adjustments to her control settings.

Three humans stood to one side of the transporter operator, all of them Starfleet personnel, alternately watching Katz work at her console and gazing at the figure on the platform. They seemed curious, no more than that.

But it had to be a lonely thing for the being inside the containment suit. It had to be hard to endure the scrutiny of others when you were so different from them, so different from anyone within a radius of several light-years.

At last Katz felt certain that her settings were what they should be. Programming in the requisite destination coordinates, she obtained a lock on the place. Then she activated the targeting scanners and verified range and relative motion, which, fortunately for her subject, were both minimal.

Checking the diagnostics monitor in the upper left quadrant of her panel, she saw that the system was functioning well within acceptable parameters. *So far so good,* the operator told herself.

Normally this would have been the point at which the transporter's molecular imaging scanners came on-line. However, Katz had already been using the scanners for the last several minutes to get an idea of what she was dealing with.

She directed the primary energizing coils to generate an annular confinement beam, which would be used in a little while. Then, with painstaking care, she encouraged the phase transition coils to convert the subject into a subatomically debonded matter stream.

This was the tricky part, the part she would at other times have left to the computer but felt compelled in this instance to carry out on her own. It wasn't that she thought she could be more exact than an electronic device. It was that if something went wrong, she had more faith in her own ability to correct it.

Come on, she thought, watching the debonded matter migrate to the system's pattern buffer. Get in there, and I mean now.

Up on the platform, the subject would be vanishing in a sparkling column of light—containment suit and all. But the transporter operator didn't have the luxury of watching the spectacle. She was too intent on her instruments, too busy with the minutiae of the matter storage process to allow herself even the slightest distraction.

Almost done, she thought. *Almost there.* Seventy-five percent, to be more precise. Eighty. Eighty-five . . .

A bead of perspiration trickled down her forehead, but she ignored it and continued to monitor the matter stream, hands on her controls in case she had to abort the process or take some other emergency measure.

Finally, after what seemed like an eternity, Katz saw the blinking green stud that verified the subject's safe arrival in the system's pattern buffer. Taking a deep breath, she let it out and gave herself permission to relax for a moment.

But only for a moment.

Then she bent to her task again and projected the annular confinement beam from the starbase's emitter array to the target coordinates. It was within the dimensions of this beam that the subject's debonded matter would travel.

Next, the operator transmitted the matter from the buffer to the emitter. Once there, it was ready to make the journey across the void of empty space.

Here goes, she thought.

And she sent the accumulated matter streaming along the confinement beam to its destination.

Katz was certain that she had done everything right. Still, she found herself staring at her instrument panel, willing it to tell her that the process would end as it was supposed to—with the subject's safe arrival and rematerialization.

Because under the most perfect conditions, one never knew—and these conditions were far from perfect.

The seconds ticked by, more of them than Katz had expected. Her teeth had begun to grind together by the time she saw the words she was hoping for: *transport successful.*

In the privacy of her mind, the operator patted herself on the back. That hadn't been easy. In fact, she wouldn't complain if that was the last such transport she was called on to make.

At last, she wiped the perspiration from her brow with the back of her hand and reset her instruments to more conventional levels. Then, turning to the trio standing next to her, she said, "Next."

As they stepped up onto the platform, Katz wished the being in the containment suit good luck. She would need it.

It wasn't until after McAteer had turned up the lights and adjourned the meeting that Picard had a chance to buttonhole him. It wasn't difficult to do so. In fact, the admiral seemed to have been expecting the captain's approach.

"You're wondering why I asked you to go after our friend the White Wolf," McAteer concluded.

"I am," Picard confirmed.

"I don't blame you," the admiral said. "In your position, I'd be wondering the same thing."

He took the captain's arm and guided him to an observation port at the far end of the room. Apparently, he wanted to conduct their conversation where others wouldn't overhear it.

"I picked you for the mission," McAteer told him, "because conventional methods haven't worked with the White Wolf. Your predecessor, Captain Ruhalter, was known for his resourcefulness, his ability to think on his feet. I'm betting that those qualities rubbed off on you."

In fact, Picard didn't think of himself as particularly resourceful. However, he refrained from saying so.

"I'll try not to let you down," he said.

The admiral chuckled. "Modesty. I like that. Then it'll look even better when you nail the bastard."

It wasn't modesty that had compelled the captain to frame his response that way. It was a sense of proportion. But he didn't tell McAteer that either.

"If you say so," he told the admiral.

Chapter Four

AS PICARD MATERIALIZED on the *Stargazer*'s transporter platform alongside his first officer, he noted that it was Lieutenant Refsland manning the facility's transporter console.

Refsland was his section chief, the most experienced of his several transporter operators. Picard always felt a little more secure in Refsland's hands.

Normally the man greeted him with a smile and a single word of greeting: "Captain." But not this time, Picard noticed. *This* time, Refsland appeared to have something on his mind.

"Something wrong?" the captain asked.

"I'm not sure, sir," Refsland told him.

"Not sure?" Picard echoed.

Refsland shrugged. "About half an hour ago, we received the new crewmen, sir. Seven of them, to be exact."

The captain found himself making a face. *New crewmen? What new crewmen?* "I haven't authorized any additions to the crew," he informed the transporter chief.

Refsland sighed. "I was afraid you were going to say that."

Picard glanced at Ben Zoma. "Gilaad?"

"Don't look at me," his friend said. "I didn't authorize any new additions either."

Certainly, Picard thought, there were berths to be filled after the casualties inflicted on them by the Nuyyad, and replacements to be arranged for officers who had subsequently left the ship. He and Ben Zoma had even considered some candidates, though they hadn't made any final decisions yet.

"Actually, sir," said an uncomfortable-looking Refsland, "the orders came from Admiral McAteer. He said you wouldn't object."

Picard scowled. *"McAteer* said that?"

"Aye, sir. He said you wouldn't want to be bothered. Otherwise, we would have contacted you immediately."

The captain had no doubt of it. The officers he had left in charge were both loyal and efficient. They wouldn't have accepted the transport if it hadn't come from a higher authority.

Placing his hand on his first officer's shoulder, Picard said, "You take care of our new crewmen. I think I need to have a word with our friend the admiral."

Then, doing his best to contain his anger, he made his way to his ready room.

Lieutenant Kochman stared at his friend Vigo across the sharash'di board. *"Another* one?"

Vigo reset the board, as oblivious to the look of discomfort on his friend's face as he was to everything else in the ship's lounge. "You go first and fourth this time."

Kochman sighed. "That's very nice of you, but . . ."

Vigo looked up. "Yes?"

The navigator held his hands up in an appeal for reason. "We've been playing for four hours straight, pal. I need a break."

Vigo blinked. "Three and a half, actually."

Kochman shot him a look.

"But," Vigo added, "that's very *nearly* four."

"I go on duty in an hour," Kochman continued. "I need to eat, wash up, grab a clean uniform . . ."

"As you should," Vigo said reasonably. "And now that you mention it, I have things to do as well. The last thing I want is to spend all my time playing a game."

But his expression said otherwise.

Kochman frowned. Little had he known what a monster he was creating when he gave his pal the sharash'di board for his birthday. *Or for that matter,* he added silently, *what a genius.*

Vigo had the same kind of knack for sharash'di that he did for weapons technology. He didn't just grasp the subject, he bonded with it—brain and muscle and bone. He *lived* it.

"You know," Kochman said, "you don't have to stop on my account. If you want, you can go on playing."

The weapons officer seemed to understand his friend's meaning. "You're suggesting I play with someone else?"

Kochman shrugged. "Well, yeah."

Vigo took in the room at a glance. "I suppose I could," he said after a while. "I would just have to teach them the game." He smiled, enthused again. "But if I could learn it, they can too."

Kochman doubted that anyone would embrace sharash'di as much as the weapons officer had. However, someone might at least give him a run for his money.

"This is what I'm saying," he told Vigo.

The Pandrilite nodded. "I think I'll follow your advice."

"Good," said Kochman, feeling a wave of relief wash over him. "Let me know how it goes, okay?"

And with that, he made good his escape.

Picard took several deep breaths before he was calm enough to proceed. Then, opting not to get his communications officer involved, he established a comm link with McAteer's office. After a second or two, the admiral's assistant appeared on the screen.

"I'd like to speak with Admiral McAteer," the captain said.

The assistant, a young man with a blond crew cut and a ruddy complexion, promised to tell McAteer that there was a call for him. Seeing the Starfleet logo come up on his screen, Picard had no choice but to wait.

As it turned out, he didn't have to wait long. But McAteer looked vaguely annoyed as he appeared on the screen, as if Picard had interrupted something important.

"Is there something I can do for you, Captain?"

Indeed there is, Picard thought. "You can help me understand something, Admiral. I've just been informed that several new crewmen have beamed aboard the *Stargazer.*"

McAteer shrugged. "As I understood it, you had several openings, owing to casualties in the course of your last mission."

It was true. Seven crewmen, including Captain Ruhalter, had died in their clash with the Nuyyad.

Also, they had lost their weapons officer, who had led a mutiny against then–Acting Captain Picard and been incarcerated as a result. And just before the *Stargazer* reached Starbase 32, Sciences Chief Angela Cariello had decided to leave the fleet to join her husband at an agricultural colony, and Security Chief Ang had accepted a position on the *Sutherland.*

"Nonetheless," Picard said, "it is highly irregular for a captain to have crewmen handed to him by a superior officer. As you know, sir, the normal procedure is for a commanding officer to review applications at his leisure before making any personnel decisions."

The admiral frowned at the remark. "I'm well aware of Starfleet procedures, Captain."

"Then you won't be surprised to learn that Commander Ben Zoma and I are already focusing on at least one candidate—a fellow who comes from a long-standing Starfleet tradition. His grandfather was an admiral, his aunt is on her way to becoming one, and his elder brother is currently serving with distinction on the *Exeter."*

McAteer looked as if he was going to cut Picard's comments short. However, the captain didn't give him the opportunity.

"He has also posted dazzling grades at the Academy, been described by his professors as driven, bright, and capable, and served as captain of the parisses squares team that beat a squad of Academy alumni just prior to graduation."

The admiral knew who he was, of course. Picard could tell by the look in his eyes.

"Frankly, sir," he continued, "I cannot imagine anyone more qualified to join the crew of the *Stargazer."*

McAteer's eyes narrowed. "Sign him on, then, Captain. Sign on anyone you want. Get rid of anyone you *don't* want. But do it *after* you catch the White Wolf. For the time being, I'd say you need all the help you can get—and that includes those seven new crewmen who have beamed aboard your starship."

"But, sir—"

"That's an order," McAteer told him.

Picard didn't like the idea, but the admiral wasn't giving him any choice in the matter. "As you say, sir."

McAteer nodded. "Again, good luck to you. McAteer out."

A moment later, his image winked off the viewscreen and was replaced by the Starfleet logo. The captain glared at it, then tapped the combadge on his chest.

"Navigation, this is Command—" He stopped abruptly, deeply embarrassed by the slip. "This is *Captain* Picard. Set a course for the Beta Barritus system."

"Aye, sir," came Gerda Asmund's reply.

"Helm," he went on, "take us out of here. Half impulse until we clear the base."

"Aye, sir," said Idun.

Through his ready room's lone observation port, Picard could see the hourglass shape of Starbase 32 receding in the distance, shrinking rapidly against the star-pricked darkness. In a matter of moments, it disappeared altogether.

Taking Admiral McAteer with it. *And none too soon,* the captain reflected angrily.

He sat in his chair a moment longer, trying to deal with his resentment. Only when he felt he had it under control did he get up and leave his ready room.

Picard reminded himself that there were seven new crewmen aboard the *Stargazer.* It wasn't *their* fault they had been foisted on an unwilling captain.

Chapter Five

ENSIGN ANDREAS NIKOLAS PRESSED the padd in the bulkhead next to his quarters, watched the duranium doors slide apart, and went inside to examine his home away from home.

Nikolas had served on other starships of this class, so he had a pretty good idea of what awaited him. He wasn't disappointed. Two beds, a couple of computer terminals, two chairs, two tiny closets, one bathroom door.

And one roommate.

In this case, the last item was of the tall, broad-shouldered, and clean-cut variety. He was in the latter stages of making his bed when Nikolas walked in on him.

The guy straightened, smiled, and held out his hand. "Guess we're going to be roommates," he said, his blue eyes twinkling beneath dark, close-cropped hair.

"Guess so," Nikolas returned. He shook the fellow's hand. "Andreas Nikolas—but my friends call me Nik. And you?"

"Joe Caber." The grin behind the words was as white and perfect as they came.

Caber, Caber . . . It sounded familiar. "Where have I heard that name before?" Nikolas wondered.

The other man looked a little uncomfortable. "My father's Neil Caber. You know, the admiral?"

Nikolas snapped his fingers. "I knew I'd heard it somewhere." He considered Caber in the light of this new information. "So you're on a fast track."

His roommate shrugged. He looked a little embarrassed. "I sure as heck hope so. I'd like to be a captain someday."

You and every crewman from here to the Neutral Zone, Nikolas thought. "And how're you doing so far?"

Caber didn't seem eager to talk about himself. Still, he answered Nikolas's question. "From what I can tell, just fine. I was second in my graduating class at the Academy. And my stint on the *Mediterranean* couldn't have worked out any better."

Obviously, Caber was a shoo-in. He'd be sitting in a center seat by his thirty-fifth birthday.

Nikolas turned his attention to his unmade bed, so the other man wouldn't see the look of bitterness on his face. "They thought *I'd* be captain material too, once upon a time."

Caber smiled, but it was the kind of smile that tried to mask pity. "And you're not anymore?"

"I got in some trouble," Nikolas told him. Of course, that was a bit of an understatement.

"Everyone gets in trouble *sometime,*" Caber said.

"I got in trouble a *lot,*" Nikolas expanded. "At the Academy they said I was reckless and headstrong. And I had a . . ." He dredged up the words they had used in his personnel file. ". . . a penchant for unbridled honesty, which was their polite way of saying I couldn't keep my damned mouth shut."

"That's not necessarily a bad thing," the other man allowed.

Nikolas chuckled. "Tell the folks at the Academy. They decided I'd be lucky not to get my butt kicked off the first ship whose captain was dumb enough to take me."

"Prove them wrong," Caber advised. No doubt, that's what *he* would have done.

The problem, Nikolas reflected, was that the Academy people were right. He was everything they said he was—stubborn, impulsive, ill-equipped to work within a command structure.

He wished he could be more of a Caber type. He wished he could be confident and cooperative, following a clear-cut path to a captain's chair.

But that wasn't the hand he had been dealt. He was who he was. And if he couldn't be a starship captain, he would be whatever fate had in store for him.

"Hey," Nikolas said, "you hungry?"

His roommate smiled that perfect smile. "I'm *always* hungry."

"Then what do you say we head down to the mess hall and see what's on the menu?"

"I say let's go," Caber told him.

"I'm already there," Nikolas said. Leaving his bed unmade, he led the way to the mess hall.

Dikembe Ulelo walked along the corridor next to his superior, Communications Chief Martin Paxton.

Paxton, a man with curly brown hair, was giving Ulelo a tour of the *Stargazer.* "You'll like it here," he said. "Captain Picard's as sharp as they come. And he treats his people well."

"That's good to hear," Ulelo responded.

But his attention was focused on the power-supply junction just ahead of them, its location easily identifiable by the little door set flush with the bulkhead. It was the second such junction they had passed since leaving the turbolift.

Ulelo's previous assignment had been on the *Copernicus,* an *Oberth*-class vessel. The *Copernicus* had had twelve power-supply junctions on each deck.

"You'll work the graveyard shift, of course." Paxton smiled sympathetically at him. "Just as I did when I was low man on the totem pole. But just for a few weeks. Then we'll all take turns."

"Of course," said Ulelo.

"So what do you like?"

Ulelo looked at him. "Like?"

"You know," said Paxton. "Food, hobbies, interests . . . ?"

"Ah." Ulelo thought for a moment, but nothing came to mind. "I don't have any real preferences."

Paxton seemed surprised. "Really?"

"Yes. Why do you ask?"

"Most people have pretty distinct likes and dislikes. Me, for instance,

I'm a coffee man. Can't wake up without it. And when it comes to hobbies, I'm a medieval history buff."

"I like to try *new* things," Ulelo said, hoping that would assuage his superior's curiosity.

Paxton nodded. "Then you're going to like it here even more. We've got some really exotic tastes on board. Take Vigo, for instance—our weapons officer. He eats this Pandrilite stuff that looks like beach sand mixed with ground glass. Swears by it. Personally, I have trouble even *looking* at it."

He laughed. Ulelo took that as his cue to laugh too.

They came to a place where the corridor crossed another corridor. Paxton turned right. So did Ulelo—at which point he saw the set of double doors at the end of the corridor.

Paxton pointed to them. "Next stop, engineering."

Ulelo nodded. There would be many things to see in engineering. Many things to learn.

"I can't wait," he said.

Carter Greyhorse was sitting at his computer terminal, going over his list of scheduled medical examinations, when his first patient of the day walked in.

She was wearing a complete Starfleet-issue containment suit, domed helmet and all. That alone set her apart from anyone else who had ever visited Greyhorse's sickbay.

But even stranger-looking was her face—if indeed it could even be *called* a face. It seemed vague, insubstantial as he viewed it through the helmet's curved, transparent faceplate, and there was only a suggestion in it of humanoid features.

She looked around for a moment, her movements stiff and awkward in the suit. Finally, she spotted Greyhorse and crossed sickbay to get to him.

As the doctor got up and came out of his office enclosure, he forced himself not to stare. But it was difficult not to. He had been looking forward to this moment from the time the newcomers beamed aboard—one of them with more trouble than the rest.

"You're Ensign Jiterica, I take it?"

"Yes," came the reply—not an actual voice but a mechanical simulation, generated by a vocalizer in the containment suit. It sounded flat, tinny, and oddly paced. "I'm here for—"

"Your exam," he said, "yes. This way, please."

Greyhorse indicated the nearest biobed, which was just outside his enclosure. He had just recalibrated it the day before.

"Have a seat," he told Jiterica.

The doctor waited for her to reach the biobed and sit down—a clumsy affair at best, given the bulk of the containment suit. Then he activated the bed's biofunction monitors, ran a routine diagnostic, and examined the monitors in front of him.

Normally they would have shown Greyhorse the status of his patient's vital functions, each of them represented by a vertical white bar against a dark blue field. In this case, the bars refused to appear. In their place, a message came up: *Reset parameters.*

Clearly the bed was baffled—and that wouldn't change even if the doctor spent his whole day resetting parameters. The device was simply incapable of tracking Jiterica's life signs.

Nor was Greyhorse surprised.

After all, his patient wasn't a creature of flesh and blood like everyone else serving on the *Stargazer.* Jiterica was an anomaly in the annals of Starfleet personnel—a being made up of nothing more than positive ions and electrons.

Her species, the Nizhrak'a, was native to Nizhara, a gas giant in the Sonada Sin system. They were low-density, plasmalike life-forms held together by powerful psychokinetic forces, nature's response to the crush of gravity and atmospheric pressure—not to mention the vicious and volatile radiation fields—that prevailed on the ensign's planet.

The Nizhrak'a were also immense—in some cases, almost as big as the *Stargazer* herself. But they could condense themselves when necessary. The ensign, for example, could pour herself into a containment suit and move through what must have seemed to her a warren of tiny spaces.

According to Jiterica's medical file, she possessed all of the biological systems—nervous, digestive, ambulatory, circulatory, sensory, and so on—found in any humanoid life-form. However, the configurations of charged particles that comprised these systems were so spread out and seemingly unrelated as to render them unrecognizable to the sensors in the biobed.

The only part of Jiterica that approached the description of a solid was the particle membrane that served as her outer skin. It gave her body shape and definition, and kept it from being ripped apart by her world's arsenal of savage, high-velocity winds.

Like every other part of her anatomy, she could psychokinetically control this membrane down to the subatomic level. That was what allowed Jiterica to assume a more or less human form and facial features, which she had been advised would minimize the differences between herself and the rest of the crew.

So why did she need a Starfleet containment suit? For several reasons, Greyhorse had learned.

First, Jiterica couldn't maintain her condensed form for long. The suit, which was specially equipped with an electromagnetic reinforcement field, enabled her to remain in a tightly packed state indefinitely without placing undue strain on her resources.

Second, the ensign's physiology was designed for maneuvering in the roiling, nightmarish atmosphere of a gas giant, not the relatively narrow corridors of a Federation starship. The suit enabled her to move as her fellow crewmen moved—on foot, in a predictable direction, and at a reasonable rate of speed—thanks to a sensor-motor technology developed specifically with the Nizhrak'a in mind. All Jiterica had to do was generate an electrical shock in a particular part of the suit's sensor net, and its motor grid would do the rest.

The containment suit's third virtue was that it maintained a felicitous environment for its wearer, simulating the kind of gravity, air pressure, and atmosphere one was likely to encounter on her world. Jiterica could have survived without these benefits, especially for a short period of time, but over the long haul it made her existence on the *Stargazer* much easier to bear.

Last, the suit enabled Jiterica to communicate. By stimulating her vocalizer with a variety of electrical shocks—much as she did to achieve locomotion—the ensign could make use of a limited vocabulary. If the doctor recalled correctly, she had more than two hundred Federation-standard words and phrases at her disposal.

Likewise, a device under her helmet received the spoken word and translated it into electrical signals. That way, Jiterica could "hear" information as well as convey it.

Of course, she could have achieved neither speech nor movement without hours of rigorous training at Starfleet headquarters in San Francisco. Greyhorse could only imagine how difficult those hours must have been. How exhausting.

How utterly frustrating.

He asked himself if he could have learned to live among Jiterica's people, amid the hellish, howling tumult of a gas giant. *Not even for a moment,* he decided.

So why had Jiterica put herself to all this trouble, exposed herself to all this pain? What did she hope to gain?

The answer, like many answers, lay in the always arcane realm of interstellar politics.

As Greyhorse understood it, Nizhara wasn't a Federation member world. However, the Federation was courting it for its strategic location near Cardassian space.

Jiterica's presence in Starfleet was therefore something of a trial run—an attempt to see if Nizhrak'a and humanoids could establish a mutually beneficial relationship. To this point, the experiment hadn't gone very well.

The ensign's previous commanding officer, Captain Cepeda of the *Manitou,* had observed that the ensign was unhappy under his command. Worse, he projected for the record that she would be unhappy on *any* ship in the fleet. He said that Jiterica hadn't sought a discharge for one simple reason—her enduring belief that her people would benefit from Federation membership.

Apparently she was willing to suffer a great deal of hardship to see that happen.

For the time being, Greyhorse decided to dispense with the idea of identifying Jiterica's vital signs. That was a problem he would have to work on when time allowed.

"You may sit up," he said.

The ensign swung her legs around—another awkward motion, thanks to her containment suit—and did as the doctor suggested. Then she fixed her ghostly gaze on him and waited.

"I've familiarized myself with your personnel file," Greyhorse told her, producing a handheld padd from the pocket of his lab coat. "Unfortunately, it doesn't tell me everything I need to know—for instance, what diseases your species is prone to, and how your body is equipped to fight them."

"I understand," she said in the same tinny voice.

Jiterica went on to inform him about the parasites of her world, which came in two basic varieties. Greyhorse likened them to the bacteria and viruses that plagued solid life-forms.

According to the ensign, her species' defense against these parasites was to create a tiny gas bubble around the offending organism, effectively isolating it from the rest of their systems. Deprived of nourishment, the parasite eventually withered and died.

"Interesting," said the doctor, making a note of the information in his padd. "And what about other forms of injury? Say, from an impact? Or exposure to radiation?"

"Only my skin can sustain injury," Jiterica told him. "When it is compromised, I reform it."

"Consciously?" he asked.

Her features fuzzed over as she concentrated on the doctor's query. "If the injury is bad enough, I do it consciously. Otherwise, my body repairs itself in due time."

He asked her several other questions in the next few minutes, and she was able to answer all of them to his satisfaction. But it wasn't just the substance of her responses that enlightened him.

The more she was compelled to speak, the shorter and blunter her sentences became. What's more, her facial features fuzzed out for longer and longer periods of time.

Apparently, the effort required to converse with Greyhorse was taking its toll on her. Not wishing to cause her any more discomfort than necessary, he said, "We'll continue this another time. For now, you can return to your duties."

Jiterica looked at him, her features still in the process of reforming behind her transparent faceplate. To his mind, they didn't create an impression of contentment. Her expression looked strained, as if she were carrying a burden much too heavy for her.

Of course, Jiterica wasn't humanoid, so her expression wasn't necessarily a window on her feelings. It might simply have represented her best attempt to look like someone else—Greyhorse himself, perhaps, or one of her trainers at Starfleet headquarters.

"Thank you," she told him.

He nodded. "You're welcome."

Then he watched as the ensign slid off the biobed and walked away. Her movements were stiff, mechanical, almost painful to watch. But Greyhorse watched anyway.

He couldn't help admiring Jiterica. As difficult as it was for her to exist under these circumstances, she never made the slightest complaint. That took courage . . .

If not a great deal of common sense, he added inwardly.

Frowning deeply, Greyhorse returned to his enclosure and prepared for his next examination. But every now and then, he thought he saw a poorly defined face in the depths of his computer screen returning his gaze with a stubborn stoicism.

And his heart went out to it.

* * *

Cortin Zweller had red hair, boyish good looks, and a spray of freckles across the bridge of his nose. Just the sight of him on the monitor in Picard's quarters—courtesy of an unexpected subspace message—brought a smile to the captain's face.

At Starfleet Academy, Zweller and Picard had been the closest of friends, guarding each other's backs in one bit of ill-considered, late-night mischief after another. It was during one of their more raucous ventures that Picard had been stabbed through the heart by an angry Nausicaan.

Of course, both men had changed since then, gradually taking on the more sober mien expected of Starfleet officers. But of the two of them, Zweller had changed a good deal less than Picard had. He still played the occasional prank—though never on a superior officer.

"In case you were wondering," the redhead said, "I like the *Ajax* just fine. I like being second officer. I even like the new dom-jot table they installed in the rec room."

Dom-jot was the game of skill at which Zweller had excelled as a cadet. However, the captain noted inwardly, his friend had never been as good as he *believed* he was.

Picard was still chuckling at the thought when he saw Zweller's demeanor change. The smile drained from the man's face, and he leaned closer to the screen.

"The only part I don't like," Zweller said, "is hearing an old buddy is sailing into a trap."

Picard frowned. His pursuit of the White Wolf appeared to have become common knowledge.

"I know what you're thinking," Zweller said. "That I'm talking about the White Wolf. But I'm not. *I'm talking about McAteer.*"

It took Picard a moment to realize that his mouth was hanging open. He closed it. *McAteer?* What the devil was his friend talking about?

Zweller was already providing an explanation. "Turns out he was against Mehdi's decision to make you captain of the *Stargazer.* In fact, he's been against a great many of Mehdi's decisions over the years. That's why McAteer's sending you on this mission, Jean-Luc—a mission he thinks you can't possibly pull off. It's to make you look bad, so he can make your benefactor Mehdi look bad as well."

Picard leaned back in his chair. He had heard that such political games were played in the upper echelons of Starfleet, but he had never experienced any of them firsthand.

Welcome to starship command, he mused.

His friend went on. "If there's any way out of the mission, grab it and hold on tight. That's what I would do." He quirked a smile, though it didn't have its usual enthusiasm behind it. "Good luck, pal. You're going to need it."

As the Starfleet logo came up, replacing Zweller's face, the captain touched a square on his keypad and erased the message. After all that his Academy chum had risked on his behalf, it wouldn't do for Picard to leave the evidence intact.

Folding his arms across his chest, he leaned back in his chair. Obviously, it was too late for him to even think about backing out of the mission. If it was true that McAteer had set a trap for him, he was firmly and inextricably caught in it.

But what if he could prove them all wrong—the admiral and anyone else who thought the White Wolf was uncatchable? What if he could do what no one expected him to do, his friend Corey Zweller included?

Picard resolved to find out.

Chapter Six

PETER "PUG" JOSEPH FELT A PIT OPEN in his stomach as he stood in the *Stargazer*'s security section and considered his newest officer.

"Is something wrong, sir?" Obal, a Binderian, looked down at his uniform and ran his hands over it, apparently thinking there might be something amiss in that department.

There was something amiss, all right. But it had nothing to do with the Binderian's clothes.

Caught off-balance, the acting security chief shook his head. "No. Nothing at all. Carry on."

Obal inclined his head slightly. "Thank you, sir."

As Joseph watched his new officer waddle away, he shook his head ruefully. There weren't any other Binderians in Starfleet, so he had never seen one before Obal arrived. Now that he had, he was appalled.

Obal resembled nothing so much as a plucked chicken. A beakless chicken to be sure, and one that had unusually big, front-facing eyes, but a chicken nonetheless.

In fact, he was the silliest thing Joseph had ever seen—and that wasn't just an aesthetic judgment. It was, unfortunately, an observation with concrete, real-world implications.

With his obvious physical limitations, the Binderian would find it hard to get others to take him seriously. In Joseph's mind, that cast doubts on Obal's ability to serve as a security officer.

After all, security personnel needed to command respect. They needed to inspire confidence. And the Binderian, well, didn't do either of those things particularly well.

Clearly, Joseph needed to do something about it. "Obal?" he said. "Could I have a word with you?"

Obal stopped in his tracks, turned to his superior again and replied, "Of course, sir. Right away." Then he waddled back across the room to Joseph's side.

The security chief took a moment to phrase his next remark. After all, he didn't want to hurt Obal's feelings. It wasn't the Binderian's fault he had been placed somewhere he didn't belong.

"You know," Joseph began, "the *Stargazer* is a big ship. A *very* big ship. It's got a whole range of career opportunities for a bright, young fellow like yourself."

Obal smiled at him. He didn't seem to have any idea what the security chief was suggesting.

"What I mean is," Joseph said, "there are lots of other sections where you could make a contribution."

This time, the Binderian spoke up. "That's good to know," he said. But he didn't say anything more.

Joseph tried again. "Sections that could profit immensely from your eagerness and your intelligence."

Obal's brow creased over the bridge of his nose. "You mean . . . you would like me to *work* in those sections? And apply my expertise to areas other than security?"

The security chief felt as if a weight had been lifted from his shoulders. "Yes! That's *exactly* what I mean."

The Binderian shrugged his scrawny shoulders. "I would be happy to do that, sir."

"You would?" said Joseph. "I mean . . . I'm glad to hear that, Obal, very glad indeed. I'll speak with the heads of the other sections the first chance I get."

"Excellent," Obal told him, clearly enthusiastic about the idea. "And when I return, I will be a better officer as a result."

Joseph's hopes fell. "When you . . . return?"

"Aye, sir. When I return to security."

The chief frowned. "To security."

"In fact, I will be happy to share what I've learned with my colleagues." Obal's brow creased again. "That is, unless you plan to lend *them* out to other sections as well."

It wasn't the response Joseph had been hoping for. Obviously, the subtle approach hadn't gotten him anywhere, so he decided to meet the matter head on.

"Obal," he said, "I was thinking you might want to transfer to another section *permanently.*"

The Binderian's brow creased deeper than ever. Then, surprisingly, the smile returned to his face.

"Why would I want to do *that?*" he asked Joseph. "My heart is in security work. And I intend to do that work better than anyone who has ever worn the uniform."

This time, Joseph sighed out loud. He could request the transfer himself, of course. But he wouldn't do that until he had given Obal a chance to prove him wrong.

Not that the chief thought that would happen. "All right, then," he told the Binderian. "Welcome aboard."

"Lieutenant Simenon?"

Simenon looked up from his console in engineering to see who had called his name. There was only one person standing anywhere near him—a middle-aged, rather plump human with kind eyes and dark hair graying at the temples.

She was smiling at him. Obviously, the engineer reflected, she didn't know him very well.

"Yes?" he hissed.

"I'm Juanita Valderrama," she said. "The new sciences chief. You asked me to come see you . . . ?"

It was true. Simenon had wanted to show her something. "Join me," he said, beckoning the woman closer.

He tapped the keys on his console that would bring up the graphic he wanted. As Valderrama leaned over his shoulder, he pointed to the screen with a scaly finger.

"I've been working on amplifying our sensors with Beta Barritus in mind," Simenon explained. "We'll have better range, especially outside the visual spectrum. Here. Take a look for yourself."

Valderrama examined the screen. It took her a couple of minutes to absorb it all, since she wasn't an engineer by training.

When she was done, she turned to Simenon and said, "All right."

He thought she was kidding. "You're happy?"

"If you are," Valderrama told him, smiling again.

Simenon considered her a moment longer. Then he said, "Fine. Thanks for your input."

"Anytime," Valderrama told him. "If there's nothing else . . . ?"

"Nothing," he assured her.

"Then I'll be getting back to my section."

"Fine," he said.

So Valderrama made her way back across engineering and headed blithely for the exit.

Simenon shook his lizardlike head as he watched the doors close behind her. Cariello, Valderrama's predecessor as sciences chief, would *never* have let him off the hook so easily. She would have thanked him for his efforts, of course—but then she would have demanded even more of him, whether he could deliver it or not.

That was how *any* good science officer would have handled it. But not Valderrama. She had simply accepted the limitations laid out for her on the screen and let it go at that.

Simenon frowned. He could tolerate a lot of things, but indifference wasn't one of them. If Valderrama had been one of his engineers, she would have been on her way back to Starbase 32 already.

Starfleet was such a big place, he mused. Surely there had been a better science officer available *somewhere.*

Gilaad Ben Zoma gazed across the shiny black briefing room table at his new second officer.

Lieutenant Commander Elizabeth Wu was a small, wiry woman with short, dark hair. If Ben Zoma hadn't known her age, he would never have guessed that she was over thirty.

"I read your file," he said. "Your record is impeccable."

Her previous captain had called her "the kind of person who gets things done." But then, Ben Zoma could see that in the cast of her eyes and the way she carried herself.

"Thank you," Wu responded, neither discounting the praise nor wallowing in it.

"I can see why Captain Rudolfini wasn't happy to see you leave the *Crazy Horse.*"

Wu's mouth pulled up at the corners—as close, apparently, as she came to a smile. "But I assure you, he understood. There wasn't any opportunity for advancement on the *Crazy Horse*. If I wanted to move up, I had no choice but to transfer."

A common motivation. "At any rate," said Ben Zoma, "I think you know why I called you here."

"Of course," she replied. "To brief me on the personalities of the people who will be reporting to me."

"Exactly." It was standard procedure. "Have you had a chance to read any of our personnel files?"

"I was just doing that when you called me."

"And whom have you read about so far?"

Wu thought for a moment. "Phigus Simenon. Your chief engineer, if I recall correctly?"

"That's right."

"He seemed capable enough," Wu remarked.

Ben Zoma smiled. "Simenon is more than capable, Commander. He's brilliant—the absolute best at what he does. But he's also as cranky as they come, so take that into account in your dealings with him."

Wu nodded, her expression indicating that she was filing the information away. "I'll do that."

"Have you gotten to Carter Greyhorse, our chief medical officer?"

She shook her head. "Not yet."

"Greyhorse is brilliant too, in his way."

"And cranky?" Wu suggested wryly.

"Actually," said Ben Zoma, "he's anything but. Greyhorse is always the same, always on an even keel, whether he's treating a splinter or third-degree radiation burns. He'd make a great poker player."

Again, the second officer looked as if she were filing his remarks away. "Noted."

Ben Zoma went on. "Idun Asmund, our helm officer?"

Wu's brow puckered. "Asmund, yes . . . I was halfway through that file. But I don't think the woman's first name was Idun."

"Her sister's name is Gerda."

The light of recognition went on in Wu's eyes. "Yes . . . Gerda. She's your navigator, I believe?"

"That she is," Ben Zoma confirmed. "And you won't find a more efficient officer in the fleet. Unless, of course, you bump into Idun, who happens to be her twin."

"Efficiency is to be commended," Wu said. "What else should I know about them?"

He smiled again. *How should I put this?*

"That they're not afraid of anything—and I mean *anything.* That they're perfectly loyal, dedicated to their work, and resourceful beyond any expectation. And that they were raised by Klingons."

That brought Wu up short. "Klingons?"

"Klingons. It's all in their files."

"I can't wait."

Who else? "Vigo?"

Wu shook her head. "Doesn't ring a bell."

"He's our weapons officer. A Pandrilite. Knows what he's doing inside and out. And he's eager to please."

"Sounds like we'll get along fine."

"I'm sure you will," Ben Zoma told her. He asked himself whom he had left out. It took a moment, but it came to him. "Then there's Pug Joseph, our security chief."

Unexpectedly, Wu's level of enthusiasm seemed to drop precipitously. "Ah, yes. Joseph."

Ben Zoma looked at her. "Something wrong?"

Wu sighed. "A few months ago, I heard some bad things about the *Stargazer*'s security section."

The first officer felt a rush of heat to his face. "Bad in what way?" he asked.

Wu shrugged. "Poor discipline, scheduling inefficiencies . . . generally, a lack of leadership."

"You don't say."

Wu's eyes brightened. "But don't worry. I'm going to crack down on Lieutenant Joseph. By the time I'm done with him, his section will be the best in the fleet."

Ben Zoma smiled halfheartedly. "I applaud your initiative, Commander. However, a few months ago, Pug Joseph wasn't the security chief on this ship. *I* was."

Wu's eyes opened wide. "I'm . . . sorry, sir. Believe me, the last thing I wanted was to offend you."

The first officer nodded. "It's all right. Really. But if I were you, I'd observe Mr. Joseph firsthand before making any judgments concerning his abilities."

"Of course," Wu responded crisply.

Ben Zoma went on with his list of command personnel. But as he did so, it occurred to him that Wu might not be quite the prize he had believed her to be.

* * *

Picard took a sip of his tea and gazed out the observation port of his ready room. The distant suns abeam of the *Stargazer* sped by him in long, straight lines of light.

Ben Zoma was sitting at the captain's computer terminal, going over the reports they had received from their section heads. For once, he wasn't smiling.

Out of the corner of his eye, Picard saw his friend push himself away from the desk and swivel his chair in the captain's direction. Picard turned to him.

"Finished?" he asked.

Ben Zoma nodded. "I see what you mean. Of our seven new crewmen, four seem to come with a bit of baggage. That's not a very good average, Jean-Luc."

Picard nodded. "An inescapable conclusion. And given what my friend Corey Zweller told me, I would not be surprised if it were more than a coincidence."

"You think McAteer stuck us with them on purpose? To give us a few distractions while we're hunting the White Wolf?"

"If you accept Corey's premise, it is difficult to ignore the possibility entirely."

Ben Zoma frowned. "I suppose."

"On the other hand," Picard said, "I'm not willing to give up on these crewmen just yet."

"You think we can help them?"

"A couple of them, at least. Ensign Nikolas, for instance. He has been labeled a discipline problem—"

"To put it mildly," Ben Zoma interjected.

"However," the captain continued, "he reminds me of myself before the incident at Bonestell that cost me my heart. He's young, brash, too full of himself to think about his future."

"But maybe, if we exercise a little more patience than Nikolas is accustomed to . . . ?"

"He may turn out to be a diamond in the rough. Precisely."

"Or," said Ben Zoma, "he may turn out to be what he's been labeled—a square peg in a very round hole."

"Then all we've lost," Picard countered, "is time and patience."

Ben Zoma didn't argue the point. Apparently, he had had enough of playing devil's advocate.

"And while we're at it," Picard said, "perhaps we can help Lieutenant Valderrama as well. True, she's been transferred twice in the last couple of years by disgruntled captains—"

"Who noted her exemplary service record but felt her level of dedication had eroded."

"Yes. But what did they do to get her motivated again? Did they challenge her or simply accept her deficiencies? That is the question, Number One."

Ben Zoma smiled. "And she's one of the easier ones. What do you think of Ensign Jiterica?"

The captain shrugged. "Apparently she was of rather limited utility in her previous assignment. Of course, we'll try to work with her. Given her people's status vis-à-vis the Federation, we don't have the option of doing otherwise."

"But you're not optimistic?"

Picard sighed. "Not terribly, no."

Given Jiterica's unusual anatomy, it was remarkable that she had come even this far. Living in the confines of that specially designed suit day in and day out, operating in an environment so different from her natural state . . .

It had to be hell.

But Picard wouldn't allow himself to mistake courage for potential. Unlike Nikolas and Valderrama, Jiterica showed no promise of fitting in on a Federation starship—not in the near term. Not *ever.*

"And Obal?" asked Ben Zoma. "From what Pug tells me, he's not especially suited to a position in security."

"That would be my judgment as well," the captain said. "Perhaps if Obal were encouraged to pursue a different sort of career . . . say, in the sciences section . . ."

"Pug's already tried encouraging him to do that. It seems he's got his heart set on being a security officer."

Picard took another sip of tea and savored it. Like Jiterica, Obal possessed a reach that drastically exceeded his grasp. "I will concede that there is a lot to be said for determination. But if I were Pug, I would try again."

Ben Zoma nodded. "I'll pass that on."

"Fortunately," the captain said, "there are the other three—Wu, Caber, and Ulelo. If McAteer had anything underhand in mind with regard to *them,* we have yet to see it."

A troubled look came over his first officer. "Actually . . ."

"Don't tell me—"

Ben Zoma dismissed the idea with a wave of his hand. "Nothing serious. It's just that Wu strikes me as a little . . . how can I put it?" He frowned for a moment, then said, "Overly enthusiastic."

"That doesn't sound so bad," Picard told him.

"It isn't," Ben Zoma agreed. "Forget I mentioned it. I'm probably just looking for problems where there aren't any."

The captain smiled wryly. "As if we did not have an ample supply of problems already."

"You know," his first officer said, "if Jiterica and the others don't pan out, you can take McAteer up on his suggestion."

"To transfer anyone with whom I'm unhappy?"

"That's what he said."

Picard thought about it. "I could do that," he agreed. "But I am not going to think about that for the moment. As far as I am concerned, a transfer is a last resort."

Because Ben Zoma was his friend, he knew better than to give the captain an argument on that count.

Chapter Seven

NIKOLAS SET HIS TRAY DOWN on the metal rack in front of the replicator opening and said, "Tuna casserole."

A moment later, the replicator went to work, transforming a small quantity of undifferentiated raw material to the parameters specified in a digitally stored molecular pattern matrix. The result was a black casserole dish full of something hot and steaming. Nikolas took it out, placed it on his tray, and looked around for an empty table.

Then he noticed Caber, who was in line behind him, looking at the casserole. Judging by the expression on Caber's face, he considered Nikolas's choice a less than desirable one.

But then, there were more than seven hundred fifty preset options on the *Stargazer*'s replicator menu, and a great deal more if one wanted to take the time to custom-program them. Tuna casserole was hardly the most exotic selection available.

"You sure you want to order that?" Caber asked.

"I know," Nikolas said. "You're surprised. Tuna casserole's for middle-aged guys in stellar cartography."

"Actually," Caber began, "I—"

"Best piece of advice I ever got," Nikolas explained, "was from an engineer on an Academy training ship. He told me replicators aren't all alike, and the worst of them are on *Constellation*-class deep-space explorers like this one. The best approach when you find yourself on one of these things is to start simple and work your way up—and what's simpler than a tuna casserole?"

"True," said Caber, "but—"

"If you're done discussing the finer points of replicator cuisine," said a blond woman waiting her turn behind them, "the rest of us would like to eat."

Nikolas frowned. "Come on," he told Caber. "I wouldn't want anyone to starve to death on my account."

Caber didn't address the woman, but neither did he seem inclined to rush. Turning to the replicator, he said, "Salmon steak. Medium rare. In béarnaise sauce."

Nikolas didn't get it. After he had given Caber the inside poop, he figured his roommate would go the tuna casserole route too. But something as tricky as salmon steak with béarnaise sauce? That was the exact opposite of what Nikolas would have recommended.

He saw the plate materialize in the replicator slot, its centerpiece a moist chunk of pinkish meat drenched in brown and translucent sauce. It looked good, all right—but thanks to that engineer on the *Copernicus,* Nikolas knew better.

There was only one explanation that he could think of. Despite appearances, Caber had allowed the woman in back of them to get him flustered. Obviously, he wasn't as self-possessed as he looked.

Nikolas found himself taking comfort in the observation. He knew he shouldn't, but he did.

"There's an empty table over there," Caber said, pointing to it with his chin.

"Sounds good," Nikolas told him. It was only after they sat down that he leaned toward his roommate and said, "You shouldn't have let that woman get you flummoxed."

Caber looked at him. "Flummoxed?"

Then, to Nikolas's surprise, Caber laughed. It was a deep, heartfelt laugh, the kind that said he hadn't been bothered by the woman at all— that, in fact, the whole idea was rather ludicrous.

"But," Nikolas asked, "if you weren't bothered by her, how did you end up ordering a salmon steak? Didn't you hear what I said about replicators on the *Constellation* class?"

"Sure," said Caber. "And I'd heard the same thing. But I checked the *Stargazer*'s specs before I came aboard, and it's been equipped with a different replicator system than the other *Constellation*-class ships. A more *advanced* system. It can handle a lot more than"—he glanced at Nikolas's plate with obvious sympathy—"the simple dishes."

Nikolas felt as if he had shot himself in the foot with a phaser rifle. The worst of it was that his roommate had tried to disabuse him of his error, but he hadn't listened.

"You don't say," he got out.

Caber shrugged. "It's only one meal. You can order the salmon for dinner if you like."

True, Nikolas thought. *But I'll still feel like a fool.*

Here he'd been thinking he had a leg up on Caber—an arena, no matter how small or insignificant, in which he could outshine the guy. *I should have known better,* he told himself.

Prodding halfheartedly at his casserole, Nikolas watched Caber dig into his salmon and lift a juicy-looking forkful into his mouth. "How is it?" he asked.

Caber nodded as he chewed. "Not bad," he said after he had swallowed and wiped his mouth with his Starfleet-issue cloth napkin. "I mean it's not the quality of the fish you get in Nova Scotia, but I've had a whole lot worse."

Nikolas knew of two places with the name Nova Scotia. Having never been to either one of them, he figured he had better ask. "Nova Scotia on Earth or on Dalarte Prime?"

Caber started to laugh. Then he seemed to realize it wasn't a joke. "There *aren't* any salmon on Dalarte Prime," he said gently. "The closest thing to it is called a second-sunset fish, and most people find it a bit too salty for their taste."

"Nova Scotia on Earth, then," Nikolas said, wishing he hadn't paraded his ignorance quite so successfully. So he hadn't traveled as much as the admiral's son, big deal. "What were you doing there anyway?"

"Ice-surfing," Caber told him, and a look of sublime contentment came over his features. "It's a passion with me. Ever try it?"

"Once," Nikolas replied.

To get a girl, he added silently. It was *always* to get a girl. But in the process, he had discovered that ice-surfing wasn't for him.

"Didn't love it?" Caber asked, taking note of his roommate's lack of enthusiasm.

"Not really," Nikolas said. "I mean, it was fun and all, and it never got as cold as they said it would, but it didn't make my toes curl. I like a sport where you're going head to head with someone, pitting your skills against someone else's."

"Winners and losers," Caber said, boiling it all down.

It sounded to Nikolas as if his roommate disapproved of the concept. But then, he reflected, an admiral's son might have a more "enlightened" view of such matters.

"So what do you play?" Caber asked.

"A lot of things," Nikolas said, steadfastly unashamed of his preference for competition. "Soccer, basketball, handball—"

"Handball?" Caber echoed, interrupting him.

Nikolas nodded, ready for what he figured would be a polite but condescending remark. "That's right."

His roommate's eyes narrowed. "Single wall?"

"It's the only kind," Nikolas said, eyeing Caber suspiciously. "Don't tell me you play?" He did his best to keep his incredulity out of his voice, but it came out anyway.

"Sure do," Caber told him. "Hell, I've been playing since I was nine or ten."

"But—" Nikolas was at a loss.

"What?" Caber prodded.

"I don't know. I guess I've always thought of single-wall handball as a street game."

Caber chuckled, his blue eyes gleaming. "And what makes you think I didn't grow up on the streets?"

Nikolas framed his answer carefully. After all, he didn't want to offend the guy. "Your father's an admiral. I figured an admiral's kid would spend a lot of time on starbases."

"He's an admiral *now*," Caber noted. "But when he was moving up through the ranks, I lived with my mother. In a place called Brooklyn."

Nikolas laughed. "You're kidding."

"Not at all. We had a place in Brooklyn Heights. The nearest courts were a few blocks away."

"I had a cousin in Brooklyn," Nikolas said. "Tommy Tsouratakis. He lived in Canarsie."

Caber leaned forward, his salmon seemingly forgotten for the moment. "I *know* Canarsie."

"I went to visit Tommy once," Nikolas recalled. It had been . . .

what? Six years ago? Seven? "He wasn't into handball himself, but he took me to the courts near his house."

"Then," said Caber, "you had to see a guy named Red O'Reilly."

"Yes!" Nikolas was tickled by the coincidence. "You know Red O'Reilly? He was king of the hill, the guy to beat."

"Did you play him?" Caber asked.

"Once. He wiped the court with me. I scored two points, maybe three if I was lucky. I was just glad he didn't shut me out."

Caber's eyes lost their focus. "O'Reilly wiped the court with me too, the first half-dozen times I played him. But I kept trying, kept challenging him. After a while, I got to understand his game better. His strengths. His weaknesses, few as they were." His mouth pulled up at the corners. "And once, just once, I squeaked by him."

Nikolas couldn't believe it. "You *beat* Red O'Reilly?"

"Fifteen-thirteen," Caber recollected. "On a completely accidental lefthanded killer. Rolled off the wall so perfectly he couldn't have returned it in a million years."

Nikolas shared in the other man's vision for a moment, savoring it as if it were he who had made the shot. Then he said with absolute earnestness, "I'm impressed."

Caber made a dismissive sound deep in his throat. "Don't be. I never came close to beating him again."

But he didn't have to, Nikolas thought. He had already accomplished the impossible—scaled Everest, won the Academy Marathon. He had conquered Red O'Reilly.

"Small world," Nikolas remarked.

"Yeah," Caber said. *"Very* small."

As he said it, Lieutenant Commander Wu approached them on her way to the mess hall's only exit. Every bit as new to the *Stargazer* as Nikolas or Caber, she didn't look right or left as she passed the other diners. But then, she obviously wasn't expecting any greetings.

Nonetheless, she got one—from Caber. "Afternoon," he said.

Wu stopped and looked surprised. "To you too," she responded, her pleasure evident in her expression. She seemed to make note of Caber's face. Then she resumed her progress.

Nikolas looked at his roommate, more envious than ever. It would never have occurred to him to say anything to a command officer unless he absolutely had to.

"Now I'm *really* impressed," he confessed.

"With what?" Caber wondered. Then he seemed to understand. "That I said hello to Commander Wu?"

"Not just that you did it," Nikolas told him. "That you sounded so earnest about it."

"You can too."

Nikolas shook his head. "Coming from me, it would sound like mockery. I'm the wild child, remember? I don't mix well with command types."

"But you *could,*" Caber insisted. "All you've got to do is make an adjustment in the way you look at them."

Nikolas looked at him askance. "An adjustment . . . ?"

"That's right. I mean, what's the difference between them and us, when you come right down to it? A couple of bars on their sleeves? A little bridge time we haven't accumulated yet?"

"The power to make us scour plasma conduits the rest of our lives?" Nikolas added.

Caber waved the notion away. "I'm telling you, they're the same kind of people we are—no better and no worse. All you've got to do is keep that in mind."

Nikolas frowned. "Easier said than done. For me at least."

"I'll tell you what," his roommate said. He looked around, as if to make sure that no one was eavesdropping on his conversation. Then he lowered his voice and went on. "I'll share a little technique I've found useful, if you promise to keep it to yourself."

Nikolas considered the offer. "Mum's the word."

"A couple of years ago," Caber began, "I was on Betazed for the wedding of a high-ranking Betazoid official. He knew my father pretty well, so he invited my whole family to the celebration. But rather than pull my mother away from work and my sisters out of school, my dad decided to just bring me."

A picture was starting to form in Nikolas's mind. "On Betazed? But don't they—?"

"That's right," Caber said. "They have naked wedding ceremonies. The bride, the groom, the guests, the guy who pronounces them soul mates for life . . . everyone. And in this case, there were also a few admirals and their staffs."

Nikolas tried unsuccessfully to suppress a smile. "Their staffs? You mean . . . their attachés?"

There was absolutely no one more stuck-up or supercilious than an admiral's attaché. They were always so straightlaced, so proper. So the idea of one of them standing there naked . . .

His smile turned into a laugh.

"Exactly," Caber said, his eyes crinkling at the corners. "They looked ridiculous. Stripped of their dignity, quite literally. And that's what gave me the idea for my technique."

Nikolas was beginning to understand what his roommate was getting at. "You think of people without their clothes?"

"Stark naked," Caber confirmed, "wearing nothing but what they were born with. Believe me, it makes it a lot easier to deal with the muckety-mucks of the world. It's hard to feel intimidated by somebody when they're standing there without a stitch."

Nikolas found it hard to disagree.

"Go ahead," Caber said. "Give it a shot."

Nikolas looked at him. "Now?"

"Why not?"

Nikolas frowned. Then he took in the mess hall at a glance, seeking a likely subject. Suddenly, one presented itself.

As the individual in question walked by, Nikolas got up from his seat and said, "Good afternoon, sir."

Chief Engineer Simenon looked up at him through slitted, ruby eyes, his scaly nostrils flaring. "Really."

Naked, Nikolas thought.

It wasn't a pretty sight. However, it had the desired effect. Whatever he might have found daunting about Simenon dematerialized along with his lab coat.

"Yes, sir," Nikolas assured him.

The Gnalish tilted his head as he regarded the ensign. "Whatever you say," he harrumphed. Then he trundled past, his tail impatiently switching back and forth behind him.

Nikolas sat down again in front of his casserole. "Not the friendliest individual I've ever met."

Caber didn't answer right away. When Nikolas turned to him to see why, he caught a glimpse of something hard in his roommate's eyes, something like disapproval but stronger.

Then the moment passed, and Caber turned to him with a smile on his face. "I've seen friendlier. But you've proven my point. You said hello to a high-ranking officer. You addressed him civilly, without even a hint of sarcasm. And you got *him* to speak to *you* civilly as well."

"If you can call that being civil," Nikolas quipped.

Caber glanced at the exit through which the engineer had departed. "That was Simenon," he said, "by all accounts the grumpiest, most mean-spirited officer on the ship. If you're going to offend someone, it's going to be *him*. And yet he left here without so much as a complaint. I'd say that constitutes success."

Nikolas saw the man's point. The technique had worked. And if Nikolas could approach Simenon, he could approach anyone—even the captain.

"And the best part," Caber told him, "is you don't feel you've kow-towed to anyone. You've still got your dignity."

Nikolas smiled. He did, didn't he?

"Thanks," he said.

Caber smiled at him. "Believe me, it's my pleasure."

Chapter Eight

PICARD HEARD THE SOUND of chimes and looked up from his terminal. "Come," he said.

The doors to his ready room slid aside with a soft exhalation of air, revealing the matronly, dark-haired form of Lieutenant Valderrama. Looking a bit tentative, the science officer came in and allowed the doors to close behind her.

"You asked to see me?" she said.

"I did indeed," the captain replied. He swiveled his chair around to face her. "Please have a seat."

Valderrama made use of the only other chair in the room, which was situated on the other side of Picard's desk. It occurred to the captain that the woman was old enough to be his mother, and for just a moment he felt awkward addressing her as a subordinate.

Then again, he mused, a great many of his subordinates were older than he was. Just not by quite so many years.

"I trust you've settled in by now?" he said, feeling the need to engage Valderrama in conversation before he began to get into anything more substantive.

"I have," the sciences chief assured him.

"Good. And your personnel?"

"Top-notch, as far as I can tell. I'm very much looking forward to working with them."

Picard nodded. "Excellent."

Valderrama seemed comfortable enough, both in her position and in his ready room. With that in mind, he put pleasantries aside and launched into the real reason he had summoned her.

Leaning forward in his chair, he said, "I hope you'll understand if I speak bluntly, Lieutenant."

Valderrama seemed to gird herself. She must have sensed this coming. "Aye, sir."

"Other captains have not been pleased with your performance of late. They have reached the conclusion that you are coasting—that you could do better if doing better still mattered to you."

Valderrama reddened. "They have said that, sir."

"However," Picard went on, "I don't care what conclusions other captains have reached. On the *Stargazer,* you'll be starting out with a clean slate."

It wasn't the kind of speech the lieutenant had expected. That much was clear from her bewildered expression.

He pressed on. "I fully expect that you will do an exemplary job here—a job of which you and I can both be proud. You will need to do no less, considering what we will soon be facing in Beta Barritus."

Valderrama stared at him for a moment. Then she lifted her chin and said, "I'm grateful for your confidence in me, sir. I'll try to be worthy of it."

"I'm sure you will," Picard replied.

Pug Joseph hadn't slept very well. He had been thinking about his new security officer all night long, turning the problem over and over in his mind and dreading the moment when he would have to confront the Binderian about his obvious inadequacies.

Maybe, he had told himself more than once in the wee hours as he lay staring at the ceiling, it would have been more merciful to nip Obal's hopes at the outset. Maybe it would have been less painful for the little fellow in the long run.

But he hadn't done that. He had shied away from what he couldn't help seeing more and more as the inevitable. And when the inevitable came, it would be that much more difficult for both of them.

As he thought that, he reached the doors to the security section. They slid apart in front of him and revealed an anteroom manned by two armed officers, Garner and Pierzynski. The officers inclined their heads and acknowledged him by name.

"Carry on," Joseph said, feeling a little silly.

Garner and Pierzynski were full lieutenants just as he was. And as soon as the captain found a permanent security chief, Joseph would be standing guard alongside them.

Beyond the anteroom lurked the hexagonal main security facility, where an officer named Horombo was sitting in front of a huge, concave bank of closed-circuit video screens. Each one showed him a different, strategically important portion of the ship—the bridge, engineering, the transporter room, and so on.

"Chief," said Horombo, sparing him a glance.

"Horombo," Joseph responded.

He proceeded across the hexagon to its opposite side, where an open doorway provided access to a short corridor. His office was located farther down that corridor. So was the *Stargazer*'s armory, which stood opposite his door and contained every phaser on the ship that wasn't currently in use somewhere.

The other doors that opened on the corridor led to a weapons diagnostics room, a weapons repair room, a target range and a storeroom full of communicators, palmlights, and other gear often needed by *Stargazer* away teams.

Joseph was so dull-witted and bleary-eyed from lack of sleep that he almost passed the diminutive figure hunched over a table in the diagnostics area without noticing him. Taking a step backward, he peered inside the room and saw that it was Obal seated there.

"Obal?" he ventured.

The Binderian turned to him. "Good morning, sir."

Joseph didn't get it. "You're not on duty for another six hours," he pointed out.

"True," Obal responded. "But I felt my time would be spent more wisely here in security."

The security chief could hardly object to such zeal. "So you've been . . . what? Testing the accuracy of our ordnance?"

The Binderian smiled at him. "Yes, sir."

"That's admirable," Joseph told him, "if unnecessary. Chief Ang made sure that was done before he left."

"In that case," Obal said cheerfully, "Chief Ang must have had something else on his mind at the time."

Joseph looked at him. "What do you mean?"

The Binderian held up the type-1 phaser in his hand. "This unit as well as several others exhibit targeting inaccuracies."

The security chief was understandably skeptical. He held out his hand and said, "May I?"

"Of course." Obal turned the phaser over to him.

Joseph placed it in the diagnostic device, closed the cover on it, and checked the digital readouts. Sure enough, the targeting mechanism was off—if only by a few hundredths of a millimeter.

"As I said," Obal noted, "there are inaccuracies."

Joseph turned to him and smiled. "Not serious ones, mind you. But I'll give you credit for finding any at all."

The Binderian inclined his head. "Thank you, sir."

"Now we've got to fix this thing. Why don't you—"

"Actually," Obal piped up, "that won't be necessary. I've already made all the necessary corrections, sir."

"You have?"

Obal nodded. "At least with regard to the type-one and type-two devices. I have yet to test the rifles."

Joseph looked at him. "You can't mean *all* the type-ones and type-twos."

"On the contrary, sir. That's exactly what I mean."

"But . . . between the type-ones and the type-twos, there are more than sixty phasers."

"Sixty-four, to be exact, sir."

"You're kidding."

"Not at all," Obal assured him.

The security chief chuckled appreciatively. "And you weren't even scheduled to be on duty."

"As I said," the Binderian reminded him, "I felt my time would be spent more wisely in security."

Under the circumstances, Joseph couldn't help but agree.

"After I check the rifles," Obal said, "I would like to take a look at the brig. In my experience, graviton polarity source field generators require frequent recalibration."

Joseph nodded. "Sure. Knock your socks off."

Obal smiled. "Thank you, sir."

The security chief left him in the diagnostics room and continued to his office, where he sat down in front of his computer screen. But before long, he found himself thinking about the Binderian again.

Sixty-four phasers, he mused. *And in his free time.*

Maybe he had been too quick to judge Obal, he told himself. Maybe the little guy was going to work out after all.

Vigo smiled to himself as he moved his tiny wagon across the winding blue ribbon of a river. Then he looked across the octagonal sharash'di board and saw Valderrama smile too, albeit a bit more ruefully.

"Looks like you've got me," she said.

Remembering his manners, the Pandrilite contained his enthusiasm. "I'll grant you, it looks that way. But it's not because you didn't pursue an interesting and effective strategy."

"It couldn't have been *that* effective," the sciences chief rejoined. "Otherwise, *you* would be the one conceding defeat."

"What hurt you," Vigo observed, "was your third-level defense. You should have chosen stone over sky."

"I would have," Valderrama told him, "if I'd had any large green stones left."

"You had two of them, actually. They were buried in the riverbed and obscured by ice."

To underscore his point, Vigo lifted the glassy overlay that represented ice and exposed the trough in the board that represented the river. It was filled halfway to the top with fine dark sand. Using a big, blue finger, he moved the sand around until he revealed a couple of smooth, blue-green stones.

"You see?" he said.

Valderrama looked surprised by his revelation. "But how did you know they were there?"

Vigo shrugged. "They had to be. When we left the first level, only three stones had turned up in the river. And on the second level, there weren't any at all. So—"

"So there had to be a couple of them on *this* level." Valderrama nodded in appreciation of his logic. "Well done, Mr. Vigo."

He inclined his head. "Thank you."

"And," she added with a gleam in her eye, "get ready for a rematch."

The remark caught Vigo off guard. "Really?"

"You don't think I'm going to just roll over and accept defeat, do you?" And with her challenge hanging in the air, Valderrama began to set up the board for another game.

The Pandrilite grinned.

He hadn't been happy about saying good-bye to Cariello, Valderrama's predecessor as head of the sciences section. Cariello was known for her drive and enthusiasm, her desire to get the most out of herself and others.

Vigo hadn't expected her replacement to be nearly as good. But fortune had smiled on the *Stargazer,* it seemed, because Valderrama was obviously made from the same mold.

"Well?" she said. "What are you waiting for?"

He chuckled. "Nothing, Lieutenant. Nothing at all."

Savoring the prospect of another match, he helped her put the game pieces back in place.

Ben Zoma forked half a stuffed grape leaf into his mouth and savored its aromatic flavor while he considered the list of Starfleet advisories on his padd.

It was midafternoon, and the *Stargazer*'s lounge was nearly empty, just as Ben Zoma liked it. Not that he wasn't the gregarious sort. On the contrary, he was probably the most gregarious person he knew.

But as the *Stargazer*'s first officer, he needed to digest everything that was happening on the ship—and in the case of a Starfleet advisory, everything that was happening *off* the ship as well. It was easier to do that in an empty lounge than in a full one.

"Commander?" someone said.

It took Ben Zoma a moment to realize that it was he who was being addressed that way. But then, he had only been a first officer for a week or so.

"Yes?" he said, looking up from his padd.

Wu was standing across the table from him, smiling politely. "Is this seat taken?" she asked, indicating one opposite Ben Zoma's.

He shrugged. "I don't think so."

"Good." Wu pulled the chair out and sat down, dispelling any notion Ben Zoma might have had about finishing his reading in peace. "I'm glad I found you here," she said. "I wanted to speak with you."

"What about?" Ben Zoma asked, putting down the padd.

Wu's brow knit. "Our last conversation included a rather . . . awkward moment. I wanted to address it."

Ben Zoma dismissed the notion with a wave of his hand. "You did that already. You said you were sorry."

"Yes," his colleague agreed. "But I wanted you to know that what I said was heartfelt."

He smiled. "I never had any reason to believe otherwise."

"You know, I *never* would have put my foot in my mouth that way on the *Crazy Horse.*"

Ben Zoma understood. "Because you knew her personnel a lot better than you know the *Stargazer*'s."

Wu nodded. "Exactly."

The first officer was able to sympathize, since the *Stargazer* hadn't been his first assignment. "It's difficult getting used to a new ship and crew, especially after you've been in one place for a long time."

"It is," his second officer confirmed.

"So let's just forget what happened," he suggested. "In fact, I've forgotten it already."

Wu looked grateful. "Thank you."

"Don't mention it," said Ben Zoma. He glanced at his padd, which was sitting next to his plate of stuffed grape leaves. "And now, if I can ask *you* a favor . . ." He let his voice trail off meaningfully.

Wu seemed to notice the padd and the grape leaves for the first time. "Of course," she replied quickly. "By all means. Sorry to have distracted you from your work."

"No problem," he assured her.

She began to withdraw as quietly as she had approached him, but before she could leave, Ben Zoma tendered an invitation.

"Any time you want to talk . . ."

Wu smiled at him again. Then she crossed the lounge and made her exit through its set of sliding doors.

Ben Zoma smiled too, Wu's overzealousness at their first meeting as forgotten as he had promised it would be. Then he went back to his padd and its advisories.

Chapter Nine

JITERICA STOOD AMID A HERD of snub-nosed silver shapes, the overhead lighting glinting off their duranium hides.

"We've got a type-eleven pod, a type-twelve pod, and three type-thirteen pods," said Lieutenant Chiang, the gray-templed officer in charge of the *Stargazer*'s lone shuttlebay. His voice rang proudly from one end of the facility to the other. "We've got a type-three personnel shuttle, two type-four personnel shuttles, and a couple of type-five personnel shuttles, and right here is a type-eight heavy cargo shuttle fresh from the yards at Utopia Planitia."

The Nizhrak knew exactly what types the vehicles were. Shuttle design was one of the myriad subjects she had studied in her crash course at Starfleet headquarters.

"Of course," the short, stocky Chiang went on, "the type-twelve is in the process of being overhauled for the umpteenth time, so it's useless to us right now."

Jiterica saw a pair of uniformed legs sticking out from under the type-12, the exterior of which was virtually identical to the type-11. It was on the inside that the two shuttles were entirely different, thanks to the type-12's 500-millicochrane impulse driver engines and its three sarium krellide storage cells.

"As you can see," said Chiang, rapping his knuckles on the type-3, "we're not exactly cutting edge here from top to bottom. This little number can barely maintain warp speed over the long haul, so we'd only use it in a dire emergency like a full-scale evacuation."

"I understand," Jiterica responded.

She had been sent here to assist the shuttlebay crew for the time being. She had no objections to the assignment. An ensign was supposed to familiarize herself with as many aspects of starship operation as possible.

"We've got another type-five on order," Chiang told her, "but between you and me, I don't expect to see her any time soon. The way they ration out new shuttlecraft, you'd think there were a million ships all clamoring for them at once."

He chortled and looked to Jiterica, as if he expected some specific reaction from her. But not knowing what it might be, she remained silent and waited for a clue.

"Rrright," Chiang said at last. He rapped on the type-3 again. "Well then, let's see if we can't—"

Before the lieutenant could finish his sentence, he was cut off by a loud clanging noise. Chiang turned grim suddenly, no longer the affable tour guide. He shouted out some orders, then pointed to the double doors that comprised the shuttlebay's entrance.

"Let's go," he said to Jiterica.

She understood the reason for his sense of urgency. The loud sound she "heard" through her audio sensors was the signal for all personnel to respond to some immediate danger—loss of air pressure, exposure to radiation, or something equally inimical to humanoid life—by unhesitatingly evacuating the shuttlebay.

Jiterica wasn't sure why such an action was necessary. To her knowledge, the ship was not under attack. Nor was it in the vicinity of any dangerous phenomena. On the other hand, anomalies cropped up from time to time in the course of subspace travel, and the *Stargazer* might have encountered one of them.

In any case, it wasn't the Nizhrak's place to determine the reason for the evacuation. Her only responsibility was to leave the area as quickly as possible.

There had been half a dozen other crewmen in the bay besides Jiterica and Chiang—two humans, a Vulcan, a Bolian, a Carpathian, and a Vobilite. They all locked down their respective control stations and scampered for the exit.

But Jiterica couldn't scamper. Her containment suit wasn't equipped to let her move that quickly. All she could do was proceed at her usual deliberate, mechanical pace—a limitation that had never been an issue until that moment.

Chiang noticed Jiterica's difficulty, stopped halfway to the exit and came back for her. But her condensed mass was more or less equal to the lieutenant's, so he didn't have the option of picking her up and carrying her. All he could do was turn her around, grab her suit under its armpits and drag her toward the double doors.

Jiterica felt feeble and embarrassed. Had she been back in the roiling chaos of her homeworld, she would simply have altered her form and ridden one of the storm winds away from peril. Here, in this place of rigidly enforced geometric boundaries, she was forced to depend on a fellow crewman for assistance.

Little by little, Chiang pulled her in the direction of safety, the heels of her bulky white suit scraping on the floor. But the lieutenant wasn't moving quickly enough. According to the evacuation protocols Jiterica had studied, they had only twenty seconds to reach the exit before a duranium barrier descended from the ceiling and sealed off the shuttlebay.

Twelve seconds had already gone by, and they hadn't even cleared the last of the shuttlepods. At this rate, they wouldn't make it. They wouldn't even come close.

"Go," she told Chiang over the sound of the klaxon. "Leave me."

"I can't," he gasped into her audio sensors, his voice ragged with effort. "You're part of my crew . . . my responsibility . . ."

Just then, the ensign saw another crewman appear on her right and grab her by the arm. A moment later, someone else appeared to grab her by the other one. Pooling their strength with Chiang's, they dragged her with greater speed over the shuttle deck.

But it wasn't going to be enough, the ensign told herself. As the ceiling rushed past her, its details framed in her faceplate, she counted down the seconds in her mind.

Seven seconds. Six. Five . . .

"Leave me," she pleaded a second time.

This time, Chiang didn't respond. Looking back at the man, Jiterica saw the rictus of strain on his face and realized he was struggling too hard to get an answer out.

Behind her, a heavy metal barrier started to descend from its slot in the ceiling. Once it closed, there would be no getting it open again. Whoever remained on the wrong side of it would be trapped.

Four, Jiterica thought. *Three. Two . . .*

The barrier was directly above, looming larger as it came down at her. At the last possible moment, she felt a jerk on her suit and saw herself shoot backward. When the sheet of metal hit the deck and locked into place, the bulky white feet of her suit were just inside it.

One.

She was safe, she realized. They were *all* safe.

Chiang and the others propped the ensign on her feet again. They were in the compartment that mediated between the shuttlebay and the corridor outside it, and one of Jiterica's colleagues was checking conditions in the ship on a computer terminal built into the bulkhead.

"Everything seems to be normal," the man said. "Power levels, hull integrity, air pressure . . ."

"Then why did we evacuate?" the Bolian asked.

That's when they heard the voice fill their compartment. "That was a drill, folks. I'm happy to say you passed."

It was difficult for Jiterica to discern one voice on the ship from another, but it seemed to her that it was Commander Ben Zoma speaking. One of the technicians alongside her, a Carpathian female, confirmed the speaker's identity.

"Ben Zoma," she said in an exasperated tone.

"Carry on," the first officer told them.

Then the duranium barrier began to slide up again, retreating into its slot in the ceiling. In the process, it showed them an undamaged and uncompromised shuttlebay, as clean and orderly as they had left it.

Jiterica turned to Chiang. He was the officer in charge of this section, and yet it seemed to her that he hadn't known about the drill. Otherwise, he wouldn't have worked so hard to get her on the safe side of the barrier.

The ensign hadn't had time to read much about drill protocol at Starfleet headquarters. She had been too busy learning more essential information, like how to walk and how to speak. However, now that she thought about it, it made sense that at least *some* drills would come as surprises even to the heads of the sections involved.

Perhaps there were drills that would even come as surprises to Commander Ben Zoma.

But it wasn't the propriety of the drill that gave Jiterica cause for concern. It was her reaction to it. Or more accurately, her *inability* to react to it.

If they had faced a real emergency instead of a false one, she would have been a burden to her colleagues. They would have been forced to risk their own lives to save hers.

Chiang wiped his brow with the back of his hand. "All right, everyone," he said, his voice echoing with something less than its usual resonance. He was still a little out of breath. "Let's get back to work."

As the others returned to their tasks, Jiterica approached him. "Excuse me, Lieutenant. I wish to speak with you."

Chiang frowned as he turned and regarded her. "Funny, Ensign . . . I was just going to tell you the same thing."

Greyhorse was sitting in his office, mulling what he had heard about Jiterica's misadventure in the shuttlebay, when he saw Phigus Simenon crossing the sickbay and coming his way.

The engineer's scaly tail switched back and forth as he walked, making him look even more driven than usual—and his "usual" was already enough to bowl most people over. Obviously, he had something on his mind.

"What can I do for you?" Greyhorse asked.

He and Simenon had gotten to know each other rather well over the last few weeks. They were alike in many ways. For one thing, neither of them was exactly steeped in the social graces.

"You can pronounce Urajel fit for duty," the Gnalish told him, depositing himself in a chair opposite the doctor's. His ruby eyes were narrowed and demanding.

Urajel was an Andorian engineer who had broken her arm in one of their encounters with the Nuyyad. The limb had healed perfectly, but Greyhorse had wanted to give it a few more days to make sure. Those extra days were now over.

"You want her?" he said. "You've got her."

No doubt, Simenon had expected more of a fight. Little by little, the muscles around his eyes relaxed. But his tail didn't stop switching. Apparently, Urajel's situation wasn't the only thing that had been bothering the engineer.

"You look troubled," Greyhorse observed dryly.

"I am," Simenon told him.

The doctor knew he would regret asking, but he asked anyway. "Any particular reason for your discontent?"

"You know the new sciences chief? Valderrama?"

"Of course I do," Greyhorse responded. "I gave the woman a physical."

"So what do you think of her?"

Greyhorse looked at him askance. "Is this a trick question?"

The engineer scowled. "What do you *think* of her?"

The doctor shrugged. "I hadn't given her much thought. She seems efficient enough, I suppose."

Simenon harrumphed, obviously not happy with that answer. "Not as far as I'm concerned."

"Is there a problem?"

"I'd say so. Yesterday I showed Valderrama some sensor enhancements in anticipation of our encounter with Beta Barritus. What do you think she said?"

"I haven't the slightest idea," Greyhorse replied. "I'm a doctor, not an engineer."

"Give it a try."

Greyhorse rolled his eyes. "She thanked you for what you'd done and said she expected you to do better."

Simenon pointed to him triumphantly. "That's what you'd expect, right? For her to goad me into enhancing the sensors even more? That's what a science officer *does.*"

Greyhorse frowned. "Am I to understand that Valderrama fell short in this regard?"

"She sure as *hell* fell short. All she did was smile and thank me for all my hard work, and go about her business. It was as if she didn't *care* how well the sensors worked."

"And this bothers you?"

Simenon's lips pulled back, exposing rows of small, sharp teeth. "It doesn't bother *you?*"

"Why should it?" Greyhorse inquired casually. "Your people are probably working on the sensors even as we speak, regardless of Valderrama's reaction."

The Gnalish snorted. "Not probably."

The doctor held his hands up, palms facing the ceiling. "So why should I be bothered?"

"Because," Simenon said, "I'm not going to be there to pick up her slack all the time. *That's* why."

As the Gnalish's remark hung in the air, Greyhorse heard the shuffle of feet in the central exam area beyond his office door. Though he couldn't catch a glimpse of anyone from where he was sitting, he could venture a guess as to the newcomer's identity. Lieutenant Paxton was scheduled to come in for a routine physical.

"Paxton?" he called out.

"Right here," came the comm officer's response.

The doctor regarded Simenon and shrugged his massive shoulders. "Duty calls, I'm afraid."

The engineer nodded his lizardlike head. "Mine too." And he left without saying another word.

As soon as Simenon was gone, Greyhorse got up from behind his desk and went out into the central exam area. Paxton was sitting on a biobed, waiting for him.

"I hope I didn't interrupt anything," the comm officer said.

"Not at all," the doctor replied.

Then, putting everything else aside—Jiterica's problem as well as Simenon's—he focused on the matter at hand. After all, even a routine exam deserved his undivided attention.

And sickbay, Greyhorse resolved, would continue to be a model of order and efficiency on the *Stargazer*—even if some of the ship's other sections were not.

Idun Asmund sat cross-legged on the floor of her quarters. Wisps of sharply scented smoke escaped from a small iron receptacle in front of her, a receptacle blackened by use and time, in which she had set fire to a tiny chunk of *s'naiah* wood.

"Uroph, son of Warrokh," she intoned.

And she added, in her thoughts, *batlh Daqawlu'taH,* meaning "you will be remembered with honor" in the Klingon tongue.

For more than a thousand years, the warriors of Clan Warrokh had recited the names of their known ancestors before taking their evening meal. It was a tradition that had been passed down from father to son and mother to daughter.

"Weyto," she said, "son of Uroph."

Batlh Daqawlu'taH.

The list was nearly a hundred names long, but Idun never forgot any of them. To do so would have brought dishonor both to her and to the mother who taught her to remember.

"Ukray'k, daughter of Weyto."

Batlh Daqawlu'taH.

They were the blood of her adopted father and mother, not her own. Still, she considered them her forebears, just as her father and mother considered her their offspring—with all the rights and privileges accorded progeny under Klingon law.

"Jitakh, son of Ukray'k."

Batlh Daqawlu'taH.

In Gerda's quarters, which were next to Idun's, her sister would be reciting the same litany of names. But then, Gerda had been raised in the same strict Klingon household, provided with the same exhaustive Klingon education.

"Hojeen, son of Jitakh."

Batlh Daqawlu'taH.

When she and Gerda were young and newly adopted, their family had spoken the names together, their father's deep, resonant voice a counterpoint to their high-pitched, childish ones. Idun could almost hear him now, giving an edge and a life to their heritage that she could never quite manage.

"Qerresh, son of Hojeen."

Batlh Daqawlu'taH.

She could feel her mother's gaze on her, full of pride and approval. Idun and her sister were truer warriors than many who had been born Klingon.

"Royyebh, daughter of Qerresh."

Batlh Daqawlu'taH.

"Dobrukh, son of Royyebh."

Batlh Daqawlu'taH.

"Rejjakh, son of—"

It was then that Idun heard something.

A chime. It alerted the helm officer to the fact that someone was seeking entrance to her quarters—and spoiling the sanctity of her meditation.

Idun frowned and opened her eyes. Her crewmates knew that she wished to be left alone at this time of day. If they were interrupting her, it had to be an emergency of some kind.

Rising to her feet, she said, "Enter."

The doors slid apart with an exhalation of air, revealing the small, wiry figure of Commander Wu. She was standing in the corridor with a data padd in her hand and a polite smile on her face.

Clearly, Idun thought, she had been wrong about the possibility of an emergency. It was just a matter of a new crewmate who was unaware of her meditation schedule.

"Commander Wu," she said. "Can I help you?"

"May I come in?" Wu asked.

Idun shrugged. "Of course."

The second officer entered Idun's quarters and looked around for a moment—first at the wood-burning artifact and the smoke issuing from it, then at everything else. There were chairs available, a couple of them designed specifically for human comfort, but Wu declined to make use of any of them.

Perhaps she was simply waiting for an invitation, Idun thought. "Would you like to sit down?" she asked.

"No, thank you," Wu replied. "This won't take long."

There was something in her tone that told Idun she wasn't going to like what her guest had to say. As it turned out, her suspicion was an accurate one.

"According to ship's records," Wu said, "you're nearly a week late in taking the requalification exam for helm duty."

At first Idun thought the second officer was making a joke—paving the way for what she had *really* come to say. Then she realized that Wu was absolutely serious.

The helm officer conceded the point. "That is correct. I *am* a bit late in requalifying."

It was something every officer was required to do in his or her area of specialization. But it wasn't a regulation that was strictly enforced—at least, not in Idun's experience.

She said so.

Wu seemed unimpressed. "Maybe that was true of your previous assignments. Maybe it was even true here on the *Stargazer.* But under my supervision, things will be different. Breaches of Starfleet regulations will not be tolerated."

It was so ludicrous that Idun was tempted to laugh. "We are in the middle of a hunt for a dangerous adversary. I can requalify as soon as it's over."

It seemed like an eminently reasonable course of action. Apparently Wu thought otherwise.

"My officers don't make their own rules," she said. "They comply with regulations. You'll either requalify immediately or you'll be removed from your post."

Idun couldn't believe what she was hearing. She felt a spurt of anger jump into her throat.

Somehow she managed to suppress it. Then she said, "That decision may not be in the best interests of this mission or this crew," pointing out what seemed to her to be the truth.

Again Wu appeared to see the matter in a different light. "Until further notice," she announced, "you're relieved of your responsibilities at the helm."

And without another word, she turned and left Idun's quarters, the sliding doors hissing closed in her wake.

For a moment, Idun was left speechless. Then she swore volubly and vividly in the Klingon tongue, filling her quarters with curses that threatened to blister the duranium bulkheads, and contacted Wu's superior via the *Stargazer*'s intercom system.

Chapter Ten

BEN ZOMA HAD JUST ARRIVED on the bridge to take over for Picard when he received Idun Asmund's impassioned call.

Her voice, normally so clipped and efficient, seethed with barely restrained anger and indignation—so much so that it attracted the attention of everyone present. Picard was no exception.

Ben Zoma frowned. Then he asked the helm officer to hold off for a moment and moved to the captain's side.

"A problem?" Picard asked.

He was beginning to look a little tense. A little grim. And Ben Zoma had no trouble understanding why that would be.

They were getting closer to Beta Barritus, closer to the White Wolf—and closer to McAteer's "trap," as Corey Zweller had described it. Picard was determined to buck the odds, to accomplish what a dozen other captains before him couldn't and turn the tables on the admiral.

But what if Picard didn't manage to complete his mission? What if he fell short and, in the process, showed everyone that Admiral Mehdi's faith in him had been misplaced?

The captain had been studying chart after chart of Beta Barritus, incomplete as they were. He had pored over every research paper he could find that dealt with the dynamics of Lazarus stars.

But what if that wasn't enough?

Then McAteer would have succeeded in his gambit—and Picard would never forgive himself for it.

Hence the beleaguered expression, the first officer reflected. In his friend's place, Ben Zoma would no doubt have looked a little beleaguered as well.

"Nothing I can't handle," he told Picard.

"I trust you are right," the captain said, easing himself out of his center seat. "But if you should require my assistance after all, you will find me in my quarters."

Ben Zoma nodded. "I won't. But thanks."

That seemed to satisfy Picard. Leaving his friend to deal with Idun's problem, he headed for his quarters and a much-needed rest.

Ben Zoma waited until the captain had left the bridge. Then he entered the captain's ready room, took a seat behind the black plastic desk, and said, "Ben Zoma to Lieutenant Idun Asmund."

Instantly the story spilled out of her, punctuated with denunciation and invective. It took the first officer a while to amass all the details and put them in what seemed like the proper order.

Then he said, "Let me get this straight, Lieutenant. Commander Wu relieved you of your duties as helm officer because you hadn't taken your requalification test?"

"That is correct," Idun responded, her voice trembling with fury she dared not release.

Ben Zoma didn't get it. "Was that the *only* reason?"

"It was the only reason she *gave* me."

The first officer frowned. It was highly unusual for anyone to be held that closely to requalification regs—especially while on a mission as potentially difficult as this one.

"I'll tell you what," he said. "For now, you'll have to comply with the commander's decision. But I'll speak with her first chance I get. And when I do, I have a feeling we'll clear this up to everyone's satisfaction—yours included."

That seemed to calm Idun a bit. "Thank you, sir."

"You're welcome," Ben Zoma replied. Then he sat back in his chair and considered what he was going to say to Commander Wu.

* * *

Pug Joseph had gotten into the habit of checking in with his monitor officer every so often, even when he wasn't on duty. Fortunately he had never caught one napping, even figuratively.

Until now.

Marching into the security section, he didn't nod to either of the armed officers standing guard in the little anteroom. He didn't even look at their faces. He just kept going until he reached the hexagon-shaped main security facility.

That's where he found Obal sitting in front of the big, concave bank of monitors with its closed-circuit views of every strategically critical area on the ship. It was the Binderian's turn to stand watch over those critical areas.

And as Joseph had feared since his routine check-in several minutes earlier, Obal was fast asleep.

The security chief stood there for a moment, watching the little fellow's chest rise and fall serenely. Then, not too roughly, he took Obal by the shoulder and shook him.

The Binderian sat bolt upright with a little cry of surprise, his eyes blinking wildly. Still, it was a second or two before he realized where he was and who was standing beside him.

"Lieutenant Joseph," he said, his eyes wide as he began to grasp the nature of his circumstances.

"Sorry to have to wake you," Joseph told him. *In more ways than one,* he added silently. "But I can't have my monitor officer catching up on his sleep."

He might as well have driven an old-fashioned arrow into Obal's chest. "I—I'm sorry, sir," the Binderian bleated. "I don't know what came over me. Nothing like this has ever happened before."

"Maybe you've never stayed up half the night checking phasers before," Joseph suggested.

Obal swallowed. "That's true. Still, I feel terrible about this. Allow me to try to atone for it somehow."

By checking the phasers again? Joseph mused. *Or maybe the photon torpedo tubes this time?* "That won't be necessary," he said. "Just do the job you're assigned, all right?"

The Binderian couldn't possibly have looked more contrite. "Of course, sir. As you wish."

Joseph felt sorry for the little guy—he couldn't help it. But he wasn't just a bystander here, he was Obal's superior. And as such, he couldn't just dismiss the incident.

Besides, if he had waited just a few more minutes to call in, one of the other officers might have discovered the Binderian before he did. Then the incident would have become the talk of the ship's lounge. And though he could have asked his people to keep it among themselves, the story might have leaked out anyway.

Joseph sighed. It wasn't just a matter of people respecting Obal anymore. Now it was a matter of people respecting *him*. Because when the captain read Joseph's report, he would be forced to wonder what kind of security section his chief was running.

"Am I relieved of my post?" Obal inquired humbly, wincing as he posed the question.

Joseph nodded. "I think that would be our best course of action under the circumstances."

Without another word, the Binderian slipped out of his chair, thrust out his scrawny chest, and stood there dutifully until his only slightly curious replacement could be called in. Then he left security and presumably made his way back to his quarters.

As Joseph watched Obal go, a sigh escaped him. He himself hadn't done a single thing wrong, but he felt every bit as bad about the incident as the Binderian did.

Maybe worse.

Picard eyed the viewscreen in front of him. It showed him a massive, dark bullet of a ship bristling with deadly armaments, half obscured by the roiling currents of Beta Barritus.

"Hail them," he said.

Paxton made the attempt at his comm console. There was no response—not that the captain had expected any.

"Sir," said Gerda Asmund, sitting at her customary spot behind the navigation controls, "they're powering weapons."

"Red alert," Picard snapped. "Shields. Phasers."

"Shields up," Gerda confirmed.

"Phasers ready," Vigo announced.

It was then that the captain noticed the two figures standing next to the weapons console, just behind his left shoulder. They comprised a mismatched pair if he had ever seen one.

One was an older man, his face lined, his hair all but gone. He wore simple, sturdy clothes, the sort one might don to work in the fields, and there were traces of dirt beneath his fingernails.

The other was a tall, athletic-looking fellow in the cranberry and cream of a Starfleet captain's uniform. His hair was thick and dark, only beginning to show signs of gray at the temples, and his smile was a beacon of confidence stretching across his face.

Or rather, across *half* his face. The other half was a charred, bubbling wound, the result of an explosion in a plasma conduit during his first and only encounter with the Nuyyad.

The fellow's name was Daithan Ruhalter. He had preceded Picard as captain of the *Stargazer.*

And the other man, the one with the plain, sturdy clothes and the dirt beneath his fingernails? He was a vintner, heir to a long line of vintners. And if he had had his way, his son Jean-Luc would have been a vintner as well.

"They're firing, sir," Gerda called out.

The viewscreen filled swiftly with a lurid barrage of phased energy emissions. A moment later the bridge bucked and shuddered with the force of the attack.

"Actually," said Maurice Picard, "I've never approved of this sort of technology. I believe man's place is on Earth, doing what his ancestors have done for centuries." He searched for a phrase. "Getting his hands dirty, if you know what I mean."

"You know," Ruhalter said judiciously, "I think you've got a point there. You can't rely too much on machines, even in a battle like this one. It's the human element that wins and loses wars."

"How so?" Maurice Picard inquired.

"Instinct," Ruhalter elaborated. "Either you've got it or you don't— and if you *don't,* no collection of sensors and shields and phaser banks is going to help you."

As if to underline the wisdom of his statement, the ship was bludgeoned again with a phaser volley. Holding on to his armrests, Picard felt his teeth rattle with the impact.

"Return fire!" he cried.

"Aye, sir!" came the crisp response.

The *Stargazer* lit up the sea of gases with a pair of ruby-red phaser beams. But somehow, though the enemy didn't seem to make any effort to evade them, they missed.

Picard's teeth ground together. "Torpedoes!" he bellowed.

Again, "Aye, sir!"

Packets of matter and antimatter plunged through swirling currents, hungry to feed on their prey. But they missed as well and were rapidly lost to sight.

The crew of the *Stargazer* paid for the miss with another round of bone-jarring torment. The deck beneath Picard's feet jerked and shivered once, twice, and again.

"Fire again!" he roared.

But nothing happened. And when he turned to Vigo, all he saw was an expression of helplessness.

"Phasers and photon torpedoes are off-line," the weapons officer reported numbly.

"Shields down seventy-five percent!" Gerda snarled.

Picard felt his teeth grate together. "Evasive maneuvers!"

Idun sent them swerving to starboard. Ever so narrowly, they avoided the pirate's next burst of fury. But without weapons, there was no possibility of their winning this battle.

"Was it a good year?" Ruhalter inquired of his companion.

"It was an *exquisite* year," said Maurice Picard. "The grapes were sweet, succulent . . . the best I have grown in a long time."

"That's good to hear. I always liked good wines."

"Ah," the vintner sighed, glancing at his son, "but it's not enough to have a promising grape. It's what one does with it that makes for success . . . or failure."

He had barely gotten the words out when the enemy found them again. The *Stargazer* lurched hard to starboard under the force of the worst assault yet.

Without warning, Idun's control console exploded in a geyser of flame and sparks and the helm officer went flying backward. Even before Picard got to her, he could tell that she was dead.

"That's what happened to me," Ruhalter said.

The elder Picard screwed up his face in grim sympathy. "It looks terribly painful."

"Only if you survive," Ruhalter noted. "In my case, death came quickly and mercifully." He stroked the side of his face that had been reduced to blackened ruin. "Good thing I remembered to shave that day. I wouldn't have wanted to make a lousy-looking corpse."

He chuckled at his own joke. And after a moment, Maurice Picard chuckled with him. The sound of their laughter provided a bizarre counterpoint to the hissing of plasma and the exclamations of the captain's bridge officers.

Not the least of which were Picard's own raw-throated shouts. "Commander Ben Zoma," he cried, "take the helm! Get us out of here!"

His friend darted to one of the aft consoles and worked like a demon to transfer helm control. In the meantime, the pirate dealt them one savage blow after another, inflicting hull breaches and casualties too numerous to report.

"I knew he wouldn't be any good at this," said Maurice Picard. The lines in his face had deepened with disapproval. "He should have stayed at home, as I advised him."

"Doesn't seem that he learned much from me either," Ruhalter remarked. "Pity, isn't it?"

"The helm!" Picard cried helplessly, perspiration collecting in the small of his back. "Damn it, Gilaad—"

Finally Ben Zoma yelled, "Got it!" and brought the *Stargazer* about. But it was too late. Picard could see that. As he watched, spellbound, the enemy fired at point-blank range.

The volley filled the viewscreen with crimson light, turning everything and everyone on the bridge blood-red. And when it hit, it seemed to plunge everything into darkness.

Some time later—a second, or was it an hour?—the captain realized that he was lying on the deck. Raising his head, he looked around, but there was nothing but sparks and black smoke and the silhouettes of what had been his officers' control consoles.

Then they came walking out of the darkness and the sizzling flashes of light. Not his bridge officers, but *they*—the two who had no business being there.

They came to stand over him, both of them. And they had the same look on their faces—a look of heartfelt *disappointment.*

"He should have listened," observed Maurice Picard.

Ruhalter nodded. "I'll say."

"He had so much promise."

"Tons of it. He could've been a great captain."

"A great *man.*"

"It was too soon," Ruhalter observed, a spurt of sparks illuminating the nightmare side of his face. "He was too damned young."

The elder Picard's eyes filled with pain, just as they had the day his son left Labarre to attend the Academy. He nodded in agreement. "Too young indeed."

The captain wanted to answer, but he couldn't. The words stuck in his throat, choking him like thick, sooty smoke, forcing him to gasp for air, for life—

Then he realized that he wasn't on the bridge at all. He was sitting up in his bed, breathing hard as if he had exerted himself, his skin covered with a sheen of sour sweat. It seemed to him that he could hear his room echoing as if he had cried out when he woke, though he couldn't retrieve any of the words.

If there had even *been* words.

A dream, Picard thought, reassuring himself. All of it, a dream. But it had seemed so real while he was dreaming it.

So hideously *real* . . .

Chapter Eleven

NORMALLY CARTER GREYHORSE MINDED his own business. But every so often—as in the case at hand—he was compelled by duty to diverge from that policy.

"I'm fine," Picard said once the doors to his ready room had closed, giving him and the doctor some privacy.

"You don't *look* fine," Greyhorse told him. "You look like you've had something big and insistent running through your brain. Something with heavy spiked boots."

"Am I that transparent, Doctor?"

"I've seen viewports that are less so."

The captain frowned. Then he walked over to his observation port and stared at it. "I didn't sleep well last night."

"Nightmares?" the doctor suggested.

Picard turned to look at him, an echo of pain and confusion in his eyes. *"A* nightmare. Just one."

"It must have been a good one."

The captain's chuckle had a distinct lack of merriment in it. "It was. We had found the White Wolf and engaged him in battle. But we didn't fare very well."

"We lost him?"

"We lost *everything,*" Picard told him.

"And that's it?"

"That's it."

Greyhorse had a feeling there was more to it, but he didn't force the issue. He just said, "Obviously, you're concerned about how we'll do when we find the White Wolf—particularly since we're operating with a new captain, a new first officer, and a new second officer."

"And that's not cause for worry?" Picard asked.

The doctor shrugged. "I'm not qualified to answer that question. What I *am* qualified to tell you is that such dreams are perfectly normal for men with command-level responsibilities—even when they're *not* about to face some legendary pirate."

"That's comforting." The captain smiled a little sheepishly. "I appreciate your putting the matter in perspective."

"It's my job," the doctor said.

"Nonetheless," Picard insisted.

Greyhorse did his best to ignore the expression of gratitude. Emotions tended to make him uncomfortable, and gratitude was perhaps the worst in that regard.

"If you have any more trouble sleeping," he said, "let me know and I'll prescribe something. Outside of that, just try to relax. I don't need to tell you that your getting all worked up won't increase our chances of success."

Picard nodded. "I'll try to remember that."

As he left the room, Greyhorse wasn't sure that he had actually accomplished anything, or that the captain would sleep any more soundly from that point on. But at least he had made the attempt.

Juanita Valderrama was examining the sensor profile of an asteroid belt on the outskirts of a nearby solar system when Lieutenant Paxton appeared in her office.

"Got a minute?" he asked her.

Valderrama swiveled away from her monitor to face him. "Of course. Please . . . have a seat."

Paxton came in and allowed the door to close behind him. Then he sat down in the seat next to hers. If his expression was any indication, it wasn't anything trivial he wanted to talk about.

It was something rather serious.

"Listen," he said, "I don't normally tell tales out of school. But in this case, I think it would benefit everyone concerned."

Valderrama regarded him for a moment, wondering what he was talking about. Then she said, "Go on."

"Just a little while ago," Paxton told her, "I overheard Chief Simenon talking to someone. It doesn't matter whom, really. He was saying that he'd had a meeting with you in engineering."

The science officer nodded. "That's right."

"You were talking about the sensors?"

"Yes. Mr. Simenon told me that he had enhanced them with Beta Barritus in mind. I thanked him."

Paxton smiled benignly. "But unless I'm mistaken, you didn't encourage him to do any better."

Valderrama's brow creased above the bridge of her nose. "He's the chief engineer. I didn't think—"

She stopped herself in midsentence. Judging by Paxton's expression, he believed he had made his point.

"I didn't think," Valderrama sighed.

"You see what I'm getting at, right?"

The lieutenant nodded. "I should have pushed him to do better."

It's what she would have done when she was younger and new to the fleet. But over the years, she had somehow stopped caring so much. She had developed some bad habits.

Habits she was about to break.

This was Valderrama's last chance to prove she still had what it took. The captain had placed his faith in her. It was up to her not to let him down.

"Thanks," she told Paxton. "I appreciate your going out on a limb for me like this."

He shrugged. "You'll do the same for me one day. Just keep it under your hat, all right? Or no one will trust me when I tell them they've got a secure channel."

Valderrama smiled. "My lips are sealed."

And they would be.

Pug Joseph was lost in thought—so much so that his colleague seemed to appear out of nowhere.

This would likely have startled him even if his colleague *hadn't* been more than seven feet tall and as blue as the sky on a summer day. "Geez,"

Joseph blurted, recoiling in his seat, "did you have to sneak up on me like that?"

Vigo, the *Stargazer*'s senior weapons officer, favored him with a broad and well-meaning grin. "I *didn't* sneak up on you. At least, that wasn't my intention."

Joseph blew out a breath and looked around the lounge. None of the dozen or so crewmen present seemed to have noticed his jumpiness. Or if they had, they weren't making it obvious to him.

He looked up at Vigo again. "Sorry. i was just thinking."

"Deeply," the Pandrilite observed. He sat down on the other side of a low-slung table, his knees coming almost to the level of Joseph's shoulders. "Any particular reason for it?"

The security chief shrugged and lowered his voice. "I was just thinking about the new guy. *Obal.*"

Vigo's brow wrinkled. "Obal?"

"The little guy. The Binderian."

"Ah," said Vigo. "That one."

"I don't think he's going to work out."

"I'm sorry to hear that."

"Not half as sorry as I am," Joseph told him.

"You like him?"

"Sure. He's as eager as they come. If he wasn't so . . ."

The weapons officer shrugged. "So *what?*"

"So *silly*-looking. Then maybe I'd be more optimistic about his chances. But he looks like—"

"I know," Vigo interjected, sparing his colleague the need to describe the Binderian's appearance. "I have seen him. He is not your typical security officer."

"That's an understatement. I mean, if Commander Ben Zoma were still in charge of the section, maybe he could do something with Obal. But me, I'm new at this."

The Pandrilite frowned. If anyone could sympathize with Joseph, it was he. They had both received their battlefield promotions a scant few weeks ago, when the *Stargazer*'s clash with a race called the Nuyyad had ripped several links from the chain of command.

Of course, the weapons section wasn't very big, and its lone vacancy had been filled by a crewman from another part of the ship. So even Vigo wasn't exactly in the same boat as Joseph.

"Listen," the weapons officer said, "Commander Ben Zoma has faith in you or he wouldn't have given you the job in the first place. You're as qualified as anyone to help Obal." Vigo paused for a moment. "That is, if he *can* be helped."

It was a big *if,* Joseph told himself. "You're not just saying that to make me feel better, right?"

"I'm saying it," Vigo insisted, "because I believe it. Whatever the task, you are equal to it."

Joseph felt a pang of gratitude. He nodded. "Thanks for the vote of confidence. But I've still got to earn it."

"And you will. Now if I were you, I would stop worrying and spend my free time doing something enjoyable—something like, say, a game of sharash'di."

Joseph looked at him askance. "Sharash'di? You mean that game Charlie Kochman got for you?"

"Yes. I could set up a board right now."

The security chief considered it for a moment, then dismissed the idea with a wave of his hand. "No, thanks. I don't think I could concentrate on a game right now."

Vigo seemed on the verge of arguing the point with him, then seemed to think better of it. "As you wish," he said. "But remember what I said—you will be equal to the task, whatever it is."

Then he moved off in the direction of Greyhorse, who had just entered the lounge. Idly, Joseph wondered what Vigo was so eager to talk to the doctor about.

Worry about that later, Joseph told himself. *Right now, you've got to figure out what to do with Obal.*

But what *could* he do? If he kicked the little guy out of security, he would be crushed. And he would know that it wasn't just his lone indiscretion that had done him in, because every officer in the section made a mistake from time to time.

Joseph thought long and hard. He considered the problem from every angle he could think of. But despite Vigo's words of encouragement, he still couldn't come up with an answer.

"Mr. Simenon?"

The Gnalish looked away from his sleek, black control console and saw Lieutenant Valderrama approaching him. He knew the look on the science officer's face, having seen it many times over the years since he came to Earth to attend Starfleet Academy.

She was about to ask a personal favor of him.

What's more, he was uniquely capable of granting it. As the ship's chief engineer, he could make a significant difference in the quality of people's lives.

What was it? Simenon wondered. Had the lieutenant's replicator gone on the blink? Or maybe her sonic shower? Had the automatic doors in her quarters gotten jammed?

Well, Valderrama would have to wait her turn in the repairs queue like everyone else. Her status as a fellow officer didn't get her any privileges in *his* book.

"Listen," Simenon said, "I'm busy right now. If—"

"This won't take long," the science officer assured him.

He scowled, swiveled on his chair and gave Valderrama his full attention. "All right," he said. "I'm listening."

And she said, "I'd like to ask a favor of you."

I knew it, Simenon thought, inwardly congratulating himself for his infallible insight into the nuances of human behavior. "And what favor is that?" he asked.

"I'd appreciate it," she said, "if you would take another stab at enhancing our sensor capabilities. I've gone over what you did and I think you can do better."

Simenon straightened. "Better?"

"That's right. A *lot* better. You're one of the most experienced engineers in the fleet, and our sensor capabilities are going to be a key to this mission. We need more from you."

"I see," the Gnalish said.

"I'm glad," Valderrama told him. She smiled. "Keep me informed, will you? I'll be in the science section if you need me."

And with that, she made her way back to the exit.

Simenon's ruby eyes narrowed as he watched the doors slide closed behind Valderrama. Obviously, someone had told the woman how he felt about their earlier conversation. Either that, or her change of heart was a colossal coincidence.

And he didn't take much stock in coincidence.

But Greyhorse was the only one with whom Simenon had discussed the matter, and the doctor wasn't the type to get involved in other people's business. He didn't believe in making what he called "uninvited appearances" in his patients' lives.

So who, then? Who had tipped Valderrama off? Someone who had overheard his conversation with the doctor. . . . Paxton, maybe? Or one of the nurses on duty at the time?

Not that I care, Simenon reflected.

In fact, he didn't give a tribble's furry hide under what circumstances Valderrama's attitude had changed, or who might possibly have been responsible. All that mattered was that her attitude *had* changed—and that the science officer would be pulling her own weight from that point on.

With that happy prospect in mind, the engineer pulled down on the lapels of his lab coat, swiveled his chair around and returned his attention to his control console.

Jean-Luc Picard roused himself from his reverie, vaguely aware that someone had spoken to him as he sat in his center seat. He turned to his right and found himself staring at Lieutenant Iulus, one of the senior men in his engineering section.

Iulus had a padd in his hand. He offered it to the captain. "Those maintenance reports you asked for?"

"Yes," said Picard, "of course." Accepting the padd, he made a point of glancing at the data contained on its screen and nodded to Iulus. "Thank you."

The engineer assured him that it was no trouble at all. Then he left the bridge, leaving the captain to wonder how long he had been adrift in his thoughts.

A minute? Several? He cursed himself softly.

He had been thinking about the White Wolf. About what sort of commander the man might be, what sort of tactical capabilities he might have at his disposal.

Picard doubted that the White Wolf's vessel would be quite as well armed as the one in his dream. But certainly the pirate had to have some tricks up his sleeve to have remained free as long as he had.

It was unfortunate that Starfleet had given him so little to go on. Just a few snippets of other ships' sensor data here and there, and more than half of it of questionable reliability.

The captain felt his hand clench into a fist. If only he knew one thing about his adversary for certain. If only the White Wolf were more than a ghost to him, haunting him, taunting and tantalizing him like a cosmic will-o'-the-wisp.

Picard sighed. He would go over the other captains' logs once again. Then he would go over their charts of Beta Barritus. Perhaps there was something he missed, something that might prove of value when he confronted the pirate.

And he *would* confront him. The captain still had every confidence of that taking place.

Turning to Gerda, he asked, "How many hours until we reach Beta Barritus, Lieutenant?"

His navigator consulted her monitors. "Eighteen, sir. Unless you'd like to increase speed to warp nine—?"

Picard shook his head. "That won't be necessary."

It wasn't the White Wolf's way to try to outrun his pursuers. Starfleet had established *that,* at least. The pirate would go to ground like a fox, and the Beta Barritus system was his favorite foxhole.

Besides, the captain didn't want to exhaust his vessel's resources by maintaining too high a rate of velocity for too long. That was why they were cruising at warp eight and no faster.

But he couldn't wait to reach Beta Barritus.

Chapter Twelve

ADMIRAL MCATEER WATCHED the Pacific sun disappear behind a blood-red frond as he negotiated one of the many cunningly shaded paths in the expansive garden behind Starfleet Academy.

The place had looked quite different when the admiral was a cadet. Stodgy, geometric, cut-and-dried. Each path had been nothing more than a way to get from one building to another.

Then he had left the Academy to serve on ships that crisscrossed the galaxy. His objective, at least in theory, was the study of stars and their attendant planets. But in reality, he had studied the men and women with whom he worked—their strengths, their failings, the reasons they did what they did. After all, his thinking had gone, if he was to become an effective leader he would need to become an expert on the people he would be leading.

And he *would* become a leader, McAteer had assured himself. Even then, he knew with grim certainty that he would rise through the ranks and guide Starfleet into a new era someday.

Finally, after many long years of dedication and achievement, after entire decades' worth of care and planning and artful maneuvering,

McAteer got what he had always envisioned. He stood on a height from which he could look out and see the end of his fated journey.

He was back on Earth, the planet of his birth. He was a Starfleet admiral, with all the trimmings. And most important, he was in a position to make his ideas about the fleet a reality.

One of the first things he noticed on his return was the Academy garden and how much it had changed. It boasted exotic plants, shrubs, and trees from dozens of alien worlds—vegetation that added life and scale and color to the place, lining each path and hiding long stretches of it from its neighbors.

It was a refreshment, an intrigue, a delight. One could walk for half an hour and not even come close to being bored.

McAteer had heard that the man responsible was someone named Boothby. A landscape architect, he had guessed, a highly trained professional who had touched this expanse with his genius and moved on.

The admiral admired the fellow for what he had accomplished—and fancied himself a like spirit. After all, what he was trying to do with Starfleet was very much what Boothby had done with this garden.

He had uprooted the old and introduced the new. He had pruned away whatever was holding him back and planted that which served his purposes. And if he had been forced to sacrifice some of the trees and hedges that had served here long and faithfully, his ruthlessness had gained him what nostalgia never could.

Soon, McAteer reflected, his garden would be free of useless undergrowth like Admiral Mehdi and unwanted weeds like that upstart Picard. It would only contain what he wanted it to contain, what he had handpicked and placed there personally.

He smiled just thinking about it. Picard had no chance to catch the White Wolf. *None.* He would look inept, inadequate—and even more so when the pirate was brought to justice.

And he *would* be brought to justice. The admiral had absolutely no doubt of it.

Noticing a stone bench just off the path, he availed himself of it. As McAteer sat, he found himself charmed by a most unusual scent—a mixture, it seemed to him, of butterscotch and vanilla. He traced it to a generous cascade of pale-blue blossoms that fell from a nearby branch almost to the ground.

He didn't know the tree's name. But the blossoms were so fragrant, so eminently pleasing, he longed to smell one close-up. Plucking a single, fat specimen from among its companions, he held it to his nose and inhaled deeply.

Yes, McAteer thought, savoring the scent. Butterscotch and vanilla. He crushed it between his fingers to get more of the smell out. And maybe a trace of cinnamon as well.

"And what do you think *you're* doing?" someone demanded.

The admiral looked around and saw a figure moving toward him, alternately drenched in sunlight and dipped in shadow. It was a man, much older than McAteer, judging by his thatch of white hair and the lines in his face. He wore black overalls and a pale-blue pullover, and there was a spray can in his hand.

"I beg your pardon?" the admiral said.

"I asked you what you thought you were doing," the man snapped, his watery blue eyes fierce and warlike. "But if that was too subtle for you, how about this—*keep your hands off the cotton-picking flowers.*"

McAteer felt a spurt of anger. No—he reserved anger for enemies of equal strength. What he felt was indignation.

"Listen, old-timer, maybe your eyesight's not what it used to be." He held up his sleeve and pointed to it. "But if you can see these bars, you ought to have some idea to whom you're speaking."

The groundskeeper—for that's obviously what he was—chuckled dryly beneath bushy eyebrows. "You're an admiral. Big deal."

McAteer felt the color drain from his face.

"I see guys like you come and go twenty times a day." The older man moved past McAteer and inspected the branch that had yielded the flower. "And the vast majority of them know better than to pick blossoms off my *darro* tree."

"I don't think you understand," the admiral told him, his tone clipped and imperious. But then, he wasn't going to take that kind of talk from a mere gardener. "I could have you fired for speaking to me that way." He snapped his fingers. "Like that."

The groundskeeper chortled as if McAteer had said something very funny. "Great. I could use a vacation. Haven't had one in longer than I can remember."

The nerve of him, McAteer thought, his teeth grinding together. *The unmitigated gall.*

He hadn't become an admiral to have a—a civilian tell him where to get off. "I'll be happy to oblige you, old-timer. Just give me your name and I assure you, you'll have nothing more to do with this place."

The old man sprayed a cloud of water at the injured branch, tilted his head to one side to see something McAteer couldn't, then turned an amused expression on him.

"The name," he said, "is Boothby."

And he walked away.

The admiral stared at the old man, sputtering. Then, no longer feeling quite so appreciative of the Academy garden, he returned to his office by the straightest route possible.

Simenon was still wondering about Valderrama's change of heart when he received a visit from Commander Wu.

"Don't tell me," he snapped in a preemptory tone. "You've spoken to Lieutenant Valderrama and you think I can do a better job of enhancing our sensor capabilities."

The second officer looked confused for a second. But *only* for a second. Then she seemed to regain her composure.

"I trust you know what you're doing here," she said.

Simenon didn't know what Wu was talking about, but he couldn't resist making use of the straight line. "We had better hope so, hadn't we? Otherwise, the warp core may blow at any time now."

He chuckled at his little joke. Unfortunately for Wu, she didn't see fit to join him.

"I'm not here about engineering expertise, Mr. Simenon. I'm here about violating Starfleet regulations."

It was another straight line, even better than the first one. "You're too late," the Gnalish said, moving along a bank of monitors. "The mutiny was last mission."

Again, he chuckled at his own jest. And again, the second officer appeared to be unamused.

"I mean it, Chief," she said as she followed him. "You're in violation of the regs."

"Oh?" he said, wondering exactly where she was going with this. "And which reg am I violating?"

"The one that says engineers are prohibited from working a double shift unless there's at least a yellow alert in effect. I count six men and women who are here for their second consecutive shift—and that's not including *you*."

Simenon looked at Wu, and saw by her frown that she was serious. "You're not kidding," he said, "are you?"

"Not at all," she confirmed.

Now it was his turn to scowl. "Look, Commander, we're trying to get something accomplished here—something that may make the difference between finding that damned pirate and going home empty-handed. If my people aren't complaining about working overtime to make that happen, why should Starfleet?"

It was as if Wu hadn't heard a word he said. "To comply with the regulation," she told him, "you'll have to—"

Simenon held up a scaly hand. He didn't have time for this nonsense. "I won't have to do a *thing*, Commander. This is my section and I'll run it any way I see fit—and if you've got a problem with that, you can take it up with the captain and Commander Ben Zoma."

Wu looked shocked by his declaration. Then her features screwed up into an expression of determination and she said, "Thanks for the advice, Chief. I think I'll do just that."

And she stalked off, presumably to find Picard or Ben Zoma.

Not that Simenon cared the least bit either way. Putting the incident aside, he took a look at the next monitor in line and muttered, "All right then . . . just where were we?"

Ben Zoma was about to get in touch with Commander Wu when Wu got in touch with *him*.

"I've just been to engineering," she told him over the intercom system, her tone one of restrained indignation. "Did you know that Chief Simenon's people are working double shifts down there?"

"I wasn't aware of that," the first officer admitted. "But it's not unusual for them to do that."

"Even in the absence of a yellow alert?" Wu asked. "Against explicit Starfleet regulations?"

It took him a moment to recall the sense of the regulation. "I see what you mean," he said. "But to tell you the truth, Commander, we often put minor regulations aside when they interfere with the smooth operation of the ship."

There was a pause. "Sir, regulations are designed to *ensure* the smooth operation of the ship."

Ben Zoma frowned. "Where are you now, Commander?"

Another pause. "I'm on my way to sickbay."

The first officer could just imagine what havoc the woman was bent on wreaking *there*.

He calculated the time it would take Wu to reach her quarters. Then he told her to meet him there in five minutes and terminated the link.

"Have you ever done this before?" Lieutenant Pierzynski asked.

It took a moment for the being in the gray-and-white containment suit to respond. "No."

"It's not difficult," the security officer assured her.

The ghostly expression behind the faceplate didn't change. "Perhaps you could demonstrate for me," Ensign Jiterica said in a flat, metallic-sounding voice.

Pierzynski shrugged, trying to act natural despite the strangeness of his visitor. "Sure."

Hunkering down on one knee, he swung open the metal plate that had been sitting flush with the bulkhead and exposed a compartment hardly bigger than his hand. Then he tapped a couple of square, colored studs inside the compartment and looked across the brig to the nearest of its eight cells.

It didn't look any different as a result of his efforts. Not yet, at least. But it would.

Jiterica leaned over in her suit to get a better look inside the compartment. "You pressed the yellow button?" she asked. "And then the red one?"

"That's right," the security officer told her. "And in that order. Otherwise, the emitters won't respond."

"I see," she said.

Pierzynski had been asked by Lieutenant Joseph to show Jiterica around the brig. It wasn't the first time Pierzynski had briefed a brand-new ensign, though it was the first time time he had done so for someone in a containment suit.

He had heard about Jiterica's problem in the shuttlebay. By then, probably everyone had heard. *Unfortunate,* he thought. But in a way, it had been for the best. Better to find out the ensign's limitations during a drill than in a real emergency.

Anyway, nothing like that would happen in the brig. Commander Ben Zoma had given Joseph his word that there wouldn't be any evac drills as long as Jiterica was stationed there.

Pierzynski got up and walked over to the cell whose generators had activated. There was a padd set into the bulkhead just to one side of it.

Tapping in the requisite code, he saw a force barrier spring into being, stretching itself like a translucent veil across the cell's doorless entrance.

"And that's how it's done," he announced. "If you want to turn it off, you just do the same thing in reverse. Or if you want to change the polarity of the fields, all you have to do is—"

Before he could finish his sentence, he heard something—a shuffling sound. Not sure what it meant, he shot a glance over his shoulder and saw Jiterica leaning against the bulkhead.

She was doubled over as if in pain.

"Are you all right?" he asked.

"I—" she began, but couldn't get any further. "I—"

The security officer didn't know what to do for her. He didn't even know what had happened. He had never had any experience with someone like Jiterica.

Tapping his combadge, he barked, "Pierzynski to sickbay! Something's wrong with Ensign Jiterica!"

"Not—" the Nizhrak said, her voice strangely flat and emotionless for someone who was so obviously involved in a struggle. "I can—"

Pierzynski didn't know what Jiterica was trying to tell him, but it really didn't matter. She needed help, and unless he was mistaken, she needed it quickly.

"Hurry!" he shouted, urging on the medical team.

Chapter Thirteen

JITERICA WAS SITTING on a biobed and peering at Greyhorse through the transparent faceplate of her containment suit. "Interference?" she repeated quizzically.

"That's right," said the doctor. He turned to Simenon, who had apparently assisted in the ensign's recovery. "Perhaps my colleague here would care to explain?"

The Gnalish shrugged his narrow shoulders. "It's simple, really. Your suit is laced with a containment field—something like the barriers we generate in the brig to keep prisoners incarcerated. In your suit, though, the field is engineered to a rather exacting standard. In the brig, there's no need for such precision, so the fields there tend to bleed a bit."

Jiterica was beginning to understand. "When Lieutenant Pierzynski activated the barrier, it bled beyond its visible parameters . . . and interacted with the field in my suit."

"With the result that your containment field went down," Simenon told her. "At least, until we could figure out what had happened and drag you away from the barrier."

"But while you were without the assistance of the field," Greyhorse noted, "it was left entirely up to you to maintain your molecular density and keep your suit from exploding. That must have been quite a burden on your physiology."

It was indeed, Jiterica reflected. Of course, she had contained herself for short periods of time before—when she beamed up to the *Stargazer,* for instance. But in this case, the lapse in her containment field had been unexpected.

"Had there been more insulation in your suit," said Greyhorse, "this might have been avoided. But as it was . . ." He frowned.

"Needless to say," Simenon assured her, "this sort of thing won't happen a second time."

The ensign didn't doubt that he was right. But there were so many *other* things that could happen . . .

"And," said the doctor, "you can leave sickbay whenever you feel rested enough. With your suit functioning again, there's no reason to keep you here."

Jiterica slid off the biobed less than gracefully. "Then I will be going. Thank you," she said, "both of you."

And she made her way out into the corridor, beset by more doubts and uncertainties than ever before.

Ben Zoma was already standing at the entrance to Wu's quarters when the second officer showed up.

"Commander," she said, looking more than a little leery.

Ben Zoma acknowledged her with a nod of his head. Then he waited while she tapped the metal plate set into the bulkhead, opening her quarters to them.

As he might have expected, the place was impeccably if minimally furnished and unutterably neat. Following Wu inside, he took a seat and waited for her to do the same.

"Well," said Wu, with admirable efficiency, "here we are. What is it you wanted to speak to me about, sir?"

Ben Zoma chose his words carefully. "I take it the captain of your previous ship was a precise observer of regulations?"

She nodded. "Of course. Captain Rudolfini was an excellent officer."

Obviously, Wu wasn't going to make it easy for him—not that he had expected her to. "At the risk of being considered a *bad* officer," he said, "I have to tell you that we do things differently here on the *Stargazer.* We don't always adhere strictly to regulations, especially when they bump heads with common sense."

The second officer didn't say anything. She just sat there and listened to him.

"And as far as I can tell," Ben Zoma continued, "we're not unusual in that respect. Most captains will overlook minor violations if they don't interfere with overall efficiency—especially when they're seen in the context of a difficult mission."

Wu just looked at him.

"Therefore," he told her, "I would appreciate it if you let up on Simenon and Idun and whoever else among your subordinates may have been guilty of a minor infraction. Of course, if you see something seriously wrong, don't hesitate to correct it. But it's got to be more than a failure to requalify or the odd double shift."

Ben Zoma expected an argument from his second officer. To his surprise, he didn't get one.

"I'll obey your orders," Wu told him evenly, "if that's what they are. But I would be remiss if I didn't tell you that I sincerely and wholeheartedly disagree with them."

He sighed. He had been right about Wu, it seemed—she was going to be trouble after all.

Jiterica dutifully moved her containment suit along the corridor in the direction of her quarters. However, the suit wasn't the heaviest burden she had to carry with her.

When Lieutenant Simenon mentioned the similarity between the field in the ensign's suit and the barriers employed in the brig, he had only meant that they drew on the same technology. But Jiterica had come to the conclusion that the similarity extended well beyond that.

After all, her containment field was a means of incarceration as well, in that it kept her from assuming the form nature had intended for her. And there were other prisons into which she had blithely and willingly placed herself.

The *Stargazer*, for instance, in that it carried her far from the milieu into which she had been born. And the vows she had made as a member of Starfleet, for they kept her from living a life in which she could find meaning.

To this point, she had managed to fool herself. Despite mounting evidence to the contrary, she had convinced herself that she might thrive in Starfleet—that she might even manage to become a viable officer someday. But her experiences on the *Stargazer* had finally put an end to that notion.

First, there was the embarrassment in the shuttlebay, where she had placed others in peril by virtue of her very existence. True, it was only theoretical peril, but the next time it might be real.

Then she had suffered an even greater embarrassment by nearly exploding her containment suit in the brig. As Simenon had indicated, the situation wasn't likely to come up a second time, but how many other venues on the ship would prove inimical to her survival?

What further humiliation would she have to endure before she accepted the inevitable—before she resigned herself to the grim reality of her prospects on the *Stargazer?*

Just as Jiterica thought this, she saw someone round the bend in the corridor ahead of her. It was a human, older than most on the ship—a female with a greater body mass than the statistical average, her hair worn loose about her shoulders.

Jiterica didn't remember meeting the woman. However, it was clear that she was a lieutenant, because there was a spool-shaped device pinned onto the right shoulder and left sleeve of her uniform. It was also clear that she worked in the science section, because those same devices were at least partly gray in color.

A full lieutenant in the science section, Jiterica thought. That would be Lieutenant Valderrama. The woman had beamed up to the ship with the group that came after the Nizhrak's.

As Valderrama approached her, Jiterica could make out the expression on the lieutenant's face. It began with curiosity, reconfigured itself almost immediately into a mask of restraint, then evolved gradually into the inevitable look of pity.

Finally, Valderrama nodded. Jiterica inclined her helmeted head in response. Then the lieutenant was past her—mercifully so—and the Nizhrak was alone in the corridor again.

Valderrama was right to pity her, Jiterica thought. All her fellow crewmen were right to do so. She was, despite her best efforts, a pitiful excuse for a Starfleet ensign.

But they wouldn't need to pity her much longer. In the morning she would tell the captain that she was quitting the fleet and ask to be returned to her homeworld.

Jiterica wouldn't find any relief in that meeting—neither then nor later. No doubt, she would regret what had happened here and on the *Manitou* for a very long time.

But in light of all her failures, a quick departure was the only reasonable option open to her.

In the short time that Nikolas had known Joe Caber, his opinion had changed a hundred percent.

Not his opinion of Caber—*that* hadn't changed one iota. Nikolas still saw his roommate as the perfect Starfleet ensign, well on his way to becoming the perfect Starfleet skipper.

What had changed was the way Nikolas saw *himself.*

When he walked into his quarters the day before, he had already resigned himself to his fate. He was going to be a loose cannon, a thorn in the side of his superiors the rest of his Starfleet career—however long it might be allowed to last.

Now Nikolas believed there might be a different fate in store for him, one that involved some success in his chosen profession. He could even see himself becoming an officer someday.

And why? Because of Joe Caber.

Because the guy had encouraged him to look beyond his limitations. Because he had shown Nikolas that they had more in common than the ensign might ever have believed.

He might never be Joe Caber, admiral's son. But if he tried, if he managed to put aside his resentments and his insecurities, he might become someone almost as good.

"Hey," said Caber, "you going to hang there all day?"

Nikolas smiled despite the increasing strain on his arms and shoulders and regripped the horizontal bar one hand at a time. "Just until I feel comfortable," he grunted.

"You sure you've done this before?" Caber gibed in a good-natured tone of voice.

In fact, Nikolas was hardly an expert on the horizontal bar. But he didn't want to admit that in front of his roommate—especially after he had boasted about his gymnastic skills all the way here.

"Just step back," he said, "and try not to gasp in awe."

Then Nikolas began swinging back and forth, all the while maintaining his hold on the chalk-covered titanium bar above him. Ignoring the pain it cost him, he swung higher and higher, until his hips were well above the bar on his backswing.

Finally, when he couldn't take it any longer, he drove forward one last time. At the apex of his swing, he let go of the bar and threw himself backward into a tightly tucked somersault.

That was the easy part, he told himself. The hard part would be sticking the landing.

As fast as the room was spinning around him, Nikolas had no real idea what he was doing. All he could do was take a stab at it and hope for the best. With that approach in mind, he released his grip at what seemed like the appropriate time.

And somehow, as if by magic, managed to land on his feet.

There was an almost overwhelming moment of vertigo, when Nikolas had the feeling that he was standing more or less upright but couldn't be certain of it. Then the dizziness passed, and he realized that he had stuck the landing.

Stuck it perfectly, in fact.

"Nice job," Caber told him.

Nikolas grinned. "All in a day's work."

Then it was his roommate's turn. He eyed the bar, rolled a bar of chalk between his hands and put it down beside the apparatus. Then he leaped up, grasped the bar, and kicked forward into a swing.

In no time, Caber was swinging as high as Nikolas had. Then higher. And he was doing it with only one hand, first the right and then the left, never both at the same time.

In a burst of energy, he swung completely around the bar, cutting a perfect circle through the air—once, twice, and a third time. Finally, without warning, he released the bar and tucked himself into a rapidly spinning somersault.

But it wasn't the single flip that Nikolas had done. It was a double, with a twist for good measure. And when Caber landed, it was with flawless grace and balance.

Nikolas whistled involuntarily. And here he thought he had impressed his roommate with his relatively rudimentary performance. The guy was amazing. Absolutely amazing.

"Nice job yourself," Nikolas told him.

But Caber didn't answer. He was staring over Nikolas's shoulder, his face frozen in an expression of disbelief. His curiosity piqued, Nikolas turned and saw what had caught his friend's attention.

It was the Binderian—the one who had beamed up to the *Stargazer* in Nikolas's group. The ensign hadn't seen him since, but he had heard that the guy was in security.

What was his name again? Obert? Obizz? *No,* Nikolas thought, remembering at last. *Obal.*

When he last saw the little guy, it was in the transporter room. They had beamed up together, along with the new science officer.

At the time, Nikolas had noted how strange-looking the Binderian was, how awkward he seemed in his Starfleet uniform. Almost comical, the ensign had thought at the time.

Now Obal was wearing Starfleet-issue black gym shorts a couple of sizes too long for him and a blue tank top that accentuated his bony shoulders and arms, and he looked even more ridiculous than he had in the transporter room.

As Nikolas watched, the Binderian went over to the weight area and picked up a couple of barbells—the lightest pair on hand, perhaps three kilograms apiece. With an effort, he brought them to shoulder height. Then, taking a deep breath between clenched teeth, he began to push them toward the ceiling.

With each push, Obal grunted. No—it was less a grunt than a wheeze, Nikolas decided. And to add to the effect, Obal's face, which was already a bright pink, turned a lush crimson.

Nikolas was sorely tempted to laugh out loud—it was that funny-looking. But he knew it would hurt the Binderian's feelings, so he managed to refrain.

Then he heard laughter after all. It seemed to fill the gym. And it came from Caber.

"Boy," he said, "that's got to be the most pitiful excuse for a body I've ever seen."

Nikolas looked at him. It wasn't like his roommate to be so critical, even in jest.

Obal, on the other hand, didn't seem to mind the remark. He just smiled as Caber was smiling and went back to his lifting.

"Come to think of it," Caber went on, "I'm not even sure that *is* a body. Bodies have muscles, don't they? I've baited *hooks* with physiques more muscular than that."

Still the Binderian seemed not to take offense. He continued his exercises without a hint of animosity, without the least sign that he was bothered by Caber's comments.

But Nikolas was bothered by them.

It wasn't that he thought Caber was trying to hurt Obal's feelings. Anyone who knew the admiral's son knew he wasn't capable of that. He was just playing around.

But the remarks still felt wrong to Nikolas. Unsporting somehow, like hunting flies with a phaser rifle.

"Hey," he said, meaning to distract his friend, "all this exercise is getting me hungry. What do you say we hit the mess hall and pump some fried chicken?"

But Caber didn't even look at him. He was still too enthralled by the sight of the Binderian.

"I wonder what he looked like *before* he started working out." Caber snickered. "Must've been hard to see him *at all.*"

"Or some ribs," said Nikolas, pushing upstream with his suggestion. "I sure could go for some nice barbecued ribs. You *are* the guy who's always hungry, right?"

It was then that Caber finally seemed to notice him. "Yeah," he replied after a moment. "Ribs. That sounds good to me too."

Nikolas indicated the doorway with a tilt of his head. "So what are we waiting for?"

Caber glanced at Obal as if he were going to shoot one more comment in the Binderian's direction. But in the end, all he did was grin and shake his head and lead the way across the gym.

Nikolas followed him, relieved that the incident was over. But before he and his roommate could reach the exit, Obal piped up.

"Have a pleasant day," he said, his voice high-pitched and tremulous and nearly as silly as his appearance.

Nikolas sighed. "You too."

But Caber didn't say anything in return. He just broke out into another wave of laughter, filling the corridor outside the gym with it as he and Nikolas made their way to their quarters.

Chapter Fourteen

PICARD HAD NEVER SEEN a Lazarus star in person. And he wasn't unusual in that respect, considering the scarcity of such stars within the bounds of Federation territory.

Nonetheless, he had studied the phenomenon long and hard since their departure from Starbase 32. He had memorized the sequence of events in the life of a Lazarus star—its unremarkable creation, its placid red-giant phase, the violent scattering of heavy elements and blinding luminosity that accompanied its seemingly suicidal supernova, and the almost miraculous birth of a new red giant in the midst of its predecessor's ample debris.

Every recorded image that Picard had seen of a Lazarus star showed it to be gauzy and colorless, the reborn sun at its heart all but occluded by the cast-off material floating around it. But as Picard watched Beta Barritus loom on his forward viewscreen, he saw that it wasn't gauzy and colorless at all.

It was a thing of sheer, unmitigated beauty—and a remarkably savage beauty at that.

The star itself was the fiery red eye of a cosmic god, glowering menacingly at the universe around it. It swam in a glittering sea of nested gases, a mammoth iridescence that boasted strands of emerald and lapis and amber.

And in the midst of that iridescence, hidden by that glittering sea, was the freebooter called the White Wolf.

Nor was there any question that he was in there. Gerda Asmund had identified his ion trail—the same sort of trail that Picard's predecessors had discovered and recorded in their sensor logs—and there was no corresponding trail to indicate the pirate's departure.

He was in there, all right. And at long last, Picard had his chance to fish the fellow out.

"Kind of takes your breath away," Ben Zoma remarked.

The captain forgot the White Wolf for the moment and again fixed his attention on the spectacle before him. "It certainly does, Number One."

Of course, Beta Barritus's beauty didn't make it any less dangerous to them. Those ionized gases surrounding it had the potential to wreak havoc with their mission.

He turned to Idun. "Reduce speed to half impulse."

"Aye, sir," said his helm officer.

"Shields at full," Picard directed.

"Shields at full," Vigo confirmed.

Slowly but surely, the system filled the viewscreen with its splendor, blotting out all evidence of more distant stars. Its outermost filaments of color blurred as the *Stargazer* came closer and finally pierced them, sending a chill up Picard's spine.

It's not the first time you've ever entered a solar system, he chastised himself. On the other hand, it was the first time he had entered *this* one.

"Lots of debris, sir," Gerda reported, "just as we were warned. The pieces are too small to see, but they're there."

Picard wasn't surprised any more than Gerda was. His predecessors' reports had all mentioned the system's debris shell—a by-product of the star's initial, explosive demise, which had destroyed whatever planets originally circled it.

"The friction is causing an increase in hull temperature," Idun noted. She glanced over her shoulder at Picard. "It's as if we're entering a Class-M atmosphere."

"See if you can find a less debris-ridden entry path," the captain told her.

Idun did as he asked. But Picard didn't hold out much hope of her finding such a path. After all, no other helm officer had found one, and plenty of them had looked.

He said as much to Ben Zoma.

"Maybe we'll be the first," his first officer told him.

"Maybe," Picard conceded.

But after half an hour, Idun still hadn't had any luck.

If the captain had wished, his helm officer would have pressed on until she dropped from exhaustion. She had been trained by her adopted family never to admit defeat.

But Picard had been brought up by members of a more practical species, and he didn't see any point in placing Idun under such stress. Besides, it wasn't as if they couldn't get through the debris field without a path of less resistance.

They could do what the White Wolf's other pursuers had done— reshape their shields to minimize the friction and plunge through the region as best they could. But the *Stargazer* would pay a price for that approach, just as all the other ships had paid a price. And in the end, it would keep them from completing their mission here.

Clearly, they needed a different strategy—one that would get them through the debris field in better shape than their predecessors. Until they had that strategy in hand, they would have to hover here on the fringes of the Beta Barritus system.

And the White Wolf would remain free.

Frowning, the captain turned to Ben Zoma and said, "Convene the senior staff, Gilaad. We've got work to do."

Admiral McAteer gazed at the mantel clock sitting on his desk, the syncopated movement of its polished brass workings visible through its thin glass walls.

McAteer loved the clock, a gift from his grandmother on the occasion of her passing. Well, not exactly a gift, he reflected. More of an inheritance, really. But he thought of it as a gift.

Truth to tell, he hadn't liked his grandmother very much, nor had she liked him. But that didn't keep him from loving the clock. It was a symbol to him of precision, of efficiency—the kind that he would instill in Starfleet little by little, until it was the Starfleet he had always had in mind.

The admiral smiled as he watched the brass gears turn in perfect coordination. Timing was everything, wasn't it?

Take his plan for Picard and the *Stargazer,* and by extension for Admiral Mehdi as well. Its success depended on everything happening just when it should.

First, he had given Picard his assignment in front of every other captain in the sector. Next, he had foisted those seven new crewmen on him, to distract him and increase the level of difficulty. Finally, with all eyes on Picard, McAteer would pull the rug out from under him.

Not that he had any choice, really. Starfleet really *did* have to get that cargo back. And even if Picard had a lifetime to recover it, he would never be equal to the task.

Contrary to what Mehdi seemed to believe, the man just wasn't captain material.

And when that became as painfully obvious to everyone else as it was to McAteer, Mehdi would be exposed as well. He would finally be seen for what he was—a man who had been in power much too long and had begun to make choices to the detriment of Starfleet.

As McAteer looked on appreciatively, the brass insides of his clock spun and whirled, oblivious to everything but the march of time. Leaning back in his overstuffed chair, the admiral tapped his combadge with a forefinger and said, "Mr. Merriweather?"

"Sir?" came the response from his assistant, whose office was in the alcove beyond.

"Send a message for me," McAteer told him. "Subspace frequency."

"To whom, sir?"

The admiral smiled again. "To Captain Jean-Luc Picard . . . on the *Stargazer.*"

Captain Picard scanned the faces of the six officers who had followed him into the *Stargazer*'s briefing room. Ben Zoma, Wu, Simenon, Valderrama, Idun Asmund, and her sister Gerda barely fit around the room's black oblong table.

The captain indicated the hologram of Beta Barritus that floated above a projector built into the center of the table. The star looked like a drop of molten fire, the vast system surrounding it a shimmering blanket of fog.

"As you're aware from your study of this system," Picard began, "the other starships that have tried to deal with the problem of the debris field have all fallen short of their goal."

"Because all they did was reshape their shields to minimize the friction," Ben Zoma offered.

"That's correct," Picard said. "Unfortunately, this approach placed a great deal of stress on their shield generators and gradually wore out their energy reserves."

Wu spelled it out for them. "Which in turn reduced their chances of continuing their efforts."

The captain nodded. "What we need is a different approach—one that allows us to penetrate the debris field *without* depleting our energy reserves." He looked around the table. "Ideas?"

For a moment, no one spoke. Then Simenon shrugged and took a stab at the problem.

"We could use our phasers to blast a path for ourselves," he offered. But the words were barely out of his mouth before he shook his head vigorously from side to side. "No, that won't work."

"Too large an energy expenditure," Ben Zoma observed.

"Yes," said Simenon. "And it would take a ridiculous amount of time to clear enough debris."

"What about a tractor beam?" asked Wu. "We could move the debris out of our way as we proceed. And it would require considerably less energy than a sustained phaser blast."

"True," said Ben Zoma. "But it would also limit our rate of speed." He turned to the chief engineer. "How fast can a tractor clear a path through that stuff?"

Simenon snorted. "Not very." His eyes slitting, he made some rough calculations in his head. "We could proceed at fifty kilometers an hour, maybe a little better than that."

"So, if the shell is a thousand kilometers deep," said Gerda, "and our data tells us that it's at least that, we're talking about as much as twenty hours."

"And during that time," Picard noted, "our sensors will be completely blind. So if the White Wolf were to exit the system, we would have no way of knowing it. He might be eighteen hours gone by the time we get through the debris field."

"Assuming," said Valderrama, "that he has a way of getting through it in better shape than those who have hunted him."

"An assumption we have to make," Idun remarked. "Otherwise, he would not have concealed himself here so often."

"So we have ruled out phasers and tractors," said the captain. "What other options do we have at our disposal?"

Again, there was silence around the table. And this time, no one spoke up to relieve it.

Picard frowned. "It's late. Perhaps if we sleep on the problem and get a jump on it in the—"

He never completed his sentence. The word *jump* had sparked a notion in his brain—one that he was even now turning over and over, inspecting it from all angles.

And the more he inspected it, the better he liked it.

"Sir?" said Wu.

"I believe I have a solution," Picard told her. "But it's not without a certain amount of risk."

"How *much* risk?" asked Simenon.

Picard planted a hand on the briefing room table, leaned toward the hologram of the solar system and pointed to a spot within its gray outer ring. "What I'm proposing is that we execute a very quick, very short subspace jump—which will, if it is successful, place us well beyond the debris field."

Glances were exchanged, some of them understandably skeptical. In fact, had someone else come up with the idea, the captain might have been skeptical as well.

"It's risky, all right," said Simenon.

"If we miscalculate," Wu told him, "we could find ourselves in the star itself."

"Yes," said the Gnalish. "Or some other inconvenient place."

Picard turned to Gerda. "How dependable is our data on the dimensions of the debris field?"

She considered the question. "Our predecessors' logs seem to differ somewhat. But they entered the system at different points, and the field may be thicker in some places than in others."

"Only a few of them ever reached the inner limits of the field," Wu chimed in, "much less explored beyond that point. For all we know, there's another debris field only a bit further in."

"If that's so," said Valderrama, "it would cut down our margin for error considerably."

"Yes," Simenon agreed. "And there's also the system's gravity well to take into account. It wouldn't be easy to pull this off inside the boundaries of a normal system. With a Lazarus star . . ." His voice trailed off ominously.

Picard turned to Idun. "What do *you* think, Lieutenant?"

The helm officer frowned at the hologram as if she were sizing up an adversary. "As Mr. Simenon says, it will not be an easy feat. There is much we do not know about this system."

"But can we do it?" Picard pressed.

Idun responded as if to a challenge, her eyes steely with resolve. "I believe we can."

That weighed more heavily in the captain's estimate than anything else that had been said. After all, Idun was the one who would have to execute the maneuver.

He looked around the table. "Any other comments?"

No one offered any. Not even Simenon, who still seemed more wary of the idea than any of the others.

"Very well, then," Picard said. "We execute the maneuver in one hour. Let's see to it that there are no delays."

Everyone got up and filed out of the room. At least, that's what Picard thought. It was only as he reached to switch off the hologram projector that he noticed someone lingering by the door.

It was Wu.

"A question?" he suggested, leaving the projector untouched for the time being.

"No question," she said. "Just an observation. It is a significant risk you're taking. I thought you were somewhat more conservative in your approach to command."

The captain smiled a wry smile. "You've been reading my personnel file, I see."

"Commander Ben Zoma made it available to me. I felt it was my duty to read it."

And so it was, Picard told himself. Nonetheless, knowing Wu had read his file made him feel vulnerable in her presence—much more so than he would have imagined.

"I will concede that I am deliberate sometimes, Commander—perhaps to a fault. And I will also concede that I have the utmost respect for the obstacles placed in front of me. But make no mistake—I will not shy away from them."

Wu looked thoughtful. "I'll remember that."

Then she left him as well.

Picard looked back at the hologram of Beta Barritus. There was only one thing missing from the three-dimensional representation—the White Wolf that lay at the heart of the solar system, daring the captain to find him.

The muscles in his jaw rippled at the thought. *One step at a time,* he counseled himself. *That is the way to catch a White Wolf—one small step at a time.*

Then he reached across the briefing room table, switched off the little hologram projector, and returned to what would undoubtedly be a very busy bridge.

The man called the White Wolf sat in the captain's chair of his ship and drummed his fingers on his armrest.

"What is it?" asked Turgis, his Klingon second-in-command, who had come to stand beside him in the lurid red light of their bridge.

The White Wolf glanced at him, as slyly narrow-eyed as his namesake. "What do you *think* it is?"

His second-in-command's expression turned into one of disgust. "Starfleet," he spat.

The White Wolf nodded, a grim smile pulling his lips back from his teeth. "They're after me."

"You've picked them up on sensors?"

"Not yet. But I don't need sensors to tell me when someone's hot on my trail." His nostrils flared. "I can feel them stalking me, Turgis. I can feel the fire in their blood."

"You're the White Wolf," the Klingon reminded him. "Any Starfleet captain would give his soul to bring you in."

"No doubt."

"But none of them ever will. Whoever's come hunting us will go home empty-handed."

"Like all the others."

"And there have been many of them."

The White Wolf grunted softly. "You make it sound as if the outcome has already been determined."

Turgis grinned, exposing knife-sharp teeth. "Hasn't it?"

And they laughed, the bridge of their ship ringing loudly with the sound of their defiance.

Chapter Fifteen

IT SEEMED LIKE JUST A FEW YEARS AGO that Picard's mother had warned him about looking directly at the sun. Now, it seemed, he did nothing *but* look at suns.

Of course, the one that burned on his viewscreen at the moment wasn't any ordinary dynamo of nuclear fusion. It was one that would test the mettle of Picard's ship, Picard's crew . . .

And, of course, Picard himself.

The hour that he had given his command staff was about to elapse. Everyone was in place, every piece of equipment checked and rechecked. All he had to do was set things in motion.

But before Picard could open his mouth to do that, he heard someone say, "Captain?"

He turned to Ulelo, who was at the comm console. "Yes?"

"I have a message, sir. It's from Admiral McAteer."

From McAteer? "On screen," Picard said, and leaned back in his chair to see what the man wanted.

A moment later, the admiral's image stretched itself across the forward viewscreen. When he spoke, his tone was as unctuous as ever. "Greetings, Captain. I trust all is going well."

Picard didn't reply. It was just a message. At this distance from Starbase 32, two-way communication simply wasn't a viable option.

"I'll get right to the point," McAteer promised. "After discussing the matter with Doctor Ibwasa of Starfleet Medical, I've been convinced that the cargo stolen by the White Wolf deserves a higher priority than I first assigned it."

"I don't like the sound of this," said Ben Zoma, who was standing alongside the captain.

"Nor do I," Picard agreed.

"Due to the increased urgency of your mission," said McAteer, "I've sent out three other captains and their crews to assist you."

But Picard hadn't heard the word "other." To him, it sounded as if the admiral had said "real." *I've sent out three* real *captains and their crews to assist you.*

Clearly, McAteer had decided that the *Stargazer* couldn't handle this assignment anymore. The conclusion left a bad taste in Picard's mouth.

A bad taste indeed.

"Help is on its way, Jean-Luc. In the meantime," said the admiral, "do your best. McAteer out."

And his image vanished from the viewscreen, giving way to the glory of Beta Barritus.

"Do your best," Ben Zoma echoed mockingly, just loud enough for his friend to hear him.

Picard scowled. "We'll do more than our best, Gilaad. We'll snare the White Wolf—and we'll do it *without* anyone's help."

His first officer glanced at him, a spreading smile on his face. "Now you're talking."

The captain took in his bridge crew with a glance. Everyone seemed intent on his or her console, unperturbed—at least on the surface—by the delicate nature of what they were about to attempt.

Satisfied, Picard turned to his helm officer. "Ready, Lieutenant?"

"Aye, sir," came Idun's reply.

The helm officer didn't have much to do anymore. Her real work, and painstaking work it had been, was already done.

Idun had programmed the warp engines to accomplish a feat no flesh-and-blood helm officer could hope to duplicate. They were to operate for precisely 0.0035 seconds—not enough time to breathe or swallow or even blink, but ample time for a vessel proceeding at warp one to clear an obstacle a thousand kilometers deep.

Picard could feel the muscles clench in his jaw. Even the slightest miscalculation could mean their doom. But he trusted Idun not to have made that miscalculation.

Ignoring the trickle of cold sweat making its way down his spine to the small of his back, he turned to the viewscreen again and pointed to the spectacle of Beta Barritus. Then he spoke a single word, eloquent in its simplicity: "Engage."

It was more than a command. It was a gesture of defiance, an announcement to himself, his crew, and the universe in general that he would accomplish his mission or die trying.

Because that was what Starfleet captains did, he reflected—the best of them, anyway. They did whatever it took to achieve their goals. They found a way.

And he would do the same.

At the helm controls, Idun tapped a single blue stud, and the *Stargazer* shot forward at the speed of light, her quartet of nacelles wildly spilling light as they carved a path through the mysterious realm known as subspace.

And then, with chilling suddenness, it was over. The warp engines were cycling down, their labors complete.

Picard released a breath he hadn't known he was holding. He felt his heart pumping blood through his body, just as it had done before he gave Idun the order to go to warp. He saw the bridge and his officers, all whole and uncompromised.

But where are we? he wondered. Where they had hoped to be, or somewhere else?

The viewscreen showed the captain the baleful eye of Beta Barritus, surrounded by a soft, pearlescent glow with bright, sharply defined tendrils of color pinwheeling through it. But it didn't tell him a thing he wanted to know.

"Report," he said, leaning forward in his chair, his voice echoing throughout the bridge.

There was a pause that seemed to stretch on forever. Finally, Gerda responded to his exhortation. "We made it, sir. We're on the other side of the debris field, approximately eleven hundred kilometers closer to Beta Barritus."

A cheer went up on the bridge among the officers at the aft stations.

Picard didn't take part in it, but by the same token he didn't feel the least bit inclined to rebuke those who did.

Even Ben Zoma was grinning from ear to ear. Glancing at the captain, he nodded his approval.

Picard nodded back. So far so good, he thought. "Scan for the White Wolf," he told Gerda.

"Aye, sir."

They weren't able to look very far. As they had been warned, the proliferation of gases and ion activity in the system made it impossible for their sensors to operate according to specs. But thanks to Simenon's enhancements, they were able to search a wider area than the ships that had come before them.

Not that it availed them anything. There was no sign whatsoever of the pirate. Of course, he hadn't gone unchecked and unfettered for so long by making it easy for his pursuers to find him.

"Chart a course based on his ion trail," Picard said. "Then we will proceed at one-half impulse."

"Aye, Captain," Gerda told him, and set to work.

"One-half impulse," Idun acknowledged.

The captain settled back into his center seat. *At last,* he thought, *the chase is on.*

Gerda Asmund frowned as she studied her navigation console. She didn't like what she saw.

"It's getting worse," said her sister Idun, who was sitting next to her at the helm controls.

Gerda nodded. "So it would seem."

In fact, it had been getting worse for the last half hour, but now it was getting worse more quickly.

Not that it came as a surprise to Gerda. The reports they had read, filed by the captains who had approached Beta Barritus before them, clearly indicated that the sensor situation would deteriorate—that once they got past the debris field, the conditions inside the system would gradually make data gathering more difficult.

Of course, there was no way of knowing *how* difficult, because none of those captains had penetrated as far into the system as they would have liked.

Gerda had thought of suggesting the use of instrumented probes to expand their sensor horizon, but that would have been a bad idea from a tactical standpoint. Though such probes might help them locate the White Wolf, they might also alert the White Wolf to their presence here.

And they didn't want the pirate to know they were after him until it was too late.

"What is it?" asked Commander Ben Zoma, who had assumed the center seat in the captain's absence.

"Sensor range is decreasing," Idun told him.

The first officer nodded. Then he looked up at the intercom grid in the ceiling. "Ben Zoma to Mr. Simenon . . ."

Ben Zoma listened to the end of his chief engineer's long and impassioned speech. Then he said, "So what you're telling me is you can't do any better."

"What I'm telling you," Simenon rejoined impatiently, "is it's not *possible* to do any better. Our sensors are better tuned than any sensors in the history of Starfleet. They're operating at absolute peak efficiency. No—*above* peak efficiency."

"I see," said Ben Zoma.

"There is no way in the universe that I or anyone else could improve on their performance."

The first officer nodded. "So you've indicated."

Simenon's eyes narrowed. "Then why," he asked, "do you have that look on your face?"

"I have a look?" Ben Zoma asked.

"You certainly do. If I didn't know better, I'd guess you were going to ask me to enhance the sensors even more—even after I've *told* you that it can't be done."

"You know me that well, do you?"

Simenon scowled. "I'm afraid I do."

"And—just hypothetically—what if I *did* ask you to enhance the sensors, however unreasonably?"

The engineer's nostrils flared, an indication that he was growing increasingly annoyed. "Why bother to speculate? Having heard me say it can't be done, you would never ask."

"Yes," said Ben Zoma. "Of course. But . . . if I *did?*"

Simenon glowered at him, then took a deep breath and said, "I'll see what I can do."

The first officer watched him return to where some of the other engineers were standing and apprise them of their latest assignment. To their credit, they didn't grumble. They just got to work, no matter how daunting their objective.

And Ben Zoma went to tell his friend Picard that they had a problem—even if Simenon *did* manage to do the impossible and squeeze a little more out of the sensors.

"I see," said Picard, leaning back into the chair behind the desk in his ready room. "And what do you recommend?"

Ben Zoma, who was seated on the other side of the black plastic desk, frowned and shook his head. "Simenon has probably done all he can. If we're going to make any strides from here on, they'll have to come from the science section."

"From Lieutenant Valderrama?" Picard asked.

"That's right."

It wasn't normally the responsibility of the science section to work on engineering issues. However, the captain could appreciate his first officer's logic.

If they had come as far as they could with what they had—and it seemed that they had—they needed a new approach to the problem. They had to devise a way of "seeing" that transcended EM flux scans, neutrino imaging, and graviton spectrometry.

The ship's science personnel would have the greatest understanding of this environment. If anyone could devise a new strategy for obtaining information under the conditions imposed by Beta Barritus, it would be the people serving under Valderrama.

Part of Picard couldn't help wishing Cariello were still with them— that she were still available to solve problems like these. He knew what Cariello could accomplish, but Valderrama was still a question mark in his mind.

Unfortunately, Cariello was no longer an option. Now it was Valderrama's turn to show what she could do to justify the faith Picard had shown in her. With luck and encouragement, perhaps she would come up with what they needed.

"Speak to Lieutenant Valderrama," the captain told Ben Zoma. "Let her know what we require of her."

"Will do," his friend assured him. However, he didn't leave to carry out the order.

"What is it?" Picard asked.

"If we're going to ask something this important of Valderrama, we should provide her with all the help we can."

The captain nodded. "Agreed. Tell Valderrama that she can have as many bodies as she needs. She has my approval in advance."

"Immediately," said the first officer. Then he got up and headed for the exit.

Suddenly Picard got an idea—a way to kill two birds with one stone, so to speak.

"Number One?" he called.

Ben Zoma stopped and looked back at him. "Sir?"

"Let's include Ensign Jiterica among the crewmen assigned to the science section."

Picard didn't see the Nizhrak catching on in a demanding environment like weapons or engineering—not when she had had so many difficulties in less problematic environments. Perhaps she would have an easier time of it under Valderrama.

"Will do," Ben Zoma told him, and left the captain's ready room the way he had entered it.

Jiterica moved her containment suit in the direction of the double doors at the end of the corridor. As the doors slid apart for her, they revealed a hallway beyond.

There were three people standing in it. Only one of them looked the least bit familiar to Jiterica. That was Lieutenant Valderrama, whom she had seen in the corridor near sickbay the day before.

As the lieutenant caught sight of the Nizhrak, she gave her companions some additional instructions—enough to send them on their way. Then she met Jiterica halfway.

"Ensign," she said in a warm, welcoming voice. "I was just informed that you'd be joining us."

Jiterica didn't know what to say to that. In the end, her response was simply, "Yes."

"We can use all the help we can get," Valderrama told her. She gestured for the ensign to follow her. "Come on. We'll find you a workstation and get you started."

"All right," said Jiterica in her tinny, artificial voice.

But she was far from optimistic that she would be of any use to Valderrama or anyone else on the ship. She also doubted that this latest assignment would change anything.

She simply didn't fit in here. Clearly, she would have to remain onboard for the duration of this mission. But the sooner she left, the better it would be for everyone concerned.

Nikolas looked around the hexagon-shaped space in which he found himself. It had pretty much the same dimensions as the main security facility through which he had passed a moment earlier, though it was equipped completely differently.

Wherever bulkhead met deck there was a sleek, dark computer terminal, its monitor alive with one graphic or another. The ensign counted twenty-four of the terminals in all, though none of them was anywhere near as elaborate as the multiscreen console in the other room.

"As you know," said Lieutenant Joseph, drawing the attention of Nikolas and the other dozen crewmen collected there, "we're hunting someone called the White Wolf. Unfortunately, we need meaningful sensor information to do that, and it's getting tougher for us to get that information the closer we get to Beta Barritus. Both the science and engineering sections are working on the problem now. But in the meantime, the captain wants more eyeballs on our incoming sensor data—so we don't miss any leads that *do* materialize."

"Which is where *we* come in," speculated Joe Caber, who was standing beside Nikolas.

"Exactly," Joseph confirmed. "You're our eyeballs. You'll be scanning from the time you get here to the time you leave—or the time you drop, whichever comes first."

It's a tedious job, Nikolas reflected archly, *but someone's got to do it.*

"Any questions at this point?" asked the security chief.

Naturally, Caber had one. "Exactly what kind of data are we looking for, sir?"

"I'd say an ion trail," Joseph told him, "but the odds of finding something like that are decreasing as we speak. Check for thermal hot spots, EM surges, unusual particle concentrations . . . anything that looks the least bit suspicious. And don't be afraid to waste the time of whoever's in charge of your shift. You never know what kind of reading might prove useful to us."

Caber nodded. "Thank you, sir."

"Find that pirate," said Joseph, "and I'll be thanking *you,* Ensign. In fact, we'll *all* be thanking you."

That inspired a chuckle from the assembled crewmen.

"To whom will we be reporting?" asked a woman with curly, dark hair. The markings on her uniform identified her as a med tech.

The security chief seemed to hesitate, as if the question involved something more than a simple answer. Then he said, "He'll be arriving at any moment. His name—"

As if on cue, someone made his way into the hexagonal enclosure. Someone short and awkward looking in his crimson tunic, whose walk strongly reminded Nikolas of a duck's waddle.

The ensign bit his lip to keep from uttering an expletive. The crewman in charge of this shift—

"—is *Obal*," Joseph finished.

Nikolas saw a grin spread over his friend Caber's face. *Perfect,* he thought. *Just perfect.*

Chapter Sixteen

NIKOLAS TAPPED OUT A COMMAND on his keyboard and called up another graphic. This one was supposed to show him neutrino concentrations at a distance of a thousand kilometers or less, each concentration represented in red on a black background.

As it was, all the ensign saw was the black background. No red, no neutrinos. Or rather, they were there, but the sensors weren't strong enough to identify them that deep into the system.

And it was getting worse, Nikolas told himself.

Every few minutes, sensor range dropped in one key area or another. If they didn't come up with something soon, the *Stargazer* would be rendered blind—unable to "see" anything at all in this mess of ionized gases and subtle radiation fields—and therefore incapable of navigating. Then the captain would have no choice but to call off the hunt.

Nikolas had barely heard of the White Wolf before he embarked on this mission. But that didn't keep him from wanting to find the guy, and not just because he had stolen something valuable from the Federation, something that could help people.

It was the challenge—the idea of doing what no one before them had ever done. Back on the handball courts of Canarsie, Nikolas had itched to take on the legendary Red O'Reilly. Now he was itching to take on the White Wolf.

Which was why Picard and his people had to come up with a new sensor arrangement—and why Nikolas would try like hell to keep them in the running in the meantime.

"Look at him," said Caber, who was sitting at the next console.

Nikolas looked up from his monitor, still lost in the data he had been scanning. "Look at who?"

Caber was staring across the room. "Who do you think?"

Nikolas followed his friend's gaze. He found himself looking at Obal, who had raised himself onto his tiptoes to peer at a monitor over an ensign's shoulder.

"I can't believe they've got him overseeing us," Caber said, his voice tinged with irony.

"Believe it," Nikolas told him, pulling up another sensor graphic on his monitor.

"This is the most ridiculous thing I've ever seen. It's like taking orders from some kind of pest."

"He's still your superior," Nikolas reminded him. "You might want to remember that."

Silence for a moment. Then Caber said, "Watch this."

By the time Nikolas looked up again, his roommate was walking across the room, headed right for Obal. *Oh man,* the ensign thought, sensing something bad in the offing.

Caber stopped when he got to the Binderian, over whom he towered the way an adult might tower over an eight-year-old. "Lieutenant?"

Obal turned and looked up at him. "Yes?"

What's he up to? Nikolas wondered.

"Sorry to bother you, sir," said Caber, "but I could use some help here." He jerked a thumb over his shoulder. "I'm not sure exactly what I'm looking at."

Obal glanced at Caber's console, then turned back to Caber himself. "We will take a look," he said agreeably.

They crossed the room together and Caber sat down in front of the screen. Unfortunately, he blocked the Binderian's view in the process, so Obal moved to the other side to see around him.

"You see what I mean?" Caber asked.

As he posed the question, he moved his chair around to the other part of the screen, again blocking Obal's view. Obal frowned, obviously a little frustrated, and moved back to his original position.

But by then, Caber had moved as well. "Sir?" he said, sounding completely innocent of any wrongdoing. "You *do* see what I'm talking about, don't you?"

Nikolas heard a sound and looked around the room. Some of his colleagues were watching Caber's antics and trying their best not to laugh at them.

"Sir?" Caber said again, provoking a snicker. He glanced back at Obal. "Can you help me, sir?"

It was only then that the Binderian got an inkling of what was going on. Looking up at the big man, he said, "This is not appropriate behavior for Starfleet personnel."

Caber turned to Obal and assumed a serious expression. "I'm not sure I know what you mean, sir."

The Binderian regarded him for a moment. Surely, thought Nikolas, he's going to issue Caber a reprimand. Under the circumstances, it's the only thing he *can* do.

But Obal didn't do it. He didn't do *anything*. He just turned from his tormentor and walked away, leaving Caber unpunished and free to repeat his antics.

Nikolas sighed.

"Hey, Nik," Caber rasped at him. He was grinning his perfect, white grin. "Did you see the look on his face? If that wasn't priceless, I don't know what is."

Nikolas frowned as he watched the Binderian sit down at his monitor and return to his work. "Yeah," the ensign said with an empty feeling in his gut. "Priceless."

Pug Joseph stood behind one of his colleagues in the main security area and considered the big, concave monitor bank.

In actuality, Joseph was only concerned with a single screen at the moment. It was the one that showed him the other hexagonal room in security, where Obal was presiding over the dozen men and women assigned to special sensor duty.

The Binderian had seemed like the perfect individual for the job. After all, he had already demonstrated a knack for detail, he could hardly manage to fall asleep in the company of so many other crewmen, and—just as important—he would free up a security officer better suited to actual security work.

On the other hand, this was an important duty, one requested by the captain himself. Joseph didn't feel so confident in Obal that he was willing to let him operate without a little scrutiny.

The security chief had been reminded of a saying he had read back in high school in Colorado, when his class was studying Aristotle: *Who watches the watchers?*

In this case, he thought, I *do.*

And it was a good thing. Though the monitor allowed him only to see and not hear what was going on, he had witnessed enough of Obal's encounter with Ensign Caber to understand the gist of it.

The ensign had ridiculed Obal, and the Binderian's response had been no response at all. He had simply let it go.

Not good, Joseph thought. *Not good at all.* He hadn't been in charge of the security section for long, but even *he* knew that an officer couldn't let a subordinate get the best of him. It was the quickest way to lose control of a section.

He was tempted, as he turned away from the monitor bank, to relieve Obal of his assignment and put someone else in charge. But he didn't do it. Part of him wanted to give Obal a chance to redeem himself.

Even though the other part was sure he wouldn't.

Nikolas was about to tell his friend Caber that he didn't like watching Obal be ridiculed, that he wished like hell that Caber wouldn't do it anymore. But before he could get the words out, he caught a glimpse of what was on his screen.

Nikolas wasn't exactly an expert at interpreting sensor data, but what he saw looked like trouble—the kind he didn't think he ought to mull over for very long. He was about to call Obal over when he realized what it would look like—a replay of Caber's antics, which was the last thing the ensign had in mind.

Getting up from his seat, Nikolas crossed the room and leaned over beside the Binderian. Obal looked up at him and said, "Yes?" every bit as pleasantly as he had responded to Caber.

Nikolas jerked a thumb over his shoulder, indicating his monitor. "I think there's something here you ought to see."

Picard felt his jaw clench as he considered the rectangular viewscreen in front of him.

It showed him and his bridge officers what Ensign Nikolas had noted mere minutes earlier on his computer monitor—an army of vicious, twis-terlike formations, each one appearing as an elongated diamond shape in a hue ranging from silver to dusky bronze. They looked as deadly as any phenomena Picard had ever seen.

"The vortices," Ben Zoma said.

The captain nodded grimly. "Yes." Their predecessors—that is, the three who had managed to venture this far—had described this obstacle in some detail.

Seeing no way around the twisters, they had attempted to negotiate a slow and careful path among them. Two of them, the captains of the *Mongoose* and the *Leningrad,* ended up turning back when the going got too rough. The third, the captain of the *Christopher,* had refused to give up until she lost a warp nacelle and no longer had a choice in the matter.

Ben Zoma frowned at the viewscreen. "Too bad we can't use your warp trick here."

"Because we don't know how far this region may extend," Picard elaborated.

"And," added Ben Zoma, "because the vortices are magnetic in na-ture. They'd wreak havoc with a subspace field. And then there's the problem of going to warp this close to a sun."

"Point taken," said Picard.

Ben Zoma looked at him. "Convene the command staff?"

The captain smiled, though he was hardly amused. "You must have read my mind, Number One."

Chapter Seventeen

AGAIN PICARD FOUND himself at the head of the long black table in the *Stargazer*'s briefing room, regarding six attentive officers.

"You are all aware of the problem, I trust."

Ben Zoma, Wu, Simenon, Valderrama, and the Asmund twins responded with nods and murmurs of confirmation.

The captain turned to the hologram hovering over the center of the table. It was different from the one he had called for last time in that the debris field and the outer precincts of the solar system had been stripped away, leaving the system's core and the vortex belt clearly visible.

"As you've learned in your readings," he said, "these magnetic vortices are what stopped the most enterprising of our colleagues. But they will not stop us. The question is: How can we get past them and continue to pursue our mission?"

Ben Zoma iterated his remark that a warp-speed jump was not an option. Then he called for suggestions.

Valderrama was the first to speak. "Magnetic forces of that intensity are going to tear up any shield they touch."

"But there's no way for us to avoid them," Wu noted.

"They're insubstantial," Gerda observed, "so we can neither punch a hole in them with weapons fire nor clear a path through them with a tractor beam."

"What about a competing force?" Idun asked.

Picard leaned forward. "What do you mean?"

"A magnetic emission of some kind," the helm officer expanded. "Something that will fight the vortices and reduce the threat they pose to our shields."

The captain looked around the table. Like him, everyone seemed intrigued by the nature of Idun's suggestion. However, no one seemed able to translate it into a workable strategy.

"It's beyond us," Ben Zoma said finally.

Picard nodded. "Let's move on."

That's when he saw the expression on his chief engineer's face. It was a surly look, a look of discontent.

The captain had seen it before. It meant Simenon was thinking about something. Thinking *hard.*

"Mr. Simenon?" he said.

The Gnalish turned to him and his ruby eyes blinked. But he didn't offer any other response.

"Mr. Sim—" Wu began.

But Ben Zoma stopped her by putting his hand on her arm. He too knew better than to interrupt Simenon when he was cogitating.

Finally, the engineer's eyes became animated again, an indication that he was finished thinking. "I've got an idea," he rasped.

Picard frowned. "And . . . ?"

Simenon frowned back at him. "What if we were to change the polarity of our shields?"

For a moment, the idea hung in the air like a second hologram, inviting everyone's scrutiny. Then the group's reactions began to manifest themselves.

"Can you *do* that?" asked Ben Zoma.

Simenon nodded. "I think so."

"If you can," said Valderrama, "it should make the shields a lot less vulnerable to the action of the vortices."

Picard hadn't trained as an engineer. However, he had a rudimentary understanding of the principles involved, and Simenon's suggestion seemed to make sense.

"Even if Mr. Simenon's approach works," said Wu, "it will still be a dangerous passage."

"Yes," Ben Zoma agreed. "But not *as* dangerous."

"I would like to see a computer model," he said.

"No problem," the engineer assured him. "I can whip one up as soon as I get back to engineering."

Taking that as his cue, the captain nodded. "By all means, Mr. Simenon." He took in his assembled officers at a glance. "You're dismissed, all of you."

He looked forward to seeing what the Gnalish came up with. If luck was still on their side, Simenon's strategy would keep alive their hope of finding the White Wolf.

If not . . .

Picard caught himself. *There is no alternative,* he reflected. At least, not one he could live with.

Greyhorse was deep in reverie when he heard the captain's voice over the intercom system.

"What is it, sir?" he asked Picard.

"I've gone over Mr. Simenon's computer models and approved his plan for getting us through the vortex belt. Mind you, I believe we will come through with minimal damage. However, I want you to be on medical alert—just in case."

Greyhorse nodded even though he knew the captain couldn't see him. "Acknowledged, sir."

"Picard out."

The doctor's first thought was always the same: *Gerda.* Would she be endangered by what Simenon had proposed? Would he see her carried into sickbay on a gurney, her body broken and bleeding?

As he had on other occasions, Greyhorse forcibly put the unwelcome image from his mind. It was his duty as a physician and as a Starfleet officer to provide medical care for *everyone* on the ship, not just a single individual.

No matter *how* he felt about her.

As Picard emerged from the turbolift, he saw everyone on the bridge glance in his direction. His officers looked as determined as he was—an encouraging sign, to be sure.

"Mr. Simenon," he said, "this is the captain."

The engineer's voice flooded the bridge with its sibilance. "Simenon here. Time to give it a go?"

As Picard approached his center seat, his first officer abdicated it and exchanged glances with him. Ben Zoma's eyes crinkled at the corners, an expression of his particular brand of fatalism.

What could possibly go wrong? he seemed to say.

"Let us indeed give it a go," the captain told Simenon.

"Reversing shield polarity," the engineer announced.

Nothing changed on the forward viewscreen. The vortices still loomed ahead of them, savage twists of magnetic force daring ship and crew to try their luck.

Picard glanced at Gerda. "Lieutenant?"

She nodded. "He's done it, sir."

"Very well, then," the captain told her, his words ringing ominously across the bridge. "Let's proceed. One-quarter impulse."

The *Stargazer* started forward, heading for the narrow gap between the two nearest vortices. Picard felt the deck shudder beneath his feet as mighty forces reached out for them.

"Steady as she goes," he said.

Idun's best bet was to follow a course midway between the vortices, keeping the ship from being savaged by either one of them. She did this with unerring accuracy, even when the magnetic phenomena tore at the *Stargazer* and her shields, causing the vessel to slide and buck and creak in protest.

The captain trusted Idun as he had never trusted any other helm officer, and he wasn't the only one who felt that way. Captain Ruhalter had said once that his right arm was less precious to him than Idun's services at the helm.

If anyone could pull this off, it was she. Of course, the captain of the *Mongoose* might have felt that way about *his* helmsman. The same for the captain of the *Leningrad* or the *Christopher,* and they had been proven dead wrong.

So where did Picard get the gall to think he could prevail over the vortices? To imagine that he and the *Stargazer* could succeed where all the rest had failed?

He didn't know. But he knew *this*—he wasn't going to stop until he had snared the White Wolf and brought him to justice.

As if in answer to his vow, the ship jerked suddenly to one side and then the other, jostling them in their seats and forcing a groan out of the deck plates. Someone cursed beneath his breath.

"Shields down eight percent," Vigo announced.

The captain frowned as the vortices on either side of them waxed immense on the forward viewscreen, two spectacular dynamos sizzling with magnetic energy. *Come on,* Picard urged his helm officer silently. *You can do it, Lieutenant.*

Sweat stood out on Idun's brow in beads. And not just Idun's brow, but Gerda's as well, for the *Stargazer*'s navigator was sifting through incoming sensor data and feeding her sister whatever tidbits she deemed most critical.

Slowly, with infinite care and patience, Idun guided them along the razor's edge. And finally, after what seemed like an eternity, the first two vortices fell away from them.

Only to reveal a great many more, rank upon rank as far as the eye could see.

Picard forced himself to take the sight in stride. After all, he was the captain now. He had to set an example.

Juanita Valderrama clung to the sides of her monitor in the science section and saw the same thing Captain Picard and his officers were seeing on the bridge.

One vortex after another muscled its way onto her screen, majestic in its deadly, dazzling splendor. The ship shivered and jerked and reeled in the phenomenon's prodigious grasp like a fish caught on a very large hook. And then, through luck or skill, they managed to wriggle free of each vortex's influence.

But the battle had to be taking its toll on the *Stargazer.* It had to be sapping their resources, just as it had sapped the resources of the other vessels that had braved this passage.

Valderrama wished she had been able to do something to help their cause back in the briefing room. It wasn't that she didn't believe that Simenon's theory could work; in fact, she did think it could. It was that the captain had placed his faith in her, made her the chief of his science section, and she was letting him down.

When he had called for suggestions, she hadn't come up with one. All she could think to do was state the obvious—that the vortices were liable to tear up their shields. For all the good she had done, she might as well not have been in the room at all.

Suddenly, the deck shot out from beneath her feet. Valderrama tried to hang on to her monitor and stay upright. But just as she thought she might be able to keep from falling, the ship lurched again and she found the floor rushing up at her.

The science officer managed to get her hand between her face and the plastic surface, cushioning the blow. Still, she felt stunned for a moment. Then she heard someone say, "Are you all right?"

The voice that had asked the question sounded strange. Metallic, almost. Valderrama couldn't imagine why, until she turned to look up and saw the ghostly semblance of a human visage floating inside the clear-faced helmet of a containment suit.

"Are you all right?" Jiterica asked a second time.

"Yes," said Valderrama. She propped herself up on an elbow. "I'm fine, Ensign. Thank you."

By then, others had gathered around them. But it was Jiterica who gently grasped Valderrama's forearm and provided the counterweight that pulled Valderrama to her feet.

It was an eerie feeling, to have those gloved hands tugging at her. But the science officer didn't show it. After all, the ensign just wanted to help her.

And Valderrama knew how it felt not to be able to help.

"Thank you," she said a second time.

"You're welcome," Jiterica replied in her tinny, computerlike voice, and returned to her terminal.

Valderrama regarded the Nizhrak a moment longer. Then she looked around at the others who had ringed her and said, "I'm all right. You can go back to your stations."

One by one, the crewmen dispersed. Brushing herself off, Valderrama got a grip on her monitor again and tried to concentrate on the images she saw there. But it wasn't easy.

Not when she felt like more of a burden to her colleagues than ever.

Picard relaxed his grip on his armrests as the vortices they were passing slid off the sides of the viewscreen. They did so reluctantly, it seemed to the captain, as if they regretted not having torn the *Stargazer* to pieces.

Ben Zoma leaned closer to him. "Are we having fun yet?"

Indeed, Picard thought. But he kept the remark to himself. What he said instead was, "Report."

Idun was the first to respond. "Impulse engines still operating at peak efficiency."

"Shields at seventy-two percent," Gerda said.

It was better than the captain might have hoped. Simenon's approach seemed to be working.

Up ahead, another pair of vortices loomed in front of them, their whirling energies wild and hungry-looking. Idun began to steer the *Stargazer* between them.

But as she did, Picard caught a glimpse of the next group of vortices, deeper in, and they were significantly more tightly packed than any the *Stargazer* had already encountered. There was barely any space between them for a *Constellation*-class starship.

Idun turned to the captain, her unspoken assessment evident in her expression. "I agree," he said. "We'll see if we have a better chance of getting through elsewhere."

Turning back to her instrument panel, Idun backed them off the gap and moved them to starboard, since one of the twisters was blocking the way to port. Nor did she stop until she came to another opening that would give them sufficient leeway on either side.

But the story there was much the same. Even if the *Stargazer* managed to get through the breach at hand, she would be unable to get through the collection of vortices beyond that. The gaps were simply too narrow for her, too rife with destructive forces.

As before, Idun was compelled to slide them to starboard in search of something more promising. However, they hadn't gone very far before another twister became visible in the distance, threatening to cut off their lateral progress before long.

There was one more opening to starboard before they reached that point—one other chance to make it through both this set of vortices and the next one. The helm officer brought the *Stargazer* to a halt in front of that opening.

Leaning forward in his center seat, Picard took stock of the situation. The gap in front of them was certainly large enough to accommodate the *Stargazer.* However, the widest channel beyond it was considerably narrower, and considerably more daunting.

On the other hand, it was broader than any of the other second-rank openings the captain had seen. Perhaps even broad enough to grant them passage if they fought long and hard enough.

Idun was looking at him again. As before, Picard nodded. "Take us through," he said.

Punching in the requisite commands, the helm officer urged the ship forward. On the viewscreen, the whirlwinds before them appeared to grow larger, exerting more and more influence as the *Stargazer* sailed boldly between them. Smaller spirals of energy spun off from the main bodies, assaulting the ship.

The deck beneath Picard's feet kicked and rolled, balking at Idun's attempts to remain in control. An aft console sparked and gave rise to a slender plume of black smoke, requiring the attention of a crewman with a fire extinguisher.

And still the *Stargazer* plunged deeper into the jaws of pure, unbridled force.

Suddenly, something whipped them in the direction of the twister to port. Idun made the correction with a burst of thrusters, forcing them back on course. Moments later, they were rocked again by magnetic forces, but they managed to get through that setback as well.

Idun was getting better at this, Picard remarked to himself. She was navigating this corridor between the vortices with more skill and confidence than she had displayed in navigating the corridors that came before it.

Finally, the worst of the passage was over. The vortices began to peel away on either side of them, relinquishing their hold on the *Stargazer*—and revealing the even greater test that lay ahead of her.

"Shields at sixty-four percent," Gerda reported, even before the captain could ask.

Sixty-four percent, Picard repeated to himself. It was remarkable, given the challenges they had met. But would it be enough to see them through the challenge to come . . .

And what lay beyond it?

Picard eyed the phenomena between which they hoped to pass. They stood there like the gates of hell, pillars of cold fire that spun and undulated and writhed in what seemed to be the most hideous torment.

As the captain had always heard, misery loved company. The *Stargazer* had no choice but to give them some.

Picard could feel the tension on his bridge as Idun took them into the opening. It was a palpable sensation, like that of a violin string stretched to its breaking point.

And the trouble they had expected wasn't long in coming. First there was a rumbling, more felt in one's bones than heard. Then the *Stargazer* was wrenched hard to starboard, throwing the captain and everyone else to the deck.

The console next to Paxton's erupted in a fountain of sparks, forcing the communications officer to recoil from it. As a crewman went to douse the fire, a second one broke out.

Picard staggered to his feet and eyed the viewscreen, where the image of the vortices had rotated a dizzying ninety degrees. Worse, the helm was unmanned. The captain started for it, ready and willing to put his once-considerable piloting skills to use.

But Idun managed to beat him to it. Dragging herself off the deck and back into her seat, she began tapping away at her controls. Little by little, she managed to right the ship.

But no sooner had the twisters turned vertical again on the screen than the *Stargazer* was bludgeoned anew. Wave after wave of magnetic energy broke over her bow, keeping her from advancing any farther.

Picard heard Idun growl as she struggled with her controls. Clearly, she needed more power.

"Mr. Simenon," he snapped. "All available power to the impulse engines!" And as he thought about it, he added, "Cut life support!"

"Aye, sir!" came the engineer's response.

The captain knew that they could survive on the air they had for as long as twenty minutes. Of course, the small amount of energy they saved might not make much of a difference, but it might also represent the margin between victory and defeat.

"Shields down to thirty-eight percent!" Gerda snarled.

Suddenly, the *Stargazer* began to make progress again. The walls of whirling energy seemed to crawl by on either side of them, yielding meter after grudging meter.

But they were far from free of the vortices' embrace. Picard felt his vessel vibrate and slew sideways, then shoot forward and veer in the other direction.

"Twenty-six percent!" Gerda announced grimly.

The captain began to doubt that they would make it—not that they had any choice but to try. They were more than halfway through now, too far to think about turning back.

The *Stargazer* lurched forward, fighting the good fight, though the vortices grabbed and tore at her with all their insane power. Yet another console began to spit sparks, and the smell of smoke became strong in Picard's nostrils, especially without the ventilation that was part of life support.

A little farther, he thought. *Just a little farther.*

And then he saw it.

Ben Zoma must have glimpsed it at the same time, because he pointed to the viewscreen and said, "Look!"

It was a narrow, vertical strip, seen between the seething near edges of the vortices. A ruddiness, as soft-looking as one of the clouds that stretched over the captain's native France at sunset.

It provided Picard and his officers with a glimpse of what lay beyond this strait—a hint that if they could only squeeze past these last two vortices, they could at last put this ordeal behind them.

"Shields at sixteen percent!" Gerda told her colleagues, inserting a note of reality into the captain's newfound optimism.

Picard felt his jaw clench. Once the shields were stripped away, there would be nothing left to protect them but their reinforced titanium hull, and no one could expect that it would last very long under such intensely adverse conditions.

"Six percent!" Gerda called out.

For just a moment, Picard had a vision of his ship being peeled like an overripe fruit, one section of hull at a time. Then, with an effort, he put the image from his mind.

Just in time to grab the back of his chair, because the vortices were clawing at them with renewed fury.

The *Stargazer* bucked and slid and bucked again, paying for every meter of headway with huge expenditures of energy. She shot forward, came up against what seemed like a tangible barrier, then pierced it and shot forward like an arrow.

And each time they made some progress, the scarlet strip ahead of them got noticeably wider, noticeably closer. *The end is in sight,* Picard assured himself. *We can do it . . .*

Gerda swiveled in her seat to look at him. "Sir," she said in a disgusted tone of voice, "the shields are down!"

The captain bit his lip. Their defenses were gone, and they were hardly out of danger yet. Had they dared too much after all? Would they falter just short of the finish line and be torn to pieces?

Picard shook his head, answering his own unspoken question. *Not today,* he insisted.

As if to dispute his conclusion, a wave of energy slammed into them head on. It sent the captain sprawling across his center seat, its armrests digging into his ribs. Then another wave hit them and another, each one fiercer and wilder than the one before it.

Without her shields to minimize the blows, the *Stargazer* was at the mercy of the vortices. She absorbed impact after impact, her lights flickering, her bulkheads keening as if in agony.

"Hull breaches on decks five, six, and seven!" Paxton announced. "Also, on decks ten and eleven!"

"Damage control teams!" Ben Zoma commanded.

There would be more breaches, Picard knew. Many more, if they lingered much longer in this confusion of colossal forces.

Get us out of here, he instructed Idun silently.

But the vortices seemed to have other ideas. They battered the ship's naked hull with assault after magnetic assault, as if they knew this would be their last chance to destroy the intruder.

And it seemed to Picard that it was just that. Never mind the damage they were taking—the ribbon of red had claimed nearly a third of the viewscreen and was claiming more with each passing second.

"Breaches on fourteen, fifteen, sixteen . . . !"

Suddenly, the lights went out and the captain felt the ship wrenched back and forth, shaken like helpless prey in the jaws of some titanic predator. He clung to his seat and watched the zagging image on the viewscreen, hoping Idun could straighten them out somehow.

Then, just as suddenly as the shaking had begun, it stopped. The lights came back on. And the viewscreen showed Picard a path all but free of the vortices.

He felt a single, small tremor, a final sickening reminder of what they had been through. But after that they were home free, sailing into the region of scarlet mist as calmly and effortlessly as if the vortex belt had never existed.

The captain drew a deep breath. Then he turned to his comm officer and said, "Casualties?"

"Nothing serious, sir," Paxton told him, relaying the latest information he had received from sickbay. "But there are hull breaches on *eleven* different decks."

"And we are defenseless," Gerda added, "until we can restore power to the shields."

"That too," said Paxton.

Picard nodded. They had taken a beating, one from which they would need time and considerable effort to recover. And somewhere beyond this placid sea of blood-red mists waited the White Wolf, who knew this system a good deal better than they did and might have come through the vortices a lot better fortified.

But they had made it through. They were alive. And for the moment, Picard reflected, that was all that mattered.

* * *

Ensign Jiterica got the news along with the rest of Lieutenant Valderrama's science section.

The ship had made it through the vortex belt. They had negotiated
the system's second major obstacle without irreparable damage to the
ship. It was a significant achievement, a tribute to the expertise of Chief
Simenon and his engineers.

What's more, everyone in the science section seemed to agree with
her. They were laughing and patting one another on the back. *Expressing
jubilation,* the ensign observed.

Jiterica was capable of jubilation as well, maybe even more so than
her colleagues were. But she wasn't jubilant at the moment. She was
too intent on something that had begun to nag at her a moment earlier,
something that lay just under the surface of her consciousness.

An idea. Or at least the beginnings of one.

Jiterica tapped out a command on her keyboard, and the image on
her monitor changed, showing her a spectrographic analysis of the wildly
churning gases surrounding the *Stargazer.* It was a different environment
than the one that existed on her homeworld, but still . . .

The ensign tapped out another command and brought up a second
analysis. It was encouraging enough for her to bring up a third analysis,
and then a fourth.

It was still a raw notion, of course. Jiterica would have to examine
it further to see if it held any real promise, and that might take a good
deal of time. On the other hand, given the simplicity of her assignment
here in the science section, time was something she seemed to possess
in great abundance.

Chapter Eighteen

Captain's log, supplemental.

Having completed our passage through the vortex belt, we have at last begun to pierce the heart of this solar system. However, we have paid a price for our progress. We have managed to resurrect only the flimsiest of deflector defenses, and it will be some time before our shields or any of our other tactical systems are back to full strength. At the same time, sensor range is steadily diminishing because of the gases through which we are compelled to travel. And we are strictly on our own now, lacking our colleagues' advice, since no other Federation vessel has managed to get this far in pursuit of the White Wolf. Of course, we have a vague idea of what to expect here, but none of it is extraordinarily promising.

STUDYING IDUN'S CONTROL PANEL over her shoulder, Ben Zoma frowned. "Then that's it?" he asked, already knowing the answer but wanting to hear it from his helm officer.

"I do not see any alternative," Idun said.

Ben Zoma nodded. "All right. I'll inform the captain."

Picard had spent the last three hours in his quarters trying to catch up on some much-needed sleep. Ben Zoma didn't like the idea of waking him. However, the captain had asked to be apprised of any significant development, and this one certainly qualified.

The first officer looked up at the intercom grid embedded in the ceiling. "Ben Zoma to Captain Picard."

No response.

"Ben Zoma to Captain Picard," he repeated.

This time he got an answer. "I heard you the first time," Picard said, his weariness evident in his voice.

"Sorry," Ben Zoma told him, smiling sympathetically. "But I thought you should know—"

"I had a dream," the captain interjected. "A wonderful dream. We had figured out a way to make the sensors work, long- and short-range, interference or no interference." He yawned. "We were hot and heavy on the trail of the White Wolf."

Ben Zoma's smile tightened a bit. "Then this is a rude awakening in more ways than one. According to Idun, sensor range has diminished too precipitously for us to continue our forward progress—especially with our deflectors in such sorry shape."

A long pause. "I see," said Picard, his voice unmistakably full of disappointment.

It had to be a bitter pill for his friend to swallow, Ben Zoma reflected. Having come so far, only to be stymied by what was really a mere technical problem . . .

"All stop," Picard commanded, "until we can devise a way to see in this muck."

The first officer turned to Idun, who looked utterly disgusted with the situation—like any Klingon denied a confrontation with her enemy. "You heard the captain," he said. "All stop."

"Aye, sir," she told him, and cut impulse power.

Without the application of braking thrusters, the *Stargazer* would continue to drift forward on momentum alone. But she wouldn't go very fast or get very far that way.

Ben Zoma swore under his breath. For the moment, it seemed, the hunt for the White Wolf was on hold.

* * *

The man called the White Wolf pushed his sensor screen away on its swivel and leaned back into his captain's chair.

"You've found them?" asked his second-in-command, the ruby-red light casting his blunt features into sharp relief.

"I have," the White Wolf told him. "They've survived the twisters in one piece."

Turgis's expression was one of grudging respect. "Really."

"Yes. But they've stopped moving. Either they've lost impulse power or their sensors have finally failed them."

"Their sensors, most likely."

The White Wolf nodded judiciously. "Most likely."

He himself had had trouble in that area for a long time. And when he finally came up with a solution, it had been a product more of good fortune than of expertise.

"They'll linger there for a while," Turgis speculated disdainfully, "then turn around and go home—and brag about how close they came to capturing us."

The White Wolf cast a sidelong look at him. "You think so? None of their colleagues have gotten even *this* far."

The Klingon sneered. "There's a big difference between beating the twisters and beating *us."*

The pirate smiled. "There is indeed."

And they laughed, as they had before whenever the subject of their pursuers came up. But this time, the White Wolf couldn't work himself up to Turgis's level of enthusiasm.

Their situation had changed. For the first time since they had begun lifting cargoes from Federation vessels, there was a chance they might have to defend themselves.

Not that the pirate had any doubt as to the outcome of an all-out encounter—especially when he had an ace wearing a Starfleet uniform up his sleeve.

Lieutenant Ulelo peered past the half-hidden form of Marion Sears, his repair-team partner, into the depths of a state-of-the-art subspace field generator.

Sears reached back, open palm extended. "Hyperspanner," she said, her voice muffled by its confinement.

"Hyperspanner," Ulelo repeated, and selected one from the assortment of handheld tools laid out in front of him. Then he laid it in his partner's palm.

"Thanks," said Sears, and pulled the hyperspanner into the shadowy nether regions of the field generator.

Ulelo had never had an opportunity like this on the *Copernicus*—a chance to inspect a key component in the deflector system at close range. And even if he'd had such an opportunity, it wouldn't have been nearly as valuable. Field generators on *Oberth*-class ships were a full level of sophistication below the *Stargazer*'s.

Sears made an unintelligible noise.

"Did you say something?" Ulelo asked her.

"No," said the engineer. "I just banged my head is all."

Ulelo didn't comment further. He just went on scrutinizing what he could see of the field generator, trying to file away everything he could about it.

According to the specs he had pulled up shortly after his arrival on the ship, the *Stargazer* boasted eight of the devices in all. Two were located on deck 10, two more on deck 26, and one in each of the ship's four warp nacelles.

Each field generator consisted of a dozen graviton polarity sources feeding a pair of 500-millicochrane subspace field distortion amplifiers. At least, that's the information Ulelo had gleaned from the pertinent computer file.

When the magnetic vortices had battered the shields down to nothing, the engineering section was left with two tasks. The first was to repair and replace whatever power linkages had been damaged. The second was to reinitialize the field generators.

Ulelo, who had received precious little training as an engineer, had been assigned to the generator initialization team. So had a number of other non-engineers—crewmen from sections as disparate as security and weapons and even sickbay—which was why this compartment was crawling with more uniformed personnel than it had seen since the *Stargazer* was commissioned.

But then, this was where the captain had decided everyone was needed—here and in the other generator compartments or in the science section. Because they couldn't complete their mission if they couldn't find a way to navigate in the gases that surrounded them, and they didn't dare move until they got their shields up.

Of course, Ulelo had a mission of his own—one that was completely different from Captain Picard's. And with that mission in mind, he dutifully resumed his studies.

Jean-Luc Picard had never been a pacer.

Certainly, he had been plagued by moments of impatience like anyone else. But he had almost always managed to find a way to channel his nervous energy into something useful.

Or, if not useful, at least diverting.

But now, with the fate of his ship and crew resting squarely on his inexperienced shoulders, he was forced to rely on others to be useful—and diversions held no appeal for him.

And without realizing it, he had begun pacing from one end of his ready room to the other.

The captain had just caught himself and resolved to discontinue the activity when he heard the sound of chimes outside his door. "Come," he said, wondering who might be calling on him.

It turned out to be Lieutenant Valderrama.

"Sit," he said. "Please." He deposited himself in the chair behind his desk, glad for the interruption.

Valderrama sat down as well. Then she smiled and said, "I think I may have come up with the solution to our problem."

It took a moment for Picard to process the information. "Our problem?" he repeated inanely. Then it sank in, making his heart beat against his ribs. "You mean our *sensor* problem?"

"Actually," said Valderrama, "I haven't been able to come up with anything regarding the sensors."

The captain's hopes fell precipitously. "I see. Then what *have* you come up with?"

"A way to see in this gas soup, sir. But it doesn't have anything to do with our sensors."

Picard looked at the science officer, making no attempt to conceal his confusion. "I'm afraid you've lost me."

"Sorry," said the lieutenant. "What I mean is, there's a data-gathering option we've overlooked. It's a bit antiquated, I'll admit, but I think it's perfectly suited to this environment."

The captain leaned forward in his chair. "I would be interested in hearing more," he told her.

Valderrama went on to explain her theory in considerable detail. Partway through the process, Picard found himself smiling. It was a brilliant idea she had come up with, and one that wouldn't be at all difficult to execute.

"And that's it," she said finally.

He nodded. "Let's put it to the test."

Obviously pleased with the captain's reaction, Valderrama said, "Aye, sir. Right away."

Picard looked up and addressed the intercom grid. "Captain Picard to Chief Simenon."

"Simenon here."

The captain glanced at his science officer. "Lieutenant Valderrama has suggested a novel alternative to our sensor scans. I would like you to assist her in implementing it."

"And what exactly *is* this novel approach?" the engineer wondered.

Picard shrugged for the science officer's benefit. "Why don't I let her tell you herself? Picard out."

Valderrama took that as her cue to stand up. "Thank you, sir," she told the captain.

Picard knew what she meant, but he shook his head. "No, Lieutenant. Thank *you.*"

He watched her depart, then sat back in his chair and experienced a surge of satisfaction. *And why shouldn't I?* he asked himself. He had shown faith in someone, and that faith had been rewarded.

Picard was proud of Juanita Valderrama. In fact, he was proud of them *both.*

Ensign Nikolas rubbed his eyes, cursed softly to himself, and focused again on his monitor screen.

He was studying the same sensor graphics as before. Except now, the areas in question were much smaller, much more proximate to the ship. And they weren't changing, because the *Stargazer* hadn't gone anywhere in the last few hours.

Still, there were reasons to keep up their watch. They didn't know enough about this system to predict what it might throw at them. And even if nature didn't come after them with a vengeance, the White Wolf might not be so accommodating.

"Tired?" asked Caber.

Nikolas shrugged. "No more than anyone else."

He wasn't sure anymore what to make of Caber. The guy couldn't have been nicer to him or more supportive. In fact, Caber seemed to be that way with *everyone.*

With one notable exception, Nikolas added silently.

He glanced across the room and saw Obal hard at work, absorbed in whatever graphic was occupying his screen at the moment. Nikolas didn't understand why Caber had it in for the Binderian. He had asked, but Caber didn't seem inclined to offer an explanation.

Maybe there *was* no explanation. Maybe it was just a matter of chemistry. But quite clearly, there was something about Obal that rubbed Caber the wrong way.

Fortunately, Nikolas had exacted a promise from his roommate—no matter how Caber felt about the Binderian, he would leave the little guy alone. No more mocking, no more instigation.

And until then, Caber had been as good as his word.

"I could use a break," he said.

"A break?" Nikolas chuckled as he turned back to his screen. "While we're sitting here without a stitch of protection? You like to live dangerously, don't you?"

"Come on," Caber rejoined. He leaned back in his chair and stretched. "The White Wolf's not even thinking of coming after us."

"How do you know that?" Nikolas asked.

"Because he knows this system and we don't. All he's got to do is stay where he is, nice and cozy in his hiding place, and we'll eventually have to give up and go home."

Nikolas frowned at the notion as he called up another graphic. "And you think that's what's going to happen? You think we're going to leave here empty-handed?"

"Don't you?"

"I don't get it," said Nikolas, forcing himself to concentrate on his work. "Aren't you the guy who kept chipping at Red O'Reilly until you finally beat him? And now you're willing to give up on the White Wolf halfway into the mission?"

"Red O'Reilly was known to lose a game here and there," Caber told him, swiveling his chair to face his roommate's. "The White Wolf has *never* lost. And believe me, when the day comes that he's caught, it won't be at the hands of a captain a couple of years older than *we* are."

Nikolas could feel his blood rising into his face. He wasn't a quitter, and he didn't like talk of quitting. And besides, Caber was distracting him from what Nikolas still considered important.

"Listen," he said, "let's talk about this later, all right? *After* this shift is over."

Caber made a sound of disdain. "This shift will *never* be over. Not as long as our captain thinks he can—"

"Ensign Caber?"

Nikolas knew who had spoken even before he turned and saw Obal waddling toward them. What's more, the ensign had a pretty good idea of what the Binderian wanted.

Caber didn't get up to acknowledge Obal's superior rank. He just folded his arms across his chest. "Yes?"

Obal frowned as he stopped in front of the big man, who looked down on the Binderian even though he was still seated. Obal looked as earnest as Nikolas had ever seen him.

"You do not appear to be approaching your assignment with the proper diligence," he observed.

"Don't I?" Caber responded.

The Binderian's frown deepened. "If we are to succeed in our mission, we must all do our part."

"Normally," said Caber, "I'd agree with you. But I just don't feel very motivated today."

Puzzled, Obal tilted his head. "And why is that?"

Caber shrugged. "I don't know. Maybe I feel funny taking orders from someone who looks like Thanksgiving dinner."

Nikolas wasn't sure if Obal knew what Thanksgiving was, much less what kind of meals were associated with it. However, he seemed to understand that he had been insulted. For a moment, he stared at Caber as if trying to decide what kind of charges to level against him.

And charges certainly seemed to be in order. Nikolas hadn't witnessed this kind of arrogance, this kind of insubordination, since the day he entered Starfleet.

But to his surprise, Obal didn't say anything about filing a report. He didn't even tell Caber that he was out of line. He simply said, "Try to be more attentive to your duties, Ensign," and walked back in the direction of his workstation.

Caber watched him go, a smile spreading across his face. Then he turned to Nikolas. "Came down on me pretty hard, didn't he?"

Nikolas sighed. "Listen, Joe—"

"The guy rules with an iron hand," Caber went on. He laughed. "I'll sure think twice before pulling *that* again."

"Joe," said Nikolas, "that's *enough*."

His voice had an edge to it that even he hadn't expected. Hearing it, Caber was brought up short. Then he grinned.

"Don't worry," he told Nikolas. "Our pal Obal's not going to take offense. He hasn't got a sensitive bone in his body. In fact, he hasn't got a bone in his body, *period."*

And Caber laughed again, making sure it was loud enough for Obal to hear him, even across the room.

But the Binderian didn't do anything about it. He just settled into his seat and regarded his screen as if nothing had happened—as if he hadn't been ridiculed in front of everyone present.

"Guess it's time to get back to work," Caber said, and swung around to face his monitor again. But the damage had been done, Nikolas reflected, and Caber knew it.

Nikolas shook his head. He didn't know with whom he was more disgusted—Caber for the abuse he was heaping on his superior, or Obal for not fighting back.

Chapter Nineteen

PICARD SAT BACK IN HIS CENTER SEAT and eyed his forward viewscreen, with its deep, daunting vision of blushing plasma seas and their continually swirling currents. He could barely make out the glowering red orb of Beta Barritus in the center of it all.

"Are we ready?" he asked.

"As ready as we'll ever be," said Ben Zoma, who was standing in his usual place beside the captain.

"And Lieutenant Valderrama?"

"On her way."

Picard had deemed it fitting that Valderrama join them on the bridge at this juncture, as it was her brainchild that had set this effort in motion.

Just as he thought that, the turbolift doors hissed open behind him. Looking back over his shoulder, the captain could see Valderrama come out onto the bridge. She was smiling, albeit a bit nervously.

"Welcome," Picard told her.

She nodded as she took up a position beside him, on the opposite side from Ben Zoma. "Thank you, sir."

The captain glanced at Gerda. "Launch probe, Lieutenant."

The navigator ran her fingers over her controls. Then she turned to him and said, "Probe away, sir."

On the viewscreen, Picard could see the probe shoot through the nest of misty, wine-colored gases. It didn't take long before it was gone— or at least, seemed to be gone, at this level of magnification.

He turned to Lieutenant Valderrama. The science officer looked tense, hopeful, and perhaps more than a little proud of herself. But then, she deserved to feel that way after she had given them their best chance to locate their prey.

Valderrama's idea had been a wonderfully simple one. The plasma soup surrounding the star made it impossible to get any more useful information out of the ship's active sensor systems.

Sensor systems consisted of proton spectrometers, gravimetric distortion scanners, and gamma ray imagers. What Picard needed—and what Valderrama had prescribed—was a sensor technology that predated the *Stargazer* by hundreds of years.

A technology called *radar.*

Radar was just a matter of bouncing ultrahigh-frequency radio waves off a distant object. And as Valderrama had so astutely pointed out, certain frequencies of radio waves could make it through almost anything, including the veils of hydrogen gas that surrounded the star in this system.

It was with this in mind that Simenon's people had spent the last day or so working on the navigational deflector and lateral sensor arrays, rerigging them so that the former could emit radio waves, which the latter could then receive and analyze.

And to enhance their prospects of success, the Gnalish had added a touch of his own. He had outfitted the probe they had just launched with radar capabilities as well.

Programmed to follow a course parallel to the *Stargazer*'s, the probe would give them additional input from a remote source and, as a result, substantially better odds of finding what they were looking for. Nor was it likely to tip off the White Wolf with its presence, since it was flying parallel to the *Stargazer* and not ahead of her.

For now, however, the probe would serve a different purpose. Its communication facilities temporarily deactivated, it would present Valderrama's idea with its first test.

"Activate radar assembly," Picard said.

"Activated," Gerda told him.

He looked forward again. "On screen."

Instantly, the image of the plasma sea gave way to a rigid green-on-black grid—the same one Gerda saw every day on her navigational console. Unfortunately, there was nothing remarkable to be seen on the grid. In fact, there was nothing at all.

Radar, Picard knew, was ploddingly slow compared to the other sensor technologies at their disposal—technologies which had, for all their quickness, proved useless here.

This might take a while, Picard told himself. Not that he minded. What they were doing here was important. No, he thought—*critical.*

Then he saw it—a bright red dot in the upper left quadrant of the grid. It flashed at the captain triumphantly, bringing a smile to his face. Nor was his smile the only one.

Unfortunately, it wasn't the White Wolf. It was just the probe. But if they could find a probe, Valderrama had reasoned, finding the pirate would be just a matter of time.

"Congratulations," Picard told the science officer. "It appears that your theory has panned out."

Valderrama's sense of accomplishment was evident in her voice as well as her expression. "Thank you, sir," she told him. "I'm pleased I could make a contribution."

So am I, the captain reflected.

Phigus Simenon hated the idea of what he was about to do. He absolutely *hated* it.

Fortunately, it wasn't difficult for him to locate Valderrama. She was standing right there in the science section, her hand on a junior officer's shoulder, lending him encouragement, it seemed, as she pointed something out on his sensor screen.

No doubt she was telling him what to expect of her radar arrangement—the one she had thought of when Simenon himself had despaired of devising any further sensor innovations. The one that would more than likely guide them to the White Wolf.

And that, of course, was what he had come to speak to her about.

Noticing his approach, Valderrama said, "Mr. Simenon. To what do I owe this pleasure?"

The engineer winced at her congenial tone. She wasn't going to make it easy for him, was she?

"I came," he said, "to . . ." It was difficult for him to get the word out—as difficult as he had imagined it would be.

Valderrama's brow creased, but she remained patient. He would have felt better if she had nudged him a little, or maybe even folded her arms and tapped her foot.

But of course, she didn't do that. She was too nice, too much like someone's mother to provoke him that way.

Simenon took a breath and started again. "I came to—" With an effort, he finally squeezed the word out: *"—apologize."* He paused. "That is, for what I said about you."

Valderrama didn't pretend not to know what he was talking about. There was that consolation, at least.

"You mean," she replied, "about my . . . apparent lack of interest in enhancing the sensors?"

Simenon nodded. "Yes. That."

"It's all right," the science officer told him. "As it happens, you were correct. I was being lax in the performance of my duties. But I'm not going to be lax anymore, I assure you."

"Good. Then . . . you accept my apology?" he asked, hoping she would say yes so he could end this debacle.

"I do," she said.

Simenon breathed a sigh of relief. "Excellent. I'll be in engineering if you need me." And he began to retreat toward the exit.

But he hadn't gotten very far before Valderrama called after him. Stopping dead in his tracks, the engineer wondered what further torment he would have to endure.

But all she said was, "How are the repairs going?"

"We're almost done," he told her. "Shields should be back to full strength within the hour."

The science officer smiled. "That's good news."

"So it is," Simenon mumbled. Then he made his way out of the science section before Valderrama could think of some *other* way to prolong his agony.

Nikolas wasn't sure at what point he realized that he had responded to the intercom greeting.

But he *had* responded to it. The ensign knew that in a distant, instinctive sort of way. Otherwise, there wouldn't have been a feminine voice in his room speaking to him as if there had already been an exchange of salutations.

"I hope I haven't disturbed you," the voice said. "I know you've been working long hours."

Nikolas sat up with an effort, shook off the warm, welcome weight of sleep, and tried to remember where he was and who in blazes was talking to him.

Stargazer, his mind said, sifting through its haze for the pertinent facts. *Commander Wu.*

"Ensign?" said the second officer.

"Yes, Commander," Nikolas responded a little shakily. He ran his fingers through his hair and suppressed a yawn. "Here. And no—you haven't disturbed me at all."

"I just wanted to assure you that your contribution has not gone unnoticed. In fact," Wu told him, "it's been brought to my attention more than once."

"It has?" the ensign said. Despite his attempt to speak clearly, he slurred the words a bit.

"Indeed," Wu replied. "Mr. Joseph informed me that you were the first to detect the vortex belt down in the security section."

That was me, all right, Nikolas thought.

"However," the second officer continued, "it was Ensign Caber who filed a report providing the full details of your diligence. Given the dedication you've shown, the seriousness with which you seem to have undertaken your assignment, I'm not surprised you were able to get wind of the vortices well before any of your colleagues."

"Ensign *Caber* said that?" Nikolas wondered.

"I know," Wu said. "It's rather unusual for an ensign to file an unsolicited personnel report, especially when it involves a crewman of equal rank. However, Mr. Caber seems possessed of a rather extraordinary sense of fairness."

And an extraordinary hostility toward a certain Binderian, Nikolas added inwardly. But all he said was, "Yes, sir."

There was a pause. "I've gone over your personnel file, Ensign, and I couldn't help noticing the strikes against you. The disciplinary action for fighting, in particular."

Nikolas felt a rush of warmth in his cheeks. "That wasn't my fault, Commander. I was just defending myself."

"Unfortunately," said Wu, "your captain saw it otherwise. Hence the disciplinary action, which didn't exactly ensure you of a successful career path."

The ensign frowned. There was nothing to be gained by arguing the point, especially with someone who had begun their conversation on a positive note.

"No, sir."

"Nonetheless, Mr. Nikolas, people change. They improve. They put their pasts behind them. And from what I've seen of your efforts so far on the *Stargazer,* you've done all those things."

Nikolas smiled. "Thank you, ma'am."

"Keep up the good work," Wu advised him. "Don't lose focus. And get some sleep, Ensign. You'll need it."

Nikolas stifled a groan. "I'll do that, Commander."

"Wu out."

Their exchange over, the ensign finally had a chance to take stock of himself. He looked down and saw that he had gone to bed still dressed in his uniform.

And his roommate, who was possessed of that "rather extraordinary sense of fairness"? There was no sign of him. Obviously, Caber hadn't been as tired as Nikolas was.

The ensign felt the urge to yawn again, and this time he gave into it. Funny, he thought. This was the last problem he had expected to have on the *Stargazer*—being woken out of a dead sleep by the second officer, who just couldn't wait to praise his devotion to duty.

Maybe Caber was right, he told himself as he slumped back against his bed and closed his eyes. Maybe he could prove those Academy guys wrong after all.

That is, if he didn't screw things up by returning to his old tricks. But he wouldn't do that, he vowed. He would be as patient and cooperative as anyone who had ever served on a Starfleet vessel.

Lieutenant Nikolas, he thought. *Captain* Nikolas. He smiled at the prospect as he drifted off.

Picard was on his way to the bridge when the doors to his turbolift compartment opened and admitted Lieutenant Valderrama.

He smiled. "Lieutenant."

She smiled back. "Sir." As the doors closed again, she said, "I understand the shields have been restored."

"Very nearly," the captain told her. "Enough for us to get under way again, so we can finish what we have begun."

Valderrama nodded. "That's good to hear."

"But we would still be in a hole if not for your brainstorm." He favored the lieutenant with a look of admiration. "Using radar in this day and age—it was an inspired idea, to say the least."

"Thank you, sir," said Valderrama.

It seemed to Picard that she was somewhat less enthusiastic than he had seen her on the bridge. But then, the novelty of her discovery and its success were probably beginning to wear off.

It occurred to him to ask Valderrama about his *other* project in her section. "Incidentally," he said in a softer voice, "how is Ensign Jiterica faring?"

The lieutenant didn't answer right away. "Unfortunately," she replied with obvious reluctance, "Ensign Jiterica could be doing better, sir. She seems listless, uninterested in the challenges we're tackling . . . even withdrawn at times. If I may be allowed to venture an opinion . . . ?"

"By all means."

"I don't think we're doing her a favor by continuing to try to make her fit in."

Valderrama sounded understandably sympathetic. She had been considered a misfit herself for the last few years.

"I'm sorry to hear that," Picard said. "I was hoping her situation would improve—for the Federation's sake as well as her own. Nonetheless, I appreciate your candor."

"I'd prefer to have been candid about *good* news," the science officer told him.

The captain smiled wistfully to himself. "Perhaps next time, Lieutenant. Carry on."

"I'll do that," Valderrama promised him.

By then, they had reached her destination—deck 6, which housed the ship's science section. The doors opened and the lieutenant departed, leaving Picard with something to think about.

In his head, he began to compose an advisory to Starfleet Command. It would contain a recommendation that Ensign Jiterica be given her unconditional discharge.

Under the circumstances, Picard reflected, it was the only humane choice open to him.

Idun Asmund heard the hiss of the turbolift doors as they parted to admit someone. *The captain,* she thought without turning. He had said he was on his way.

"Helm," said Picard, confirming her suspicion. He took his seat behind her. "Activate impulse drive."

"Aye, sir," Idun responded. Her long, slender fingers tapped the requisite studs on her control console. "Ready."

There was a pause, as if the captain was savoring this moment. And no doubt he was. "Full impulse," he said finally.

"Full impulse," she confirmed.

"Engage," Picard ordered, his voice the crack of a whip.

Idun sent them hurtling through the gases and ion clouds of Beta Barritus, depending on a kind of sensor operation she had never heard of before this mission. Not that it mattered that she was unfamiliar with this thing called *radar*.

If it got them closer to their prey, Idun Asmund was all for it.

The White Wolf frowned as he peered at his personal sensor screen, where a single blue dot was drifting slowly across a white grid. "They're moving again," he announced. "Obviously, whatever problems they had have been solved."

His second-in-command's thick brows met over the bridge of his nose as he considered the news. Then, with a curt backhanded gesture, he dismissed the threat posed by their pursuer.

"I'm *glad* they're moving," the Klingon snarled. "I'm tired of hiding here like a mewling *p'takh.*"

The White Wolf shook his head slowly as he studied his screen. "There are no cowards on this ship, Turgis. If there were, I would've gotten rid of them a long time ago."

The Klingon rumbled on as if he hadn't heard his captain's comment. "My heart yearns for battle—for *blood!* It's been too long since I raised my hand against an enemy!"

The White Wolf saw others on the bridge turn to Turgis, wary of the edge in his voice. On the other hand, he mused, some of them probably felt the same way.

"We're not operating a warship," he insisted—and not for the Klingon's benefit alone. "We're privateers. Our victory comes in not getting caught."

A sound of disgust tore from Turgis's throat. "That's no victory! That's mere *survival!*"

The White Wolf's eyes narrowed as he turned to look at his second-in-command. "What are you saying? That you've had enough of this life? Of what we do here?"

It put the Klingon on the spot. But then, that was exactly what the pirate had meant to do.

"Well?" he asked.

Turgis turned red in the face, but he contained his fury—just as the White Wolf had expected he would. He hadn't shared a bridge with the Klingon all this time without getting to know him a little.

As Turgis stalked off to drown his defiance in a bottle of bloodwine, the pirate turned to the others. "What are you looking at?" he asked them. "The hunt's on again—and we've still got work to do."

One by one they went back to their business. And a moment later, so did the man known as the White Wolf, for he had played a poker game or two in his day.

And he knew that a hidden ace wasn't always a guarantee of victory.

Chapter Twenty

CHIEF COMMUNICATIONS OFFICER MARTIN PAXTON wasn't a stickler about much, but he did have a thing about punctuality.

So when his relief had yet to show up a full ten minutes after Paxton's shift had ended, it bugged him. And it bugged him even more that the tardy officer was Ulelo.

He had taken Ulelo off the graveyard shift sooner than any other comm chief would have. He had treated the new guy with warmth and respect. In Ulelo's place, Paxton would have made damned sure he didn't bite the hand that fed him.

Finally, the comm chief had had enough. Tapping his insignia, he said, "Paxton to Ulelo."

There was no answer.

Again he said, "Paxton to Ulelo."

Still no response.

"Computer," he said, "locate Mr. Ulelo."

The computer's soft, feminine voice informed him that "Mr. Ulelo is in the shuttlebay."

The comm chief frowned. "Paxton to Ch—"

158   *Michael Jan Friedman*

"Mr. Paxton?" someone said over the comm link. But it didn't sound like Ulelo.

"This is Paxton," he said. "Who's this?"

"It's Andarko, sir. Technician first class. I'm speaking into Mr. Ulelo's communicator."

"And why isn't Mr. Ulelo speaking into his communicator?" Paxton inquired, figuring it was a reasonable question.

"He took off his tunic to work on one of the shuttles with Lieutenant Chiang," said Andarko. "But when I heard a voice coming from his communicator, I came over to see what was going on."

"I see," said Paxton.

Had he spoken directly into the intercom grid, Ulelo's name would have rung throughout the shuttlebay. But, not wanting to embarrass Ulelo any more than was necessary, he had chosen to use the more private method of communicator-to-communicator, so Andarko was the only one who had ended up hearing him.

"Would you be so kind," Paxton asked the technician, "as to get Mr. Ulelo for me? I need to speak with him right away."

"Actually," Andarko said, "he's right here, sir."

A moment later, the comm chief heard a voice that he recognized as Ulelo's. "Sir?"

"Mr. Ulelo," Paxton said evenly, "are you aware of the fact that you were supposed to report to the bridge almost fifteen minutes ago?"

"Actually," a third voice chimed in, "it's my fault Ulelo's late."

It took Paxton a moment to place it. "Chiang?"

"That's right," the shuttle chief confirmed. "And I'll take the blame for Mr. Ulelo's tardiness. You see, he asked for a look at the newer shuttles. And while we were going over them, he found a comm problem with the type-eight. I asked if he could stay awhile and fix it, and, unfortunately, we both lost track of the time."

"Sorry, sir," said Ulelo.

"Same here," Chiang added. "I didn't mean to keep your man that long."

Under the circumstances, Paxton could hardly be angry. It wasn't as if Ulelo had been goofing off. He had been working—just not where he was *scheduled* to be working.

"Don't give it a second thought," said the comm chief. "Just tell me when to expect him."

"Immediately," Ulelo assured him. "I'm done with the shuttle. Mr. Chiang shouldn't have any more problems with it from here on."

"I wouldn't even have known it *had* a problem," the shuttle chief remarked, "if Ulelo here hadn't mentioned it."

"Then it's a good thing he was there," Paxton said. "See you later, Chiang. Paxton out."

With a private chuckle, he turned his attention back to his comm console. Chiang was lucky Ulelo was so curious by nature. In fact, they were *all* lucky.

Considering the dangerous nature of their mission, the last thing they needed was a shuttle malfunction.

As Gilaad Ben Zoma entered his captain's ready room, he saw a figure standing on the other side of the room, gazing out the observation port. For just a moment, he could have sworn that the figure was that of the late Daithan Ruhalter.

But of course, it wasn't. It was that of Jean-Luc Picard.

Strange, the first officer thought. Picard wasn't as tall as Ruhalter or as broad, and Ruhalter's hair had been gray where Picard's was still brown. And yet, for just a moment, Picard had put him in mind of their former captain.

It was something about Picard's bearing, Ben Zoma decided. Something about the set of his shoulders. Ruhalter had been a confident man, a confident captain. It seemed to Ben Zoma that his friend was becoming a confident captain as well.

And why not? They had already accomplished what no one else could. They had gotten through the debris field and the vortex belt, and now—thanks to Valderrama—they had come up with a way to see in a place where standard sensors were of no use to them.

With a little luck, they would accomplish one more task—the one they had come here for. They would catch the infamous, elusive White Wolf.

"You're staring out that port again," Ben Zoma noted.

Picard chuckled grimly. "I find I do my best thinking here."

"You used to do your best thinking in the shower," said the first officer. "Or so you told me."

"That," said the captain, "was *before* I had an observation port to stare out of."

Ben Zoma found himself smiling. "So what's on your mind at this advanced hour?"

160   Michael Jan Friedman

"Our approach to catching the White Wolf. I think we need to re-consider it."

The first officer pulled up a chair. "I'm all ears."

Picard made a fist with his right hand and used his left forefinger to describe a circle above it. As he spoke the circle moved down until it described an equatorial orbit.

"Right now," Picard said, "we are descending toward Beta Barritus in a shallow spiral—the textbook approach to finding something in a solar system under less than optimum sensor conditions. The virtue of that approach is the likelihood that we will eventually come across the White Wolf's position."

But there was a downside as well. Picard articulated it.

"Unfortunately, this may take a very long time. And if the White Wolf is hiding on the other side of the star, which he may well be, catching him will take even longer."

Ben Zoma nodded. "No argument there."

"What I'm considering," the captain told him, "is going directly to Beta Barritus—a trip that should take no more than three hours at full impulse. Then, when we've come within perhaps a thousand kilometers of the star, we can follow an *upward* spiral."

"Because the White Wolf is probably hiding as close to Beta Barritus as he can," the first officer noted thoughtfully. "I mean, that's what *I* would do—make it as difficult as possible for my pursuers to reach me, much less find me."

"Precisely. And if it happens that his sensor capabilities are superior to our radar and he finds *us* before we find *him,* he will probably take flight in an outward direction."

"Which will eventually flush him out of the system—and make him easy prey for McAteer's armada." Ben Zoma grinned appreciatively. "Obviously, you've done more than consider this. You've thought it through pretty damned thoroughly."

"I have," Picard admitted as he took the seat behind his desk. "So what do you think?"

Ben Zoma shrugged. "What I think, Jean-Luc, is we ought to put your strategy into action."

The captain looked pleased with his friend's response. "I am glad to hear you say that, Number One." He tapped his communicator. "Helm, this is Picard . . ."

And he gave the order to head directly for Beta Barritus.

"Aye, sir," said Idun.

Ben Zoma glanced at the observation port and saw the ruddy glare of the star grow more intense. Idun was bringing them about, putting them on the course Picard had described.

The captain noticed as well. "There," he said, and turned back to his friend. "That's done."

Ben Zoma regarded the man on the other side of the desk. "You know," he remarked, "I'm glad to see you feeling so enthusiastic. For a while there when we first entered this system, you were frowning so hard I thought your face would crack."

Picard looked skeptical. "Really."

"Really," said the first officer.

"Well," said the captain, "I do feel more in control of the situation. Though, to be honest, I'm anything *but* in control. I still don't know what tricks our adversary may be holding in reserve."

He had a point, Ben Zoma conceded. It was hard to know how to fight someone when you knew so little about him.

"Funny," Picard went on. "I thought our battle against the Nuyyad was our baptism of fire—a fight to the death against a ruthless and powerful enemy. Yet I feel so raw, so untested."

"Maybe that's the way a captain *always* feels," Ben Zoma suggested. "No matter *how* long he's been in command."

Judging by the expression on Picard's face, that possibility hadn't occurred to him. "Perhaps," he allowed.

The two of them sat in unhurried silence. Finally, it was the captain who spoke up.

"I should take another look at what we know of the White Wolf. I may find something I have overlooked."

Ben Zoma shook his head. "You've gone over those logs for days on end. It's enough. You may be the man in charge here, but there's nothing more you can do."

"There must be *something* I can—"

"Go to bed," Ben Zoma advised him. "That's what Captain Ruhalter would've done."

The captain mulled it over, then rejected the notion. "Perhaps not just yet, Gilaad."

Ben Zoma's eyes narrowed suspiciously. "You just can't stay away from those logs, can you? You're going to stay up into the wee hours trying to find something you missed."

"Not into the wee hours, I assure you."

"You'll turn in shortly, then?"

"Absolutely. In just a few minutes."

"Scout's honor?"

"Without question."

Ben Zoma leaned back in his chair and folded his arms across his chest. "Good. I'll wait."

Picard began to protest. "There's no need to—"

His friend stopped him with a raised hand. "Honestly, what kind of first officer would I be if I didn't look after my captain's health and well-being?"

Picard shook his head. "Gilaad, I—"

"And what kind of friend would I be if I let you sit here all by yourself, trying to find a needle's worth of something useful in a haystack of command logs?"

The captain sighed. "Believe me, I'm not looking forward to it. I would go to bed if I could."

"I'm sure you would," Ben Zoma replied evenly. But he didn't move out of his chair.

Picard was reminded again of why he held his first officer in such high regard. "Can I at least offer you something to drink?" He indicated the half-empty cup on his desk. "Tea, perhaps?"

Ben Zoma shook his head. "No, thanks. Puts me to sleep. How about a cup of black coffee?"

The captain rose from his chair to fill his friend's request. "Coming right up."

Gerda Asmund watched the seething red expanse of Beta Barritus slide off the edge of the viewscreen. She didn't think she would miss it, either—not after staring at its steadily swelling girth for the last three hours.

The star's lurid light was replaced by cottony clusters of soft rose and lavender, too dense for Gerda to see through. Fortunately, she didn't have to see anything. Valderrama's radar was working like a carefully honed *bat'leth,* slicing through anything and everything in its way.

Soon, the navigator thought, they would find the White Wolf. She could feel it in the marrow of her bones. They would find him and put an end to the myth of his invincibility, adding to the glory already associated with the name *Stargazer.*

And glory was what made the difference between bloodwine and water, between life and mere existence. Any Klingon knew that.

Gerda was in the process of refining the course she had laid out for her sister when she noticed something on her radar monitor, something represented by a green blip on the otherwise black field.

There weren't any planets or moons in this solar system. There weren't even any asteroids. They had all been reduced to ions when their original star went nova.

And it couldn't be their radar-assist companion probe because that was elsewhere. So if there was an object out there, it was neither one they had brought with them nor a naturally occurring body.

Which left Gerda with just one inescapable conclusion.

She turned to her sister and saw that Idun had noticed the green blip as well. Her eyes, which were locked intently on her monitors, were alight with a warrior's anticipation.

The navigator looked to the intercom grid. "Captain Picard, this is Lieutenant Asmund."

"Picard here," the captain said a moment later.

He sounded tired to Gerda. But then, none of them was getting much sleep these days.

"There's something on radar," she told him.

A pause. "I'll be right there," the captain replied. And he no longer sounded the least bit fatigued.

Chapter Twenty-one

PICARD WAS A STEP AHEAD of Ben Zoma as they emerged from his ready room and crossed the bridge.

"How far?" he asked as he approached Gerda's console.

"Slightly more than a million kilometers," his navigator told him.

"Is it a ship?"

Gerda nodded. "I believe so, yes."

Picard looked up at the viewscreen. All it showed him was a nest of blood-red gases.

Then he peered past his navigator at the screen on her console that had tipped her off. It showed him a black field with a green blip prominently displayed on it.

There was something there all right, Picard thought. Something that might be the White Wolf. And thanks to Valderrama's radar, the *Stargazer* could track it down.

"Red alert," he said.

"Raise shields and power weapons," Ben Zoma added.

"Shields up, sir," Vigo assured him from his weapons console. "Phasers and photon torpedoes ready."

Of course, the torpedoes were a last resort. Picard still wanted to bring that cargo home intact—and the White Wolf as well, if he could.

"Bring us closer," he told Idun.

She saw to it. "Aye, sir."

His helm officer made the necessary adjustment in their heading. Nothing changed on the viewscreen, but Gerda's monitors told the captain a different story. There, the object of their attentions was getting closer by the second.

"Four hundred thousand kilometers," Gerda announced.

If it *was* the White Wolf, he didn't seem to know he had company yet—and that meant Picard held a big advantage. He could get even closer before his prey knew it was being hunted.

Unless it's a trap.

Picard's mouth went dry at the unwelcome thought. Could that be it? Could his adversary be biding his time, every bit as aware of the *Stargazer* as the *Stargazer* was of him?

"Three hundred thousand kilometers, sir."

Still no reaction from the White Wolf—if it *was* the White Wolf. The captain was beginning to harbor some doubts.

"Two hundred thousand," Gerda reported.

"Fire when ready!" Picard barked.

"One hundred thousand . . ."

And their adversary woke up.

The White Wolf's phaser salvo seemed to erupt from out of nowhere. It loomed rapidly on the main viewer, growing in volcanic splendor and magnitude until it blanched the entire screen.

"Evasive maneuvers!" Picard called out.

But it was too late.

The phaser attack bludgeoned the *Stargazer* with bone-rattling force, causing the deck to lurch beneath the captain's feet. Grabbing the back of Gerda's chair, he managed to stay upright, but only barely.

As Idun sent them twisting away from the enemy, Vigo launched a counterstrike. The *Stargazer*'s phased energy bolts vanished into the crimson haze, reaching for their unseen enemy.

"Missed!" Gerda hissed, consulting her radar in conjunction with a computer model of their phaser strike.

A second time, a ruby-red barrage loomed on their viewscreen. But this time, it swept past them without taking a toll. Obviously, Idun's helm work was baffling the enemy's weapons batteries.

Vigo unleashed another volley of his own. The captain tracked it on Gerda's monitor, watching it stab across the screen at the green dot that represented the enemy ship. It was as true an attack as a phaser cannon could make.

But at the last possible moment, the White Wolf banked sharply and escaped unscathed.

At that point, the pirate might have turned tail and tried to shake them. But he didn't do anything of the sort. He switched back and went for the *Stargazer*'s throat.

Picard glanced at Idun. She was accepting the enemy's challenge, refusing to change their heading a single degree. But then, she had been raised by Klingons, and Klingons didn't flinch when an adversary attacked them head-on.

As a collision became imminent, the captain wished his helm officer had been raised in a slightly less aggressive culture. And he wished so even more when the White Wolf's vessel became visible on their viewscreen, no longer an abstraction but a fact.

And yet, for a fact it seemed remarkably ethereal—a ghostly specter emerging from a sea of blood and fire, swimming up from an impossible red depth. Not a massive black bullet like the ship of his nightmare, but a slender, pale wraith.

And like Idun, the vessel's helm officer wasn't flinching. The pirate was on a course that threatened to ram the *Stargazer* into oblivion.

"Fire!" Picard barked.

But the White Wolf had already foiled him by veering off to starboard. And as he darted past the *Stargazer,* he unleashed a series of phaser blasts at close range.

The captain was sent sprawling by the fury of the attack. Somewhere behind him a console exploded, spewing sparks and billows of smoke, and he could hear groans of pain.

But Ben Zoma would see to the console and the injured, Picard thought as he dragged himself to his feet. It was the captain's job to see to it they didn't absorb such punishment a second time.

"Report!" he commanded.

"Shields down thirty-eight percent!" Gerda growled.

"Casualties on decks seven, ten, and eleven!" Paxton reported. "Hull breaches on twelve and thirteen!"

Picard cursed under his breath. They had taken a beating. And to that point, they hadn't even dealt the enemy a glancing blow.

The problem was that the pirate was more maneuverable than the larger and more powerful *Stargazer.* The White Wolf might not have been able to match their firepower or their defenses, but he could certainly fly rings around them.

Clearly, they needed a new tactic. Gritting his teeth, Picard tried to come up with one.

But all he could think about was Daithan Ruhalter—not the heroic and inspirational human being under whom he had served, but the strangely wistful Daithan Ruhalter of his nightmare. The latter's words came to the captain anew, surging from the depths of his memory . . .

Instinct, the nightmare Ruhalter had said. *Either you've got it or you don't. And if you don't, no collection of sensors and shields and phaser banks is going to help you.*

Picard could feel a bead of sweat meandering down the side of his face. He felt as if all eyes were upon him, waiting for him to say the words that would turn the battle around.

But he had no such words at his disposal.

It was too soon, the nightmare Ruhalter had said of Picard. *He was too damned young.*

No, thought the captain. He glared defiantly at the viewscreen, which showed him nothing more than billowing scarlet gas clouds. *I am* not *too young,* he insisted. *I* will *beat the White Wolf.*

And suddenly, it came to him how he would do it.

Turning to Idun, Picard said, "Retreat! Full impulse!"

His helm officer looked at him with an expression of horror on her face. It seemed to him that she was about to protest, right there in the middle of their encounter with the enemy.

But in the end, she kept from commenting on his choice of tactic. She simply worked her helm controls and carried out her captain's command.

A moment later, he saw the gas clouds ahead of them swing to port. Idun was bringing them about, moving them away from the enemy as fast as their impulse drive would take them.

Joining Gerda at her navigation console, Picard inspected her radar monitor. It showed him that the pirate wasn't content to let them go—not after they had smoked him from his lair. He was following the *Stargazer,* pursuing her as quickly as she was running away.

And why not? The White Wolf had already proven his tactical superiority. He wanted to end this hunt and end it quickly, just as Picard would have done if their roles were reversed.

The captain gauged the distance between the two ships—a bit too far for effective phaser fire, he judged. But that could change—and with a grim smile, he demonstrated just how quickly it could happen.

"All stop!" he bellowed. Then, to Vigo: "Fire phasers!"

Everything happened so quickly, Picard couldn't be certain at first whether his gambit had worked or failed. The White Wolf's ship seemed to surge out of nowhere, looming impossibly large on the viewscreen, even as the *Stargazer* stabbed it with two seething red phaser bolts at appallingly close range.

The twin energy lances sent the pirate ship skittering past them at a terrifyingly oblique angle. Picard could almost imagine the White Wolf's hull scraping that of the Federation vessel. But the miss, narrow as it may have been, was unquestionably a miss. The *Stargazer* and what was left of her shields remained intact.

Which was more than the captain imagined could be said of their adversary. Of course, without traditional sensor readings, he had no way of knowing how badly he had damaged the White Wolf. But there was a way to find out.

"Go after him!" Picard commanded Idun. Then, as the helm officer's fingers flew over her controls, the captain glanced at Vigo and added, "Ready phasers!"

The gas clouds slid sideways on the viewscreen as the *Stargazer* came about and offered pursuit. Turning to Gerda's monitor, Picard saw the green blip in full flight.

"Range?" he asked.

"One hundred twenty-five thousand kilometers," his navigator informed him.

Farther than they would normally have attempted weapons fire, even with their normal array of sensors in operation. However, the White Wolf wasn't bobbing and weaving at this point. His attempt at escape was straight and unswerving.

Picard gave the order. "Target and fire!"

A moment later, his forward phaser banks belched crimson fury. It pierced the softly tinted gas clouds ahead of them and was almost immediately lost to sight.

However, the phaser beams hadn't ceased to exist. With luck, the White Wolf would soon find that out.

"Fire again!" the captain said.

As before, two seething beams of phased energy poured out of the

Stargazer and buried themselves in the sea of gases. And as before, he could only imagine their effect.

But this time, Gerda gave him something more concrete than his imagination. "The enemy is slowing down," she announced triumphantly. "Half impulse at best."

Glancing at her monitor, Picard could see the gap between them and their prey diminishing precipitously. One hundred thousand kilometers. Eighty thousand. Sixty thousand.

"Match their speed and fire!" he said, his voice sounding stentorian in the narrow confines of the bridge.

Idun slowed them down, and the *Stargazer*'s phaser batteries poured destruction into the roiling clouds. As the captain watched them vanish, he was joined by Ben Zoma.

"How are we doing?" the first officer asked.

Picard kept his eyes on Gerda's radar monitor. "Better than before, Number One. *Much* better."

"So what made you think of that stop-and-fire tactic?"

What indeed? "I was thinking of Captain Ruhalter. We used to fence, as you know, and one of his favorite moves was something called a stop-thrust. It often began with a retreat."

Ben Zoma seemed impressed. "I see."

"We must have hit them again," Gerda said. "They've slowed to a crawl, sir."

Indeed, the behavior of the green blip bore out her observation. The pirate was hardly making any progress at all.

"Looks like he's had it," Ben Zoma remarked.

Something occurred to the captain. "Unless our friend the White Wolf is laying a trap for us."

Ben Zoma looked at him. "Feigning disability to bring the *Stargazer* in closer, so he can let us have it with both barrels?"

Picard nodded. "Precisely."

"Our regular sensors aren't *completely* dead," Ben Zoma reminded him. "If we get within fifty kilometers of the bastard, I'll bet we can get a full scan of him."

The captain considered the option. If the White Wolf attacked them with phasers at a range of fifty kilometers, it could leave the *Stargazer* a shambles. But they had a mission to complete, and they weren't going to complete it by hanging back.

"Slow to one-eighth impulse," he said.

"One-eighth impulse," Idun confirmed.

Picard watched Gerda's radar screen. The pirate ship's behavior wasn't changing one iota. She was still moving through gas-drenched space at a snail's pace.

When they got within sixty kilometers, the captain called for thrusters only. At fifty-six kilometers, some of the traditional sensors began to kick in. By the time they reached fifty-two kilometers, they had enough information to know where they stood.

The White Wolf's shields were down, her weapons were off-line, and her propulsion systems were all but useless. The *Stargazer* had won. Her prey was hers for the taking.

The White Wolf swept away some of the smoke issuing from his helmsman's flaming control console, situated just ahead of his captain's chair. Then he peered at the still-functioning radar screen attached to his armrest.

Their pursuer, represented by a blue icon on a white grid, was creeping closer to them by the moment.

"Damn them," growled Turgis, who had been injured and was using the back of the center seat to hold himself up.

"Yes," said the pirate. "Damn them indeed."

His vessel was absolutely helpless, rendered so by their Starfleet enemy's surprise tactics. There was nothing he could do to keep his hold from being emptied of its stolen cargo, or his crew from being tried at the nearest starbase.

The prospect left a bitter taste in his mouth—even more bitter than the acrid taste of burning plastic.

But he still had his hidden ace. As long as that individual hadn't come into play yet, there was still a chance that the White Wolf would come out on top.

Picard was tempted to smile as he savored his victory.

But he couldn't, of course. There was still work to be done and lots of it. For one thing, he doubted that he could tractor the pirate's ship back through the obstacles Beta Barritus had thrown at them, so he would have to board the pale, slim vessel in order to remove her crew and cargo.

And the captain couldn't depend on his transporters. The gas clouds and free-floating ions in the vicinity were creating too much interference for that. So the only way to remove anybody or anything—

"Captain?" said Gerda, interrupting his thoughts.

He looked at her. "What is it, Lieutenant?"

The navigator pointed to her radar screen, which now showed not one blip but two. "Sir," she said, her voice low and grim, "radar shows a *second* ship in the area."

Chapter Twenty-two

PICARD TURNED TO BEN ZOMA. "A *second* ship?"

They had been expecting only one ship when they went after the White Wolf. If there were two or three of the pirates or perhaps even more, it would mean trouble.

Ben Zoma frowned. "Doesn't sound good."

"Evasive maneuvers," the captain told Idun.

But as the *Stargazer* began to swing around the White Wolf, Paxton spoke up from his comm console.

"They're hailing us," he informed Picard.

The captain felt a muscle spasm in his jaw as he considered the situation. "Discontinue maneuvers," he told Idun. "But be ready to resume them on my command."

"Aye, sir," came the helm officer's response.

Picard glanced at Paxton. "Return their hail, Lieutenant."

Paxton turned to his console and did as he was told. A moment later, he turned around again, an unmistakable look of disbelief on his face. "Sir," he said, "it's the *Cochise*."

Picard wasn't ready to believe it. "Are you certain?" he asked his comm officer.

Paxton shrugged. "That's what they claim, sir."

"Then they should be able to show me Captain Greenbriar," the captain concluded. "Tell them I want to see him. *Now.*"

Paxton went to work again at his console, and before Picard could draw another breath, the craggy visage of a Starfleet captain filled his viewscreen. It was static-riddled and it wavered occasionally, but there was no question that it was Greenbriar.

"Picard," he said, "are you all right?"

"I am," the captain told him. He looked around his bridge at the damage it had taken. "Though somewhat the worse for wear."

"And the White Wolf?"

"Disabled, apparently. We were about to put together a boarding party when you arrived."

"That's good news," said Greenbriar.

Picard should have been happy to see his colleague, happy to have a little support in such a perilous setting. But something about the *Cochise*'s presence here felt wrong to him.

Before the *Stargazer,* no one had ever managed to get this far. Not in dozens of previous attempts. *No one.*

Yet here was the *Cochise,* basking in the proximate, ruddy light of Beta Barritus. It seemed like an awfully big coincidence—a little too big for Picard to swallow.

"I hadn't expected to see you here," he told Greenbriar.

"I hadn't expected to *be* here," Greenbriar replied in a comradely tone of voice. "At the last minute, Admiral McAteer changed his mind and dispatched us to back you up."

"Yes," said Picard, "I knew that. I meant I didn't think you would be able to penetrate this far into the system."

As he spoke, his mind raced headlong. *What is going on here?* he demanded of himself.

Picard's friend Corey Zweller had warned him that McAteer wanted to see him fail, so that Admiral Mehdi could be seen to fail as well. But how badly did McAteer want it?

Badly enough to take the lives of Picard and his crew?

And if the *Stargazer* and all its hands were to be lost here, in this dangerous place, who would question it? Who would know that the *Cochise* had followed her in?

No one but the captain and crew of the *Cochise*—and Admiral McAteer, of course.

Suddenly, the captain realized what he was saying—and rejected the idea. *I'm being paranoid,* he thought. *I've been on edge so long, I've begun tilting at shadows.*

McAteer might have been a lot of things, but he was also a high-ranking Starfleet officer, a man trusted implicitly by other men of good judgment. It was unthinkable that he would sacrifice the *Stargazer* just to further his personal ambitions.

Wasn't it?

As he asked himself that question, he noticed Ben Zoma leaning over Gerda's console. A glance told him that Greenbriar's ship had come within their limited sensor range—although it wasn't as limited as the *Cochise*'s sensor range, since Greenbriar's instruments hadn't been enhanced by the *Stargazer*'s Chief Simenon.

Ben Zoma was scrutinizing the *Cochise* intently, examining her power levels, her structural integrity, her crew, anything that might have told him something was wrong. And Gerda was following his every move.

Inwardly, Picard smiled. It seemed he wasn't the only one wary of Greenbriar's appearance here.

"How *did* you make it this far?" he inquired of Greenbriar.

"The same way you did, I expect," came the man's reply. "We warp-jumped the debris field, then altered the polarity of our shields to make it through the vortex belt. And when we couldn't see in this muck, my chief engineer came up with the idea of—"

Without warning, Gerda whirled in her seat. "Captain," she said, her eyes hard and angry, "the *Cochise* is powering up her weapons!"

Picard didn't even have time to utter a curse. "All available power to the shields!"

They made the adjustment just in time to ward off a blinding red phaser barrage. Nonetheless, the impact sent everyone on the bridge reeling hard to starboard and tore one of their plasma conduits free of its moorings.

"Return fire!" the captain bellowed as the conduit whipped back and forth capriciously, spraying superheated plasma at a bulkhead.

Vigo punched back at the *Constellation*-class *Cochise* with his forward phaser banks, but Greenbriar's ship was already executing evasive maneuvers. Only one of the energy beams managed to strike her.

And a moment or two later, Picard's colleague came about for another pass at him.

"Shields down fifty-four percent," Gerda noted.

The captain absorbed the information. His ship was at a distinct disadvantage. She had already been battered by the White Wolf, whereas Greenbriar's vessel was all but unscathed.

And Greenbriar himself was one of the most experienced captains in the fleet, while Picard had been given command of the *Stargazer* only a few short weeks ago.

A lopsided match if ever there was one, Picard thought. He had to find a way to pull off an upset.

"Evasive maneuvers," he told Idun. Then he glanced at Vigo and said, "Fire at will."

Picard's helm officer moved them off the bull's-eye, giving the *Cochise* a running, twisting target. And as soon as Greenbriar's ship came within range, Vigo greeted her with a sizzling phaser salvo.

But the *Stargazer* was brutalized as well. The captain was thrown back into his chair as an aft control bank erupted in flames.

"Shields down seventy-six percent," Gerda reported.

"Casualties on decks seven and eight," Paxton added. "Sickbay is sending out teams."

Picard felt a familiar hand on his shoulder. "We can't just trade volleys with them," Ben Zoma said, his voice so low that only his friend could hear it. "That's what Greenbriar *wants* us to do."

The captain frowned as he considered his options. In the meantime, the *Cochise* wheeled and came at them again with full fury. As before, Idun made it difficult for Greenbriar to hit them, but he still got in a solid phaser shot.

"Shields down eighty-seven percent," Gerda announced, a hint of frustration in her voice.

And the *Cochise,* her captain undaunted, was coming about for another charge at them.

The *Stargazer* could withstand only one more barrage before she lost her defenses altogether. If Picard was going to turn the tide, this would be his last chance to do so.

Perspiration collected in the small of his back. He had to do *something.* But *what?*

And then it came to him. *Of course,* he thought. It was so simple, he was amazed that he hadn't thought of it before.

"Mr. Vigo," Picard said.

The weapons officer turned to him.

"Target the center of the *Cochise*'s navigational deflector and hit it with the narrowest, most intense beam you can manage. And don't let up until I tell you."

Vigo smiled, a sign that he had some idea of what his captain was up to. "Aye, sir."

The captain glanced at his helm officer. "Give us a good look at our target, Lieutenant."

Idun nodded, as steady as ever. "I will, sir."

As they closed with Greenbriar's ship, Idun banked sharply and un-expectedly, taking the *Stargazer* across the *Cochise*'s bow. It seemed like a reckless move in that it exposed their flank to their adversary's phasers for an awkward amount of time.

And the *Stargazer* paid for it.

Raked by Greenbriar's directed energy beams, she lost more than what was left of her shields. She suffered hull breaches and severed power linkages and ceased to function in a thousand small ways.

Picard didn't need to hear the damage reports. He could feel what had happened in his bones.

But Idun's maneuver also gave Vigo the opening he needed. The *Stargazer*'s powerful crimson phaser beams plunged mercilessly into the heart of their adversary's navigational deflector, cutting through layer upon layer of graviton-contained spatial distortion in the merest fraction of a second.

Fortunately, they didn't have to take out the entire deflector. Their objective was the small, long-range signal emitter at the center of it, a shallow, bowl-like structure currently being used for one purpose and one purpose only . . .

To transmit the special-frequency radio waves that drove Greenbriar's radar system.

As Obal rushed into the shuttlebay with the other members of his security team, he took in the scene as calmly and objectively as his Academy trainers had advised him to do.

There were three crewmen down. *No,* he thought, as he came around a cargo shuttle and saw another pair of legs protruding beyond it, *make that four crewmen down.*

Racing across the bay as fast as he could, he reached the unidentified legs and saw the body to which they were attached. It belonged to Lieu-tenant Chiang, the chief of this section.

The man was unconscious, bleeding from a cut on his forehead. There was blood on the shuttle next to him as well. Apparently, Chiang had struck his head on it during one of the phaser impacts the *Stargazer* had suffered.

It was Obal's job to get him out of here, just as his comrades were removing the other crewmen in the bay. Of course, Chiang was much bigger and heavier than the Binderian, but he believed he could manage.

He had already hooked his hands under the man's armpits and begun to drag him toward the exit when he noticed something—a red light on the lonely-looking console not twenty meters away.

It gave Obal pause. If he recalled correctly, a red light only came on in case of trouble, and very specific trouble at that. It signaled that the semipermeable force field between the bay and the tinted sea of gases outside was about to fizzle out.

If that happened, all the air in the bay would rush out into inter-planetary space. And along with it would go any crewmen and equipment that happened to be present at the time.

Could the light have gone on due to a circuitry malfunction? It was certainly possible, with all the punishment the ship was taking.

Or, Obal asked himself, a chill running down his spine, might it be that the light was working perfectly? In that case, the problem would be in the mechanism that maintained the force field.

"Lands of fire," he breathed, invoking an image from his people's most primitive belief system.

He couldn't take the chance that it was a simple short circuit. He had to do something, and do it quickly.

Easing Chiang to the smooth, hard surface of the deck, Obal darted in the direction of the console. But even as he did this, he saw the barrier begin to buckle and spark, and felt the tug of something hideously powerful.

Was he too late? he wondered. Would everyone in the bay, rescued as well as rescuers, be sucked out of the ship?

No, he vowed. *I won't let it happen.*

Gritting his teeth, Obal hunkered down and drove his slender legs as hard as he could. Little by little, he made his way across the bay to the freestanding control console.

He ignored the cries of his fellow security officers as they realized what was happening. He even managed to ignore the sight of Lieutenant Chiang sliding toward the failing barrier.

Slowly but insistently, Obal plied the last couple of meters of his journey and reached the console. Then he hung on to it against the pull of space as he surveyed its colored studs and touch-sensitive pads.

In his Academy class he had had no trouble remembering which stud did what. Now, with so much riding on his actions, he found the task a bit more difficult.

That one, he decided at last, singling out a square blue stud. And he pushed it down as hard as he could.

For a moment, Obal feared he had made the wrong decision. Then he felt a let-up in the force that had been tugging at him. Looking up in the direction of the force field, he saw by the silver gleam along its perimeter that the back-up emitters had been activated.

There was a second force field in place, stopping the air from leaving the bay—along with everyone and everything in it. Obal drew a deep breath and expelled it. He was just glad he had noticed the red light in time.

Releasing the console with an understandable reluctance, he returned to Lieutenant Chiang's still-unconscious form. Then he began dragging the man toward the exit again.

Jean-Luc Picard looked around his bridge at the devastation he and his officers had endured—the flaming control panels and the clouds of black smoke and the persistent blasts of white plasma—and hoped it had all been worth it.

He turned to Vigo. "Did you get it—the signal emitter?"

The Pandrilite shrugged his massive shoulders. "I don't know, sir. I think . . ." But he couldn't finish his sentence. All he could do was shrug a second time.

Picard turned to Gerda's control console, which had survived the battle to this point. Her radar monitor still showed the movements of the *Cochise* as a green blip.

But unless the captain was mistaken, the *Cochise* wasn't coming around for another pass at its finally defenseless adversary. In fact, Greenbriar's ship wasn't going anywhere at all.

Picard looked to Gerda for confirmation. Looking up at him, she said, "They're dead in the water, sir."

And there could be only one reason for that. The *Stargazer*'s phaser assault had disabled the *Cochise*'s signal emitter. Greenbriar's ship, though still well shielded and well powered, was completely and utterly blind.

Instinct, he thought. *Either you've got it or you don't.*

The captain nodded in recognition of Gerda's remark, then turned to Vigo. "Well done, Lieutenant."

The weapons officer smiled at him. "Thank you, sir."

Picard took in his other officers at a glance, settling on Idun last of all. "Well done, all of you."

His helm officer nodded, a glint of satisfaction in her eyes. This was the sort of thing she lived for—she and Gerda both.

Finally, the captain considered the viewscreen, which had reverted to an image of the gas clouds surrounding them. "Mr. Paxton," he said, "see if you can raise Captain Greenbriar."

In a matter of moments, Greenbriar appeared on the viewscreen. For a man who had just lost a space battle, he didn't look very disappointed. He seemed as pleasant and easygoing as if he and Picard were standing around the punch bowl at McAteer's cocktail party.

"Good shooting," Greenbriar told him. "My compliments to your weapons officer."

Picard didn't feel inclined to join in the jocularity. "What's going on here, Captain?"

The other man frowned, accentuating the lines in his seamed face. "I guess there's no point in trying to conceal it any longer."

But Greenbriar's tone of voice belied his expression of resignation. It suggested that he was stalling for time, still looking for a way to secure the victory.

Picard glared at him. He was through playing games, especially the sort that put the welfare of his ship and crew at risk. "The truth, Captain. And I mean *now.*"

Greenbriar regarded him for a moment. Then he nodded soberly, appearing to accept the fact that he was out of options.

"I'd appreciate it if we could speak in private," he said.

Picard considered it for a moment. Then he turned to Ben Zoma. "I'll be in my ready room. You've got the bridge."

His first officer nodded, though he would no doubt have preferred to hear what Greenbriar had to say. "Aye, sir."

Casting a last wary glance at the viewscreen, Picard repaired to his ready room.

Chapter Twenty-Three

PICARD SAT BACK IN HIS CHAIR and studied the same craggy visage that he had seen on the viewscreen. Except now, it filled the computer screen on his desk.

"You must be a little confused," Greenbriar said.

"To say the least," Picard responded. "Try as I might, I cannot imagine why you would attack a Starfleet vessel, unless you have aligned yourself with a pirate who has become the bane of this entire sector. And if you have, that begs yet an even *greater* question."

Greenbriar nodded. "It's difficult to explain. Maybe it would be better if I let the pirate speak for himself."

Picard shrugged. "If that is what it takes."

A moment later, Greenbriar's image was shunted to the left side of the screen, making way for the image of another man on the right. *The White Wolf,* Picard thought.

But the pirate wasn't at all what the captain had expected.

For one thing, his hair wasn't white; it wasn't even gray. And he wasn't the crafty old veteran he was cracked up to be. The White Wolf was a baby-faced young man, barely out of his twenties if Picard was any judge of such things.

"Captain," said the pirate in a soft, cultured voice. "I wish I could say it was a pleasure to meet you. But under the circumstances . . ."

Picard frowned. "Captain Greenbriar promised me an explanation. I'm waiting to hear it."

The White Wolf nodded. "Of course. My name is Carridine. And contrary to what you may have heard about me, I'm more of an exobiologist than I am a pirate."

It sounded familiar. *"Emil* Carridine?" Picard asked.

The pirate looked at him. "I see you've heard of me."

"If I recall correctly, you come from a wealthy family on Earth. Some years back, you embarked on a series of planetary surveys in a previously unexplored part of space—"

"And was never heard from again," the White Wolf said. "But I hadn't disappeared. Not really. I had only assumed a different identity."

"So I gather," Picard told him. "The question is, *why?"*

Isn't it always? Carridine's expression seemed to say.

"During one of my routine planetary surveys," he said, "I found a world I called Daribund. It was ridiculously rich in latinum—a huge prize for anyone with a yen to get rich quick."

The White Wolf's eyes lost their focus as he remembered. "If it had been a barren world, I wouldn't have thought twice about it. But Daribund was populated by a pre-sentient species with an extremely fragile niche in the planet's ecosystem. Any mining enterprise on that world would have doomed that species to extinction."

Picard saw the problem. "And you wanted to prevent that."

"In the worst way," Carridine told him.

"And he couldn't go to the Federation," said Greenbriar, "because the planet's dominant species was a pre-spaceflight culture."

Picard nodded. "The Prime Directive."

"So," Carridine continued, "I bought a ship and put a crew together and took the matter into my own hands."

"And defended this world on your own," Picard concluded.

"Not that it was easy. I wasn't Starfleet, so it was difficult to acquire much in the way of firepower. So I took a different tack."

Carridine went on to describe his boyhood fascination with Earth's twentieth-century buccaneers—men like Bluebeard and Jean Lafitte. Inspired by them, he set out to create a situation that would keep unsavory characters from strip-mining Daribund.

"If I became a pirate," he said, "if I raided the ships of Federation member worlds, Starfleet was bound to come after me eventually. And if Starfleet was focusing its attention on this part of space, what pirate in his right mind would try to horn in?"

Picard followed the reasoning. "And as long as real pirates stayed away, Daribund's pre-sentients would remain safe."

It was a clever scheme. And more important, it had worked, up to then. The *Stargazer*'s presence here was evidence of that.

Picard regarded Greenbriar. "And just how did *you* become involved in this enterprise?"

Greenbriar shrugged. "I caught the White Wolf, just as you did. But as I was about to take him in, he told me the story he's telling you—and I changed my mind."

Picard frowned. "You let him go."

"He did more than that," said Carridine.

"I became his ally," Greenbriar told them without remorse. "I became his informant. Whenever Starfleet sent a ship after him, I let him know about it in advance. Until now, that was the extent of my involvement. By making it here, you compelled me to do more."

"To attack a colleague," Picard said.

Greenbriar nodded. "Yes."

"Unfortunately," Carridine said, "I've now been apprehended a second time, and I don't imagine you'll be as open-minded as Captain Greenbriar was. It seems Daribund is about to lose its defender."

He paused, no doubt waiting for his comment—and its implications—to sink in. When he spoke again to the captain, it was as one reasonable man to another.

"On the other hand, Captain Greenbriar saw the injustice in apprehending the White Wolf. I hope you will see the injustice as well, Captain—and act accordingly."

Picard looked at him. "You're suggesting that I let you go? After all we've gone through to apprehend you?"

"What I'm suggesting," said Carridine, "is that you follow the impulses that led you to become a Starfleet officer in the first place. No more, no less."

Picard frowned. He hated the idea of deceiving his superiors as Greenbriar had. He hated even the suggestion of it. He had taken a vow when he entered Starfleet, and he had every intention of remaining true to it.

And yet . . .

It was difficult not to see Carridine's point. The man was protecting something worthwhile, something no one else was inclined to protect, and harming no one in the process.

The White Wolf was on the side of the angels, strange as it seemed. And if Picard wanted to be on the side of the angels as well, there was only one choice he could make.

With a sigh, he tapped his communicator and summoned Ben Zoma. Then he tapped it again and said, "Picard to Simenon."

The reply came a moment later. "Simenon here."

"I'd like to see you in my ready room," Picard told him. "You and I have an important matter to discuss."

"What's that?" asked the engineer.

"In my ready room," the captain maintained.

Simenon grumbled. "As you wish."

Picard turned to Carridine. "I'm going to arrange a shutdown of the *Stargazer*'s impulse engines. An *accidental* shutdown, of course. It will present only a minor inconvenience to my engineering staff, but its timing will be most unfortunate, as it will allow the legendary White Wolf to slip through my fingers."

Carridine smiled in relief. "Thank you, Captain."

"But there's a condition," the captain added. "I want the Federation's cargo returned. I don't care how."

The White Wolf nodded, only too glad to comply. "Whatever you say. I've got no use for it anyway."

Greenbriar nodded approvingly. "You're a good man, Picard. Just as I had heard."

Picard took some solace in the knowledge that he had at least one true ally among his fellow captains. Also, it occurred to him, he understood something he only *thought* he had understood before.

"People are often not what they seem," he said, quoting Greenbriar word for word.

The other captain smiled. "You've got a hell of a memory."

"Yes," said Picard. "But this is one day I may want to forget."

Idun didn't know anything about Picard's conversation with Captain Greenbriar. She didn't know why he had summoned Ben Zoma and Simenon and then dispatched them again.

But when Picard finally emerged from his ready room, the helm officer was certain that his orders would involve phasers and boarding

parties and the incarceration of all who had committed crimes against
the Federation.

That is, until the captain actually spoke.

"You know," he said, "this is not a good situation."

She looked at him. "I beg your pardon, sir?"

"I was referring to the impulse engines," Picard told her. "This is
a very bad time for them to have shut down."

Idun looked at her console, trying to figure out what the captain
was talking about. As far as she could tell, the ship's impulse engines
were working perfectly.

"Sir," she said, "I don't see any problem with the—"

The helm officer stopped in midsentence. Suddenly, all her monitors
were flashing, indicating that they had lost impulse power. She turned
to Picard again.

"I don't understand," she said. "How did you—?"

"In fact, the timing couldn't have been much worse," Picard remarked, his voice now loud enough for everyone on the bridge to hear
him. "No doubt the White Wolf will take advantage of this unexpected
opportunity to escape us. And without working impulse engines, there's
no possibility of our offering pursuit."

Idun didn't understand. The captain didn't seem very disappointed,
considering how hard they had worked to find the pirate and disable his
vessel. Then she realized what he was doing.

He was letting the White Wolf go.

"Had another starship tracked us down and joined the fray," Picard
continued, "it might have been a different story. However, we faced the
pirate alone." He looked around at his bridge personnel, eyeing each of
them in turn. "Completely alone," he added for emphasis.

Idun didn't know why the captain was doing this. But clearly, it had
something to do with what he had learned in his ready room.

She had been raised by Klingons to be a warrior, and a warrior
didn't allow a defeated enemy to slip through her fingers. Her every
instinct cried out against this.

Yet she remained silent, because it was Captain Picard who had implicitly asked her to do so. Her respect for him went beyond instinct,
beyond protocol, beyond her understanding of right and wrong.

If Picard wanted to allow the enemy to escape, Idun wouldn't do
anything to stand in his way. Nor, she decided, would she include any
of this in her helm report.

Her sister darted a glance at her from her place at navigation. Judging from Gerda's expression, she felt the same way.

"It's too bad," Lieutenant Paxton said, taking his cue from the captain. "We came so close."

"So *very* close," Picard sighed.

"I guess we have no choice but to repair the engines and go home with our tail between our legs," Vigo said.

"No choice at all," the captain agreed.

He looked around the bridge, waiting for one of his officers to object. No one did.

Least of all Idun Asmund.

Obal was taking his turn at the big concave bank of security monitors when Pug Joseph approached him.

"Mr. Obal," said the security chief.

The Binderian turned to him and smiled. "Good morning, sir."

"How's it going?" Joseph asked, though that wasn't exactly the question he had come to ask.

"Fine, sir," said Obal. "I understand the impulse engines are running perfectly again."

"Uh . . . yes, I guess they are. I'm told we'll be leaving Beta Barritus before we know it."

Obal shrugged his narrow shoulders. "It's a pity the White Wolf got away. But at least we managed to recover the stolen cargo."

Joseph looked at the Binderian and couldn't tell if there was any irony in his comments or not.

"Listen," the security chief said, feeling the need to change the subject, "I wanted to tell you what a great job you did down there in the shuttlebay. If not for you, we might have had a real tragedy on our hands."

Obal smiled. "I was happy to help. But then, isn't that what a security officer does—provide help in times of crisis?"

Joseph didn't have the heart to tell the Binderian that he still didn't have what it took, or to reprise his advice that Obal's talents would be better served elsewhere. Not now, after he had made such a hero of himself.

Unfortunately, there was more to security work than cataloging phasers or securing the shuttlebay. One had to have the respect of others, and Joseph just didn't see how Obal could earn that respect.

"Yes," the chief replied grudgingly. "That's what a security officer does."

Picard smiled when he saw the stars.

They were long, bright streaks rather than points of brilliance, a function of the *Stargazer*'s faster-than-light velocity. But they were a welcome sight nonetheless.

"You know," said Ben Zoma, who was standing at the captain's side, "I could go a long time without missing Beta Barritus again."

Picard nodded in agreement. "A *long* time."

"Sir," said Gerda, putting a damper on the moment, "sensors are picking up a vessel."

Picard turned to her, his eyes narrowing. "What *kind* of vessel?"

His navigator consulted her monitors. "It's a Federation starship—the *Antares*. Two hundred million kilometers and closing."

Normally, Picard would have treated this as good news. Or at the very least, not *bad* news. But after his experience with the *Cochise*, he couldn't help feeling a little gun-shy.

"Hail them," he said.

"Actually," Paxton told him, "they're hailing *us.*"

Picard nodded. "On screen."

The viewer filled with the image of a Starfleet captain—a swarthy man with a neat dark goatee. Picard believed he had seen the fellow at the admiral's soiree on Starbase 32.

"This is Captain Vayishra of the *Antares*," the man said. "The *Grissom* and the *Reliant* will be here within the hour."

"I see," Picard replied.

Vayishra looked sympathetic, in a vaguely condescending sort of way. "Had trouble getting in, did you?"

Picard shrugged. "Some."

"Don't take it too hard," Vayishra told him. "From what I've heard, it's a mess in there."

"That it is," Picard confirmed.

"When we're all here," said Vayishra, "follow our lead. We'll find the White Wolf no matter what it takes."

"Actually," said Picard, "we already found him."

The other captain looked skeptical for a moment. Then he laughed. "Of course you have. You've got him in your brig even as we speak."

"I'm afraid we don't," Picard told him. "However, we *do* have the cargo he lifted."

Vayishra's brow furrowed. "You're being facetious, of course."

"I'm not," Picard assured him.

Vayishra shook his head. "But how did you—?"

"It will all be in my report. Picard out."

As Vayishra's perplexed expression vanished from the screen, giving way to the field of streaming stars, Ben Zoma moved to the captain's side. "That was more fun than you deserve," he said.

"Is it?" Picard responded. "I *am* the only captain who's ever cornered the White Wolf."

"Also the only one who's ever let him go."

Picard glanced at his first officer. "You would have done the same thing in my place."

Ben Zoma smiled. "Probably."

"Which makes us . . . what?" the captain wondered. "Soft touches?"

His friend considered the question for a moment. "I prefer to think of us as men who can tell where orders end and justice begins."

"Very poetic," Picard said appreciatively. "But what kind of captain ignores his orders?"

"In this case?" Ben Zoma said. He clapped his friend on the shoulder. "The best kind."

Chapter Twenty-four

As OBAL WORKED OUT with a set of weights in the ship's gymnasium, he reflected on how happy he was.

He had pleased Lieutenant Joseph with his work in the shuttlebay. And if Lieutenant Joseph was pleased, Obal was pleased. In fact, he was smiling to himself when he heard a hiss and saw the doors to the gym slide apart.

They revealed someone in exercise togs. Someone tall and muscular. Someone obviously human.

Caber, he thought.

The ensign didn't notice the Binderian right away. He was too intent on something, too wrapped up in his own thoughts. In fact, he was half-way to the parallel bars when he seemed to realize that there was someone else in the room.

Caber turned to see who it was. When he caught sight of Obal, a grin spread across his face. A *cruel* grin, if the Binderian was any judge of such things.

The human stood there for a second, staring across the room. Then, like a predator who has caught the scent of his prey, he started in Obal's direction.

The Binderian wasn't surprised. Caber had taken advantage of every opportunity to ridicule and belittle him. Why would he miss out on this one?

Obal eased his weights to the ground and sighed. He wasn't looking forward to the abuse that was sure to follow. He wasn't eager to be humiliated again. However, he had tolerated his treatment to this point for the sake of decorum—and, for the sake of decorum, he would continue to do so.

His superiors had more important things to do than mediate petty differences between crewmen. Obal was determined not to be a burden to them. He would endure whatever he had to for as long as he had to.

And eventually, Caber's hostility would wane. At least, that was the Binderian's plan.

But as the human approached him, the curl in his lip seemed to undercut Obal's expectations. "Imagine finding *you* here," he spat.

The Binderian didn't say anything at all. He just stood there, stoic and uncomplaining.

"Nothing to say?" Caber laughed. It was a short, ugly sound without any humor in it. "Funny, you seemed to have *plenty* to say when we were in security."

Seeing he hadn't gotten a reaction, the human bent down and poked a rigid forefinger into Obal's bony chest.

"Where the hell do you get off telling me what to do?" he demanded through clenched teeth. "Where does a squirt like *you* get the gall to lord it over someone like *me?*"

The Binderian's chest hurt where he'd been poked, but he managed to remain silent.

It only made Caber that much angrier. "You don't even have the guts to stand up for yourself. You think you deserve to give orders to people who *do?*"

Again he poked Obal in the chest. This time, it was all the Binderian could do to keep from crying out.

"Why don't you find yourself another ship?" Caber demanded, his saliva striking Obal in the face. "One where they *like* taking orders from skinny little cowards?"

Another poke, stabbing deep into the Binderian's flesh. His eyes watered from the pain, but he kept it to himself.

"You hear me?" Caber snapped, his voice echoing, his eyes mere inches from Obal's. "You get your scrawny butt off this ship or I'll make you wish you *had!*"

As the gym doors slid open, Nikolas caught sight of Caber. He was about to offer an excuse for his lateness when he realized that his friend wasn't alone.

Obal was with him. And it looked as if Caber were trying to ram his forefinger right through the Binderian's anatomy.

"You hear me?" Caber snarled, either oblivious to Nikolas's presence or purposely ignoring it.

"Hey, Joe!" Nikolas snapped. He loped across the gym to intervene before the situation could deteriorate any further. "Come on, leave the poor guy alone!"

Caber didn't respond. Instead, he poked Obal in his scrawny chest again and said, "Get lost—and I mean now!"

Nikolas felt a spurt of anger. Obviously, his roommate had let his feelings about the Binderian run amok. Grabbing Caber's arm, he spun him around.

"You can't do that," Nikolas told him, meeting his friend's red-rimmed gaze with equal intensity. "He's a crewman on this ship, just like you and—"

Before he could finish, Caber's fist came flying at him. Nikolas couldn't believe it. The next thing he knew, he was lying on his back, his jaw feeling as if it had been broken in a dozen places.

Caber came to stand over him, the angle accentuating the difference in their sizes. He pointed a thick, trembling finger at Nikolas and growled, "Stay out of this!"

"I can't," Nikolas insisted, his words slurred by the pain and stiffness in his jaw. He began to get up, hoping he could still keep Obal from harm.

But Caber had other ideas. As Nikolas got his feet underneath him, the other man launched a kick at his friend's face. Nikolas was too surprised by the unrestrained viciousness of the attack to defend himself. All he had time to do was turn his face away.

Caber's kick wound up smashing Nikolas in the side of the head with the fury of a phaser blast, putting him on his back again. For a moment, the ensign was too dazed to move. Then, his ear a fiery agony, he rolled over on his belly in an attempt to get up and stop the other man.

But it seemed that Caber was done with him for the moment. He was going after Obal again, his finger pointed at the helpless Binderian in an unmistakable promise of violence.

Nikolas groped for his combadge, found it, and tapped it. "Security to the gym," he mumbled through his pain, his voice sounding strange and distant, as if it were someone else's.

Then he thrust himself up onto all fours. It would take security a few minutes to get there, he told himself. In that time, Caber could inflict on Obal what he had inflicted on Nikolas.

Or worse.

Staggering to his feet, he saw Caber close with Obal. *Too late,* he thought. *Too late.*

Caber was going to take out the rest of his anger on the Binderian. And as fragile as Obal looked, there was no guarantee he would survive the beating.

But as Caber reached for Obal's neck, something unexpected happened: the Binderian flung up one of his skinny arms and deflected the human's attempt to grab him. Then, turning sideways, he lashed out awkwardly with one of his feet and speared Caber in the knee, eliciting a deep-throated cry of pain.

As Caber leaned over to grasp his injured joint, Obal struck again. He drove the heel of his hand into the ensign's forehead, straightening him up and causing him to stagger backward a couple of steps.

Pressing his advantage, the Binderian rushed forward and, with blinding quickness, bounded feet first into Caber's chest. The impact slammed the human into the bulkhead behind him, snapping his head back and forcing a groan out of him.

It was then that Nikolas realized that the doors to the gym were open and that Pug Joseph and a couple of his security officers were already across the threshold, their mouths hanging open as they watched Obal in action.

Caber, meanwhile, was no longer a threat. He slid down the bulkhead like a bag of assorted and unrelated bones, his eyes closed, a trickle of blood visible in the corner of his mouth.

Nikolas wondered if he had lost consciousness and dreamed it all. He was still wondering when Obal scurried to his side and put his spindly arm around him.

Michael Jan Friedman

"Are you all right?" the Binderian wheezed.

Nikolas nodded. "Fine," he wheezed.

By that time, Joseph had joined them. The other security officers were attending to Caber.

"What just happened?" the security chief asked Obal.

Looking apologetic, the Binderian shrugged his narrow, rounded shoulders. "I regret to inform you that Mr. Caber and I have had disagreements in the past. However—"

"They weren't disagreements," Nikolas interjected. "Caber didn't like him. He bullied him."

Joseph frowned at him. "I'd appreciate it if you would let Ensign Obal speak for himself."

Nikolas controlled himself. "Aye, sir."

The security chief turned to the Binderian again. "Go ahead," he said. "I'm listening."

Obal sighed. "As I said, we have had disagreements. I ignored them for the sake of decorum." He glanced at Nikolas. "However, Ensign Nikolas chose this occasion to come to my aid, and was injured for his trouble. On Binderia, we call someone who comes to our aid a *kellis dagh*. It is the height of cowardice on my world to let an assault on a *kellis dagh* go unavenged."

Nikolas was still stunned from the beating he had taken, but he had enough of his faculties about him to understand what Obal was saying. He couldn't abandon someone who had defended him, no matter what repercussions might have followed.

Might yet follow, Nikolas amended inwardly.

After all, Caber was an admiral's son with a spotless record. If anyone was going to get the benefit of the doubt, it would be him. But Nikolas and the Binderian had the truth on their side.

Surely, the ensign thought, *that has to count for something.*

Joseph nodded. "I'll be sure to include that in my report."

Obal turned to Nikolas. "Come. I'll help you get to sickbay."

Smiling through his pain, the ensign thanked him.

"You're welcome," said Obal, smiling back.

Nikolas didn't think the little guy would be able to help him much, considering the difference in their weights. But after what Obal had done for him, the ensign certainly wasn't going to turn him down.

With the help of Joseph and his new friend, Nikolas got to his feet and began the arduous trip to sickbay.

* * *

Picard was going over repair reports in his ready room when he heard a familiar chime. "Come," he said.

It was Valderrama. As always, she looked a little tentative as she entered the room.

"Please," the captain told her. "Sit down."

The science officer took the seat opposite his and smiled warmly. "What can I do for you, sir?"

"Nothing at the moment," he said. "I just wanted to ask you a question, if that's all right."

She shrugged. "Of course, sir."

Picard leaned forward. "Tell me, Lieutenant, how did you get the idea to use radar as a replacement for our sensor devices?"

Valderrama shrugged. "I'm not sure, sir. I guess you could say it was an inspiration."

The captain wished she had given him a more concrete response. "What would you say if I told you that Ensign Jiterica claims otherwise? That she says *she* had the inspiration first?"

The science officer reddened. "I don't understand."

Picard frowned. "A little while ago, Ensign Jiterica ran into Commander Ben Zoma and asked if her radar idea had proven useful. Commander Ben Zoma told her that, to the best of his knowledge, it was *your* radar idea."

"Which it was, sir."

"Nonetheless," the captain continued, "Ensign Jiterica insisted that *she* had come up with it. She insisted that she had given it to you, trusted you with it. Nor did she understand why you were trying to take credit for it."

The science officer shook her head. "That's not the way it happened, sir. I hate to say it, but Jiterica is lying."

"Normally," Picard said, "I'd be inclined to give you the benefit of the doubt. However, Jiterica's personal logs, which are time-coded, corroborated her story. The ensign had the idea first and gave it to you, her superior. And you claimed it for yourself."

Valderrama didn't try to defend herself this time. She just stood there, looking at him.

The captain frowned. "Can you enlighten me as to why you would do something like that?"

Valderrama looked away. It took her a few seconds to get a reply out, and when she did it was husky with remorse.

"I didn't think you would keep me on unless I did something spectacular," she said. "All I did was grasp at the first straw presented to me."

Picard took a deep breath. "I can tolerate a great many things from my crew," he told Valderrama. "However, a lack of ethics isn't one of them. I would advise you to repair to your quarters and begin packing your things."

The woman's brow creased down the middle.

"If I were you," the captain went on, "I would resign my commission rather than face charges. But either way, I can assure you that you'll be leaving the *Stargazer.*"

Valderrama didn't object to his decision. She just turned and left his ready room.

As Picard watched the doors slide closed behind her, he couldn't help thinking that he had witnessed a tragedy. He couldn't absolve Valderrama of her guilt. Clearly, she had brought her troubles on herself.

But that didn't make the outcome any less tragic.

The captain had begun dictating a commendation of Jiterica into his log when he heard the sound of chimes again. *Valderrama?* he wondered.

"Come," he said.

When the doors parted, he saw that it wasn't Valderrama after all. It was Commander Wu.

"Yes?" Picard said.

The second officer stepped into the room and spoke without preamble. "Sir, it's come to my attention that you're operating as commanding officer of this vessel in clear violation of Starfleet regulations."

"Indeed," the captain responded. "And if I may ask, precisely which regulations am I violating?"

She told him. As it turned out, there were a good deal more of them than he would have guessed, ranging from insufficient expertise in weapons systems to a lack of certain inoculations.

"I promised Commander Ben Zoma that I wouldn't hold any of my subordinates to regulations. But I believe that, as you're the captain, you at least should be held to a stricter standard."

Picard felt himself stiffen at the rebuke. Nonetheless, he said, "I appreciate your pointing that out, Commander. I'll take it under advisement."

Wu nodded. "Thank you, sir." And she turned to go.

"Commander?" he said, stopping her in her tracks.

She faced him again. "Captain?"

No doubt she expected him to comment on her overzealousness. He surprised her. "You handled yourself well while we were hunting the White Wolf."

Wu smiled. "It pleases me to hear that, sir."

He smiled back. "Dismissed."

Picard waited until she had left the room and the titanium doors had closed behind her. Then he contacted his first officer via the ship's intercom system.

Apparently, he still had one more problem to take care of.

Wu didn't understand. She said so, her voice echoing throughout sickbay.

Greyhorse shrugged. "There's no question about it. You're due for a physical."

She frowned. "But you already gave me a physical."

"That was when you first came onboard."

"It wasn't that long ago," she pointed out.

"Long enough," Greyhorse told her. "Lie down, please." And he indicated the nearest biobed.

Wu got up on the bed and lay down. Then she watched the doctor scan the bio monitors.

"You know," she said, "I have reports to file. I hope this won't take long."

"It shouldn't," he told her. Suddenly, his brow creased.

"Is something wrong?" she asked.

Greyhorse shrugged. "Nothing serious." But he continued to regard the monitors.

"Don't be mysterious," Wu told him. "If there's something I need to know about—"

"It's your blood pressure," he said, looking up at her. "It's a little high."

"How high?"

The doctor told her. Indeed it *was* a little high. But just a little—hardly worth discussing.

And now that Wu thought about it, she had an explanation. "I had black bean soup for lunch. It was very salty."

"That might be the culprit," Greyhorse allowed.

The second officer swung her legs around and sat up. "And everything else is in order?"

He nodded. "Very much so."

"Good," said Wu, slipping off the table. "Then, if you don't mind, I'll get back to my duties."

She was halfway to the exit when Greyhorse spoke up again. "Actually, Commander, I can't allow that."

Wu turned and looked at him. "I beg your pardon?"

"I can't allow you to return to your duties," he said. "Not with excessively high blood pressure."

"But we agreed that it's from the black bean soup."

"We agreed that it *might* be. The only way to know for certain is to test you again later this evening."

"But in the meantime, you're telling me I can't resume my duties as second officer?"

"That's what I'm telling you."

Wu scowled. "This is ridiculous. You're splitting hairs."

"It's a regulation," Greyhorse maintained.

"But you don't need to take it quite so literally, Doctor. There's no way I'm unfit for—"

She was halfway through her declaration when she realized what she was saying. And a moment later, she realized why she was saying it.

"The captain put you up to this," she said accusingly. "Didn't he? Or was it Ben Zoma?"

"Ben Zoma," Greyhorse replied.

And Wu knew why he had done it.

She had tried to hold Lieutenant Asmund, Chief Simenon, and Captain Picard to the letter of the law. This was Ben Zoma's attempt to show her how it felt to be held to that kind of standard.

The second officer regarded Greyhorse. "Thank you for your honesty," she told him. Then she left sickbay, already beginning to fashion an appropriate response.

Ulelo was on his way to the bridge when he heard someone call his name. Glancing back over his shoulder, he saw that the greeting had come from Lieutenant Vigo.

"Yes?" Ulelo said.

The weapons chief smiled at him as he caught up with his overlong strides. "Headed for the bridge?"

"That's right."

"So am I."

They walked together for a moment, Vigo reducing his strides to match his companion's. Then he spoke up again.

"So tell me, Lieutenant, do you have anything planned when your shift is over?"

Ulelo nodded. "I have some reading to catch up on."

It was his stock answer to such a question—and a valuable answer it was, enabling him to keep his options open in case the Pandrilite's suggestion didn't serve his purposes.

Vigo looked disappointed. "That's too bad."

"Why's that?" Ulelo asked.

The weapons chief shrugged. "I was hoping to engage you in a session of sharash'di. You're familiar with the game, aren't you?"

Ulelo had to admit that he wasn't.

"It's easy to learn," Vigo assured him, the twinkle returning to his eye. "If you like, I could teach you sometime."

Ulelo considered the offer. On one hand, the idea of learning sharash'di held no appeal for him. He had no patience for trivial pursuits these days.

On the other hand, it would give him a chance to spend time with the Pandrilite. And that might garner him some insights into the ship's weapons systems.

"I would like that," Ulelo said.

Vigo smiled, exposing blunt, white teeth. "Good. Maybe tomorrow, then, after our shifts are over."

"Tomorrow," Ulelo echoed, and made a mental note of it.

His shift over, Ben Zoma was plying a corridor en route to his quarters when he ran into Commander Wu.

"Sir," said Wu.

"Commander," said Ben Zoma.

"I'm glad I found you," Wu said.

"You are?" he asked, wondering why that might be.

"Yes. Apparently, Lieutenant Asmund isn't the only one overdue for a helm test. Your qualification's expired as well."

Ben Zoma hadn't been aware of that. "Are you sure?"

"Quite sure," the second officer told him. And she handed him her data padd to prove it.

He scanned it and saw that his qualification had expired, all right—at midnight the night before. He eyed Wu, hoping to find some evidence that the woman had learned her lesson.

But he couldn't see it in her expression.

"According to regulations," said Wu, "you're not permitted to take the helm until you requalify."

Ben Zoma sighed. He didn't much care whether he was permitted to take the helm or not. What he *did* care about was his second officer's attitude. Apparently, neither his advice nor her episode with the doctor had done anything to change it.

"Is that an order?" he asked halfheartedly.

As he waited for her response, something marvelous happened. Wu laughed—actually *laughed.* Then she said, "Let's call it a suggestion, Commander, and leave it at that."

Ben Zoma was only too happy to oblige.

PROGENITOR

Chapter One

JEAN-LUC PICARD HAD LOST his fencing partner.

His name was Daithan Ruhalter. Ruhalter had also been Picard's captain, his predecessor as commanding officer of the *Stargazer.*

Picard had been happy to discover that there was another fencer on the ship, a security officer by the name of Pierzynski, who had a good few inches on Picard and outweighed him by perhaps thirty pounds. Unfortunately, as Pierzynski had subsequently discovered, size and skill didn't always go hand in hand.

At the moment, Picard enjoyed a four-touches-to-none advantage in a five-touch match. To this point, Pierzynski had failed to take advantage of his longer reach, just as he had failed to do so in the four matches that preceded this one.

Picard could have postponed the inevitable and toyed with the fellow for a while. However, he didn't want to give Pierzynski the illusion that they were competitive enough for the captain to consider doing this on a regular basis.

It was unfortunate. Picard had hoped a good fencing session would

distract him from what he was obliged to do when the *Stargazer* reached
Starbase 42.

But Pierzynski hadn't provided much of a distraction for him. The
disposition of Caber and Valderrama still weighed heavily on the captain's
mind, making him wonder how he could ever have allowed himself to
embrace those individuals in the first place.

Picard sighed. "En garde."

Pierzynski raised his blade in response. Then, aggressive by nature,
he took a step toward the captain.

Picard frowned. He didn't even have to parry to create an opening.
Taking a couple of steps back, he waited for Pierzynski to follow him.
Then he planted his back foot, extended his point and launched himself
forward—all in one quick, fluid motion.

He hit Pierzynski in the ribs, just below his elbow. Point and match.
"Alas," he said.

Pierzynski reached for the top of his mask and pulled it down, exposing his flushed, fatigued-looking face. Then he tucked the mask under
his sword arm and extended his hand to the captain.

"Good one, sir. One more?"

Picard removed his own mask and clasped the security officer's hand.
"Perhaps some other time, Mr. Pierzynski. I'm due on the bridge in half
an hour."

Pierzynski nodded. "Of course, sir." He smiled sheepishly. "I hope
I didn't disappoint you *too* much, sir."

The captain smiled back and lied through his teeth. "You didn't disappoint me at all, Lieutenant. I simply had a good day."

That seemed to make Pierzynski feel a little better. At least, it seemed
that way to Picard as he showered, dressed, and made his way to the
bridge.

He arrived just in time to receive word from his communications
officer that a message was arriving for him. Naturally, the captain reckoned it was from Starfleet Command, since his only orders at the moment
were to exchange personnel at Starbase 42.

He was wrong. It wasn't from Command, after all. Apparently, it
was from the *Crazy Horse*.

"Really," Picard said, wondering what it might be about.

"Really, sir," Lt. Paxton confirmed for him.

"I'll take it in my ready room," Picard told his comm officer, and
went there to receive the message.

* * *

Phigus Simenon, chief engineer of the Federation starship *Stargazer,* eyed the knot of scarlet-clad specialists standing at attention in front of him. There were twelve of them in all, males and females representing six different species.

They didn't seem happy. But then, he didn't *want* them to be happy. Not after what he had just seen.

"Disgraceful," he spat, feeling his anger constrict the flow of blood in his throat vessels. "Absolutely disgraceful."

"Sir," said Dubinski, one of Simenon's senior officers, "in all fairness—"

Simenon cut the man short with a snap of his tail. "Fairness?" he repeated, giving the word a bitter twist as it echoed throughout the engineering section. "You want fairness after you let this ship go up in a ball of matter–antimatter fury?"

In reality, the *Stargazer* hadn't suffered so much as a scratch. But that was because the events of the last several minutes had only been a simulation of a warp core containment failure, not a real one.

Simenon ticked off his section's failings on the digits of one scaly clawlike hand. Each accusation snapped and cut like the business end of a very sharp whip.

"First," he hissed, "you relaxed and assumed the internal sensors would detect the beginnings of the failure. Second, you allowed the computer to respond to the situation, when you should have taken the initiative yourselves."

Both were grievous errors, considering Simenon had shut down the sensors and the computers for a five-minute period. But then, what good was a test if it was too easy?

"And third," he finished, "you hung onto the core too long when you should have ejected it immediately."

The assembled engineers seemed to strain under the weight of their superior's charges. They weren't used to this kind of talk—even from the likes of *him.*

But it wasn't Simenon's job to mollycoddle them. His job was to make sure the ship got what it needed in the way of power and propulsion and a number of other critical areas, and he would be damned if he was going to fall short of accomplishing that.

That was why he was ripping into his engineers, right? To ensure that they didn't falter in their vigilance? To make sure the *Stargazer* didn't fall victim to some ridiculous and avoidable oversight?

"Sir," said Dubinski, now that Simenon had vented the worst of his figurative spleen, "I'd like permission to speak."

Simenon fixed the fellow with his lizardlike gaze. "Permission granted, Mr. Dubinski. I can't wait to hear the excuse you're going to give me."

The engineer frowned. "It's not an excuse, sir. I'd just like to try to put this . . . exercise . . . in perspective."

Simenon shrugged. "By all means."

"First off, sir, we *did* conduct periodic checks of the core—even more frequently than Starfleet directives recommend. And while it's true we gave the computer a chance to respond to the situation, we had every reason to believe it would do so—since our boards told us it was running fine."

The engineering chief harrumphed. "And your slowness in dumping the warp core once you realized the computer wouldn't do it?"

"It just didn't feel right," Dubinski explained. "After all, complete, irreparable and rapid failure is virtually unheard of without apparent cause—enemy fire, a collision with another ship, *something*—and we couldn't identify anything that might have triggered a breach of the containment vessel."

It was a good answer. Simenon had to admit that, if only to himself. In fact, it bothered him that he hadn't considered it.

Just as he hadn't considered that every control console in engineering would show the computer was online—something the chief should have taken into account if he were to make the test a fair assessment of his people's preparedness.

It wasn't like him to gloss over important details. But then, it wasn't like him to conduct unannounced drills in the first place. He had always judged the efficiency of his section by virtue of daily observations, not contrived exercises.

So what had come over him? A sudden lack of confidence in his security measures? Or something else—something unrelated to the continued welfare of the *Stargazer?*

Something that had been bothering him more and more over the last several days, keeping him awake at nights and insinuating itself into his thoughts during his waking hours.

Inwardly, Simenon cursed and crossed the room to a sleek, black control console, where he made a show of inspecting what was on its various screens. It gave him time to think—to gain that sense of perspective of which Dubinski had spoken.

Maybe he hadn't been fair to his engineers, he thought. Maybe—gods help him—an apology was in order, as hideously distasteful as the concept seemed to him.

Then Urajel, the Andorian on his staff, breathed something to the woman next to her. Obviously, she hadn't intended for Simenon to hear it. But he heard it, all right.

He heard it all too well.

Turning from the console and glowering at the Andorian with slitted yellow eyes, he said, *"What* was that, Ms. Urajel?"

The engineer's face suffused with blood, giving it a dark blue tinge beneath her fringe of silver-white hair. No doubt, she was tempted to deny she had said anything. But she couldn't do that.

Urajel steeled herself. "I said I wonder what crawled up your hindquarters, sir."

Another time, Simenon might have let the remark slide, insubordinate as it was. But not *this* time.

This time, his anger surged. "You'll run safety drills for the balance of this shift," he rasped, not just to Urajel but to all of her colleagues as well. "And for the next shift, and the one after that and the one after that, until I'm confident that what I saw today won't happen again."

Simenon knew he wasn't being fair to them. He knew he was abusing his power as engineering chief. But even knowing these things, he couldn't help it.

Before he said something he would *really* regret, he whirled and made his way to his office.

Picard considered Starbase 42 as it loomed ever larger on his bridge's main viewscreen.

Like many of the interstellar bases Starfleet had built in the last twenty years, 42 was comprised of a long cylinder, a protruding ring in the vicinity of its midsection and an even more prominent ring near what was generally recognized as its top.

Both rings were liberally dotted with brightly lit observation ports. At this distance, the captain imagined he could see uniformed figures framed in the ports, peering out at him in curiosity even as he was peering in at them.

Where had all those figures come from? Where were they going?

There were so many uniformed personnel in the fleet, it was barely possible to keep track of even a fraction of them. . . .

Much less to know who would become an asset to his crew and who would become a burden. Or who would choose to leave just when she seemed to have found her niche.

"You look positively grim," said Gilaad Ben Zoma, Picard's friend and first officer.

"Do I?" the captain asked.

"If I didn't know better, I'd think your shields were down and you'd just fired off your last photon torpedo."

Under most circumstances, Picard would have smiled at the metaphor. But not under *these* circumstances.

"I'll do my best to cheer up," he said.

Ben Zoma leaned a little closer. "That would be nice. And while you're at it, you may want to give the order to establish orbit."

The captain glanced at Idun Asmund, his primary helm officer, and realized that she was waiting patiently for instructions. Feeling his face flush, he said, "Establish orbit, helm."

"Aye, sir," came the response.

Picard frowned at his lapse as he watched Idun manipulate her controls and activate the ship's braking thrusters. *Keep your mind on what you're doing,* he told himself.

"You know," Ben Zoma said in a voice only the captain could hear, "none of this is your fault. It wasn't even your decision to bring these people aboard."

"I know that," the captain replied. "But that doesn't mean they're not my responsibility."

"And as for that *other* personnel situation—"

Picard stopped Ben Zoma with a gesture. "Let's contemplate that later, shall we? I can only take so much change in one day."

"Orbit established," reported Idun's twin sister Gerda, who was seated at the bridge's navigation console.

The captain nodded. "Hail the base."

"Aye, sir," said Ulelo, who had minutes earlier taken over for Paxton at the comm panel.

In a matter of moments, the officer in command of Starbase 42 appeared on the viewscreen. He was a broad, squared-off fellow with pronounced crow's feet at the corners of his eyes and a thatch of thick, gray hair. And though he gave Picard his name readily enough, the captain couldn't have repeated it if his life depended on it.

Despite what he had told himself, he was still distracted by what was happening to his crew. More to the point, he was still wondering if he could have done anything to prevent it.

There's one *thing you could have done,* he reflected. *You could have denied the captain of the* Crazy Horse *his request to speak with one of your officers.* But that would have been neither fair nor in keeping with Starfleet protocol.

The commander of the starbase asked if Picard would be beaming down himself. When he indicated that he would not be, the man said something polite and signed off.

As the image of the base was restored to the screen, the captain turned to Ben Zoma. "Shall we?"

The first officer stood aside for him. "After you."

Reluctantly, Picard got up from his seat and made his way across the bridge to the turbolift.

Chapter Two

AS PICARD AND BEN ZOMA ENTERED Transporter Room Three, one of half a dozen such facilities on the *Stargazer,* the captain saw that there were two uniformed figures waiting for them beside the hexagon-shaped transporter platform.

One of them was Juanita Valderrama, a middle-aged woman with a kind, round face and dark hair. The other, a man in an ensign's uniform, was the tall, sturdy-looking Joe Caber.

Picard turned to the morning-shift transporter officer, who was standing off to the side at his black, streamlined console. "Mr. Refsland," he said, "is the base prepared to receive Lieutenant Valderrama and Ensign Caber?"

"They are, sir," confirmed Refsland, a husky, blond fellow in his middle twenties.

The captain nodded. "Good." He indicated the platform with a gesture. "If you please."

Caber ascended without any further encouragement. Valderrama, on the other hand, hesitated.

"Is something wrong?" Picard asked her.

The lieutenant lifted her chin. "May I speak candidly, sir?"

The muscles worked in Picard's jaw. *Here it comes,* he thought. *The disclaimer. The "I was wrongly accused" speech.*

"By all means," he responded.

Valderrama's nostrils flared. "I want to apologize," she said softly. "Not only to you and First Officer Ben Zoma, but to Ensign Jiterica as well. What I did was reprehensible. I wish the idea had never even occurred to me."

It was the last thing that Picard had expected to hear after Valderrama tried to take credit for someone else's idea—in this case, Ensign Jiterica's. Glancing at Ben Zoma, he saw a look of surprise on his friend's face—although it must have been only a faint shadow of the surprise visible on his own.

Still, he couldn't accept Valderrama's apology. What she had done truly *was* reprehensible, and there was nothing she could do now that would change that.

Meeting her gaze, the captain said, "I'll be sure to relay your apology to Ensign Jiterica."

If Valderrama had hoped for absolution from him, she didn't show it. In fact, she looked considerably more at ease simply for having made her peace with her commanding officer.

"Thank you," the lieutenant said. Then she joined Caber on the transporter platform.

A part of Picard naturally disapproved of what she had done. However, another part of him wished her well and hoped she might regain what she had lost of herself.

Unlike Valderrama, Ensign Caber had yet to make a sound. He looked bored as he stood on the platform, as if his being there were something of an inconvenience to him.

The captain could have let him go on that way. But he didn't. He approached the ensign and said, "What about you, Mr. Caber? Do you have any regrets concerning your actions?"

The young man smiled thinly, exposing perfectly spaced white teeth. "None at all, sir," he replied with undisguised arrogance. "And when my father hears what happened here, I don't think *I'll* be the one with cause for regret."

The threat wasn't lost on Picard. Caber's father was an admiral in Starfleet. Never having met the fellow, the captain had no idea how he would react.

Not that he could allow it to affect his decision. Caber had assaulted another member of the crew, exhibiting a certain amount of what appeared to be bigotry in the process. His presence would no longer be tolerated on the *Stargazer.*

Picard turned to Refsland and said, "Energize."

"Energizing," Refsland responded.

Almost instantly, Valderrama and Caber were reduced by the transporter to shimmering columns of light. Then they vanished altogether, their molecules dispatched through space to their destination.

Picard sighed. Ben Zoma was right, of course. Valderrama and Caber had brought this fate on themselves. Their departure wasn't anyone's fault but their own.

Nonetheless, the captain regretted the loss of his most promising ensign and his science officer. Any commanding officer in the fleet would have felt the same way.

Fortunately, Caber and Valderrama were not his only reason for being there that morning. "Mr. Refsland," he said, "are our new crewmen ready to beam up?"

The transporter operator nodded. "Aye, sir."

"Then," said the captain, "advise the base that we are ready to receive them."

As Refsland relayed the information to his counterpart at Starbase 42, Picard turned to Ben Zoma. "Feeling lucky?"

His friend smiled. "I was just going to ask *you* that."

The two who would replace Caber and Valderrama, unlike their predecessors, had been handpicked by the captain and his first officer. In fact, they were the first additions to the crew Picard had made since the day he assumed command.

He regarded the empty transporter platform. "To tell you the truth, Number One—"

"Too late," said Ben Zoma. "Here they come."

In a reversal of the dazzling effects that had accompanied the departures of Valderrama and Caber, two brilliant columns of light appeared on the platform. Moments later, a pair of figures materialized in the midst of them.

One of them was human, a fair-haired young man with boyish features that contrasted with the seriousness of his expression. The other was a Kandilkari, his long, striated face distinguished by the heavy, purple jowls characteristic of his species.

"Welcome aboard," the captain said.

"Thank you, sir," the human replied crisply. "It's a genuine pleasure to be here."

This was the crewman Picard and Ben Zoma had had their eyes on weeks earlier, before Admiral McAteer foisted his own choices on them. Like Caber, the fellow came from a Starfleet family with a long and prestigious track record. And like Caber, he was an ensign with a high career ceiling.

But that, the captain hoped, was where the resemblance between the two men ended. Caber had been an anomaly, an aberration. Picard expected much more from the likes of Cole Paris.

"I, too, take pleasure in joining this crew," said the Kandilkari in a slow, surprisingly musical voice.

Stepping down from the transporter platform, he extended a long, four-fingered hand in Picard's direction. His eyes, which were as purple as his jowls, seemed to dance with enthusiasm as he spoke.

"Lieutenant Nol Kastiigan," he added by way of an introduction. "At your service, sir."

The captain shook Kastiigan's hand, feeling the unusual metacarpal structure. "You come highly recommended, Lieutenant."

"Captain Sannek and I had the utmost respect for one another," Kastiigan told him. "I only regret that he chose to retire when the *Antares* was decommissioned."

Picard smiled. "Captain Sannek spent more than forty years in the center seat of one Starfleet vessel or another. His retirement is no doubt well-deserved."

He turned to Ensign Paris again, who was waiting to be invited before he descended from the transporter disc. It was a formality few observed in this day and age.

"Please," the captain told him, indicating the deck beside him.

Only then did Paris come down from the platform. "If it's all right with you, sir," he said, "I'd like to take the first available shift. No time like the present and all that."

Picard glanced at Ben Zoma, who looked equally impressed. It was difficult to decide who was more eager, their new lieutenant or their new ensign.

"I think we can arrange that," said the captain.

Ben Zoma nodded. "Absolutely. But you'll want to settle in first," he told the ensign.

The fellow smiled a little. "Of course, sir."

"Come on," said Ben Zoma, heading for the exit. "I'll see to it you're shown to your quarters. Both of you."

The newcomers fell in behind the first officer, leaving Picard alone with Refsland. He turned to the transporter operator, who was already in the process of locking down his console.

Refsland looked up at him. "I guess that's it, sir."

Picard nodded and replied, "So it would seem, Mr. Refsland." But inwardly he added, *For now.*

Nikolas was lying in his bed with his uniform on, enjoying the feeling of just doing nothing, when the doors to his quarters slid apart. Reluctantly, he opened his eyes.

The guy that came in was his new roommate. He had to be. Otherwise, he wouldn't have walked in as if he owned the place.

As Nikolas watched, the guy made his way to the naked mattress that had been Joe Caber's and took stock of the linens piled on top of it. Then he began unfolding them.

"You don't waste any time," said Nikolas, "do you?"

His roommate looked at him as if noticing him for the first time. "Excuse me?"

Nikolas smiled and sat up. "Sorry," he said, offering the guy his hand. "Andreas Nikolas, widely known as the only indispensable member of the crew."

The newcomer just looked at him.

"That was a joke," Nikolas told him.

Finally, the guy cracked a smile, albeit a weak one, and shook Nikolas's hand. "Cole Paris. Pleased to meet you."

"Just so you know," Nikolas said, "I haven't had much luck with roommies lately. The last one got himself kicked off the ship. But then," he quipped, "what do you expect from an admiral's son?"

Paris's smile faded.

"What?" said Nikolas.

"I'm an admiral's *grand*son."

Nikolas felt a rush of heat in his cheeks. *Nice going,* he thought. *Offend the guy right off the bat.*

"Tell you what," he said, "just give me a moment and I'll get my foot out of my mouth."

The new guy dismissed the notion with a wave of his hand. "Don't give it another thought," he said with the utmost seriousness. "I'm sure I'll make my share of stupid remarks."

Nikolas didn't know Paris very well, but he had a premonition that the guy was right. Paris seemed a little off somehow, a little too stiff for his own good—like a toy soldier Nikolas had seen once in the window of an antiques store.

Different from Caber, he thought. That was for *damned* sure. As different as high noon and midnight.

"So what do you do," Nikolas wondered, "when you're not busy saving the universe?"

Paris stared at him for a second, a knot of flesh gathering over the bridge of his nose. Then he said, "Another joke?"

Nikolas nodded. "Sort of. But a question, too."

His roommate shrugged. "I do like to read."

Now we're getting somewhere, Nikolas told himself. "Anything in particular?"

"Uh huh. Piloting manuals. That sort of thing."

Inwardly, Nikolas cringed. "Really."

"Can't get enough of them."

Nikolas managed a smile. "How about that."

Paris looked thoughtful. "You know," he said, "I could go for something to eat."

The guy was talking Nikolas's language. "Why don't we head for the mess," he said, "and I'll—"

"But I've got an orientation meeting with Commander Wu," his roommate finished, "and I don't want to be late. First impressions and all that. See you later, all right?"

"Yeah," said Nikolas. "See ya."

As he watched Paris leave their quarters, he couldn't help thinking how much Paris and Wu were going to love serving together. Between them, they didn't have a relaxed bone in their bodies.

To a casual observer, Dikembe Ulelo would appear to be sitting at his console on the bridge of the *Stargazer,* exchanging routine data with the comm officer on Starbase 42.

But in reality, he was focused on another matter entirely. He was reflecting on the progress of his mission.

The junior communications officer had accomplished quite a bit since his arrival on the *Stargazer* a few weeks earlier. He had examined the engineering section, the shuttlebay, and a critical component of the deflector array. However, there was still a good deal more that he could learn.

For instance, Ulelo had yet to get a look at the ship's weapons control center. Vigo, the chief weapons officer, had agreed to give him a tour of the place when an occasion presented itself, but to date that hadn't happened.

Ulelo might have expressed a stronger desire to take Vigo's tour, but he didn't want to arouse the weapons chief's suspicion. So he had decided to wait until the next time Vigo invited him to play sharash'di, and then remind his colleague about his invitation.

Eventually, he reflected, he would get Vigo to show him what he wanted to see. It was just a matter of time.

A green light began to flash in the corner of one of Ulelo's communications monitors. It alerted him that the ship was in the process of receiving a subspace packet from the nearest Starfleet relay station.

It was part of his job to go through the packet and distribute its component messages to the appropriate parties. After all, only some of it represented official business. Much of it was personal mail intended for individual members of the crew.

The comm officer would also make a copy of each message for his own use. Then he would download the lot of them to the computer terminal provided in his quarters.

Of course, this would constitute a clear-cut violation of Starfleet regulations. But he would accept the risk if it meant knowing just a bit more about his colleagues—because knowing them better might gain him easier access to key operating areas of the ship.

And the more Ulelo learned about the *Stargazer,* the better equipped he would be when the time came.

Chapter Three

As JEAN-LUC PICARD CONTEMPLATED the computer screen in his ready room, he heard a chime. "Come," he said.

The doors parted and Ben Zoma walked in. "There's a rumor going around that that last packet contained new orders. Any truth to it?"

The captain smiled. "Quite a bit, actually."

Ben Zoma sat down opposite Picard. "So where are we going?"

"The Egreggedor system. There are a couple of planets there that Admiral McAteer would like us to survey."

The first officer looked skeptical. "Wasn't that system surveyed less than a decade ago?"

Picard shrugged. "Slow day at the office, I suppose."

"Must have been." Ben Zoma frowned thoughtfully. "You think McAteer's trying to take another shot at us somehow?"

"I wouldn't put it past him," the captain said. "Not after he unleashed us on the trail of the White Wolf, hoping to make us look bad when we failed to find him."

"Unfortunately for our friend the admiral, we managed to disappoint him in that regard."

Picard nodded. "Which no doubt made him feel that much more bitter toward us."

Ben Zoma seemed to take pleasure in the notion. "No doubt," he said with a mischievous gleam in his eyes.

The captain clucked in mock disapproval. "I don't think you're showing the proper respect, Number One."

"You're probably right," the first officer told him. "And believe me, I feel terrible about it."

"You don't *look* like you feel terrible about it."

"I hide it well," said Ben Zoma. He got to his feet. "Well, I would love to stay and gloat some more, but I think it's time we started out for Egreggedor."

"I would appreciate it," Picard responded.

He watched his friend leave the room to apprise Idun and Gerda of their destination. Then he turned back to his screen and sent a message to Admiral McAteer, confirming that the *Stargazer* had received her orders and would endeavor to carry them out.

No matter *what* the admiral had in mind for them.

Second Officer Elizabeth Wu of the Federation ship *Stargazer* sat down at the desk in her quiet, tastefully decorated quarters and opened the message that had come for her just that morning.

Wu had learned of it when she arrived on the bridge to go over supply reports with Captain Picard. As she passed Ulelo at his comm station, he had told her, "You've got mail, Commander. From Captain Rudolfini on the *Crazy Horse.*"

Picard was the only one close enough to hear Ulelo. At the mention of Rudolfini, it seemed to Wu, a shadow crossed the captain's face. Of course, it might just have been her imagination.

In any case, her curiosity was piqued. In fact, it was increasingly difficult for her to keep her mind on her work until her shift was finally over.

Then she went straight to her quarters. And now here she was, opening the message—wondering what her former captain had to say as his image filled her monitor screen.

Enzo Rudolfini was tall, painfully thin and almost completely bald, with a prominent nose and a chin that seemed to want desperately to crawl into the flesh of his neck.

But if his looks were less than felicitous, his ability to command a starship more than made up for them. Rudolfini had a way of drawing people to him that Wu had never seen in any other human being. A week after she came aboard the *Crazy Horse* as a raw ensign, she would have given her life for the man.

And she wasn't alone in that regard. People loved Rudolfini. They adored him—enough to stay on his ship for the duration of their Starfleet careers in some cases. And Wu had envisioned doing exactly that her-self—at least, in the beginning.

But after her third year as head of security on the *Crazy Horse,* she had craved a change—a challenge. And with the second-officer and first-officer slots filled with individuals as enamored of the captain as she was, it wouldn't be possible for her to find that challenge under Rudol-fini's command.

So she applied for a transfer to a ship willing to give her a chance to serve as second officer. And she had found that opportunity here on the *Stargazer.*

Rudolfini hadn't been happy about it. He had loved Wu like a daugh-ter. But what could he do? He couldn't offer her what she wanted. So like the good man he was, he had wished her well as she embarked on a new phase of her career.

He smiled at her from the screen. "Hello, Elizabeth. I hope this message finds you well."

It was good to hear Rudolfini's voice. Wu had only been gone a few weeks, but it felt like forever.

"Before I go on," he said, "I should tell you I've already discussed this with Captain Picard and received his permission to speak to you. So don't feel like you have to sneak around."

Wu's heart began to pound—and her heart *never* pounded, not even in the midst of a space battle.

"When you left the *Crazy Horse,* you said it was because you had nowhere to go. T'lar and Omalayak had locked down the first and second officers' slots and it seemed they would stay there for the long haul. Well, guess what?"

They're leaving, Wu thought wildly.

"They're leaving," Rudolfini said. "T'lar accepted a captaincy on the *Resilient* and she's taking Omalayak along as her first officer. Looks to me like I've got not one but *two* slots open. That is, if I can find someone capable of filling them."

Wu couldn't believe it.

"I had Mecir in mind for the second officer's post. If anyone deserves it, she does. But I don't have anyone qualified to be an exec, and I'd sure hate to have to look outside the family. . . ."

Wu knew exactly where he was going with this. He was going to ask what she had dreamed about for years.

"So what do you say, Elizabeth? I know you just got used to being a second officer, but they say it's easier to be a Number One than a Number Two. And I can't think of anyone I'd rather have standing beside me on the bridge of the *Crazy Horse.*"

Wu drew a deep breath and let it out slowly.

"Get back to me as soon as you can, all right? Rudolfini out."

A moment later, his image blinked off and was replaced by the Star-fleet logo. Wu sank back in her chair, stunned.

She had given up on the possibility of ever receiving another pro-motion on the *Crazy Horse.* And suddenly, a promotion had fallen right into her lap.

The question was . . . did she dare pass it up?

Phigus Simenon stood in his quarters and contemplated the small white stone in his scaly hand.

The stone, which had come from his homeworld, had a series of black characters carved into its otherwise smooth surface. As Simenon wasn't an expert in the area of ancient writings, he had no idea what the characters meant.

Nor did his father, to whom the stone had been given three long decades ago. But then, one didn't have to understand the characters to appreciate their significance in the scheme of things.

Simenon glanced at the computer terminal on the opposite side of the room. He had known this day would come. Hell, how could he *not* know? But he had put the prospect from his mind, concentrating instead on his duties as a Starfleet engineer.

Now he had no choice. He had received the summons. He was com-pelled to answer it.

With a sigh, Simenon crossed the room, pulled out the chair in front of his terminal, and sat down. Then he placed the stone on the desk beside his keyboard and called up the message he had received from Gnala earlier in the day.

Typing out a return message, he had the terminal translate it into a language his people would understand—one that bore a vague resem-blance to the characters on the stone.

Then he dispatched it to the communications queue for inclusion in the next subspace packet to that part of space, sat back in his chair, and absorbed the import of what he had done.

Carter Greyhorse, the *Stargazer*'s chief medical officer, blew on a spoonful of steaming hot corn chowder. "Yes, Pug," he replied, "I remember your misgivings."

"Well," said Pug Joseph, the ship's acting chief of security, "I think I'm getting past them. The way my people respond to me lately, I feel sometimes like I'm the *permanent* chief of security."

Joseph was sitting across the table from Greyhorse, twirling his fork in a plateful of pasta. To that point, the doctor noticed, Joseph had been too talkative to actually place any of it into his mouth.

"That's good," said Greyhorse.

"I'm gaining confidence," Joseph told him.

"I hear it in your voice."

Joseph grinned. "Really?"

"Would I lie to you?"

The physician took a mouthful of soup, savored its taste, and glanced across the mess hall. Right on schedule, Gerda Asmund was sitting down to eat with her sister Idun and a couple of other officers.

Greyhorse could have been one of them if he wished. But it would have been torture for him to share Gerda with others, to engage in conversations he didn't care about when what he really wanted was to take her in his arms.

And she knew how he felt about her. He had told her himself, right there in one of the ship's corridors less than a month earlier—just after she had lashed out at him in anger.

"You're all I can think of," the doctor had confessed, the bulkheads echoing with his pain. *"All I want to think of. I can't go on like this. If I haven't got a chance, I need to hear you say it."*

That's when Gerda had told him to meet her in the gym, where she would teach him "to fight like a warrior." It wasn't exactly an answer to his question. But then, in a way it *was*.

So Greyhorse met her in the gym as she suggested, and continued to meet her afterward at regular intervals. And little by little, despite his pronounced lack of athleticism, he was beginning to learn what she taught him.

But it wasn't his thirst for learning that kept him coming back. It was the chance to touch her, however fleetingly—to smell her scent, to hear her voice, to feel her intoxicating presence.

In the gym, where they were alone. Where it was just the two of them, locked in a dance of violence and grace—at least on her part.

But Greyhorse didn't sit with her in the mess hall. He sat with men like Joseph and listened to them go on about their personal trials while he kept his own very much to himself.

"So what's going on with you?" Joseph asked.

The doctor turned back to him and shrugged. "The usual."

Picard smiled politely at Wu as he regarded her across the sleek, black expanse of his ready room desk. "I believe I know why you asked to see me," he said.

Wu smiled back. "Captain Rudolfini asked me to respond on a timely basis. I did that."

"And what was your decision?" Picard asked, though he believed he already knew.

"I told him," said Wu, "that I would accept the position of first officer aboard the *Crazy Horse.*"

The captain felt a sting of disappointment—no less sharp for his anticipation of it. "I see. As of when?"

"Your earliest convenience," said his second officer.

Picard nodded. "I will ask Mr. Paxton to contact the *Crazy Horse* and arrange a meeting in accordance with our schedules. I don't imagine it will take more than a week or two before we can get together."

"Thank you, sir," said Wu. She looked contrite for a moment. "I hope I haven't given you cause to disapprove of me."

"Disapprove?" he echoed.

"Yes, sir. For leaving so soon after I arrived."

Picard shook his head from side to side. "Not at all, Commander. Opportunity knocked. You answered."

Wu looked relieved. "Thank you for putting it that way, sir."

"If there's nothing else?" he said.

"Nothing," she confirmed.

"Then you are dismissed, Commander."

With a slight inclination of her head, Wu got up and left the captain's ready room. As soon as the door closed behind her, Picard sat back in his chair and shook his head.

In fact, he thought, he *did* resent Wu's coming and going in so short a time. He *did* disapprove of her behavior.

However, it wouldn't have accomplished anything if he had stood in the way of her transfer. The *Crazy Horse* would have missed out on Rudolfini's first choice of exec and the *Stargazer* would have been stuck with a disgruntled second officer.

It was too bad, Picard thought. He liked Wu. He had come to appreciate her dedication and efficiency, and she had even begun to overcome her tendency to be overzealous at times.

He tapped his communicator. "Picard to Commander Ben Zoma."

"Ben Zoma here," came the response.

"We've got a personnel matter to discuss, Gilaad."

There was a pause on the other end. *"The one you mentioned to me earlier?"*

The captain frowned. "Yes. *That* one."

"I'll be right there," his first officer promised. *"Ben Zoma out."*

The disappointment in his voice was unmistakable. But then, Ben Zoma had come to value Wu's contributions as well.

Picard swiveled in his chair to face his computer terminal. Tapping out a command, he called up Starfleet's periodically updated list of qualified second-officer candidates.

Unfortunately, there was no one on the *Stargazer* whom the captain could name as Wu's replacement. With so many of his officers having received battlefield promotions, command experience was in drastically short supply.

Funny, Picard thought. When Wu had been foisted on him by Admiral McAteer prior to their hunt for the White Wolf, he hadn't looked forward to working with a stranger. Now he wasn't looking forward to seeking out a candidate on his own.

Nonetheless, the captain reflected with a sense of resignation, *that is* precisely *what I will have to do.*

Chapter Four

GERDA ASMUND WAS RUNNING a long-range sensor diagnostic at navigation when she saw a fair-haired young man approach the helm console manned by her twin sister.

Idun looked up at the fellow—an ensign she had never seen before—as he stopped beside her. "Yes?" she said, posing a challenge as much as a question.

"I'm your replacement," the ensign told her.

Gerda glanced at the chronometer readout in the upper right-hand corner of her control panel. In fact, Idun's shift was over, though Gerda's still had two hours to go.

It was the captain who had decided to stagger the schedules of the helm and navigation officers. What's more, it made perfect sense. The remaining officer could apprise the new one of any concerns that had arisen in the last couple of hours.

Nonetheless, Gerda hated to see anyone but her sister at the helm. Idun was a skilled pilot and a cool head in an emergency—and one never knew when a crisis might arise.

"So you are," Idun told the ensign.

She got up and gave him her seat. Then, with a glance at her sister, she left the bridge. Knowing Idun, Gerda imagined she would be in the gym in a matter of minutes.

Turning her attention to the new helmsman, Gerda watched him go over his monitors to make sure everything was in order. The navigator felt a rush of indignation. Did he think that someone like Idun would leave a mess for him?

Ben Zoma, who had the center seat, glanced at the ensign. "Steady as she goes, Mr. Paris."

The ensign nodded. "Aye, sir."

Paris, Gerda repeated to herself.

So *this* was the new crewman she had heard about. The one whose Starfleet lineage went back to the Stone Age, or so it seemed. He didn't look like much to Gerda.

But then, *no* human did.

Gerda had grown up among Klingons after the death of her natural parents. Her *human* parents. In the process, she had adopted a Klingon's way of looking at things—a Klingon's appreciation for the drama and spectacle of life.

Her Klingon father had been an impressive individual. He had carried himself with confidence, with dignity. One had but to look at him to know one was in the presence of a warrior.

Very few humans possessed that kind of bearing. Captain Ruhalter was one of them, though his spirit had gone to *Sto-Vo-Kor.* Captain Picard was another, at least at times.

And Greyhorse . . .

The navigator didn't know what to make of him. He was often passive, willing to let others make his decisions for him. But he showed a certain *promise,* she was forced to concede.

Ensign Paris, on the other hand, looked to the navigator like any other human—fragile, timid, too focused on expediency to give any thought to matters like dignity and honor. If he had a warrior's spirit, he concealed it well.

Abruptly, Paris's fingers began crawling over his control console. Clearly, he was busy with something. But to Gerda's knowledge, he hadn't been given an order to make changes.

"What are you doing?" she asked.

He looked at her. "I beg your pardon?"

Gerda pointed to the ensign's console. "You did something to the thrusters. What was it?"

He shrugged. "I changed the timing."

"Who told you to do that?"

Paris hesitated. "No one."

"Then why did you do it?" the navigator asked.

"To make the ship more responsive," he explained.

"Thruster timing is a delicate matter—one that requires special ex-pertise. By tampering with it, you have likely made it necessary for some-one to spend hours readjusting it."

"That's certainly a possibility," Paris conceded. "And if the thruster timing was all I'd worked on, it *would* be out of sync."

Gerda scowled. "You worked on *other* flight functions as well?"

"Sure," he said.

He tapped out a command and Gerda saw a graphic come up on her monitor. It showed her a bright yellow cross section of the *Stargazer*'s shield configuration.

Paris leaned over and pointed to the graphic. "By making comple-mentary changes in thruster timing and shield geometry, I've picked up a tenth of a second of response time."

The navigator made some quick calculations, which—to her great surprise—precisely supported the ensign's contention. She looked at him with new respect.

"Of course," the ensign said, "it'll only make a difference if we find ourselves in a battle. And who knows when *that* will happen."

In her short time on the *Stargazer,* Gerda had already taken part in her share. "Soon enough," she assured him. She eyed his controls. "Where did you learn to do that?"

"Back at the Academy," said Paris.

"A professor taught it to you," Gerda concluded.

"Professor Rehling," he told her. "But he didn't teach it to me. We came up with it *together.* In fact, the professor insisted that my name appear above his when the monograph comes out."

"The monograph . . . ?" Gerda echoed.

The ensign nodded. "They say it'll be required reading for all Star-fleet helm officers."

"Impressive," the navigator muttered.

And Gerda Asmund wasn't easily impressed.

* * *

Vigo, the *Stargazer*'s Pandrilite weapons officer, had a bit of a problem on his hands.

His friend Charlie Kochman had introduced him to a clever diversion called sharash'di, having purchased it for Vigo from an Yridian merchant at a bazaar on Beta Nopterix. However, Kochman no longer seemed to wish to play the game.

In fact, he told Vigo he wished he had never bought it for him in the first place.

Of course, the weapons officer had challenged his friend to a sharash'di match a couple of times a day for the last several weeks. In retrospect, it was to this that he attributed Kochman's growing disaffection with the game.

Vigo, on the other hand, never seemed to grow tired of it. Every time he played sharash'di it was as if he were playing for the first time, discovering new complexities and new delights.

So when Kochman's interest in the game began to flag, Vigo found other opponents—among them the ill-fated Lt. Valderrama and Ulelo, the new man in communications. But the weapons officer was finding that none of these others wished to play him again, either. Valderrama, the only one who had seemed at all eager for a rematch, had changed her mind when Captain Picard stripped her of her responsibilities.

Hence, Vigo's problem.

But a few hours earlier, while he was still at his post, the *Stargazer* had picked up a couple of new crewmen—a new science officer and a new ensign. To Vigo's colleagues, the newcomers might have represented a great many things—expertise, reliability, new viewpoints to spice up mess hall banter.

To the Pandrilite, they represented only *one* thing: prospective sharash'di partners.

Which was why he had made it his business to get to this place as soon as his shift was over. The other newcomer was on the bridge according to the ship's computer. But *this* one was in his quarters.

Pressing the metallic pad set into the bulkhead, Vigo stepped back and waited. *Nol Kastiigan,* he repeated to himself. *Science officer first class. Formerly of the* Antares.

A moment later, the duranium doors to Kastiigan's quarters whispered open, revealing the science officer's anteroom. But the science officer himself was not in evidence.

"I will be right there," someone called in an oddly musical voice from the next room.

Kastiigan, Vigo thought.

"Don't hurry on my account," he advised the newcomer. Then he came in and looked around—and to his surprise, found himself wondering about what he was looking at.

The Pandrilite wasn't sure what he had expected to see here, but he was pretty certain this wasn't it.

"Thank you for your patience," said Kastiigan as he entered the room, wearing a black-and-white tunic and loose-fitting pants that featured the same color scheme. "As it happens, you are my first visitor."

Vigo nodded, still wondering. "I guess you haven't had a chance to unpack," he allowed.

His host looked at him. "I beg your pardon?"

Vigo indicated Kastiigan's quarters with a sweep of his hand. "There's nothing here."

The newcomer followed his gesture, but seemed at a loss. "On the contrary," he maintained, "there is quite a bit here. Chairs, computer, carpet . . . and that is in this room alone. In the next room, there is a bed, a set of drawers and a closet. And in the bathroom—"

"That's not what I mean," said the weapons officer. "Those things were here before you got here. They're permanent furnishings. I'm talking about *your* things."

Kastiigan seemed even more perplexed.

"You know," Vigo elaborated, "the items you brought with you from your previous assignment. Standing sculptures, hanging artwork, images of your loved ones . . ."

The science officer smiled. "I did not bring any such items."

Vigo looked at him askance. "You didn't bring any mementos from your homeworld? Or from the planets you've visited? No parting gifts from friends or family?"

Kastiigan shook his head from side to side, indicating that he had done nothing of the sort.

It was a big galaxy, the weapons officer reminded himself. Different cultures had different customs. Still, he was curious as to the reasoning behind the Kandilkari's behavior.

"Why *not?*" he asked.

"Because," Kastiigan explained, "such possessions would only be a burden to my crewmates after I perish."

For a moment, Vigo thought he was kidding. "Are you planning on perishing sometime soon?"

"Oh, yes," the newcomer responded cheerfully.

Vigo blanched. "You *are?*"

"Most definitely. As soon as possible. And when I do, I will consider it my great honor to give my life for my captain and my comrades—you included, Lieutenant."

"Er . . . thanks," said Vigo.

"You are quite welcome. Perhaps we will even have the opportunity to perish *together.*"

The Pandrilite managed a smile, albeit a weak one. "That would be . . . something to look forward to, wouldn't it?"

"It would indeed," said Kastiigan. "Now, what was it you wished to speak to me about?"

It wasn't often that Vigo could say he didn't have a yen to play sharash'di. This was one of those rare times.

"Nothing," he assured the Kandilkari. "Really. I just wanted to . . . welcome you aboard."

Kastiigan inclined his head. "You are kind to do so. Would you care to stay and join me in meditation?"

Vigo had never been one for meditation. He said so.

"I understand," the science officer told him. "For some, the manner of one's death is a personal matter."

"Right," said Vigo, jumping on the excuse with both feet. "It's personal. *Very* personal. So if you don't mind, I'll go back to my quarters and meditate on my own."

"May you find fulfillment in your meditation."

"You, too," the weapons officer told him. Then he backed out of Kastiigan's quarters and made his way down the corridor as quickly as he was able.

Phigus Simenon took a deep breath, waited for the turbolift doors to open, and headed directly for Picard's ready room.

He knew the captain was there because the ship's computer had told him so. Still, he glanced at the bridge's center seat to make sure the situation hadn't changed.

Picard wasn't there, but Commander Wu was. And in Simenon's experience, Wu was the sort of individual who wanted to know everything that was going on.

Everything. Without exception.

Seeing Wu's head turn in his direction, Simenon looked away again. The last thing he wanted to do was engage the second officer in conversation. He just wanted to take care of what he had come to the bridge for and beat a hasty retreat.

But Wu didn't seem inclined to let him do that. Rising from her seat, she intercepted the engineer and asked, "Can I help you?"

She couldn't. Only Picard or Commander Ben Zoma could do that. "No," Simenon told her emphatically.

He must have surprised Wu with the forcefulness of his response, because she recoiled a bit. What's more, the other bridge officers turned to look at him.

It was exactly what he had hoped to avoid.

"All right," Wu said, regaining her composure. "Then perhaps—"

The engineer didn't wait for her to finish her suggestion. Instead, he turned and made his way back to the turbolift, having embarrassed himself quite enough.

As he reached the double doors, they slid apart for him. He was about to enter the lift compartment when he heard a familiar hiss.

Picard's ready room door was opening. Simenon turned his head in time to see the captain and Ben Zoma emerge.

Before they could go anywhere, the Gnalish hurried over and planted himself in front of them. Picard looked surprised. But then, he had probably never seen his chief engineer move so quickly before.

"Mr. Simenon," he said.

Ben Zoma smiled. "Everything all right?"

The Gnalish wasn't in the mood for niceties. "Can I see you in private?" he rasped. "Both of you?"

Picard's eyes narrowed. No doubt, he was trying to divine the reason for Simenon's discomfort.

"Of course," he said at last.

"Good," the engineer snapped, and led his superiors back into the captain's ready room.

* * *

Ensign Nikolas was whistling to himself as he made his way to the bridge for his training session with Commander Wu.

Wu wasn't exactly known as an easy taskmaster. People didn't often whistle on their way to meetings with her. But this once, Nikolas felt justified in doing so.

To that point in his career on the *Stargazer,* he had earned a reputation for arriving at his training sessions just in the nick of time, raising the eyebrows of the officers in charge of them. In fact, some of the ensign's friends had picked up on his habit and given him the obvious moniker: "Nik of Time."

But this time he wasn't going to show up exactly when he was due. For once, he was going to be early for something.

That was his intention, at least.

But as Nikolas passed the doors to the ship's gymnasium, which were situated between his quarters and the nearest turbolift, he saw them slide open. And out of the corner of his eye, he saw a feminine figure come out of the gym.

Of course, he wouldn't have allowed himself to be detained if it was just *any* feminine figure. But it wasn't. It was Idun Asmund, her cheeks flushed with evidence of her exertions, her skin glistening with a thin sheen of sweat.

Nikolas didn't know he was slowing down to acknowledge her until he had already done it. "Lieutenant," he said a little awkwardly.

She glanced at him, her eyes the blue of polar ice, and said, "Ensign." Then she made her way down the corridor.

As he watched her retreat, he couldn't help smiling. Idun Asmund was a living work of art. No, he corrected himself—*better* than that. She was a genuine masterpiece.

"Nikolas?" said a familiar, high-pitched voice.

The ensign looked away from the object of his admiration just long enough to see who had greeted him. He found himself peering down at a small, pink humanoid who—as the ever-sensitive Joe Caber had gleefully pointed out—looked a lot like a plucked chicken.

In this case, a plucked chicken in midnight-blue gym togs.

"Obal," said Nikolas.

The Binderian, who worked in security under Pug Joseph, looked up at him with a distinct glint of curiosity in his eyes. "What are you doing?" he asked.

Nikolas resumed his admiration of Idun Asmund. "Appreciating one of the finer things in life."

A moment later, the helm officer vanished around a bend in the corridor. The ensign sighed. *All good things come to an end,* he mused, and he couldn't think of anything better than the sight of such an attractive woman.

Nikolas turned to his friend—and realized something. "Hey . . . you were working out in the gym just now, weren't you?"

"Why, yes," said Obal.

The ensign smiled. "You know what? You're one lucky guy."

"And why is that?"

"Well," said Nikolas, "it's not everybody who gets a chance to share a gym with one of the Asmund twins."

The Binderian's brow wrinkled over his big, round eyes. "What does luck have to do with it? Are the Asmunds less likely to make use of the gym than other crewmen?"

Nikolas chuckled. "You don't get it, do you?"

Obal shrugged his bony shoulders. "I suppose not."

The ensign wasn't all that surprised. As humanoid development went, Obal's people were pretty far off the beaten track. Nonetheless, he did his best to explain.

"You see, buddy, by human standards, the Asmund twins are hot. I mean *really* hot."

Obal looked just as perplexed as before. "Hot?"

Nikolas sighed. "They're . . . how can I put it? Extremely desirable mating partners. Get it?"

A light went on in the Binderian's eyes. "Ah," he said knowingly. *"Hot.* Of course."

Nikolas pointed to his friend's chest. "And *you* got to get sweaty with her. You know what that makes you? The envy of every human male on board—me included."

Obal shrugged again. "If you say so. But, you understand, we didn't engage in any mating practices. We merely fought."

It was the human's turn to be perplexed. "You mean you . . . sparred with her? With Idun Asmund?"

The security officer nodded. "It was her idea, actually. She said she had heard of my prowess as a hand-to-hand combatant and wished to see if the stories were true. As it turned out, it was an exhilarating experience for both of us."

Nikolas smiled. After all, he had seen Obal in action. His friend was as fast as lightning and twice as devastating.

"Then you must have pulled your punches, my friend. Otherwise, the lieutenant wouldn't have walked out under her own power."

Obal let a smile of his own leak out. "I suppose I did pull my punches a *little.*"

It had to be more than just a little, Nikolas mused. But what he said was, "That's what I thought." Then an idea came to him—a brillant, absolutely inspired idea. "Say, do you think you could set up a sparring session for *me?*"

The Binderian looked at him. "With Lieutenant Asmund?"

"Yup. With Lieutenant Asmund."

Obal thought about it. "You're sure you'd like that?"

"I know I would. It would give me a chance to get to know her a little better—and there are few things I would rather do in life than get to know Idun Asmund."

Obal seemed to understand. "All right. I'll try."

"That's the spirit," Nikolas told him. "And if she agrees, I'll treat you to dinner."

His friend eyed him suspiciously. "But dinner is available to all crewmen free of charge."

"Picky, picky," said Nikolas, already dreaming about his sparring session with the statuesque helm officer.

Unexpectedly, Obal made a face. "Wait a second . . ."

"What is it?" the ensign asked.

"Shouldn't you be on the bridge? I distinctly recall your saying that you had a training session scheduled with Commander Wu."

Nikolas felt the blood drain from his face. "Gotta go," he blurted and sprinted down the corridor, hoping he could catch a turbolift before it was too late.

Picard sat down behind his desk and watched Ben Zoma fill the chair on the other side of it. But their chief engineer remained on his feet, pacing back and forth across the captain's ready room with his hands clasped behind his back.

Picard had seen Simenon agitated before, but seldom like this. It worried him.

"Won't you sit down?" he asked Simenon.

The Gnalish shook his head. "That won't be necessary." Suddenly, he stopped and looked directly at Picard. "I need a leave of absence. For personal reasons."

"Personal reasons?" Ben Zoma echoed.

Simenon hesitated, his ruby eyes blinking. "Yes," he said finally.

It was clear that he didn't wish to go into any detail regarding his request. However, the captain felt compelled to make sure his officer was all right.

"Is there a problem?" he asked.

Again, Simenon hesitated, as if that were a difficult question to answer. Then he said, "Everything is fine."

Picard frowned. "You're not ill, are you?"

The engineer looked at him askance. "Why do you ask?"

The captain smiled. "Isn't it obvious? You seem to have something on your mind."

"That's for sure," Ben Zoma chimed in. "Come on, Simenon. You're among friends. What's going on?"

Leave it to Ben Zoma to cut to the chase, Picard reflected. He regarded the engineer. "Phigus?"

For a moment, he thought Simenon might let them in on his problem. Then the Gnalish's lizardlike features hardened with resolve. "I have to go back to Gnala," he said. "That's all. And if you're my friends, you won't ask me any more questions."

Picard and his first officer exchanged glances. The captain didn't like the idea of letting the matter drop. However, Simenon wasn't leaving him any other option.

"Very well," Picard said reluctantly. "I'll respect your privacy. And I'll grant your request for a leave of absence."

Ben Zoma looked at him and shrugged. "There's nothing urgent about Egreggedor, is there?"

"Nothing," the captain agreed. He glanced at the intercom grid. "Picard to Gerda Asmund."

"Asmund here," came the response.

"Chart a course for Gnala, Lieutenant. Best speed."

"Aye, sir," said Gerda.

The Gnalish looked from one of them to the other. "Thank you," he told them. Then, before they could engage him in further conversation, he left Picard's ready room.

As the door whispered closed in Simenon's wake, Ben Zoma whistled. "I've never seen him like that."

"Nor have I," the captain noted.

"I wonder what's bugging him," said Ben Zoma.

So did Picard. But he had given his word not to pry into Simenon's business and he meant to keep that promise unconditionally.

Chapter Five

Captain's Personal Log, supplemental. We are more than halfway to Gnala, the world of Simenon's birth, and he has yet to volunteer any additional information regarding his business there. In fact, he has become rather close-mouthed in general, leading me to believe that what awaits him on Gnala may be something less than pleasant for him. Still, I continue to respect Simenon's wishes and allow him to deal with the matter on his own.

FOR THE UMPTEENTH TIME THAT DAY, Elizabeth Wu's thoughts wandered in the direction of her return to the *Crazy Horse*. And for the umpteenth time, she reeled them back in.

For the time being, she was still serving on the *Stargazer.* Captain Picard and everyone else on the ship were depending on her to carry out her duties faithfully and efficiently, and she would be damned if she would fail them in any way.

Hence, her decision to visit the science section. It wasn't that she didn't trust Lt. Kastiigan, who appeared to be a capable individual. It was just that new section chiefs often had questions, and it was the second officer's job to answer them.

Just as soon as the double doors slid open in front of her, Wu began to look around for Kastiigan. As it turned out, he was nowhere in sight. All she could see was the section's horseshoe-shaped bank of sleek, black sensor stations, through which all incoming data was available.

Half the stations were occupied—in every case but one by a science technician who had received prior authorization to access sensor data. The crewman who represented the exception was easy to identify, even when seen from the back.

After all, most of the 240 people serving on the *Stargazer* only donned a Starfleet-issue containment suit when they went *outside* the ship. Only one of them—a Nizhrak ensign named Jiterica, whose molecular structure was radically different from any of her colleagues'—was in the habit of wearing a suit on board.

Wu crossed the room to join Jiterica. But it wasn't until she was standing beside the ensign that her presence was noted.

Turning in her chair, Jiterica looked up at the second officer. There was an expression of surprise imposed on the ghostly visage visible through her transparent faceplate.

"Commander," she said, her voice sounding tinny as it emerged from her specially designed vocalization unit.

"Ensign," Wu responded with the same note of formality.

Jiterica glanced at the monitor, then at Wu again. "I apologize. I accessed sensor data without the proper authorization."

She was right. And the fact that she had violated regulations with full knowledge of what she was doing made her violation an even more grievous one.

The second officer's first impulse was to come down on Jiterica for blatantly breaking the rules. However, she managed to hold that impulse in check.

Not so long ago, Ben Zoma had made Wu the object of a strict interpretation of the rules, giving her a taste of how it felt. Since then, she had become less of a stickler about regulations, and her relationships with the crew had improved as a result.

Nor, to her surprise, had anyone's efficiency suffered. It was a lesson Wu now wished she had learned years earlier.

"It's all right," she told Jiterica. "It's a minor infraction. There's no need to apologize."

The ensign gazed at her for a moment, her ghostly visage unreadable. "Thank you," she said at last.

"Don't mention it," Wu assured her.

Peering over Jiterica's shoulder at the monitor, she saw that the ensign was studying the file on Gamma Barchedden V, a gas giant in a distant star system. She wondered why—until she remembered that Jiterica had grown up in the atmosphere of a gas giant.

When Wu regarded Jiterica again, she thought she saw a sadness in her strange, translucent eyes. A melancholy, as if she had lost something dear to her.

"Are you . . . homesick?" Wu asked.

Jiterica didn't give her an answer right away. And when she did, it was an elusive one. "I was just trying to gain a better understanding of Gamma Barchedden."

Understanding that the subject might be an emotional one, the second officer didn't probe any deeper. "I see," was all she said.

The ensign got to her feet—a less than graceful maneuver, thanks to the cumbersome suit she wore. "I'm due on the bridge in a few minutes," she told Wu. Then she brushed past her and made for the exit.

Wu's heart went out to Jiterica. After all, the Nizhrak hadn't had an easy time of it on her last vessel, nor had she made any friends to this point on the *Stargazer.*

And yet, if not for her contribution to their search for the White Wolf, they might never have had an opportunity to find the pirate. Obviously, the ensign had a lot to offer.

But she might never get the chance unless someone took her under her wing. *Someone like me,* Wu thought.

She might not have planned to serve on the *Stargazer* much longer, but while she was there she was going to see what she could do on behalf of Ensign Jiterica.

Vigo wasn't exactly a stranger to the *Stargazer's* engineering section. As chief weapons officer, he often had occasion to check on the various systems that generated and delivered the energy used in phaser and photon torpedo barrages.

But he hadn't come to engineering to check on any systems this time. He had come to see his friend Pug Joseph.

Vigo found him in his office, a small cubicle that lay just past the weapons diagnostic room and opposite the locked phaser armory. As the Pandrilite filled the doorway with his bulk, he saw Joseph look up from whatever work he was doing on his computer terminal.

"Vigo," said the security chief. He swiveled around in his chair. "What's up?"

"I . . . wanted to speak with you," the Pandrilite told him.

Joseph's brow pinched over the bridge of his nose. "You don't look so good. Is everything all right?"

Vigo averted his eyes. "Perhaps not everything."

The human leaned forward. "What's the matter?"

"I've had a . . . bad experience," Vigo said.

"Bad in what way?"

Vigo frowned. It was an awkward expression for him. A smile would have felt much more natural.

"I just spoke with Lieutenant Kastiigan in his quarters. Apparently, he intends to die."

Joseph stared at his friend. "I hate to tell you, buddy, but I don't think any of us has a choice in the matter."

"No," said Vigo, struggling to explain. "He doesn't *expect* to die. He *intends* to die."

The security officer looked strained as he tried to figure out the difference. "I'm not sure I follow you."

The Pandrilite heaved a sigh. "I don't suppose I'm explaining this very well."

"Why don't we try it again? You spoke with Kastiigan, right? And he told you . . . ?" Joseph held his hands out, palms up, indicating that it was Vigo's turn to speak.

"He told me that he wanted to die. He wanted to give his life for his captain and comrades."

Joseph shrugged. "People say those kinds of things."

"And he wanted to do it *as soon as possible.*"

Finally, the security officer began to show signs of concern. "As soon as possible? You mean he's in a hurry?"

"So it would seem."

Joseph grunted. "Are you saying Kastiigan is . . . suicidal?"

Vigo shook his hairless, blue head. "I don't think so. I just think he's got a warped sense of duty."

Joseph looked at him with a hint of suspicion in his expression. "Then why are you so shaken up?"

The weapons officer frowned again. "On Pandril, we don't speak of . . . the sort of event Kastiigan is contemplating. It's considered bad luck. Tempting fate, a human would say."

The security chief seemed to see the entire picture now. "He's giving you the heebie-jeebies."

"That would be another way of putting it."

"So what are you going to do? Try to avoid Kastiigan?"

"As much as I can," Vigo told him.

"It's a big ship," Joseph said, "but it's not *that* big. You're going to run into him sooner or later."

"I thought you might suggest a way for me to avoid doing so."

The security officer considered the question for a while. Then he said, "You could find out what shift he's working and work a different one. But that's not going to work all the time."

"I know," said Vigo, who had already discarded that option on his own. "As the senior weapons officer, I have to be available when the captain *wants* me to be available."

Joseph gave it some more thought. "Well," he said finally, "you could try talking to him. You could let him know that all his talk of dying is disturbing you."

That had occurred to Vigo as well. He had rejected it because he was a Pandrilite—because his people weren't the kind to impose their values on others. But maybe it was time to break with tradition.

"Perhaps I will do that," he told Joseph. "Thank you."

"Hey," said the security officer, "I'm glad to help. Let me know how it goes, will you?"

Vigo agreed that he would do that.

As Dikembe Ulelo waited for a turbolift on Deck 10, his hands locked behind his back, he considered the contents of the subspace mail he had read to that point.

Commander Wu had been offered a position on another vessel. Lt. Iulus's sister had given birth to a girl. And Ensign Montenegro's father had survived a serious illness.

None of this news succeeded in moving the comm officer to any great degree. However, he filed it all away in his mind, knowing he might need to draw on it sometime.

"Dikembe?" someone said, intruding on his thoughts.

Ulelo turned and saw a woman approaching him. A crewman in the science section, judging by her uniform.

But she didn't look at all familiar to him. And judging by the pucker in the woman's brow, she wasn't entirely certain that *he* looked familiar to *her.*

Ulelo's first impulse was to leave the vicinity. To *escape.* But how could he do that? The *Stargazer* wasn't so big a place that he could lose himself once he had been identified.

Eventually, the woman would find him. Better to face her now, the comm officer told himself, than have to explain his abrupt departure at some later date.

The woman's expression of uncertainty became a smile as she came closer. "It *is* you," she said.

"Yes," Ulelo responded, not knowing what else to say.

"What are you doing here on the *Stargazer?*" she asked. "I thought you were still working for Lovejoy on the *Copernicus.*"

The comm officer frowned. Lovejoy was his former captain, the *Copernicus* his previous assignment.

The woman tilted her head playfully as she regarded him. "What's the matter?" she said. "Cat got your tongue?"

His frown deepened. Apparently, she had met him prior to his coming to the *Stargazer.* It was evident from her tone and choice of references. But he still didn't have a clue as to who she was.

Before he could consider the wisdom of saying so, it came out. "I'm sorry," he said, "but I don't know who you are."

The woman's smile faded a bit. "Since when did you become such a joker, Dikembe?"

Ulelo had no choice but to remain steadfast in his position. "I'm not joking. If we've met before, I don't recall it."

The woman's smile faded the rest of the way. "Stop it. We spent *hours* together at the Academy. You, me, Angela, Ragnar . . ."

He didn't remember Angela or Ragnar either. "I'm sorry."

She held her hands out in an appeal for reason. "It's *Emily,* Dikembe. Emily *Bender.*"

Ulelo just shrugged.

Her gaze went cold. "Right. Whatever you say." And with that, she turned and began to walk away.

But the woman didn't get far before she stopped and looked at him again. This time, her expression was one of unconcealed resentment. Clearly, he had caused her some discomfort.

"I don't know why you're pretending not to know me," she said, "but it's rude. Damned rude."

Then she walked away.

Chapter Six

"MIND YOU," SAID PICARD, "I didn't bring you aboard for this reason alone. But I would be lying if I told you I haven't been looking forward to this moment."

Ensign Paris inclined his head slightly. "That's high praise, sir. I'll do my best to prove worthy of it."

With that, he slipped on his fencing mask, raised his sword vertically in a gesture of respect, and dropped into an en garde position.

Picard smiled approvingly. If Paris was even half as good a fencer as his personnel file had indicated, this was going to be a most enjoyable bout indeed.

And it would have the added benefit of taking Picard's mind off other matters—the sort that hadn't even occurred to him before Admiral Mehdi made him a captain.

Personnel matters, for instance. Caber and Valderrama might be history, gone if not quite forgotten. But Picard was plagued more and more by the looming prospect of Commander Wu's departure.

The woman had just begun to feel at home here, it seemed to him. She had just begun to accept the way her superiors conducted themselves on the *Stargazer.*

And what does Rudolfini do? He reels her back to the Crazy Horse *like a prize fish.*

Then there was Simenon. Though Picard had promised not to pry into the engineer's personal affairs, he wished he knew more about Simenon's reasons for visiting his homeworld.

But there was nothing he could do in either case, Wu's or Simenon's. They weren't children, after all. They had the right to make their own decisions, just as he did.

And right now, he chose to test his new ensign's mettle.

The captain slipped on his own mask and returned Paris's salute. Then he lowered himself into a crouch and extended his blade, savoring what was to come.

He wasn't disappointed. The ensign's initial attack was a flurry of high and low angles that drove Picard back almost to the limit of the strip. But before he could be driven off it, the captain launched a counterattack. Inspired by his opponent's speed and aggressiveness, he matched it lunge for lunge.

And Paris warded off each thrust. In fact, he almost turned the last one into a point with a deadly-quick riposte.

Again, Picard smiled. This was nothing like fencing with Lt. Pierzynski. Nothing at *all.*

Paris launched another assault, probing what he must have perceived as the captain's weaknesses. His point darted at Picard's lead shoulder, then his lead hip, then his shoulder again.

But the captain parried each move and answered it with a thrust of his own. It gave the ensign pause, forced him to think about what he would try next.

And in that moment, Picard struck.

His attack wasn't just quick, it was devilishly precise—a long, low lunge of which his fencing instructors back in France would have been proud. As Paris retreated in desperation, the captain's point came at his chest like an angry viper.

But just when Picard thought he had won the touch, the ensign flung his bell-shaped guard in the way. It deflected the captain's weapon just enough to keep it from grazing his opponent.

Picard swore softly to himself and tried it again. This time, his attack was more explosive than precise. But as before, Paris managed to deflect it enough to save himself.

The captain was tempted to make the attempt a third time since Paris seemed to be off-balance. But the ensign recovered more quickly than Picard would have thought possible and nearly caught him off guard with a lunge of his own.

They were back in the center of the strip, the captain noticed, right where they had started. As if in mutual recognition of that fact, the combatants paused for a moment.

"Well played," Picard said, his breath coming hard.

Paris inclined his head. "Thank you, Captain."

"Especially that last counter. Brilliant, I thought."

"You're too kind," said the ensign. "Shall we have another go at it?"

"I'd like that," Picard replied sincerely.

And they went at each other again.

As Admiral Arlen McAteer gazed out the observation port of the modest and all-but-empty officer's lounge at Starbase 37, he was reminded of how little he had enjoyed living on starbases.

Unfortunately, he had been forced to do so at various times in his career—including an eighteen-month stint shortly after graduation at Starbase 68. He had worked there as the attaché of Admiral Bailey, a man with an unsightly paunch, thick white hair, and an equally white mustache.

Bailey, as McAteer recalled, hadn't tried any new approaches to the management of his sector. He hadn't made adjustments in personnel and their responsibilities. All he had done, it seemed, was let matters follow their natural course.

Early on, McAteer decided that Bailey wasn't very impressive, either as a man or as an admiral. He figured he could do better—a lot better. It was while he was working at Starbase 68 that McAteer decided he would become an admiral himself one day.

He had reached that objective precisely according to plan. Of course, the admiral still felt compelled now and then to leave Starfleet Headquarters on Earth and visit a starbase, but that was an inescapable part of his job.

And sometimes it wasn't McAteer's job at all but he did it anyway, for reasons that might be considered more personal than professional. This was one of those times.

His thoughts were interrupted by the hiss of the lounge doors and the sight of a woman in officer's garb. *It's her,* the admiral thought, recognizing the woman from her file picture.

Her name was Rachel Garrett. She was the second officer on the Federation starship *Excelsior.*

McAteer decided that Garrett's file image hadn't done her justice. *She's a damned impressive-looking woman,* he reflected. Part of him wondered if she had dinner plans.

But then, he could have more easily obtained a dinner date back on Earth, if that was all he was after. He had traveled all the way to this base for a much more important reason, and one that precluded any kind of romantic liaison.

"Admiral," said Garrett as she approached him.

"Pleased to meet you," he said, offering the woman his hand.

She took it. "Likewise, sir."

"Something to drink?" McAteer asked.

Garrett shook her head. "No. Nothing, thanks."

"Please," he said, "sit down."

He indicated a chair across a low table from his. The commander took it and gave him her attention.

McAteer smiled at her, doing his best impression of a doting uncle. "I've been looking forward to meeting you, Commander. I've heard good things about you."

She looked pleased to hear it. "Thank you, sir."

He wrinkled his nose. "Nasty business with the Orazwari last month."

Garrett nodded soberly. "It was. I suppose my captain told you all about it."

"I read his report. He said he had no choice but to leave his landing party behind until he could regroup and determine what he was up against. He also said the party wouldn't have survived without the courage of its ranking officer."

Garrett shrugged. "I was in charge, sir. I did what anyone would have done in my place."

"As I recall," said McAteer, "you did a bit more than that. When you saw that the Orazwari were getting close to your hiding place, you led them in another direction single-handedly—risking your own life so that the crewmen in your care could survive."

"Most of them were wounded," she explained. "They weren't in any shape to lead the Orazwari away."

"Nonetheless," said the admiral, "a remarkable effort. And all the more remarkable when one considers the fact that you survived."

"I was lucky, sir."

"I don't believe that for a minute," he told Garrett, "and unless I'm mistaken, neither do you." He leaned back in his chair and regarded his monitor screen, which the commander couldn't see. "After all, this isn't the first time you've demonstrated remarkable courage or inventiveness. In fact, you've pretty much made a habit of it."

Garrett didn't seem to know how to respond to that.

"You know," said McAteer, approaching the real reason he had arranged to see her, "a woman with your extraordinary abilities should be moving up the chain of command. But I see that you've been a second officer for some time now."

His guest shrugged. "I like it on the *Excelsior.* It's a wonderful ship with a wonderful captain."

"So I understand," the admiral told her. "And I don't doubt that he values your services. But your fleet would benefit more if you were to make a change."

Garrett looked at him askance. "Such as?"

"Second officer on another ship."

Her brow creased ever so slightly. "I don't understand, sir. I'm *already* a second officer."

"Of course you are," said McAteer. "But on the *Excelsior,* there aren't any opportunities for advancement. Whereas, if you were to make a lateral move to another ship . . . you might find such opportunities materializing before you know it."

Garrett looked at him. "Is this a hypothetical question? Or did you have a ship in mind?"

"I have a ship in mind, all right. But for the moment, I prefer to conduct our conversation as if we *were* speaking hypothetically."

"I see," the commander said.

"So what would you do," the admiral asked, "if I were to say that I could arrange a berth for you on another vessel . . . where you would be the recipient of a captaincy in a short amount of time?"

Garrett looked tempted—just as he had predicted. "A captaincy," she said. "That would be quite a move."

"Are you saying you don't deserve it? Or that you're not eminently capable of commanding a starship?"

"I'm saying it would be most unusual, sir. In fact, this entire conversation strikes me as most unusual. I find myself asking why a Starfleet admiral would go to the trouble of meeting me out here in the hinterlands, much less making the kind of assurances you're making." She paused. "Hypothetical or otherwise."

McAteer smiled again. "You're a shrewd woman, Commander. But then, that doesn't surprise me in the least. If you were any less shrewd, I might be speaking with someone else."

"Obviously," said Garrett, "you want something. What is it?"

He continued smiling. "All I want is to help you help yourself—by supplying me with information on the officers with whom you'll share your new ship. When we've accumulated enough of it, I'll have them disciplined and stripped of their ranks. And you will move in to fill the breach created by their absence."

"And if I don't find anything objectionable?"

"You will," he told her. "Believe me."

Garrett seemed to consider the admiral's offer for a moment. Then she frowned. "Permission to speak freely, sir?"

McAteer held his arms out in an expression of magnanimity. "By all means, Commander."

His guest leaned forward. "I'll be blunt, Admiral. I want to move up in the world as much as anyone in the fleet—but not at the expense of other qualified officers."

"They're *not* qualified," he interjected.

Garrett chuckled. "Why don't I believe that?"

"You need to trust me," McAteer said.

"Sorry," she replied. "I don't. And just for the record, Admiral, I don't ever plan on allowing myself to be used as a political pawn—yours or anyone else's."

McAteer had the distinct impression that his offer had been spurned. *Imagine that,* he thought.

"I don't suppose it would make any difference if I sweetened the pot?" he said.

Garrett smiled stubbornly. "There's nothing sweet enough in this galaxy to make me your puppet, Admiral."

McAteer scowled. Obviously, this conversation wasn't going anywhere. There was just one thing left to do.

"I'm sorry we couldn't help each other, Commander. I think you'll come to regret that in time. But in any case, what we've discussed here today is not for public consumption. If I learn that you've even mentioned this conversation to anyone—and I mean *anyone*—you'll be drummed out of the fleet. Understood?"

"What I understand," Garrett said, "is that you'll probably drum me out of the fleet anyway. Otherwise I'll be a danger to you—someone who can expose you for what you are."

"Come now," the admiral told her. "Do you really think I'd leave myself open like that? We haven't mentioned a name, remember? We haven't even mentioned a ship. So what is there to expose?"

That seemed to give Garrett pause.

"Besides," he added, "this sort of maneuvering happens a lot more often than you might imagine. You might say it's the *business* of admirals to maneuver."

"Not being an admiral," she said, "I wouldn't know."

He couldn't resist a gibe after the way she'd refused him. "And you probably never will. Dismissed, Commander."

Garrett stared at McAteer for a moment. Then she got up and left the room.

A pity, the admiral thought. The second officer of the *Excelsior* had seemed like the perfect candidate for what he was trying to accomplish. The perfect inside informant—though she might have suggested a slightly different term for it.

McAteer sighed. He would just have to find someone else to torpedo Jean-Luc Picard.

Chapter Seven

ELIZABETH WU WAS A WOMAN OF HER WORD, even if no one had heard her give it.

Stopping in front of Ensign Jiterica's quarters, she touched the security pad in the bulkhead. A moment later, the doors parted and gave her access to what lay within.

As it turned out, the ensign was seated at her workstation, the blue glare of its screen superimposed over the gray, vaguely human face she effected. Though her chair was bigger than the standard, she looked uncomfortable in her containment suit. Cramped, Wu thought.

"Hello," she said.

"Hello," Jiterica echoed.

"Doing some reading?"

The ensign paused for a moment before answering. "I am not accessing the sensors."

Wu waved away the notion. "I wasn't accusing you of anything."

"Then why are you here?" Jiterica asked.

The second officer shrugged. "If you have no plans tonight, I thought you might like to join me for dinner."

Jiterica looked at her. "I don't eat."

It hadn't occurred to Wu to consider that possibility. "You must eat *something*," she said.

The ensign pointed to a valve on her containment suit—one that the second officer hadn't noticed before. "This mechanism allows me to create an aperture in my containment field. Through it, I can ingest air molecules, which my body is able to break down into their component atoms and use as sustenance."

Wu nodded. "I see. But humans—and a great many other species— don't just go to the mess hall to eat. We go to socialize, to—" She searched for the right word.

"Commune?" Jiterica suggested.

Wu breathed a sigh of relief. "Yes. May I assume that your people have an equivalent activity?"

"We gather in groups at certain times of day," the ensign explained. "We share experiences."

"That's exactly what I'm talking about," Wu said. "Even though your planet and your people are far away, you need to commune with someone. You need to share your experiences."

Jiterica seemed to absorb the advice. However, there was no indication in the cast of her ghostly features as to whether the second officer had swayed her.

"What do you think?" Wu asked, trying not to be too pushy. "Would you like to give it a try?"

The ensign considered it for a moment longer. Then she said, "When would you like to do this?"

Wu smiled. "I'll meet you back here as soon as our shifts are over. How does that sound?"

"As soon as our shifts are over," Jiterica echoed.

As the second officer left the Nizhrak's quarters, she felt a distinct sense of accomplishment. And for good reason.

She was about to make a difference in someone's life. She had convinced a lonely outsider to take the first step on a journey of immense personal enrichment.

Even after she was gone, she thought, Jiterica would remember the woman who had helped her find her place on the *Stargazer*.

Nikolas was sitting at the computer station he shared with his roommate, going over his new schedule of assignments, when he heard the sound of chimes.

Someone was calling on him. He hoped it was Obal.

After all, the Binderian had promised to try to get him a sparring session with Idun Asmund. And when Nikolas had looked his friend up at the end of his shift, the computer had informed him that Obal wasn't in his quarters.

He was in Idun's.

"Come in," said Nikolas, rising to his feet.

The doors opened and Obal entered. "Nikolas," he said, greeting the ensign exactly as he usually did.

"There you are," said Nikolas. "How did it go?"

He could tell from the change in the Binderian's expression that he wouldn't like the answer to his question. "Not well, my friend."

"What happened?" the ensign asked.

Obal shrugged his narrow shoulders. "Lieutenant Asmund declined your invitation to spar."

Nikolas was disappointed. Obviously, the woman was intimidated by the prospect of fighting with him.

"Maybe it would help," he said, "if you promised her I would go easy on her."

The Binderian didn't look very optimistic. "I doubt it."

Nikolas considered the lack of enthusiasm in his friend's response. "It's worth a try, isn't it?"

Obal's expression told the ensign he didn't think so.

"Okay," said Nikolas. "I'll tell her myself."

"She will not agree," Obal told him.

"We'll see about that," the ensign replied. And with that, he left his friend to pay a visit to Idun Asmund.

Gilaad Ben Zoma had met Tanya Tresh on his first day at Starfleet Academy.

Though their relationship had begun as a heated love affair, it had cooled off more quickly than either of them would have imagined, and settled into the kind of warm, intimate friendship only former lovers could enjoy.

Unfortunately, Ben Zoma hadn't actually seen his friend Tanya in more than a year. But then, he was the first officer of the *Stargazer,* and she was doing what she had always wanted to do—serving as an exobiologist on a Starfleet research vessel.

Still, they corresponded often by subspace packet. Usually it was just to say hello or send news of a mutual acquaintance. But this time, Ben Zoma had contacted his friend for a different reason.

"Gilaad," she said, as beautiful as ever beneath a fashionable pile of long, blond hair. "It was good to hear from you as always—even if all you wanted was to pick my brain."

The first officer smiled. Once, he had had other things in mind, but those days were long past. And Tanya did possess the particular expertise he needed.

"I don't know why you've suddenly developed such an interest in this subject, but here's your answer," she said. And she went on to tell him exactly what he wanted to know.

Ben Zoma frowned. He hadn't expected good news, but this was even worse than he had imagined.

"I hope that helps," Tanya told him. "Take care. And say hello to your pal Jean-Luc for me. I always did have a soft spot for Frenchmen."

Ben Zoma was so occupied with the information she had given him, he barely took notice of her teasing. He sat there for a moment as his friend's face gave way to the Starfleet insignia.

Then he got up and made his way to the captain's ready room.

Commander Wu looked around the surprisingly crowded mess hall for some open seats. Finding a couple at the far end of the room, she turned to her companion and pointed.

"We can sit there," she suggested.

Ensign Jiterica turned the transparent faceplate of her containment suit in the indicated direction. "If you say so," she responded, her voice as flat and tinny as ever.

"Good," said the second officer, making a conscious effort to sound cheerful for Jiterica's sake. "Let's go." And she led the way, threading a path between two rows of tables.

Glancing over her shoulder, she made sure that the ensign was following her. After all, Jiterica hadn't looked eager to accompany her here in the first place. And whenever Wu happened to glance at the Nizhrak's ghostly features, she had seen indications of uncertainty and trepidation.

On the other hand, that might not have meant anything. Wu wasn't one of the exobiologists who had worked with Jiterica at the Academy. She didn't know whether there was any real correlation between the Nizhrak's expression and her emotional state.

For that matter, Wu couldn't be sure Jiterica's people were even capable of emotion. Could they feel loyalty? Gratitude? Disappointment? Only Jiterica could answer those questions with any confidence.

Wu had believed that the ensign's actions back in the science section had their roots in a feeling of loneliness. But even that assumption might have been in error—a case of a human interpreting an alien's behavior on the basis of her own.

All the more reason for me to get to know Jiterica, the second officer told herself. *If I can reach her, understand her, I can help others to do the same.*

As she and her charge approached their seats, Wu became aware that they were being watched—and not just by a few crewmen here and there. Nearly everyone in the mess hall was staring at them, perhaps wondering what Jiterica was doing here.

Wu wondered if the ensign was aware of the scrutiny. For her sake, the commander hoped not.

"Here we are," she said, pulling out a chair for the Nizhrak. "Go ahead and sit down."

Jiterica studied the chair as if it were a rare celestial phenomenon, something she had never seen before. Then she tried to turn her suit around and settle into it.

It was a difficult maneuver—much more difficult than Wu would have thought. After all, Jiterica hadn't seemed to have any trouble sitting down in the science section or in her quarters.

But now that the commander thought about it, those places had swivel chairs without armrests. None of the chairs in the mess hall were of the swivel variety and they *all* had armrests. She bit her lip, wishing she had anticipated the problem before she invited the ensign to have dinner with her.

But she hadn't. She had acted blithely, confident that her good intentions would be sufficient. And now the ensign was paying the price for her shortsightedness, striving with the chair as if she were wrestling a *mugato.*

Wu looked around and saw people wincing in sympathy with Jiterica's efforts. She had to wince a little herself.

Finally, the ensign inserted her suit securely between the armrests. But her trials weren't over, because she then had to turn the chair around and slip it under the table.

Wu did her best to help, but it was still an arduous task. It took a full minute for the two of them to pivot Jiterica's chair ninety degrees and push it up to the table. And even then, she didn't look comfortable.

The containment suit was too bulky to permit much movement, so the Nizhrak just sat there as if she were paralyzed.

Fortunately, she didn't *need* to move. As Jiterica had pointed out to the second officer in her quarters, she didn't take in nutrients the way that humanoids did.

Walking around the table, Wu sat down opposite her companion. It was then that she received an answer to at least one of her questions about the ensign.

Jiterica's face, pale and insubstantial-looking as it was, showed definite signs of embarrassment. Her brow was pinched and her eyes moved from one onlooker to another, making it clear that she was all too aware of them.

"So," said Wu, "how do you like it on the ship so far?"

The ensign looked at her. "I have no complaints."

It wasn't the kind of response Wu had hoped for. Obviously, this was going to take some work.

"You've been in every section of the ship by now," the commander noted. "You must have made some pretty interesting observations."

Jiterica seemed to weigh the remark for a long time. "I have made observations," she agreed at last. "However, it is difficult for me to say which of them you may find interesting."

Wu shrugged. "Try me."

The Nizhrak's ghost-visage frowned. "All right. Two days ago, I was assigned to the security section."

The second officer recalled the assignment. But then, one of her duties was to put together the weekly training schedules for all junior officers serving on the *Stargazer.*

"When I arrived, Lieutenant Joseph was engaged in phaser practice. Rather than interrupt him, which I thought would be rude, I stood and watched him."

Wu nodded. "And?"

"And," Jiterica continued, "I saw that his aim left something to be desired. Though his objective was to hit the center of his target, he occasionally missed."

The commander waited for the ensign to go on. But she didn't. She just sat there.

It was only after they had stared at each other in silence for several long seconds that the commander realized something: Jiterica had come to the end of her story.

"Really," said Wu, trying her best to seem enthusiastic.

"Yes," Jiterica replied.

"Any . . . other observations?" Wu asked hopefully.

With an effort, the Nizhrak extracted a handful from memory. However, none of them was any more entertaining than the first one. In fact, a couple were actually less so.

"How about that," said Wu.

Jiterica's eyes seemed to narrow. For a moment, the second officer had the feeling that her companion was onto her—that Jiterica had realized how uninteresting her stories were and how hard Wu was working to make it seem otherwise.

Then the ensign said, "You should eat, Commander. Otherwise, you'll be hungry when you start your next shift."

Wu *was* getting hungry—and she had a not-so-inexplicable desire to stretch her legs. "I'll tell you what," she told her companion. "You wait here and I'll be back in a moment or two."

"Agreed," said Jiterica.

As the commander got up and headed for the replicator slot, she considered the size of the gap she was trying to bridge in inviting the Nizhrak to dinner. Too large, perhaps.

But she wasn't about to give up. If there was a way to relate to Jiterica, a way to make her feel more at home here on the *Stargazer,* Wu was going to find it.

And she was going to do it *before* she claimed her post on the *Crazy Horse.*

Chapter Eight

As Jiterica made her way down the corridor, most of her attention was focused on coaxing her containment suit forward in a rhythm that accommodated ambulation.

She gave the rest of it to Commander Wu, who was walking alongside her. "Yes," she said, answering the question the second officer had just asked her, in a way calculated to spare Wu's feelings. "I *did* find our dinner a worthwhile experience."

"Good," Wu returned. "We'll have to do it again sometime."

But Jiterica didn't think that the human was quite as eager as her comment indicated. In fact, she was reasonably certain of it.

"Yes," Jiterica agreed, trying to be polite.

Truthfully, she hadn't been optimistic about the idea of a dinner exercise in the first place. However, she had gone along with it, partly to please the commander and partly to see if it might actually have a beneficial effect.

But from the moment Jiterica saw the chair in which she would be sitting, she suspected that she had made a mistake. And when she caught the look on Wu's face and realized how uninteresting the commander found her stories, she was sure of it.

She had been foolish to imagine that she could ever relate to humanoids the way they related to each other. Even species as divergent as Pandrilites and Gnalish might find a common ground here on the *Stargazer,* but not a being compelled to wear a containment suit merely to get around.

"See you later," said Wu.

"Yes," Jiterica responded. "Later."

The second officer's intentions had been good ones. The Nizhrak had no doubt of that. But they could never become friends.

Jiterica was gratified by the knowledge that she was making a contribution as a member of the crew. To expect anything more than that was simply unrealistic.

She watched Wu vanish around a bend in the corridor and recalled what real companionship had been like—how easy it had been, how effortless. Perhaps someday she would know such companionship again.

But not here, Jiterica thought. *Not on the* Stargazer.

Nikolas found the person he was looking for in the ship's gymnasium. *As if she would have been anywhere else,* he mused as he walked into the high-ceilinged chamber.

Idun was working out on the parallel bars, swinging her long legs back and forth with apparently effortless grace and precision. And as if that didn't make her tantalizing enough, she was wearing a form-fitting black warm-up suit that accentuated every luscious weapon in her arsenal.

The ensign didn't say anything right away. He just walked up to the bars and watched with undisguised admiration.

After a while, Idun noticed him. Finishing her routine with a simple side dismount, she went to the towel she had left on the floor and dried herself off. Then she glanced at him.

"Is there something I can do for you?" she asked.

"Well," said Nikolas, "our mutual friend Obal tells me you've decided not to spar with me."

Asmund nodded. "That's correct."

"I understand," he told her. "You're concerned that you'll get hurt. But I'm here to tell you that you needn't worry. I'm used to sparring with weaker opponents."

Her eyes narrowed. "Really."

"That's right," Nikolas assured her. "And if I can pull my punches for them, I can pull them for you, too."

The helm officer nodded. "I see."

"So," he went on, "there's really no reason not to—"

"Name the time and place," she said, interrupting him in the middle of his pitch.

Nikolas smiled. "Really? I mean . . . great. How about tomorrow, after second shift?"

Asmund's eyes seemed to glitter. "Fine."

"And afterward," he suggested, pushing his luck, "a cup of coffee in the rec? And a little friendly conversation?"

Her mouth pulled up at the corners, making her look even more desirable. "One thing at a time," she advised him.

The ensign was perfectly willing to go along with that. "One thing at a time," he agreed.

"I'll see you tomorrow, then."

"Absolutely," he told her. "Tomorrow."

Nikolas watched the doors to the lieutenant's quarters slide shut. Then, rather pleased with himself, he started to retrace his steps along the corridor.

This is good, he mused. This is very good. And it wasn't anywhere near as difficult as he had thought it would be.

Wouldn't Obal be surprised.

As soon as his shift was over, Ulelo returned to his quarters, stretched out across his bed and tried his best to concentrate on his mission. However, it was difficult to do so. Thoughts of Emily Bender kept intruding.

He had no reason to doubt that she had known him at the Academy as she had claimed. His memories of that time were incomplete, hazy at best. All he remembered was what he had learned in his classes.

It hadn't bothered Ulelo that it should be so. But it had bothered Emily Bender. It had bothered her a lot.

The question was . . . what would she do with her resentment? Would she discuss the matter with her fellow science officers? Would they think it strange that the junior comm officer couldn't—or wouldn't—acknowledge the experiences he had shared with Emily Bender?

And would the story spread eventually to Captain Picard and his command staff, raising doubts in their mind as to Ulelo's character . . . if not his sanity?

He couldn't afford that.

But what could he do about it? How could he keep Emily Bender from shining a light on his odd behavior?

He had barely posed the question when he heard the chimes that told him someone was standing in the corridor outside his quarters. Ulelo sat up on his bed and wondered who it might be. After all, no one had called on him before.

"Come in," he said. Then he left his bedroom and entered the smaller enclosure that served as an anteroom—just in time to see the doors part and reveal Emily Bender.

"May I come in?" she asked.

Ulelo frowned. "I don't—"

Before he could get the rest out, she slipped past him. "Thanks a bunch, Dikembe."

As the doors to his quarters hissed closed behind him, Ulelo watched his unwanted visitor take a look around. After a moment or two, she seemed disappointed.

"You know," she said, "I was hoping to find something from the Academy so I could pin you down. But you don't seem to have anything of that sort on display here." She turned to look at him. "Still, it's you. I know—I found your name in the personnel files."

Ulelo sighed. "Maybe we did know each other at the Academy. It's certainly possible—I met lots of people there. It's just that I don't remember you."

Emily Bender's eyes narrowed. "I don't believe you. We were a tight-knit group. Maybe we haven't kept up with each other very well, but there's no way you could have forgotten me."

He shrugged. "I'm sorry, but I—"

She put her forefinger to his mouth, silencing him. "Don't, Dikembe. I don't know why you're trying to give me the brush-off, but it's not going to work."

Ulelo moved her finger away from his lips. "It's not a brush-off. I just don't remember."

Emily Bender smiled. "Do you believe in Fate, Dikembe?"

He frowned. "What does that have to do with—"

Her finger slid back across his lips. "You probably don't know this, but I had a crush on you back at the Academy. A *big* crush, and I always regretted not doing anything about it. Then I saw you in the corridor and I realized that I'd been given some kind of second chance."

Before he knew it, before he could say or do a thing to stop her, Emily Bender slipped her arms around his neck and kissed him. He couldn't say he didn't enjoy it. She was a woman, after all, and a rather attractive woman at that.

But Ulelo wasn't in a position to follow his instincts. Removing her arms from his neck, he shook his head.

"You're making a mistake," he said.

She looked at him disbelievingly. "What—?"

"A mistake," he repeated. "I'm going to have to ask you to leave."

Emily Bender stared at him for a moment longer. Then, her cheeks flushed with embarrassment, she said in an injured voice, "All right. If that's the way you want it."

And she left Ulelo standing there in his quarters, feeling that he hadn't merely failed to solve his problem. Somehow, he had increased the complexity of it.

Picard looked at his first officer as they stood in his ready room. "You did *what?*"

Ben Zoma shrugged. "I contacted my friend Tanya, who studied the Gnalish a number of years ago."

The captain winced. *"Please* tell me you didn't speak to her about Simenon."

"Actually," Ben Zoma said a little sheepishly, "I did. I wanted to find out what he was holding back from us."

Picard held his hands out in an appeal for reason. "Gilaad, that is *precisely* what he asked us *not* to do."

Ben Zoma nodded. "I know. I butted into his business. I betrayed the trust of a friend and a fellow officer."

"To say the least," Picard told him.

"But I may also have saved his miserable life."

That brought the captain up short. "What do you mean?"

Ben Zoma explained. In detail.

Picard frowned as he realized what his engineer was up against. The odds against him were considerable. But that didn't excuse what his first officer had done.

"We agreed not to pry into Simenon's affairs," Picard said. "You and I both. For pity's sake, we gave him our *word.*"

"So," Ben Zoma responded matter-of-factly, "does that mean you're not going to talk with him?"

The captain wrestled with the question. Finally, he came to the only conclusion possible. "Simenon is going to hate us for lying to him," he told his first officer.

"I know," Ben Zoma conceded. "But if you can't depend on your *friends* to lie to you, who *can* you depend on?"

Picard grunted. *Who indeed?*

Admiral McAteer sat back in his chair and tapped the rim of the bar glass on the table beside him. The previously clear liquid inside the glass began blushing with a host of different colors.

The admiral smiled appreciatively. "Best damned Samarian Sunset I ever saw. If it tastes as good as it looks, we're all set."

Of course, there was no answer. The replicator that had produced the cocktail had no more to say in response to his remark than any other inanimate object in the room.

McAteer didn't mind in the least. The truth was he *liked* being by himself once in a while.

Not everyone understood that, he thought, as he picked up the Sunset and conveyed it to his lips. Just because he was good with people, because he could *influence* them, didn't mean he wanted to be surrounded by them all the time.

The cocktail was sour and dusky sweet and a little bitter all at the same time, a riot of unexpectedly complementary tastes. And it went to his head like an exploding photon torpedo, exactly the way it was supposed to.

"Perfect," the admiral said out loud. "My compliments to the bartender." His words of praise echoed in the room for a moment, then faded to nothing.

He didn't normally drink by himself, especially when he was on a starship far from home. On the other hand, he seldom found himself in such a good mood.

Finding someone to undermine Picard hadn't been as simple as he had expected it would be. He had begun to realize that after he failed to enlist the services of Rachel Garrett.

After that, McAteer had felt the need to be careful. *Very* careful.

Any other strategy would invite the possibility of yet another second officer turning down his offer, and in that case he would be asking for trouble. The admiral was confident that Garrett, at least, wouldn't say anything about their discussion. But someone with less control or common sense might flap his jaws at the wrong time and expose McAteer's vendetta.

If it became common knowledge that he was after someone for personal reasons, it would be a difficult matter to explain away. He could ill afford that kind of embarrassment at this critical juncture in his Starfleet career.

So the admiral had resolved that his next attempt would be a successful one. That meant putting a lot more work into the winnowing-out process. A lot more research.

More than once, he had come close to his goal—or thought he had. But time after time, there had been something about the candidate that forced McAteer to rule him or her out.

Some weren't ambitious enough. Some were *too* ambitious. Some were too righteous while others couldn't be trusted, and still others simply lacked what it took to command a starship.

At one point, the admiral thought he had found his man in the person of Donald Varley, second officer on the *Invincible*. Varley had started out as a fast-tracker just like Picard, a fellow who would inevitably be placed in command of a starship.

Then he had slipped off the fast track by offending a superior officer. Judging from what McAteer had read of the incident, it wasn't really Varley's fault. Nonetheless, it had gone against him.

The experience appeared to make Varley a little more cynical—and a great deal more practical. McAteer got the impression that the fellow would compromise a few ethics if it meant obtaining the captaincy he had always wanted.

In the admiral's mind, Varley had been perfect—perhaps even more perfect than Rachel Garrett.

He had been all set to approach Varley with his offer. Then he had discovered one more tidbit of information—that Varley and Picard had become the best of friends in their last year at the Academy.

So much for perfect.

But McAteer hadn't given up. He had continued to rifle through personnel file after personnel file—and finally, his work had paid off. He found a candidate he believed would not only embrace his plan but act discreetly in carrying it out.

Then and only then had he made arrangements to meet the fellow at a mutually convenient starbase—the one he was headed for now, Samarian Sunset well in hand.

"It's only a matter of time now," the admiral told himself gleefully. "Only a matter of time."

And if his assessment wasn't greeted with encouragement, neither was it met with skepticism. But then, that was the way it went when one conversed in an empty room.

Chapter Nine

IN HIS SMALL BUT NEATLY KEPT OFFICE in sickbay, Carter Greyhorse considered what he was about to do. Then he tapped his combadge and said, "Greyhorse to Gerda Asmund."

The navigator's response came a moment later—from her quarters, according to the ship's computer. "Asmund here. What is it, Doctor?"

She still called him that—*Doctor* instead of Carter or even Greyhorse. Even in the aftermath of their most exhausting lessons, when they were both standing there on the gym floor with their chests heaving and their faces flushed and the musky scent of Gerda's sweat like perfume in his nostrils . . . even then, it was *Doctor.*

"It appears I won't be able to make our lesson this week," Greyhorse informed her.

He listened carefully for the tone of her reaction. *Please,* he thought, *give me a crumb. Even a hint of disappointment.*

"Oh?" Gerda said.

"I'm going on an away mission," he elaborated.

"In the next few days?"

"Yes," Greyhorse told her.

In fact, all chief medical officers went on away missions at one time

or another, so there was nothing inherently impressive about his announcement. But this was the doctor's first such mission since joining
the *Stargazer.*

"I haven't been apprised of any away mission," she said, a hint of
annoyance in her voice. "Is it classified?"

"It's not," Greyhorse assured her. And he described the endeavor in
broad strokes, trying his best to wring some mystery and importance
out of them.

Gerda chuckled, making his heart sink. "Oh, *that.* I wouldn't call it
much of an away mission."

"There's danger involved," the doctor maintained. "I've been warned
to expect casualties."

"Casualties?" she echoed.

He licked his lips. "Yes. The captain informed me that they were a
distinct possibility."

Gerda paused, causing Greyhorse's heart to soar. Was it possible that
she was actually *worried* about him? Was she perhaps wondering how
she might feel if he didn't come back?

"Tell me more," Gerda said curtly.

The doctor savored the words as he might an exotic elixir. Then he
did as the navigator asked.

Picard regarded the peaceful-looking sphere pictured on his
viewscreen, half of its surface brilliant with sunlight and the other half
blanketed in shadow.

He had never seen this particular world before, but he had seen others
very much like it. In fact, it was a good deal like his native Earth except
for the predominance of red-leafed vegetation that gave its landmasses
their striking crimson color.

"We've established orbit, sir," Gerda announced.

Picard nodded. "Thank you, Lieutenant." He glanced at Ulelo. "Contact the authorities, Lieutenant. Let them know we're here."

"Aye, sir," said the comm officer.

Next, the captain addressed his second officer, who was waiting patiently beside his center seat. "Commander Wu," he said, "you've got
the bridge."

Wu inclined her head slightly. "Acknowledged, sir."

Picard had already briefed her thoroughly on his intentions. If she
had had any questions, she would have asked them then.

He got up from his seat and headed for the turbolift. But before he could get there, he heard Wu say, "Captain?"

Surprised, he turned back to her. "Yes, Commander?"

She smiled. At least, it *looked* like a smile. "Good luck."

"Thank you," said Picard.

If his luck were *really* good, Wu would have been remaining with him on the *Stargazer* instead of returning to the *Crazy Horse*. But the captain didn't tell her that.

Instead, he entered the turbolift, watched the doors close, and punched in his destination. Then he waited for the compartment to take him to Transporter Room Two.

Phigus Simenon stood in the corridor outside his quarters, watched the duranium doors hiss closed behind him, and frowned at the thought that he might never see this place again.

Not that he was leaving behind the most *comfortable* living arrangement in the galaxy. At best, his suite was plain and uninspired, just like that of every other officer on the ship. At worst, it was poorly designed for someone of his size and physiology, not to mention his unique esthetic preferences.

But Simenon had called his quarters home, however briefly. He had looked forward to remaining in them for a while as a key component of the *Stargazer*'s command staff. And for that reason, he was reluctant to put the place behind him.

On the other hand, there was nothing he could do about the situation. He had received the summons. It was time to go.

Turning, he made his way down the corridor. But as much as he would have liked to reach the nearest turbolift without running into anyone en route, he hadn't even reached the first bend before two of his engineers appeared in front of him.

Urajel and Dubinski. The pair who had borne the brunt of his tirade a few days earlier.

Simenon put his head down and tried to walk past them. He desperately didn't want to engage them in conversation right now. He didn't want to engage *anyone* in conversation.

But of course, Urajel and Dubinski didn't know that.

"Sir?" said Dubinski.

I'm going to walk right past him, Simenon told himself. *I'm going to put my head down and pretend he doesn't exist.*

But of course, he couldn't do that. No matter how much he wanted to avoid contact with anyone, Dubinski was one of his engineers. If the man had something to say, it was Simenon's job to listen.

At least until he reached the transporter room.

"Yes?" he responded.

Dubinski shrugged. "I just wanted to apologize. I thought about what you said in engineering the other day." He glanced at Urajel. "We all did. And we came to the conclusion that you were right."

Simenon looked at him. "I was? I mean . . . of course I was."

Urajel nodded, her antennae dipping in the process. "No matter how many times we checked the warp core, we shouldn't have assumed there was nothing to worry about. Just as we shouldn't have assumed the computer was on top of the situation."

"And," Dubinski added, "while irreparable core failure is rare without an apparent cause, I'm sure there are causes out there we've never even heard of."

"In short," said Urajel, "we acknowledge our errors and we're going to try to do better." Her face turned a deeper shade of blue. "And I personally regret the—"

"Question you asked?" Simenon suggested, getting her off the hook. "About my hindquarters and what might have invaded them?"

Urajel nodded stiffly. "Yes, sir."

Normally, the chief engineer would have simply accepted their apology and moved on. But as he didn't believe he would be the chief engineer much longer, he said, "Don't give it a second thought. *Any* of it."

Dubinski looked perplexed. "I beg your pardon, sir?"

Simenon dismissed it all with a snap of his wrist. "You did fine, all of you. I was holding you to an unreasonable standard." He eyed Urajel in particular. "And for your information, something *had* crawled up my hindquarters—a personal matter. It was astute of you to notice."

Neither engineer seemed to know what to say to that. Taking unexpected pleasure in the looks on their faces, the Gnalish walked around them and resumed his trek to the transporter room.

If he wasn't coming back to the *Stargazer,* he thought, he would at least leave here with his conscience in good shape.

Ensign Nikolas put his tray full of food down on the table in front of him and pulled up a chair.

"Man," he said, "those replicator lines seem to get longer every day. Is the captain taking on new crewmen in secret or something?"

His friend Obal, who was sitting across the black plastic table from him, chuckled good-naturedly. "If he is, he is keeping it secret from me as well."

Nikolas savored the smell of his salmon in béarnaise sauce. And who did he have to thank for it? His old roommate, Joe Caber. It was Caber who had advised him to trust the mess hall's replicator and try some of the more challenging dishes.

Caber wasn't all *bad,* the ensign told himself archly. *Just* mostly.

He wondered what Caber would have said if he knew Nikolas had convinced Idun Asmund to spar with him. More than likely, the guy's jaw would have dropped—just as Obal's was going to.

Nikolas was still thinking about his old roommate when his new one walked into the mess hall. Paris wasn't alone, either. He was accompanied by Lt. Paxton and Lt. Pierzynski, the latter being the number two officer in Pug Joseph's security section.

And Paris had only beamed aboard a couple of days ago. "Like I said," he muttered, "the guy doesn't waste any time."

"Of whom are you speaking?" asked Obal, who wasn't facing the entrance to the mess hall as Nikolas was.

"Paris. My roommate."

"Ah," said the Binderian. He swiveled in his chair and spotted the newcomer as he joined the end of the replicator line. "Ensign Paris is quite impressive."

Nikolas wasn't certain he had heard right. He looked at his friend questioningly. "Excuse me?"

"He's quite impressive," Obal repeated. He twirled some spaghetti around his fork. "Quite innovative."

Nikolas looked at the Binderian as he deposited the cluster of spaghetti into his mouth. It wasn't like his friend to use words like "impressive" and "innovative."

"Why do you say that?" the ensign asked.

Obal shrugged. "I heard Gerda Asmund say so. And the captain as well. I have no reason to doubt their judgment."

Nikolas frowned. "The *captain* said Paris was impressive?"

The Binderian nodded. "He did."

"In what way?"

"In the way he participates in a sport called fencing," Obal explained.

"Apparently, he presented Captain Picard with a considerable challenge in that regard."

"Did Paris beat him?" Nikolas asked.

"It was never made clear to me who won. Only that the competitors were more or less evenly matched."

The ensign's frown deepened. "The captain was probably being generous, that's all. Gerda, too."

Obal seemed to find the comment interesting. He cocked his head to one side. "Is this an example of what humans refer to as jealousy?"

Nikolas made a sound of disdain. "What are you talking about?"

"You're normally generous with your praise for people, my friend. However, in Ensign Paris's case, you are denigrating his accomplishments. This suggests that you are jealous of him."

"Does it really?" asked Nikolas. He chuckled to show Obal how off base he was. "I'd only be jealous of Ensign Paris if *he* was sparring with Idun Asmund instead of *me*."

The Binderian looked surprised. In fact, he looked *exactly* the way Nikolas had expected him to look. "Are you saying you convinced Lieutenant Asmund to meet you, after all?"

The ensign nodded. "It wasn't even all that difficult."

Obal made a face. "I'm not sure this is wise, my friend."

"You're concerned that someone might get hurt," Nikolas speculated.

"Well," said the security officer, "yes."

The ensign dismissed the possibility with a wave of his hand. "I already discussed that with Idun and it's not going to happen, so don't give it a second thought."

Obal frowned. "You're sure?"

Nikolas nodded. "Absolutely."

He shot a glance in Paris's direction. His roommate was describing what looked like a space battle to Paxton and Pierzynski, who watched him with rapt expressions.

Jealous indeed, Nikolas thought, and let his mind drift in the direction of his appointment with the beautiful Idun Asmund.

As Simenon approached the double doors of the transporter room, he was pretty certain that the captain would be waiting for him inside. Probably Ben Zoma as well.

After all, he was leaving them. And though they didn't have any inkling of how permanent that departure might be, they had to know he wasn't looking forward to what he was facing on Gnala and would therefore want to wish him luck.

The doors whispered apart for him as he came in range of an unseen sensor. They seemed a little sluggish, though. *I should have someone check the trigger mechanism,* Simenon reflected.

And then he remembered—more than likely, that would be someone else's problem, not his.

The hard, unyielding nature of that reality stuck in his throat like a bone. Still, the engineer managed to swallow it back and enter the transporter room, his eyes trained on the floor so he wouldn't have to face anyone until the last possible second.

Finally, when he believed he had almost reached the transporter pad, he looked up. After all, he had to say his good-byes.

But to his surprise, the hexagonal platform was already occupied. The captain and four of Simenon's colleagues were standing on it in rugged civilian clothing.

It took the engineer a second to figure out what was going on. Once he had done that, he shook his head emphatically from side to side. "No, you don't," he rasped at them. "I'm going down to Gnala alone. This is none of your business."

"Wrong on both counts," Greyhorse told him flatly. "And that's the advice of your physician."

"We're your friends," Vigo said.

"Yes," Picard chipped in. "And this is a time when you need your friends around you."

"Come on," Ben Zoma advised him. "Lighten up." His expression turned arch. "That's an order."

Joseph didn't say anything. He just smiled.

Simenon took a deep breath and let it out again. He had never been so touched in his entire life—not that he would ever say so. But what his friends were doing wasn't right. They didn't have any idea of what they were getting into.

"You're all proud of yourselves," he observed, "aren't you? You think you're going to save me from a grisly end. But all you're going to do is get yourselves killed along with me."

"Nice speech," Greyhorse told him.

"Very nice," said Picard. "Now get on the platform and let's get this over with."

"Fools," Simenon spat.

"Careful," said Ben Zoma. "We don't like you *that* much." But the Gnalish knew the human didn't mean it.

Obviously, there was no dissuading them. Swearing under his breath, Simenon climbed onto the platform and took an empty spot. Then he turned to Refsland, the transporter operator on duty, and uttered a single word.

"Energize."

Chapter Ten

ONCE, SHORTLY AFTER PICARD had been accepted at Starfleet Academy, someone had told him that a man in a transporter could actually feel his molecules being dismantled and zapped through space.

Nothing could have been further from the truth.

There was no awareness of the process, no sensation associated with it. One moment, you were in one place. A moment later, you were somewhere else. It was that simple.

It's *so* simple, in fact, that it often surprised those unaccustomed to transporter travel. After all, they expected some intermediary state, some time to prepare oneself for the change in environment, and they didn't get even a fraction of a second in that regard.

Picard, on the other hand, had traveled by transporter more times than he could easily remember. But even a veteran of such travel could occasionally wish he had had a moment to prepare for what he was about to see.

He found himself wishing that now.

Ben Zoma whistled softly. "I've never seen anything like *this.*"

"Nor have I," Picard confessed.

"It's beautiful," Vigo observed.

Joseph nodded. "You can say that again."

They were in an immense stone chamber, one that seemed to soar skyward with irresistible grace and power and majesty. And every inch of it, every twisting column and fluted wall, was the deep, scarlet color of human blood.

There were no energy-powered lights that the captain could discern, neither globes nor open flames. The only apparent source of illumination was a series of towering, splinter-thin windows that filtered the planet's sunlight and cast it in long, elegant shafts on the smooth stone floor.

It took him a moment to realize that he and his away team weren't alone in the place. At the far end of the chamber, a ceremonial gathering of some kind stood in a slash of light.

Shading his eyes from the glare of the windows, Picard was able to make out six elderly, white-robed Gnalish surrounded by at least a dozen towering individuals in loose-fitting black garments. The larger figures wore their hoods drawn low over their faces, so the captain couldn't tell what they looked like underneath them. However, the image they brought to mind was that of a team of medieval executioners.

Impossible, Picard told himself. Gnala was a civilized world. Its government didn't execute anyone, even for capital crimes. Then he noticed the long, deadly-looking blades that seemed to grow out of the larger figures' black sleeves.

For a moment, neither the white-robed Gnalish nor their companions said a thing. They just stood there, eyeing the away team much as the away team was eyeing them.

Finally, one of the Gnalish whispered something to one of his colleagues, his voice too low for Picard to discern individual words. The whisper was returned, its echoes fading on the air. Finally, one of the white-robed figures made his way toward Simenon and his companions and extended a scaly finger in their direction.

His mouth twisting, he rasped a single word of accusation: "Offworlders!"

It sent the hooded ones rushing at the newcomers like a powerful black tide. Before the away team knew what was happening, it had been surrounded. The captain saw that their captors were every bit as big as Vigo.

And of course, they had those *blades* in their hands.

"Tell me Refsland got the coordinates wrong," Ben Zoma whispered.

Joseph shook his head. "No such luck, Commander."

"Don't move," Simenon told his comrades.

"Believe me," said Greyhorse, "I hadn't even considered it."

Picard found himself wishing that they had brought phaser pistols. But Ben Zoma's friend Tanya Tresh had been explicit about the need to leave such weapons behind.

"What now?" Joseph asked Simenon.

The engineer didn't answer him. He just watched and waited.

Slowly and with great dignity, the Gnalish in the white robes advanced across the scarlet stones of the floor. And as they moved, they made hushed comments one to the other.

By the time they stopped in front of the away team, Picard could see that one of the Gnalish—the one who had pointed to them and initiated the stampede of black hoods—had a sickle-like blue mark on the front of his robe. The captain guessed that this one enjoyed a higher rank than the others.

The Gnalish with the blue mark regarded Simenon, ignoring the four humans and the Pandrilite. "Who are they?" he hissed imperiously, indicating Picard and the others with a sweep of his spindly hand. "And why in the name of Magdalassar have they come?"

Picard glanced at his first officer. He had an uneasy feeling that Ben Zoma's friend Tanya hadn't told them *everything*.

Elizabeth Wu felt awkward in Captain Picard's chair.

She hadn't expected to feel that way. After all, she had been in command of the *Stargazer*'s bridge at least once a day since the moment she beamed aboard.

So why the change?

In her heart, Wu knew the answer. To that point, she had felt like a legitimate part of the *Stargazer*'s crew. She had felt like she belonged there. Now she had one foot out the door, her return to the *Crazy Horse* imminent. It made her feel like an intruder, an interloper who had no right commanding these people.

Of course, she was the only qualified second officer present. In the absence of her superiors she *had* to command the *Stargazer*, and her subordinates had to obey her. But Wu didn't feel right about it and she wouldn't blame her officers if *they* didn't feel right about it, either.

"Commander?" said Paxton, who had returned to the bridge only a few minutes earlier.

She turned to the comm officer. "Lieutenant?"

"I have a communication for you from Starfleet Command."

Command? "Put it through."

A moment later, the image of an admiral popped up on the viewscreen—a woman with long, gray hair gathered into a ponytail. She looked vaguely familiar to the second officer.

What was her name again? Reagan? Rayburn?

"This is Admiral Rayfield at Starbase Sixty-three," the admiral said, putting an end to the commander's speculation. She looked around the bridge. "Where's Captain Picard?"

"The captain," said Wu, "is on Gnala."

"What's he doing there?"

Wu frowned. She didn't want to make Picard look like the kind of officer who abandoned his ship to take care of personal matters, no matter how well-intentioned.

"He's pursuing a matter of some importance to the Gnalish," she said finally. "First Officer Ben Zoma went with him. I'm Commander Wu. May I be of assistance?"

"I'd rather speak with Captain Picard," the admiral insisted.

The second officer felt her spine stiffen. "Unfortunately," she said truthfully, "any attempt on our part to contact the captain would be seen as a breach of Gnalish custom. And even if we were to ignore that consideration, it might take a while to get hold of him."

Rayfield looked as if she were about to ask for details. After all, Wu's responses to that point had been rather vague. In the end, however, the admiral seemed willing to accept the situation at face value.

"All right," she said. "Commander Wu, you say?"

"That's correct, Admiral."

"An Andorian cargo vessel has relayed us a distress call from the *Belladonna,* a research vessel assigned to the Oneo Madrin system. Familiar with it?"

"I've heard of Oneo Madrin," Wu told Rayfield. "Unfortunately, I've never seen it firsthand."

Rayfield frowned. Obviously, it wasn't the answer she had been hoping for. "It's a binary system with an accretion bridge. You've seen those before, haven't you?"

"I have," the second officer assured her. "Twice, in fact. At Aescalapios and Wells-Parvat."

The admiral seemed to take some comfort in that. "Good. Then you know how tricky they can be."

"You think the *Belladonna* got too close?" Wu asked.

"It's a reasonable assumption in the absence of any real data. The *Belladonna*'s distress call was garbled, to say the least."

As would have been the case if the vessel's comm system had been damaged by unexpected radiation from the accretion bridge. And if her captain had called for help, communications probably wasn't the only system that had been damaged.

But if the *Belladonna*'s shields were functioning, her crew had a fighting chance. They could still be alive—as long as a rescue effort was launched in time.

Apparently, that was where the *Stargazer* came in.

"You're the closest Starfleet ship," said Rayfield. "You know how that works."

"I do," Wu replied.

"Keep me posted," said the admiral. "Rayfield out."

As the admiral's face vanished from the screen and was replaced by their view of Gnala, Wu turned to her helm officer.

"Lieutenant," she said, "take us out of this system."

"Aye," Idun replied.

The commander was under orders not to contact Picard and the away team. The captain had been crystal clear on that point. But with luck, they would be back before Simenon's ritual ordeal was over.

"Navigator," Wu said, "chart a course for the Oneo Madrin system." She watched Simenon's planet slide unceremoniously off the starboard side of the viewscreen. "Best speed."

"Charting," said Gerda, who had begun tapping out commands at her console as soon as she heard the admiral's orders.

Leaning back, the second officer took a deep breath. She would have ample opportunity to get comfortable in the captain's chair. After all, she was going to be seeing a lot of it.

Picard took his right leg, which had been lying across his left one for too long, and planted it on the floor. Then he picked up his left leg and laid it across his right.

Ben Zoma was sitting next to him on a ledge built into the wall. "So," he said, "how do you like your visit to Gnala *so* far?"

The captain frowned. "Just fine, Number One." He indicated the small, high-ceilinged chamber in which they had spent the last two hours. "I was *hoping* I'd be incarcerated in a windowless chamber while this region's Council of Elders—"

"Assemblage of Elders," Greyhorse interjected from his seat on the other side of the room.

"While this *Assemblage,"* Picard amended, "inflicts who-knows-what-sort of miseries on my chief engineer."

Pug Joseph, who had steadfastly refused to sit since they were herded here, shook his head. "I still can't believe those monsters in the black pajamas were Gnalish."

"I know what you mean," said Vigo, who sat beside the doctor with his massive arms folded across his chest. "I thought all Gnalish were small of stature like Mr. Simenon."

"You learn something new every day," Joseph remarked.

Suddenly, the door to the chamber creaked open. As the captain watched, he saw Simenon cross the threshold.

Picard sat up. "Where have you been?"

"Are you all right?" Joseph wanted to know.

"Of course I'm all right," the Gnalish told him. "No one's going to injure someone in my position."

Vigo grunted. "What did they tell you?"

Simenon made a sound of disgust. "They didn't tell me *anything."*

Picard looked at him. "Then where have you been all this time?"

The engineer scowled. "I've been meditating. So has the Assemblage—so when we finally discuss your presence here, we can do it rationally and with all of our arguments clear in our heads."

"And when will you make these arguments?" asked Greyhorse.

Simenon jerked his head in the direction of the open doorway. "That, I'm told, would be *now."*

Ulelo was aware of the conversation taking place around him as he sat in the mess hall, but he wasn't paying attention to it. He was too intent on what had taken place in his quarters a few short hours ago.

"Do you believe in Fate?" Emily Bender had asked.

He should have seen it coming, but he hadn't. He had stared at her, barely managing a protest.

"It was *Rayfield,"* said Paxton, Ulelo's superior in the communications section. He placed such an emphasis on the name that it broke in on Ulelo's reverie. "You know, the one with the gray ponytail."

Dubinski, the officer in charge of engineering in Simenon's absence, looked skeptical. "Wait a minute. I thought Takahiro was the one with the gray ponytail."

Paxton shook his head. "Takahiro is the one with the short hair and the mole."

"I thought that was Saturria," remarked Refsland, the *Stargazer*'s senior transporter operator.

"No," said Paxton. "Definitely Takahiro."

Ulelo began to settle back into his thoughts. He could feel Emily Bender's finger pressing gently on his lips. He could hear the huskiness in her voice as she moved closer to him.

"I had a crush on you back at the Academy," she had told him. *"A big crush."*

"So we're headed for Oneo Madrin," said Garner, one of Pug Joseph's senior security officers.

"That's right," said Paxton.

Refsland grunted thoughtfully. "Both those suns are Sol-class, aren't they?"

Paxton nodded appreciatively. "Good memory, Bill. With seventeen planets, none of them habitable."

"Any idea what the distress call is about?" asked Urajel, Dubinski's colleague in engineering.

Paxton shook his head. "None."

"Command must be concerned," said Refsland, "or it wouldn't have asked us to investigate."

"It's a distress call," Urajel told him with a typically Andorian lack of patience. "Of *course* they're concerned."

"It'll probably turn out to be engine trouble," said Dubinski.

Garner, who had served with Dubinski on another ship before this one, chuckled at the comment. "You *always* think it's engine trouble."

"It's the most common cause of distress calls," Dubinski told her. "You can look it up."

"Never mind all that," said Urajel. She looked around the table. "What are Simenon and the others up to on Gnala?"

Paxton smiled. "That's the billion-credit question, isn't it?"

"It's not a diplomatic problem," Refsland noted. "The captain wouldn't have needed the doctor and Pug and Vigo along for that."

"Then what?" asked Urajel. She turned to Ulelo. "You've been awfully quiet. Care to venture a guess?"

The comm officer shrugged. "I wouldn't know where to begin."

It was at least half a lie.

Ulelo had perused Ben Zoma's correspondence with Tanya Tresh just as he had perused every other correspondence received on the *Stargazer,* so he knew exactly what Simenon was facing on Gnala. He just didn't know what Picard and his officers had planned to do about it.

"I've got a hunch I know what they're up to," said Dubinski. And he went on to describe his theory.

As it turned out, he couldn't have been farther from the truth. But Ulelo didn't say so because it would have meant exposing himself as something other than what he seemed.

The others eventually discarded Dubinski's hunch and offered a half dozen of their own. But by then, the comm officer wasn't really listening to them anymore.

He had rediscovered the thread of his ruminations. He found himself remembering Emily Bender's kiss, the soft insistence of it. He remembered too the smell of her as she pressed against him.

And he remembered the look on her face when he denied her what she wanted of him. It was a look of pain, of humiliation, of deep and abiding disappointment.

If she had posed a threat to Ulelo before, he had magnified it with the clumsiness of his response. He needed to do something before she placed his mission in jeopardy.

As his colleagues prattled on about Simenon and Gnala, he gradually came up with a plan.

Chapter Eleven

UNTIL HE BEAMED DOWN from the *Stargazer,* Simenon had only heard about his people's ancient Northern Sanctum from his father and his uncles. He himself had never had occasion to set foot in the place.

Now he found himself in the sanctum's Great Hall, an imperious, torturously angular chamber with floors pitted by age and slanted windows ablaze with the glory of the setting sun.

The Assemblage of Elders sat in front of him on a raised stone bench, their High One occupying its center with three of his colleagues on either side. Some Gnalish found it daunting merely to stand in the presence of those august figures, and even more so when they were flanked by their gigantic guards.

But Simenon wasn't here just to stand in their presence. He was here to fight for the future of his family.

Fortunately, he wasn't alone in the effort. His comrades from the *Stargazer* were seated behind him on one of the stone shelves that hugged the perimeter of the chamber. It wasn't as if they could say anything on his behalf, but he was grateful for the moral support.

Not that he would ever have confessed that to them.

There were several others in attendance as well, a few dozen Gnalish

with personal stakes in the outcome of the proceedings. The law allowed
them to observe and participate as long as the Assemblage had no ob-
jection to their doing so.

The High One, who was also the oldest and most loose-skinned of
the councillors, got to his feet. Simenon could see the blue mark on the
front of his robe.

"The Assemblage has meditated," the High One announced. He eyed
Simenon. "I trust you've done the same."

The engineer nodded. "I have."

"You have brought offworlders to engage in the ritual," the High
One noted, wasting no time in addressing the matter at hand. "However,
the ritual is restricted to Gnalish."

Here goes, thought Simenon. "Normally, that's true. But as I'm sure
you know, exceptions have been made in the past."

The councillor frowned, stretching the sac of loose skin under his
chin. "Only under the most extenuating circumstances."

"These are extenuating circumstances as well," Simenon said.

The High One's eyes narrowed. "In what way?"

"I have no brothers to take along on my journey. An accident claimed
both their lives a few years ago."

The councillor shrugged. "The law states that you may take first
cousins in their place."

"I have no first cousins either," said Simenon. "My parents had no
siblings who survived to adulthood."

The High One didn't have an answer for that. Sensing that he had
gained an advantage, Simenon pressed on.

"As a result," he said, "I have invited the assistance of some of my
friends, all of whom are male and roughly my age and should therefore
be admissible to the ritual."

Another Gnalish, as tall and heavy and pale of skin as the black-
garbed guards, rose from the midst of the onlookers. "I would like to
speak," he said in a deep, harsh voice.

The High One nodded. "You have leave."

"I disagree with the one called Simenon. The laws governing the
ritual are explicit." His fiery eyes flashed with indignation as he glanced
in the engineer's direction. "It's not enough for someone to be the right
age and sex. He must also be a blood relative of the individual under-
taking the journey."

A second Gnalish got to his feet. He was considerably smaller than
either Simenon or his fellow protester, and his skin had a light and dark

pattern to it. He too asked to be recognized by the Assemblage and was granted the privilege.

"Kasaelek is right," the diminutive one snapped. "The ritual is intended for Gnalish and their blood kin, not for strangers to our ways—and certainly not for the offspring of other worlds."

Simenon smiled grimly. It was no secret why these two would have a problem with his choice of comrades. In their place, he might have objected with the same vehemence—and maybe even the same arguments.

"My competitors can hardly be considered unbiased judges," he told the Assemblage, his voice ringing passionately throughout the chamber. "It's in their interest to see me undertake the ritual on my own."

"I merely seek justice," countered the giant.

"We must honor our traditions," the light and dark one insisted.

"Of course," said Simenon, his eyes narrowing. "Especially when justice and tradition favor your causes."

His rivals glowered at him. He glowered back, measure for measure.

"The fact remains," Simenon went on, "that it's in the Assemblage's power to grant my request—to give me the help I need to compete on an even footing. Anything less would ensure my defeat."

The High One looked pensive. "What you're suggesting is unprecedented, Simenon. But you're correct in your contention that all competitors should have an equal chance to win."

"High One," the giant spat, "this is—"

The councillor whirled and hissed, imposing silence on the speaker. "You will address us when you're given permission to do so."

The giant inclined his head in contrition. "Of course," he said. "I meant no disrespect."

It was then that someone new entered the chamber through its only door. As Simenon was facing the Assemblage, he couldn't turn to see who it was. It was only after the newcomer had sat down alongside the other Gnalish that the engineer caught a glimpse of him.

And cursed in the privacy of his mind.

"I would like to speak," said the newcomer.

The High One nodded. "You may do so."

Simenon sighed. He hadn't prepared for this possibility, though in retrospect he realized he should have.

"I'm Lennil Ornitharen," the newcomer told the Assemblage. "Phigus Simenon's cousin. Despite his claim to the contrary, he doesn't have to recruit offworlders to help him in the ritual. He has living kin on *this* world. He has *me."*

The councillors muttered beneath their collective breath and exchanged meaningful glances. Only the High One withheld comment until he could present Simenon with the obvious question.

"Is it possible you have a cousin, after all?"

The engineer heaved a sigh. "Ornitharen is my cousin, yes. But he's my *second* cousin. And believe me, I'm grateful for his offer of assistance, which—as you know—extends above and beyond the mandate of our customs and traditions.

"However, I decline to include him in my entourage, which the ritual laws limit to six companions—not as a matter of affection, but as a practical matter. I know from experience that Ornitharen isn't made for physical exertion. He pales in comparison even with other Gnalish of my subspecies, whereas my human and Pandrilite friends are hardy examples of their kind."

He regarded his cousin with an expression of regret. "I don't have the luxury of worrying about his feelings, High One. I've got to think about survival—-not only my own, but that of my bloodline."

Ornitharen began to protest the decision, but the High One stopped him. "Simenon is the generational leader of your clan. You lack the standing to argue with him."

If the look on Ornitharen's face was any indication, he wasn't happy about the High One's remark. Nonetheless, he managed to remain silent, bending to his cousin's will.

Apparently satisfied with Ornitharen's response—or rather, his lack of one—the High One told Simenon, "We of the Assemblage must weigh what we have heard here. We will let you know when we've come to a decision in this matter."

The engineer would have preferred an answer then and there—but only if it was the *right* answer. As he had indicated to the Assemblage, the wrong one would ensure his defeat.

"I wait patiently," he told the High One, "trusting in your wisdom." As if he had a choice.

McAteer regarded the Bolian seated on the other side of the black plastic table. Like all Bolians, he had light blue skin and a ridge that ran from the nape of his neck to somewhere under his chin.

His name was Shalay. He was the second officer on the *New Orleans,* a starship that had once been a state-of-the-art prototype and was now far from it.

By human standards, the fellow was quite handsome, quite charming. No doubt, he did well with the ladies. And if the admiral's reports were accurate, Shalay was prepared to make a career move.

"You know," said McAteer, "I've been looking forward to meeting you, Mr. Shalay. I've heard good things about you."

Truthfully, Shalay's file hadn't contained anything spectacular. It wasn't nearly as impressive as Garrett's had been. However, the Bolian had demonstrated a talent for politics that had moved him briskly up the chain of command.

He reminded McAteer of someone: himself.

Shalay nodded, taking the compliment in stride. "It's kind of you to say so, Admiral."

"Kindness has nothing to do with it, Commander. To be blunt, I hate to see an individual with your unlimited potential languishing as second officer on a third-rate ship."

The Bolian smiled—warily, McAteer thought. "That's blunt, all right."

"How do you like serving on the *New Orleans?*"

Shalay shrugged his muscular shoulders. "It's been a valuable experience. I benefited from every minute of it."

He was politic, too. The admiral liked that.

"But you wouldn't be adverse to making a change? Moving to another vessel where there was a greater chance of moving up?"

Shalay's brow puckered. "A *chance* of moving up?"

McAteer smiled. "You were hoping to move right into a first officer's slot. I understand. However, the post I'm thinking of is just as good as a first officer's slot."

"Begging the admiral's pardon," said the Bolian, "I don't see how that could be the case."

McAteer leaned forward and rubbed his hands together. "On the vessel I have in mind, the captain and first officer leave something to be desired. My problem is I'm not present to document their inadequacies. But," he added pointedly, "if I had someone who *was . . .*"

Shalay seemed to get it. "You want me to transfer to another ship as second officer. Then you want me to supply you with ammunition so you can sink that ship's captain and first officer."

"At which point," the admiral said, "I will see to it that you move up to take their place."

"As first officer? Or as captain?"

McAteer smiled. "Need you ask?"

Shalay's eyes crinkled at the corners. "I've never received an offer like this."

"And you never will again," the admiral told him pointedly. "Not from me, at least."

"So it's take it or leave it."

McAteer nodded. "That's correct."

Shalay pondered the quid pro quo. Finally, he said, "You've got yourself a deal."

The admiral was pleased—he had been right about the Bolian. "I'm glad to hear it," he said.

"Where am I going, anyway?"

McAteer saw no reason to keep it a secret. After all, Shalay had to give his captain the information.

"The name of the ship," he said, "is the *Stargazer.*"

Picard stood outside the door to the Great Hall, in the gargantuan lobby where he and his officers had beamed down, and asked Simenon the question they all had on their minds.

"Do you think the Assemblage has been persuaded?"

His engineer shrugged. "I don't know. They're the Assemblage. They can do anything they like."

His cousin, who bore a striking resemblance to Simenon but was rounder and softer looking, stood by himself in a fluted alcove. It was difficult to tell if he was praying or just thinking.

Greyhorse tilted his head in Ornitharen's direction. "Your chances seemed good until *he* walked in."

Simenon glanced in his cousin's direction. "I can't fault him for what he did. We had the same grandfather. He feels it's his responsibility to help me."

Joseph grunted. "Even if you don't *want* his help?"

The engineer frowned. "Even then."

Picard noticed that Simenon's detractors were standing around as well, each with his own small contingent of supporters. In both cases, those who had spoken in the Great Hall were of the same stature as those who surrounded them.

The captain understood why. But then, once the hearing was over, Simenon had had a chance to enlighten them a bit in that regard.

"Hey," said Joseph, "the door's opening!"

Picard followed his security officer's gesture and saw that the door to the Great Hall—a ponderous wooden affair on ancient metal hinges— was indeed swinging open. Apparently, the Assemblage of Elders had completed its deliberations.

But it hadn't been more than a couple of minutes since the Assemblage had begun them. The captain wondered if that boded well or ill for Simenon's cause.

A hulking bailiff in a black robe emerged from the Great Hall. "You may enter," he told everyone present.

"Let's go," said Ben Zoma, leading the way.

Simenon paused for a moment, seemingly reluctant to go back into the Great Hall. Then he followed Ben Zoma and the rest of their colleagues fell in behind them.

Picard went through the doorway last. But then, he wanted to see the expressions on the faces of Simenon's adversaries. As it turned out, they didn't look any more confident than Simenon did. The captain drew encouragement from that.

The Assemblage of Elders was just where the captain had seen it last, occupying the bench in the center of the room. Simenon walked up to them and stood before them, while Picard and the others again took seats on the stone shelves that protruded from the walls.

It took a moment for everyone to get settled. Then, as before, the High One spoke for the entire Assemblage.

"We have heard the arguments and made our decision," he said, his voice echoing lavishly. "And it is this—that the offworlders will be allowed to participate in the ritual."

The announcement was met with muttered protests and expressions of disgust from the camps that had spoken against Simenon. The High One didn't respond to them. He simply stood there and waited patiently for them to subside.

"However," he added at last, gazing directly at Simenon, "it will be up to you to keep your companions from violating the ancient laws that govern the ritual—for if they do, rest assured that you will be the one held accountable."

Simenon nodded. "I understand."

The High One regarded him for a little while longer. Then he turned to Picard. "Accommodations will be provided for all participants. However, I cannot guarantee they will be to your liking."

"I'm sure they will be just fine," the captain assured him.

But then, what else could he say? The Gnalish weren't about to build a new wing on their majestic Northern Sanctum expressly for the comfort of meddling offworlders.

"Then," said the High One, "this hearing is over." He took in everyone present at a glance. "As always, the trial begins at first light. May all participants in the ancient ritual face the challenges ahead of them with skill and courage."

There was a chorus of agreement with what was no doubt a traditional blessing. But, clearly, not everyone was happy with the Assemblage's decision. The two who had spoken against Simenon earlier glared at him now with unabashed animosity.

But Ornitharen didn't glare at his cousin. He walked over to him and put his scaly hand on Simenon's shoulder as Picard and the others closed in on them.

"I think you're making a mistake by not including me among your companions," Ornitharen said. "But I'll still be cheering more loudly than anyone for you to make it to the egg nest first."

Simenon harrumphed—about as close as he ever came to a laugh. "Thanks," he told his cousin. "I'll feel better knowing that."

He sounded sincere, Picard thought. However, it seemed to him that his engineer was simply trying to take the edge off Ornitharen's humiliation. Nothing would truly make Simenon feel better except the knowledge that his ordeal was over. . . .

And that it had ended in victory.

Chapter Twelve

CARTER GREYHORSE FOUND HIMSELF in a dark, drafty place, surrounded by an eerie landscape of blanketed bodies. It took him a moment to get his wits about him—to figure out where he was and what the devil he was doing there.

Finally, he figured it out. Gnala. The Northern Sanctum. He and his colleagues had been given this chamber so they could rest in preparation for Simenon's ritual.

He raised his head and looked out past the last prone body, which was too large to belong to anyone but Vigo. Greyhorse remembered the weapons officer saying he liked to sleep by the exit. Apparently, he had done just that.

But the doctor couldn't make out the outline of the door, which meant one of two things: either it fit its frame too perfectly to let any light in, or it was still the middle of the night. In a place this ancient, the doctor guessed that it was the latter.

He sighed and laid his head back against the wad of clothes he had employed as a pillow. Everyone else appeared to be sleeping soundly, despite the hardness of the surface beneath them. *So why am I awake?* Greyhorse asked himself.

He didn't have to think for very long to come up with the answer. Her name was Gerda.

He had dreamed of her before he woke—dreamed of the two of them, actually. They were embracing in the cloistered confines of a scarlet forest, her face turned up willingly toward his, her blue eyes glittering like sapphires in the moonlight.

Even here, Greyhorse was preoccupied with her, obsessed with her. She invaded his every thought, day and night.

If one of his patients had come to him and described such an obsession, he would have prescribed therapy. It wasn't healthy to dwell on someone so often and so intensely.

He probably needed a psychiatric counselor. Unfortunately, Starfleet crews didn't include such people, and he wasn't going to leave the *Stargazer* to gain access to one of them—because if he did, he would be giving up his only chance to be with Gerda. *A vicious cycle,* he mused, *if ever there was one.*

The doctor propped himself up on an elbow. Whenever he woke in the middle of the night—which was often—he had a difficult time getting back to sleep unless he took a nice, long walk. He had a feeling that this instance would be no exception.

Of course, he reflected, he wouldn't be walking the predictable, temperature-controlled corridors of a starship down here. He would be outside in the open, unfiltered air of Gnala. But then, that might actually make him sleepier.

Besides, his only alternative was to lie there until the others woke up, which might not be for hours, and that was a bleak prospect indeed. Rather than contemplate it, he unrolled his clothes, put them on as quietly as he could, and threaded his way softly past his colleagues until he reached the door.

Fortunately, it didn't creak as he opened it. Feeling a breath of warm, moist air on his face, he knew he had made the right choice. As he stepped out into the darkness, he closed the door behind him.

As luck would have it, the sky was clear and crowded with stars, the air redolent with scents that reminded him of mint and sage and other Earthly spices. A near-full moon frosted the mossy ground underfoot as if eager to guide his steps.

By the light of Gnala's setting sun, the Northern Sanctum had looked like a colossal bloody dagger. By moonlight, it seemed even larger and more ominous. Likewise, the shaggy, wind-driven growth of forest surrounding it, where Greyhorse and the rest of the away team would be toiling after daybreak on Simenon's behalf.

He didn't want to lose his way in the depths of that forest—not after Ben Zoma had briefed him on the perils that awaited the unwary traveler. However, he wasn't ready to go back inside their sleeping chamber yet, so he decided to simply walk a circuit around the sanctum.

As the doctor did this, the architecture of the place revealed itself to him line by craggy line. If the sanctum had seemed intricate and intriguing on the inside, its exterior was even more so.

What's more, it featured a series of little alcoves, each one paved with small, flat stones and separated from the mossy ground by red walls. Greyhorse inspected a couple of the alcoves and found that there was nothing to see in them. By the time he got to the third one, he was ready to assume the same of it.

But he gave it a glance anyway—and discovered that it wasn't quite the same as its predecessors, after all. For one thing, the ground wasn't paved. It was the same mossy stuff that the doctor had been walking on.

For another thing, there was something embedded in it—something oval in outline, its surface rounded like a small hill, and so pale as to appear luminescent in the moonlight. His curiosity aroused, Greyhorse entered the alcove to take a closer look.

And saw that it was a stone.

At first, he thought it had been milled by a machine—that's how smooth and regularly shaped it was. Then he saw the tiny imperfections in its surface. He also noticed a complex network of glyphs that had been incised into it and darkened for greater legibility.

Greyhorse didn't read Gnalish, so he had no idea what sort of wisdom the glyphs were meant to impart. However, he was intrigued by the patterns that seemed to emerge for him.

In fact, the more he looked for them, the more they seemed to reveal themselves to him. And the more they revealed themselves, the more he got the feeling that he had seen them somewhere before.

It can't be, the doctor told himself. *I've never set foot on Gnala before. And I've never seen anything of Simenon's that might have borne these markings.*

But he had seen them *somewhere.* He was certain of it.

Greyhorse had to stare at the stone for some time, kneeling before it and examining it in the moonlight, before he realized why the markings seemed so familiar. They were reminiscent of a genetic data map he had helped to compile back in medical school.

The doctor recalled it as if it were yesterday. He and his classmates had been given tiny batches of cellular material that belonged to an eel-bird, a denizen of the fifth planet in the Regulus system, and were asked to identify each of the creature's genes by its unique sequence of purine and pyrimidine bases.

He had learned more from that simple exercise than almost any other facet of his medical education, perhaps because the professor involved was so passionate about his work. He had promised his students that they would never forget what eel-bird genes looked like—and, in fact, Greyhorse had never forgotten.

He nodded to himself now as he gazed at the markings on the moon-lit stone. *Yes,* he told himself, *there is a remarkable similarity to that eel-bird map.*

Was it just a coincidence—or something else? After all, the ritual in which he and his companions were about to take part would determine whose traits would survive in the Gnalish gene pool and whose would be lost to the pool forever.

Could Simenon's ancestors have understood the concept of genetics—and not just at the relatively superficial level of common sense? Could they have had the wherewithal to track the makeup of the species from generation to generation?

The medical officer sat back on his haunches and ran his fingertips over the markings. They were sharp-edged enough to have been carved just the day before. But this was an ancient complex according to Simenon, one that had been used for thousands of years. More than likely, the stone was as ancient as the rest of it.

And if that were so . . .

Greyhorse frowned. The Gnalish hadn't climbed the ladder of technological development any more quickly than his forebears on Earth. If anything, Simenon's people had been a little slower. To suggest that they'd enjoyed a grasp of advanced genetics thousands of years ago didn't seem likely.

But then, things weren't always what they seemed. A good scientist had to keep an open mind.

Greyhorse resolved to ask Simenon about the stone in the morning. Maybe he could shed some light on it.

Standing, the doctor stared at it some more, tilting his head so he could appraise it from another angle. Now that he knew where to look for the patterns, they were hard to miss.

Just then, a chill invaded the alcove—a sharp breath of unexpectedly cold air. It reminded Greyhorse that it was time he got back to the sleeping chamber. He would need his strength if he were going to be of any help to his colleagues in the morning.

And he had to be of considerable help to them if he were going to impress Gerda with his accomplishments.

With some reluctance, Greyhorse left the stone behind. Then he made his way back around the perimeter of the sanctum, Gnala's moon diligently lighting his way.

As Errigo Shalay entered his captain's ready room, he saw that she was intent on her monitor.

"Have a seat," said DeMontreville, a stern-looking woman with a square jaw and short, dirty-blond hair.

Shalay sat down opposite his superior and watched her eyes move back and forth in the glare of her screen. *A message from Starfleet,* he thought. *It had to be.*

Finally, DeMontreville grunted, leaned back in her seat, and said, "Damned Romulans."

"Romulans?" the Bolian echoed.

The cold-blooded bastards hadn't been seen in or near the Federation in almost thirty years, ever since they signed the Treaty of Algeron. And as far as Shalay could tell, no one missed them.

DeMontreville nodded. "Every so often, Command receives a report of a Romulan vessel in our space. They all turn out to be false alarms when they're investigated, but we're still apprised of them."

"I see," said Shalay.

His captain regarded him. "So how was your shore leave?"

"Fine," he told her, leaving out the details. After all, his meeting with Admiral McAteer was supposed to be a secret.

DeMontreville looked at him askance. "I know that look, Shalay. You've got something on your mind."

The second officer smiled. "You know me too well." He leaned forward in his chair. "I've heard through the grapevine that there's a position opening for a second officer on the *Stargazer.*"

An expression of disappointment crossed the captain's face. But then, no commanding officer liked to lose a valued officer, and Shalay had done an exemplary job on the *New Orleans.*

"And you'd like to apply for it?" she said.

"I would," he confirmed.

DeMontreville sighed. "I hate to lose you, Commander. But if that's what you want, you've got my permission."

Shalay smiled again. "Thank you, Captain."

"Just remember, there are no guarantees. The *Stargazer*'s a new ship. I'm sure you're not the only one eyeing that post."

"No guarantees," he acknowledged.

What DeMontreville didn't know was that it wouldn't be any contest. The *Stargazer* position was Shalay's, hands down.

Admiral McAteer would make certain of that.

Picard hunkered down next to Greyhorse in the darkness of the sleeping chamber and shook the big man's shoulder. "Doctor?"

Greyhorse looked up at him with eyes so wide they looked almost comical. "Is it time already?"

"It is," the captain confirmed.

The doctor sat up. "All right," he said firmly, as much to himself as to the captain. "I'm awake."

That is a matter of opinion, Picard thought.

Simenon was standing by the door to the chamber already, a scowl on his face, his arms folded impatiently across his chest. Obviously, he was eager to get going, eager to get his ordeal under way.

However, the captain's wrist chronometer told him they had almost three quarters of an hour before the ritual was scheduled to begin. Certainly, that was ample time for a quick bite and some last-minute mental preparation.

Clearly, Simenon could use some calming down. With that in mind, Picard started across the room to join him.

As he passed Ben Zoma and Joseph, he saw that they were just beginning to pull their clothes on. "Let's go, gentlemen," he told them. "We've got work to do."

Ben Zoma grunted good-naturedly. "And here I was thinking we were on shore leave."

"No such luck," the captain told him.

Joseph stretched his arms out and groaned. "I feel like I just went to bed," he complained to no one in particular.

"You *did,*" said Ben Zoma. "This time of year, the nights here are only five hours long."

Joseph sighed. "Now you tell me."

As Picard approached his engineer, he could more clearly see the nervousness in Simenon's eyes. It was certainly understandable. If the future of the captain's family were at stake, *he* would have been nervous as well.

The ritual, as Simenon had described it to them the night before, was really a foot race that took place in the wilderness surrounding the Northern Sanctum. Three teams started from the same point but were compelled to negotiate divergent courses.

However, the winners of the race didn't get a trophy, as Picard had done when he came in first in the Academy marathon on Danula II. Instead, they won the right for one of their number to fertilize a cache of two dozen newly hatched eggs, the majority of which would then grow into a clutch of bouncing baby Gnalish.

Earlier in the evolutionary development of Simenon's people, this competition had been a good deal more chaotic. Instead of a few hand-picked teams trying to negotiate a prescribed course in an orderly fashion, it had been a free-for-all, pitting huge packs of instinct-driven Gnalish against each other.

Unfortunately, each pack was more or less decimated in the struggle. Few males emerged from the struggle whole and even fewer reached a ripe old age.

As time went on and civilization took hold on Gnala, the impulse to fertilize was channeled into other pursuits. It became less of a bio-logical imperative and more a matter of personal pride. Finally, a couple of thousand years earlier, the ritual began to resemble its current, con-siderably less bloody form.

Not that Gnalish didn't get hurt in the course of the ritual; they did. And on occasion, their injuries were fatal. But at least most of them survived to tell the tale.

On the other hand, as Simenon had told them, those who lost the race sometimes didn't wish to survive. That was because each Gnalish male had one chance and one chance only to succeed in the ritual—and the prospect of never seeing one's progeny walk the earth was sometimes too much for them to bear.

So if Simenon seemed grim and fidgety, he had a right to be that way. In a sense, countless generations of his bloodline were depending on him—both those who had come before him and those who might come after. Picard didn't envy him that burden.

And to complicate the matter, Simenon wouldn't be racing against his equals. He would be racing against representatives of Gnala's two other subspecies, the Aklaash and the Fejjimaera.

In this case, they were the Gnalish who had spoken against the engineer in the Great Hall. Kasaelek, the pale-skinned giant at whom the elder had hissed, was a product of the towering subspecies called the Aklaash. The light-and-dark specimen was Banyohla, who represented the small, slender Fejjimaera.

Simenon had outlined the other subspecies' advantages for his colleagues. The captain recalled his engineer's words as if he had spoken them only moments earlier.

"The Aklaash are big and unspeakably strong and they tend to fare well in the ritual, which is why they're easily the most populous subspecies on Gnala."

"I see. And the Fejjimaera?" Picard had asked.

"They're smaller than I am, but a hell of a lot quicker. Also, they have a considerable talent for camouflage."

"And do they fare well in the ritual also?"

"Almost as well as the Aklaash, as a matter of fact. Finally, there's the subspecies to which I belong—the Mazzereht. We perform the worst of all, and by a wide margin."

"I'm sorry to hear that," the captain had said.

Simenon had frowned. *"So am I. But there's no way around it. Strength and speed are big assets in the wild."*

"But if your subspecies has survived at all, Nature must have given it some assets of its own."

"She did," Simenon had told him.

"And what are they?"

"She gave us . . . brains."

Simenon hadn't said it with any real optimism. Clearly, for the purposes of the ritual, he would have preferred that his people possess some more physical attribute.

Nor could Picard blame him.

He regarded Simenon now. The engineer's eyes were hard and alert, the eyes of a being about to meet the challenge of his life. And not just a challenge, but a test of his ability to survive.

The captain and the others could help him here and there. They could lend him support in his struggle. But ultimately, the test was Simenon's to pass or fail.

"Well?" Ben Zoma asked, inadvertently breaking into the captain's reverie. "What are we waiting for?"

The first officer had finished getting dressed and seemed eager to get going. They all seemed that way—even Dr. Greyhorse, though he still looked a little bleary-eyed.

Picard looked back at Simenon. "Are you ready?" he asked as gently as he could.

The Gnalish scowled at him. "I'd better be, hadn't I?"

Chapter Thirteen

As PICARD AND THE OTHERS ISSUED from their sleeping chamber in the thin morning light, a white-robed Elder and two of his Aklaash bodyguards were already waiting for them.

"You will follow me," said the figure in the white robe.

Simenon agreed that he and his comrades would do this. Then they followed their guides into the embrace of the undulating, dawn-speckled forest, leaving the pride and majesty of the Northern Sanctum behind.

Insects chittered at them over the sighing of the wind. There were scraping sounds of tiny creatures making their way from hiding place to hiding place. *The occupants of the lowest rungs on the food chain,* the captain thought, *gathering to witness the trial of the beings on the highest rung.*

Before long, they came to a large clearing ringed by immense crimson trees with mottled bark and broad, spade-shaped leaves. Picard had seen sequoias on the western coast of North America; it seemed to him that these behemoths were bigger.

As the captain and his officers entered the clearing, he saw that they were the last to do so. The other two teams were already standing in closely knit circles, munching on something that smelled vaguely like bananas but sounded a lot crunchier.

Seen in briefer and more informal attire, Kasaelek and his bunch looked even more imposing than they had in the sanctum—more massive and thickly muscled under their scales. The smallest of them was as tall or taller than Vigo, and Vigo was a head taller than Picard. It was difficult for an offworlder like the captain to believe the Aklaash and Simenon belonged to the same species.

The Fejjimaera group was decidedly less impressive-looking, their informal garb revealing small, slender physiques. However, as Ben Zoma had pointed out, it was their speed that had earned them a good track record in the ritual event—and quickness wasn't likely to manifest itself in a display of bulging muscles.

But it wasn't just their body types that distinguished the Aklaash from the Fejjimaera. While Kasaelek and his comrades seemed very much at ease, almost lethargic, Banyohla's team looked fidgety. They kept darting looks at the other two groups and hissing their observations in each other's ears.

Perhaps that was just the way they acted, Picard thought. Or perhaps they were actually worried about the competition the offworlders might offer them.

He chose to believe the latter.

Of course, the Gnalish in the white robes were in evidence here as well. There were three of them in all, including the individual who had led Simenon here—each of them followed closely by a couple of Aklaash in black garb.

According to Simenon, the rest of the Assemblage would be waiting for them at the "finish line." They would sit there patiently, telling stories of their forebears and humming ancient melodies, until a victor appeared—the first of the three competitors to reach the nest of unfertilized eggs.

And when he did, they would oversee the fertilization process, as he added his DNA to that of the eggs. Apparently, *that* was one of the Assemblage's duties as well.

Picard was hardly an expert on Gnalish biology, but he could imagine what the fertilization process might be like. It made him cringe a little to think of his engineer performing such an act in full view of both the Assemblage and his colleagues.

But then, he wasn't a Gnalish. No doubt, there were human behaviors that occasionally made Simenon squirm as well.

As Picard thought this, a black-garbed Aklaash came over to the engineers' group and distributed something small and flat to each of its members, with Simenon receiving an extra package of the stuff. When it was the captain's turn, he saw that he had been given a couple of crackers with a strong, bananalike scent to them—the same sort of food the other teams were eating.

"Lovely," said Greyhorse, an expression of displeasure on his face as he inspected the crackers more closely. "What are they?"

"Layfid," Simenon replied, as he tucked the extra package into an interior pocket of his shirt.

"And what's that?" asked Ben Zoma.

"Reconstituted worm waste," said the engineer. He took a bite of one of his crackers and nodded approvingly. "And nutritious worm waste at that."

Vigo swallowed back his revulsion. "I don't suppose there's an alternative of some kind?"

Joseph grunted. "This from the guy who shoves sturrd down his throat? I'll take worm waste over that stuff any day." And to prove his point, he began munching on one of his crackers.

Picard tried one of his own and found it wasn't nearly as bad as Simenon had made it sound. Besides, they were going to be in the woods for some time, and he would sooner trust a cracker than something he found growing in the wild.

Another black-robed guard came by and gave each of them something else—not food this time, but a tapered wooden club about a meter long and a belted sheath to go with it. The captain turned the club over in his hands.

Then he glanced at Simenon. "This is a *tellek?"*

The engineer nodded. "The only weapon any of us is allowed."

Simenon had described it to Picard and the others the night before. It had sounded formidable. But now that the captain held it in his hands and saw how light it was, he was a good deal less confident about its effectiveness. Nonetheless, he put on the belt and stuck the *tellek* in its sheath, and watched his companions do the same.

For a few minutes, they ate their crackers and watched Gnala's sun come up through the branches of the densely packed forest. Then one of the white-robed ones made his way to the center of the clearing and raised his bony hand.

"Come on," said Simenon.

He led the way to a narrow trail radiating from the clearing—one of three distinct pathways through the woods that began just a few meters apart. Kasaelek approached the trail on their left. Banyohla approached the one on their right.

The Assemblage's representative said something slow and rhythmic, something that seemed to find willing accompaniment in the soft plaint of the morning breeze. Picard's universal translator had a devil of a time making any sense of it.

But then, he didn't have to understand the words. All he had to do was watch for the fall of the elder's hand, because that was the gesture that would signal the start of the race.

The captain glanced at Simenon. He looked like a Markoffian sea lizard, coiled and ready to strike.

As Picard thought this, the elder in the white robe stopped singing. His hand fell like a dying bird. And the captain plunged forward alongside Simenon, for the ritual had begun.

Gerda Asmund was checking her monitors for unexpected obstacles on the course she had plotted when her sister spoke up.

"All right, what is it?" asked Idun, who was sitting beside her at the helm console.

Gerda glanced at her. "What do you mean?"

"Your expression," her sister said knowingly. "You seem concerned about something."

The navigator frowned. Was it that obvious?

"I was wondering how the captain and the others were faring on Gnala," she said. It was the truth, more or less.

"They've been in my thoughts as well." Idun made a sound of disgust, loud enough only for her twin to hear. "They should have taken us with them."

"They couldn't," Gerda reminded her. "The ritual in which they're participating is restricted to males."

Her sister dismissed the idea with a sound of disgust. "If it were a Klingon ritual, there would be no such restriction."

Gerda nodded. "True."

Klingons were more egalitarian than most other species in that regard. When it came to fighting, to killing and being killed, males and females were on the same footing.

"Nonetheless," said Idun, "they will acquit themselves well—I am certain of it. The captain is a brave and clever individual. Likewise, Ben Zoma and Simenon."

"What about the others?" Gerda asked.

Her sister shrugged. "What Joseph lacks in experience he makes up in determination. And Vigo . . . few humanoids have his strength."

She had failed to mention only one member of the party. What's more, Gerda understood the omission. Despite Greyhorse's size and the handful of lessons she had given him, he wasn't much of a fighter.

Then why had she tutored him in the martial arts? Why had she spent precious hours with him in the gym when she could have been honing her own fighting skills or studying her navigation charts?

Yes, she thought. *That is the question.*

Gerda and Idun had always shared everything with each other. Even their deepest secrets.

When the two of them were taken in by the House of Warrokh, tiny stripling girls in the midst of huge, menacing warriors who roared and snarled at each other for no apparent reason, they had cried themselves to sleep—and shared each other's tears, for they were wrapped in each other's arms.

When they were older and a gang of sneering boys had thought to push "the human girls" around, they had stood back to back and endured their beating together. And in the end, they obtained their revenge together as well, cornering the offenders one by one and returning their injuries measure for measure.

And when their father died defending his family's honor, they had howled together over his ruined body and shared the joy of knowing he would go to join Kahless in Sto-Vo-Kor.

We have shared everything, Gerda thought. *But I cannot share my feelings in the matter of Carter Greyhorse.*

And what was worse, she couldn't bring herself to say why.

Ulelo stopped when he got to the set of doors he had been looking for and waited for his presence to be announced.

It took longer to get a response than he had expected. But then, having never called on any of his crewmates, his only point of reference was how it felt on the other side of the doors.

Finally, the duranium panels slid aside, giving him a view of an anteroom much like his own. However, this anteroom looked a good deal warmer, decorated as it was with Japanese watercolors and a grouping of Vulcan statuettes.

Emily Bender looked at him. She was standing in front of an unusually shaped teakwood chair, a padd in her hand. "Yes?"

Ulelo recited the words he had rehearsed. "I wanted to apologize for my behavior. I treated you rudely and I'm sorry."

His host regarded him for a moment. "I don't know whether to forgive you or detest you."

"I wouldn't blame you either way," he said.

That seemed to soften her up a bit. "Have a seat," she told him, clearly still a little wary. *Of being hurt again.*

"Thank you," he said.

Emily Bender stepped aside and Ulelo entered her quarters. Once inside, he noticed a number of other personal touches—a geode filled with brilliant violet crystals, a woven wall hanging done in more muted violets, an artifact that might have been a ceramic oil lamp a very long time ago.

And a picture of Emily Bender with two people who seemed to be her parents.

She indicated a Starfleet-issue chair. The communications officer sat. For a heartbeat or two, neither of them spoke, until he realized that she wasn't going to make this easy for him. It was incumbent on him to begin the exchange.

He did so.

"What I said before must have seemed strange to you," Ulelo ventured. "Both in the corridor and in my quarters. After all, you were certain that you knew me, but I wasn't acknowledging that I knew *you.*"

Emily Bender nodded. "It was strange, all right." She was still holding herself back, waiting to hear what he had to say.

"I'm sure everything you told me was true," he continued. "About the Academy, our friends there, how close we were . . . I don't doubt it for a minute. But what I was saying . . . that's true too. I honestly don't remember any of it."

She tilted her head to one side as she studied him. "You're saying you have amnesia . . . ?"

Ulelo shrugged. "I was in an accident a little while ago. I lost pieces of my memory. Apparently, my relationships with you and the others you mentioned were some of the pieces I lost."

It was a lie, of course. He hadn't had an accident at all.

So why was he misleading her? Heaven knew it wasn't because he wanted to torment the woman. It would have been a lot easier on him if he could have simply told her the truth.

But that wasn't an option.

"An accident," Emily Bender echoed, making it clear she was skeptical about the information.

He nodded. "I'm not supposed to talk about it." Another lie. He was getting good at telling them. "But it wasn't pleasant," Ulelo added for good measure.

She sighed. "So you really don't remember me?"

"Not at all." That part, at least, was true. "And I don't remember any of the people you mentioned."

Emily Bender seemed to weigh his claims for a while, her eyes searching his. Then she drew a breath and slowly let it out.

"Look," she said, "if you don't remember me, you don't remember me. I guess that's the way it is."

"It's frustrating," Ulelo allowed. "For me more than anyone."

"I'm sure it is. And lonely, I imagine."

"That too." *Painfully so.*

Emily Bender leaned forward in her chair. "So let me get this straight. When you asked me to leave your quarters . . . you weren't giving me the brush-off after all?"

He started to answer in the affirmative—until he saw where his response might lead her. As before, he acknowledged the fact of her beauty, if only to himself. He tortured himself with the idea that he could bring some joy into his life, just by giving in to a woman who obviously wanted him as much as he wanted her.

A woman who was willing to accept him unconditionally, it seemed. Without reservations. Without *questions.*

Fortunately, Ulelo was still strong. He could still do what his duty—and his sanity—demanded of him.

"I wasn't giving you the brush-off," he conceded. "But please understand . . . I would feel awkward getting involved with you romantically, given the fact that you know me and I don't—"

Emily Bender held up her hand. "Don't. I can already hear what you're going to say."

Ulelo frowned. "And what's that?"

"That you could use a friend."

He hadn't planned on saying that at all. However, he saw no way to deny it.

She considered him for a moment. Then, looking a little bitter, she shook her head. "If we can't be what I'd like us to be . . ." Her voice trailed off wistfully.

The comm officer was grateful that the matter had resolved itself without his having to engage in further maneuvers. "I understand," he said softly. Then he added, "I guess I'll be going."

She didn't stop him. In fact, she didn't even turn her head to watch him go.

Picard and his colleagues had been jogging down their ritual trail for less than twenty minutes before Simenon slowed them to a walk.

The captain himself could have continued at a trot for another hour, if necessary. However, it was clear that at least one member of their party could not.

And that member was Greyhorse.

The doctor was breathing heavily even now, still feeling the effects of the quicker pace. But then, he was a big man, not exactly made for long-distance running, and to Picard's knowledge he had never dedicated himself to a fitness regimen.

Of course, Greyhorse had prescribed such regimens for others. Why was it that physicians so seldom practiced what they preached?

Simenon glanced back at the doctor. Then he muttered something beneath his breath.

"What's that?" asked Greyhorse.

Simenon shook his head. "Nothing."

"Don't give me that," Greyhorse said. "You don't mutter at someone that way and then not tell them what you're thinking."

The Gnalish rolled his eyes. "All right. I admit it. I was wishing that you were in better shape."

The doctor frowned. "Really."

"Really. And," Simenon added, "while I was at it, I wished one of the Asmunds could have come in your place."

Picard would have expected Greyhorse to react negatively to such a statement. But if his feelings were hurt, he didn't show it.

Instead, he told Simenon, "Believe me, so do I."

Clearly, the admission caught Simenon by surprise. "You know," he said, "no one told you you had to come."

Greyhorse chuckled derisively. "As usual, my friend, your gratitude knows no bounds."

"Gentlemen," said Picard, "I suggest we table this discussion for the time being. As you may have noticed, the Asmunds are not in evidence here, nor is there any possibility that they will arrive before the start of the ritual."

"And as for the doctor's conditioning," Ben Zoma chimed in optimistically, "I expect him to catch his second wind any moment now."

Simenon looked at Greyhorse. "Maybe you're right."

"That's the spirit," said Ben Zoma.

"But," Simenon added as he forged ahead, "I doubt it."

Chapter Fourteen

COMMANDER WU HAD HER HELM OFFICER drop the *Stargazer* out of warp near the center of the gargantuan Oneo Madrin system, at a point more or less equidistant from its twin stars.

It was a tricky maneuver, considering the complex balance of planets and gravity wells in the system. However, Idun pulled it off without any apparent difficulty.

"Proceed at half impulse," said the second officer.

"Half impulse," Idun confirmed.

Wu advanced toward the viewscreen, which showed her a substantial section of the slender, golden accretion bridge that linked the system's two young suns. One sun was substantially bigger than the other, which was why it was able to steal a stream of charged particles from its neighbor's photosphere.

Not surprisingly, there was no sign of the *Belladonna*. But then, the research vessel was less than a hundred meters in length. Trying to pick her out visually against the vast backdrop of a binary star system made finding a needle in a haystack seem ridiculously easy by comparison.

Fortunately, the ship's sensors weren't restricted to the visible spec-

trum. They also included wideband electromagnetic scanners, virtual neutrino spectrometers, and a host of other devices.

It was the nonvisual array that Wu was relying on to pick out the
Belladonna. She glanced at Gerda, who had primary responsibility for
sensor operations.

"Got them?" she asked.

The navigator frowned as she worked at her console. "Not yet," she
was forced to report.

Wu was surprised. Turning back to the image on the viewscreen,
she wondered what the problem was. The *Belladonna's* captain had sent
out a high-priority distress call. He wouldn't have resorted to that option
if his ship had been in any shape to leave Oneo Madrin.

According to that logic, the research ship should still have been here,
and Gerda's sensors should have identified it in a matter of moments.
But they hadn't done that.

Wu's mind raced, going through the possibilities. None of them was
very promising—and the ones that involved hostile intervention were the
least promising of all.

She could think of half a dozen species in this part of space that
might have been tempted to attack the *Belladonna*—among them the
Enniac, the Azhuridai and the Topoli. It was unlikely that any of them
would have done so for fear of the repercussions, but one never knew.

Fortunately, there was a way to see if the research vessel might have
met with foul play. "Scan for ion trails," she told Gerda.

The navigator looked up at her. "You think they were attacked?"

Wu shrugged. "Let's find out."

It didn't take long. In a matter of seconds, Gerda had called up a
graphic identifying ion concentrations in the area.

As it happened, there was only one discernible trail. That pretty much
ruled out the possibility of an assault. But the exercise was a valuable
one nevertheless, because it showed them the route the *Belladonna* had
taken through the system.

And in the process, it gave them a pretty clear picture of where she
had gone—a picture that, as it sank in, turned out to be as disheartening
as it was unexpected.

Gerda muttered something harsh in the Klingon tongue. Wu didn't
speak a word of Klingon, but she had no trouble understanding the gist
of the navigator's remark.

"They're in the accretion bridge," Idun said for the benefit of anyone
who hadn't figured it out.

Wu nodded. "It seems that way, all right."

She considered the conditions the *Belladonna* would be facing, ticking them off one by one in her mind. *High levels of radiation. Powerful magnetic fields. Near-solar temperatures, mitigated only by the scarcity of material in which thermal energy could be stored.* No one could survive in that environment for long.

"We've got to get her out of there," she said.

Of course, it might already have been too late. If the *Belladonna*'s shields had been compromised even a little . . .

Nonetheless, they had to try.

The second officer turned to Gerda. "Can you identify them?"

The navigator shook her head. She was rotating sensor modalities, one after the other. "I'm picking up some kind of solid object. But it doesn't look like a ship. At least, not a *whole* one."

Wu bit her lip. Was it possible that the vessel had already blown up? Or been vaporized?

"There's a reason for that," said Kastiigan.

He was standing at the tiny science station aft of the captain's chair, his jowly face caught in the crawl of a moving graphic. Apparently, he had joined his colleagues on the bridge without Wu's noticing it.

"A reason?" she prodded.

"Yes," said the science officer. "According to my readings, only a portion of the *Belladonna* exists within the accretion bridge. The rest . . . does not."

"You mean she's been ripped apart?" the commander asked, trying to get a handle on the situation.

"No," said Kastiigan. "There's no indication that the *Belladonna* has sustained that sort of damage. Her sensor profile just seems to go so far and no farther."

"Where is she?" Wu demanded. "I want to see her for myself."

"I'll relay the coordinates to Lieutenant Asmund's station," the Kandilkari said obligingly.

A moment later, Wu saw what Kastiigan was talking about. The *Stargazer*'s sensors were picking up a fragment of what might have been a Federation research ship. But it showed no signs of the carbonization or twisted metal that would have resulted from a hull-rending decompression.

It was just as the science officer had said—the *Belladonna* simply wasn't all there.

Wu shook her head. It didn't make sense. She was tempted to say so until she remembered something—that she was the one in charge of the ship at the moment. She had to keep her head if she expected her subordinates to do so.

"Good work," she told Kastiigan.

"Thank you," he responded.

The second officer stared at Gerda's monitor, coming up with question after question for which she had no ready answers. For instance, how had a piece of the *Belladonna* wound up in the accretion bridge? And what had happened to the rest of the ship?

Then she got something new—an answer for which she had no question. "Commander," said Gerda, "we're detecting life signs."

Wu watched as Gerda magnified the surviving portion of the research ship on her monitor. It was covered with red blips, each of them representing a viable, functioning life-form.

Without question, there were living beings aboard—humanoid, judging from their biochemical makeup. But how could that be? This was only a *section* of the *Belladonna*.

Or was it?

"Commander," said Idun, her voice taut with concern, "we're being drawn in the direction of the accretion bridge."

The second officer eyed the viewscreen and saw a confirmation of what Idun had told her. The accretion bridge was growing larger at a slow but noticeable rate.

Wu didn't get it. Accretion bridges didn't have enough mass to generate gravitic forces. So what in the name of Zefram Cochrane was tugging at them?

As calmly as she could, she made her way to the helm. "Reverse engines," she said. "Full power."

Idun carried out the command. For a tense moment or two, it wasn't clear whether she would win the battle or not. Then she turned to Wu and reported that the *Stargazer* was moving backward, returning to her original position.

Indeed, the commander could see it on the screen. The accretion bridge was gradually diminishing in size.

"Maintain thrusters," Wu told her, "until we're two thousand kilometers from the accretion bridge."

"Aye, Commander," said the helm officer, and they continued to retreat from the phenomenon.

Wu returned to her seat and regarded the image on the viewscreen. She no longer wondered how the *Belladonna* had wound up in the accretion bridge. Obviously, it had succumbed to the forces the *Stargazer* had just managed to overcome.

But where in blazes were those forces coming from? She couldn't say—just as she couldn't say how all those people had survived on a mere piece of a ship, or how it had become merely a *piece* of a ship in the first place.

Maybe the *Belladonna*'s crew could tell her. "Hail them," the commander told Paxton.

The comm officer did as she asked. But after a moment, he said, "No response."

Obviously, she would have to take another tack.

"Launch a probe into the accretion bridge," Wu commanded, determined to obtain some answers while there was still time to help the living on the *Belladonna*.

Back in his Academy days, Picard had run marathons. What's more, he had fared rather well in them, regardless of whether the course before him was crumbly desert dirt or rocky mountain turf or some smooth artificial surface.

But then, he hadn't run those races on anything even remotely like the stuff he now found underfoot.

"There's a rhythm to it," Simenon told him. "All you've got to do is find it."

Picard frowned and tried to follow his engineer's instructions. However, the springy, reddish-brown moss beneath his feet seemed to want to bounce when he didn't, and vice versa.

"Easy for you to say," he told his engineer.

When they had begun this race, the ground had been pretty much what one found in most forests—an uneven but generally reliable mixture of whatever substances the surrounding trees cared to contribute. But a few minutes ago, that had changed.

"This is most unsettling," Vigo observed. Obviously, he was having trouble making the adjustment, too.

"Get used to it," Simenon told them. "From here on in, the trail will be like this more often than not."

And that wouldn't be a disadvantage to the Aklaash or the Fejjimaera, Picard reflected. But it would be a disadvantage to *them*—a group made up mostly of offworlders unaccustomed to this kind of terrain—as if they weren't laboring under enough of a disadvantage already.

Suddenly, the trees up ahead seemed to explode into a million frag-ments and the sky was filled with a flight of green and purple avians. Shading his eyes from the shafts of sunlight that penetrated the forest, the captain saw that the creatures were vaguely reminiscent of a flock of Terran geese.

As they flew, their wings flapping in graceful unison, they shed their plumage over the forest. The green and purple feathers wafted and rolled lazily, glinting with iridescent majesty.

"The colunnu?" Picard asked.

"That's right," Simenon confirmed.

"They're beautiful," Vigo observed, squinting so he could see. "And so fragile-looking."

"Yes," said Ben Zoma. "Hard to believe they would pick us clean if we let our guard down."

Thanks to Simenon, Picard knew exactly what his first officer meant. The colunnu's feathers were extremely poisonous. If any of them were to prick his unprotected skin, they would paralyze him in twenty seconds and shut down his nervous system in another ten.

And the colunnu, who had an uncanny knack for knowing when one of their feathers had claimed a victim, would be on him almost instantly. If Simenon's cautions weren't exaggerations, his bones would be picked clean even before the poison finished its work.

"A gruesome end," said the captain, "to be sure."

That, he mused, was why they were all wearing thick, sturdy boots—to make certain they didn't step on any green and purple feathers and come to regret it.

Suddenly, Joseph stopped in his tracks and looked around. "What's that?" he asked.

Greyhorse stopped, too. "I didn't hear anything," he said.

"Listen," the security officer insisted.

They stopped and listened—all of them, Picard included. That's when he heard it—a barking sound in the distance.

"Simenon?" said Ben Zoma.

"Sanjarra," the Gnalish told them.

"Which ones were those again?" asked the doctor.

Simenon shot him a disparaging look. "Four-legged predators, travel in packs . . . starting to sound familiar?"

Greyhorse's brow furrowed. "These aren't the ones that can snap our bones with their teeth, are they?"

"In fact," said the engineer, "they are."

"What are the odds they'll pass us by?" asked Vigo.

"Not very good," Simenon told him.

The barking was getting louder. "As I recall," Picard said, "sanjarra hate water."

"That's correct," the Gnalish rasped. "Unfortunately, we're not *near* any water."

"So what do we do?" asked Greyhorse. "Take to the trees?"

Simenon shook his scaly head. "It wouldn't help. Sanjarra are *born* in the trees."

"Then what?" the doctor demanded.

Simenon looked grim. "We get our sticks out and stand our ground— and hope they've eaten recently."

Picard drew his stick from its sheath and watched his officers do the same. Then, without anyone telling them to do so, they put their backs together and formed a knot.

As the beasts got closer, their growling grew louder and more frenzied. They were within a hundred meters now, the captain judged, though the forest still hid them from view.

His heart was pounding and he could feel a trickle of sweat running down the side of his face. Primitive reactions, he noted. But then, this was a primitive confrontation.

Picard would have given much for the reassuring weight of a phaser pistol in his hand. Unfortunately, the nearest directed energy weapon was in orbit high above the planet's surface, securely locked in the *Stargazer's* armory.

More growling, closer still. Without question, the sanjarra had caught their scent.

"As soon as you see them," said Simenon, "go on the offensive. Keep them off-balance. Once they leap, we're as good as dead."

Another flight of colunnu crossed the sky in close formation. But this time, the captain didn't look up to appreciate them.

He had a more immediate concern.

Chapter Fifteen

WU FELT AS IF she had been watching the streaming splendor of Oneo Madrin's accretion bridge for hours before the *Stargazer* finally got some telemetry from its class IV probe. In fact, though, it could only have been seven or eight minutes.

"We're receiving," Paxton announced.

"What have we got?" asked the second officer, getting up to join him at his console.

Paxton frowned as he studied his communications monitors. "There's interference from all the radiation, Commander. I'm trying to eliminate it . . ."

Wu leaned over his shoulder to see how he was doing. Little by little, the comm officer was cleaning up the image on his central monitor. As he did this, Wu could see the outline of a ship emerging.

Or rather, *part* of a ship.

But the part she could make out appeared undamaged, just as their sensors had already indicated. It was as if something had sheared the *Belladonna* in half.

Then Wu saw that there was something else in the accretion bridge— a churning maelstrom of energy that had no business being there, but was dancing around the severed end of the research ship. "What's that?" she asked Paxton.

The comm officer peered at his monitor, its glare casting crimson shadows on his face. "It looks like a graviton storm—though I don't think I've ever seen one of this intensity."

"Is it intense enough to have drawn us toward the accretion bridge?" Wu asked.

"I don't believe so," Kastiigan told her. "Nor do I believe it is intense enough to have trapped the *Belladonna.*"

The second officer frowned. *Something* had exerted an attractive force on them. If not the graviton storm, what then?

As if he had read her mind, Kastiigan said, "Graviton storms seldom occur spontaneously. They are usually an incidental effect of some other sort of disturbance."

"So maybe this one is concealing something," Paxton speculated.

"Something that has an attractive force all its own," Wu remarked.

Paxton nodded. "A kind of cosmic sinkhole."

"An interesting thesis," Kastiigan noted. "It would explain why we are only seeing part of the research vessel."

Wu felt a trickle of cold sweat in the small of her back. "You mean because the rest has already been swallowed up by the sinkhole."

Paxton shrugged. "Makes as much sense as anything else."

The second officer studied the telemetry some more. She had heard of gaps in space–time that pulled matter from her universe into another. They had been documented in the logs of starship captains as far back as the twenty-second century.

"All right," she said at last. "If this is a sinkhole, where does it lead?" She challenged her bridge officers with a look. "What's on the other side?"

"That is difficult to say," Kastiigan responded. "But one thing seems certain, Commander—the *Belladonna* won't have the wherewithal to survive the journey."

Wu didn't like hearing that. However, it was hard to argue the point. The stresses associated with space–time rifts were such that few vessels had a chance of getting through them intact.

She stood up and eyed the viewscreen. "Mr. Paxton," she said, "do you think you can use the probe to punch a comm signal through that mess?"

"I think so," said the communications officer.

"Good," Wu replied. "Try hailing them again."

Paxton's fingers crawled over his controls. Then he sat back and watched his screens for a reply.

"Anything?" she asked.

Paxton shook his head. "I'm afraid not."

Wu frowned. A lack of response could mean one of two things: either their signal still hadn't gotten through to the *Belladonna* or there was no one in a position to answer it.

She hoped it was the former.

"Commander," Kastiigan said abruptly, "we have a problem. The probe is being drawn into the phenomenon as well."

Wu turned to Paxton. "Get it out of there."

The comm officer tried. But after a while, he shook his head. "It's not responding. The pull is too strong."

The second officer considered their options. They were too far away from the probe to get a tractor beam on it. And if they got much closer, they would be putting the *Stargazer* in jeopardy again.

Had the class IV been a manned probe, Wu would have gone after it without a second thought. But it was just a set of instruments surrounded by a duranium hull. And instruments—no matter how valuable—could be replaced.

"Try a sudden acceleration," Wu suggested.

Paxton looked at her. "You mean slingshot it out the other side of the accretion bridge?"

"If you can."

"It's worth a try," the comm officer said.

His fingers moving with practiced ease, he tapped out the second officer's order on his control panel. Then he implemented it.

On Paxton's monitor, the yellow blip that represented the probe suddenly leaped past the research ship, striving to free itself from the phenomenon's embrace. And for a moment, it appeared to Wu that it might make it.

Then, slowly but certainly, the probe was dragged backward. Paxton gave it all the thrust he could, but it didn't seem to help. Finally, the class IV device vanished from the screen altogether.

Paxton turned to Wu, looking apologetic. "We've lost contact with the probe, Commander."

She sighed. Clearly, she needed more information, and she wasn't going to get it by sending in more unmanned probes.

Wu gazed at the main viewscreen, where all she could see was the accretion bridge. Somewhere inside it, the *Belladonna* was slowly but inexorably slipping into the stormy maw of the phenomenon.

If she were going to do a better job with the research vessel than she had with the probe, she had to do something—and soon. But this wasn't a problem with a simple solution. She couldn't just transport the survivors off the *Belladonna*—not when she couldn't even get a comm signal through.

Turning to the rest of the bridge contingent, Wu said, "I need a plan—and I need it *now.*"

The sanjarra were already within twenty meters of Simenon's party when Picard got his first glimpse of the beasts through a gap in the screen of crimson trees.

They looked like sleek, black greyhounds with blood-red tiger stripes and faces like fruit bats. Their eyes were like shiny, black pebbles and their mouths were full of long, curved teeth. A strange combination to be sure, but hardly the strangest the captain had seen in the course of hundreds of planetary surveys.

It was difficult to tell precisely how many there were, but Picard reckoned that there might be a dozen. As they got closer, their growls deepened and they bared their fangs.

The sanjarra looked completely undaunted by the fact that they had never seen the likes of the offworlders before. But then, the captain supposed, meat was meat.

As they emerged from cover, they got lower to the ground and their muscles seemed to bunch. Picard was reminded of Simenon's instructions: *"As soon as you see them, go on the offensive. Keep them off-balance. Once they leap, we're as good as dead."*

Taking the Gnalish's advice to heart, the captain lunged as if he were on a fencing strip and swung his *tellek* at the nearest bat-face. Its plans interrupted, the beast gave a deep-throated snarl and jumped back out of harm's way.

Picard's companions lashed out as well, with much the same results. The sanjarra looked angry, discomfited by the turn of events. But then, they were predators. They weren't accustomed to defending themselves from their prey.

Again, the captain leaped forward and took a swing at the nearest of the bat-faces. And again, it withdrew with a dangerous-sounding rumbling deep in its throat.

Ben Zoma narrowly swung and missed another one. "When do we get to the part where they run away?" he asked.

Picard had been wondering the same thing. "Why do I get the feeling we're just making them madder?"

"Keep at it," Simenon told them, "and they'll get the idea." Taking his own advice, he drove back one of the beasts with a vicious two-handed attack. Then he added, "Eventually."

Suddenly, someone cried out and fell in a heap. Glancing to his left, the captain saw that it was Greyhorse who had gone down, his leg caught in a thick, leafy vine.

Nor was Picard the only one who had noticed. A couple of sanjarra appeared to have taken note of the doctor's fall as well. Their tiny eyes glittered with a fierce, undeniable hunger.

As the captain looked on, the beasts coiled to spring. *Not good,* he thought. *Not good at all.* Once they pounced on Greyhorse, he was as good as dead.

Someone would have to stop them before they could spring. Determined that he would be the one to do that, Picard started to move in the doctor's direction.

But Joseph beat him to the punch. Leaping forward and swinging his *tellek* in big, savage arcs, the security officer made the beasts think twice about claiming their prey.

Then help came in the form of Simenon and Ben Zoma. Over-matched now, the sanjarra who had been eyeing Greyhorse grudgingly gave ground. But at the same time, it gave some of the other beasts an opening.

And when Picard and Vigo went after *those* bat-faces, it created an opportunity for the sanjarra to attack from still another quarter. It was as if the bat-faced predators were a deadly flood and Picard's people were trying to maintain a leaky seawall in which they could only plug one hole at a time.

"Watch out!" someone cried, his voice thick with urgency.

"Behind you!" shouted someone else.

They whirled, swung their *telleks,* whirled again to face a new threat. None of them ever quite managed to hit anything, but neither did they let the sanjarra gain the advantage.

Picard blinked away sweat that had fallen into his eyes and tried desperately to hold up his end of the bargain. They all did—Greyhorse too, now that he was on his feet again.

Finally, after what seemed like a very long time, the beasts' frustration seemed to overcome their hunger. They didn't growl any less loudly or viciously when they were beaten back, but they also weren't as quick to come forward again.

Then the breakthrough came. One of the bat-faces, perhaps the largest of them, appeared to lose interest in his prey. He turned around and began to pad away through the forest, not even bothering to give Simenon's party a second look.

A moment later, a second beast admitted defeat as well. And as if by tacit agreement, the rest of the sanjarra followed suit.

In a matter of moments, they were gone. It was only then that Picard realized how much his arms hurt. Taking a deep breath, he looked around at his comrades. They were breathing hard but no one seemed to have sustained any damage.

Not even Greyhorse.

"Everyone all right?" Ben Zoma asked.

His question was met with tired murmurs of assent.

Vigo slipped his *tellek* back into its sheath. "Well," he said, grpping Joseph's shoulder, "that could have turned out worse."

Joseph nodded. *"Much* worse."

Ben Zoma swiped perspiration from his brow with the back of his hand. "I'd call it a good omen."

Simenon cast a skeptical look at him. "That is," he amended, "if you believe in such things."

"Come on," the first officer told him. "Even you have to admit we did well just now."

Simenon's nostrils flared stubbornly. "All right," he said at last. "I'll admit it."

Then he started off down the path again.

As he fell in behind the engineer, Picard smiled through his weariness. If even Simenon could show a hint of optimism, their venture might turn out well after all.

Chapter Sixteen

"WELL?" SAID WU, scanning the faces of her bridge officers.

She could feel the hum of the *Stargazer*'s engines through the deck plates, hear the control consoles' unrelenting chorus of beeps and chirps. Normally, she tuned those things out the way any veteran officer would, but they seemed all too obtrusive now in the silence that followed her challenge.

"Who's got a way to get those people off the *Belladonna?*" she asked, her voice echoing throughout the bridge.

No one spoke for a moment. Then Paxton broke the ice.

"We could try using a tractor beam. But that would require us to get a lot closer to the accretion bridge."

"And we can't do that," said Idun, "because the pull would drag *us* into the phenomenon as well."

Kastiigan nodded at his science console. "True."

"We can't transport them off," Gerda thought out loud. "Not when we can't get a reliable lock on them."

"And," Kastiigan added, "the radiation and the magnetic fields in the accretion bridge would wreak havoc with a confinement beam."

"So the transporter isn't an option," Wu concluded. "What *is?*"

Silence ruled the bridge again. Wu found herself missing the captain, Ben Zoma, Simenon, and Vigo. Had they been aboard, there would no doubt have been a few more suggestions in the air.

Paris, who was manning the weapons station in Vigo's absence, hadn't spoken to that point. But now he said, "We've established that we can't use our tractor beam to pull the *Belladonna* out. But why couldn't we use it to send in an unmanned shuttle?"

Wu looked at him. "You mean as a rescue vehicle?"

The ensign nodded. "If we can get it to the *Belladonna*, they can offload their people one group at a time."

The second officer considered the notion. It was interesting, all right. She turned to Lt. Dubinski, Simenon's stand-in at the engineering console. "What do you think?"

The engineer took a moment to run some calculations. When he looked up, it wasn't with a great deal of optimism. And when he spoke, it was with even less.

"Even if a tractor beam could be effective in an accretion bridge environment, we'd have to stretch it pretty thin to keep the *Stargazer* out of trouble. It wouldn't be able to handle the mass of a shuttle *pod,* much less a full-fledged passenger craft." Dubinski glanced at Paris. "Good try."

But the ensign didn't seem especially gratified by the compliment. His expression said he wouldn't be content until he had come up with something better.

Wu looked around the bridge. "Anyone else?"

No one seemed to have an idea—not even Paris, for all his obvious determination. Under different circumstances, that might not have bothered the second officer so much.

But under *these* circumstances, with a ship full of lives hanging in the balance, it bothered her a lot.

Picard sat down heavily and rested his back against the rough bark of a tree trunk.

"I just need a minute," Greyhorse gasped, collapsing against another tree on the opposite side of the path.

Of course, this was the fourth time the doctor had said that since the beginning of the race a few hours earlier. Though no one had complained out loud, it was growing difficult to ignore the fact that he was slowing their team down.

To Simenon's credit, he was managing to withhold comment on Greyhorse like everyone else. He just stood there a little farther up the trail, glancing occasionally at the paths of their adversaries to either side of them and frowning.

"Thanks a lot," Greyhorse rasped in the Gnalish's direction.

Simenon turned. "For what? I haven't said a word."

"You don't have to," the big man told him. "The way you're standing there is comment enough."

The engineer's ruby eyes narrowed. "What would you have me do? There's nothing more important to a Gnalish than winning this race. *Nothing.* And we're sitting here wasting time when we could be looking after the future of my clan."

"No one's trying harder than I am," Greyhorse wheezed.

"I didn't say you weren't *trying,*" Simenon shot back. "All I'm saying is that—"

He stopped in midsentence as something dark darted across the path and leaped into his backpack. Muttering a curse, the Gnalish reached for the pack, but he was too late.

Whatever it was had emerged with Simenon's package of extra crackers and was dragging it off into the forest.

"Stop it!" the Gnalish cried.

Picard, who was closest to it, managed to head the thing off. It was then that he got his first good look at it.

The creature was small and slender with black, matted fur, a long reddish tail, and tiny paws. Picard would have sworn it was a Terran rat if not for the high, bony ridge in the center of its skull.

It stopped and looked at him for a second with its black, oval eyes, as if it were wondering what kind of smooth-skinned monstrosity had wandered into its forest. Then, with blinding speed, the creature whirled and darted back toward the path, still dragging Simenon's cracker package along with it.

By then, the others had come after it as well. But when the thing scampered back into their midst, it made them spin and dance with the awkward determination of Tellarites at a Regency ball.

"It's behind you!"

"Over there!"

"No," said Picard, pointing to the thing as it scurried past him, "over *there!*"

Every time the creature made a move to elude them, someone blocked its escape route. And after a while, their efforts began to take a toll on the rodent. It moved less quickly and unpredictably, became easier to track with one's eyes.

It still could have slipped into the brush and eluded its pursuers if it had relinquished its hold on their food supply. But having come this far, the creature seemed reluctant to part with its prize.

Finally, Picard and his officers surrounded it, blocking its escape at every turn. At that point, it was just a matter of retrieving the package of crackers.

"Stay where you are," the Gnalish snapped. "I'll get it." And he moved in to recover what was his.

"Feel free," said Ben Zoma.

"It's all yours," Joseph told him.

Hunkering down low, Simenon eyed the rodent. Then he advanced on it with a hunter's purposefulness. "I'll teach you to steal my food," he said softly.

"You can teach him to steal mine, too," Greyhorse remarked dryly.

The rodent didn't move a muscle. It just sat there on its hind legs, its furry, ridged head tilted to one side, watching the engineer as if mesmerized by him.

"That's right," Simenon hissed approvingly. "Just stay there *one* moment longer, you filthy duwiijuc—"

Suddenly, he darted forward and grabbed for the creature. But as he did so, the rodent darted forward, too—right between the Gnalish's legs. And before Simenon could do anything about it, the thing had grabbed hold of his tail.

A cry of rage and indignation boiling up from his throat, the engineer switched his appendage back and forth in an attempt to dislodge his tormentor. But it didn't work. The rodent hung on as if its life depended on it—and maybe it did.

Cursing like a drunken Klingon, Simenon bent over and tried to reach for it through his legs. But that didn't work very well either. The rodent managed to remain just out of reach.

By then, everyone was laughing so hard it hurt. They couldn't help themselves. The only exceptions were Greyhorse, who *never* laughed, and of course Simenon himself.

Finally, Picard couldn't stand it any longer. "Stay in one spot," he told his engineer, "and I'll get it off."

"Easy for you to say!" Simenon hissed. "You haven't got a duwiijuc eating you inch by inch!"

Nonetheless, he managed to remain still until the captain could grab the rodent by its furry torso. Trying not to get bitten himself, Picard pulled the creature off Simenon's appendage. Then he flung it into the crimson brush.

As soon as Simenon was free of the thing, he brought his tail up and inspected it. "The damned thing drew blood!" he groaned.

"Stay where you are!" mimicked Ben Zoma, "I'll get it!" And with that, he incited another wave of laughter.

"Thank you," said the engineer, stoically watching his superior guffaw at his expense. "Thank you very much. I'll remember your compassion next time *you're* injured."

"Oh, don't be such a baby," Greyhorse told him. He grabbed hold of Simenon's tail and took a look at it. "It barely broke the epidermis. I'll bandage it and you'll be fine."

By then, the laughter had begun to die down. Joseph and Ben Zoma had to wipe tears from their eyes as they made an uphill attempt to recover their sobriety.

The security officer took in a deep breath. "Now that," he said, "was worth the price of admission."

"Twice the price," Greyhorse decided as he delved into his pack for a plastiskin bandage and a dressing.

"Don't let anyone ever tell you you're not a good host," Ben Zoma chipped in.

Simenon scowled. "I'm glad I had the opportunity to provide you with some entertainment."

The doctor managed to keep his expression deadpan as he approached his colleague with the bandage he had found. "So am I. Now stand still. I can't treat a moving tail."

And they started laughing all over again.

Wu leaned back in Captain Picard's chair in the captain's ready room and pondered what she had learned from Lt. Kastiigan.

The *Belladonna*'s descent into the sinkhole was slower than she would have guessed. Assuming the research vessel's shields continued to hold up, it probably had a few hours before it was lost forever.

That was good news. It gave her some breathing room, some time to come up with an option she and her officers hadn't considered yet. *If there is one,* she found herself adding.

There is, she insisted. There had to be.

But there were only so many methods of getting a crew off an endangered ship. She ran down the list again in her mind, hoping to somehow find something she had missed.

One way was to beam them off. However, she and her bridge officers had already ruled out that possibility because of the conditions that prevailed inside the accretion bridge.

The other method was to put them in a shuttlecraft. But that was an impossibility as well because a shuttle couldn't escape the pull of the sinkhole.

Wu leaned back in her chair and closed her eyes. She had always found it easier to think with her eyes closed, even as a little girl back at the Aramis III agricultural colony. Her younger sister, Victoria, had made fun of her for that all the time. Then Victoria saw some of the things her sister was accomplishing in school and she secretly began to close her eyes as well.

Wu sighed. Her accomplishments in school had meant a lot to her—much more than they might have to other children her age. They had paved the way for her to realize her dream of joining Starfleet, of ascending the chain of command—of reaching a moment like this one, when people depended on her for their survival.

I can't let those scientists down, she told herself stubbornly. *I've got to get them out of there. Any other outcome is unacceptable.*

Of course, there *was* a third way; there had been one all along. If the *Belladonna* could generate enough thrust, and the *Stargazer* brought her tractors to bear at the right moment, they might be able to wrench the research ship free of the sinkhole.

But that required a willing partner in the *Belladonna,* not to mention a considerable contribution from her impulse drive. And so far, they had been unable to obtain a response to their hails, much less any evidence that the *Belladonna*'s engines were still in working order.

Wu frowned to herself. If not for those two small problems, the plan couldn't miss.

If only Ensign Paris's idea had proven workable. They would already have sent out a shuttlecraft on a tractor beam, offering the crew of the *Belladonna* a lifeline. The survivors might have been boarding it at that very moment.

But Dubinski's calculations had thrown a wrench into the ensign's plan. Too much mass on the end of the beam. Too much radiation, too many uncertainties presented by those magnetic fields.

Even a pod would have been too much, the engineer said. But then, even the smallest one weighed nearly a metric ton. And there wasn't anything lighter than a pod. . . .

Or was there?

Wu's eyes snapped open.

Could they send in a probe with instructions for the scientists? Maybe one they had stripped of its instruments and propulsion capabilities, to reduce the mass their tractor beam had to handle?

For a moment, it sounded as if it might work. Then the commander thought about it some more and her heart sank. Sure, they could send in a probe. But what would it do when it got there? How would it gain access to the interior of the *Belladonna?*

Probes couldn't open hatches. Probes couldn't canvass the research ship for survivors among the crew regardless of where they might have decided to gather.

Only a rescue team could do that. And no rescue team Wu had ever heard of could survive in a radiation-shot environment full of fierce, bone-crushing graviton waves.

All of a sudden, it came to her that she was wrong about that. Dead wrong. There *was* such a rescue team. And it was waiting for her in blissful ignorance on a lower deck of the *Stargazer.*

Chapter Seventeen

PICARD WAS JOGGING side by side with Simenon, the rest of their party a bit behind them, when he remarked that the trees ahead of them seemed to be thinning.

"You're right," the Gnalish observed.

It wasn't until a few minutes later that Picard saw the reason for it. That was when he found himself standing at the brink of a narrow but remarkably deep crevasse that appeared to cut the wild tangle of forest-land in half.

Fortunately, there was a way at hand for the group to make their way across the half-dozen meters of treeless space. But it wasn't one that inspired a great deal of confidence.

"A bridge," said Greyhorse, a lock of his dark hair lifting in the swirling winds that held sway here.

"If one can call it that," Ben Zoma added.

To Picard, it looked more like a quartet of thick, scarlet ropes, two above and two below, with the latter supporting a series of short, wooden planks and the former serving as crude handrails. There were also a few short lines that connected the upper ropes with the lower ones.

"Looks old," said Vigo.

"And rickety," Joseph added.

"It was built some time ago," Simenon confirmed.

"Decades?" Greyhorse asked.

"Centuries," the Gnalish told them.

Picard looked at him, an expression of surprise on his face. "And it's still standing?"

"It was built to last," Simenon explained. "Also, it's maintained on a regular basis."

"What's *regular?*" Joseph asked.

"Every few weeks," the engineer replied.

"So it should be safe," the captain concluded, though he didn't sound as sure of himself as he might have intended.

"Should be," Simenon agreed.

"You think it can hold me?" Vigo asked.

"If it can hold an Aklaash," the Gnalish reasoned, "I would think it can hold a Pandrilite."

Joseph looked at him. "How do you know it can hold an Aklaash? I thought this route was just for Mazzereht."

"This time it's for Mazzereht," Simenon told him. "Last time, it might have been for a party of Aklaash, or Fejjimaera. The routes are doled out at random."

"Hey!" said Joseph. He was standing on the brink of the ravine and pointing to something far to their right. "There's another bridge down that way. Maybe it's sturdier than this one."

"It's not," the engineer assured him. "And even if it were, we couldn't use it."

"Why not?" asked Greyhorse.

"Because," said Simenon, "that's the one the Fejjimaera are going to use. We've all got to cross the ravine somewhere. The Fejjimaera are going to cross it down *there.*"

Ben Zoma grunted. "So we're stuck with *this* bridge."

"In a manner of speaking," said the Gnalish, "yes."

As he said that, the wind whistled a little more insistently and the bridge swayed drunkenly under its influence. Seeing it, they all fell silent—Simenon included.

"Listen," said Picard, breaking the spell, "it's not as if we have a lot of choice in the matter."

Greyhorse shaded his eyes as he examined the bridge from one end to the other. "So it would seem."

The captain took his companions in at a glance. "So what are we waiting for?"

There were murmurs of agreement. However, no one seemed very eager to try the span.

"I'll go first," Simenon volunteered.

He didn't get any arguments from the others.

Jiterica was sitting at her workstation in the science section, dutifully inspecting yet another set of sensor readings, when she heard someone call her name.

Turning, she saw that it was Commander Wu. The second officer was crossing the science section, headed her way.

"Commander?" Jiterica said in response.

Wu looked serious. "I need your help with the research vessel," she told the Nizhrak.

Her curiosity piqued, Jiterica swiveled to face her superior. "I will assist you in any way I can."

Wu held a hand up. "Don't say that until you've heard me out. What I have in mind will involve considerable personal risk. If you decline, I'll understand."

"I would like to help," Jiterica maintained.

Wu nodded. "I was hoping you would say that."

"What do you need me to do?" the ensign asked.

The commander didn't tell her right away. Instead, she described Ensign Paris's idea. Its flaw, apparently, was that a shuttle would have too much mass to be manipulated by a tractor beam under the conditions that existed in the accretion bridge.

"But not a single crewman," Wu continued pointedly. "That would be a different story entirely."

Jiterica looked at her. "A single crewman," she repeated thoughtfully. The conclusion was an obvious one. "You mean *me*."

Wu nodded. "That's right."

"Because I'm accustomed to the conditions in a gas giant."

"Exactly. Radiation and magnetic fields aren't a problem for you and neither is high gravity, and your mass is no greater than that of the average human being."

Jiterica took a moment to consider the idea. The more she thought about it, the more sense it made—except for one fairly significant problem.

"Given the inefficiencies of projecting a tractor beam into the accretion bridge, the ship will have to come rather close to it. Won't she run the risk of being drawn inside?"

"She would," Wu agreed, "if she had to come that close. But what if she simply maintained a tractor lifeline to a shuttle . . . and it was the shuttle that sent in the crewman on a beam of its own?"

"Two tractor beams," Jiterica said. "One from the ship and one from the shuttle. An interesting approach."

"I'm glad you think so," Wu told her. "Of course, the beam would only get you so far. You would still have to find a hatch and gain access to the *Belladonna.*"

It seemed to Jiterica that she was capable of doing that. Then something occurred to her. "Commander . . . unless I'm mistaken, our shuttlecraft aren't equipped with tractor assemblies."

"Normally," said Wu, "that's true. But we're going to take one of ours and make it an exception."

The ensign nodded. "I see." She had just one other question. "Who will pilot the shuttle?"

Wu told her who she had in mind.

Simenon wasn't nearly as matter-of-fact about crossing the crevasse as he had made himself out to be.

Like most Mazzereht, he was discomfited by heights. It was one of the reasons his subspecies didn't succeed in the ritual more often.

On the other hand, what was the point of mentioning such a shortcoming? He had to cross the chasm. They all did. It was just a matter of looking straight ahead and doing it.

All right, Simenon told himself, *you can do this.*

Clenching his jaw, he grasped the rope rail on the right side and took a step onto the bridge. Then another. And another.

As it turned out, the span wasn't half as wobbly as it looked. It wasn't as easy as walking down a corridor on the *Stargazer*—after all, corridors didn't bounce as one negotiated them—but neither did it require a particularly sophisticated sense of balance.

After Simenon had advanced a couple of meters, he was inspired to turn around and look back at his comrades. "Coming?" he asked them.

Joseph frowned and ever so carefully followed the engineer onto the bridge. It didn't appear to take him long to discover what Simenon had discovered—that the crossing simply wasn't as prodigious a feat as it had appeared.

"This isn't bad at all," the security officer observed.

"All the same," Picard said, "let's not all pile on at once. We'll go no more than two at a time."

"You're the captain," Simenon told him.

Or rather, that was what he meant to say. Before he could quite get the words out, he felt the bridge give way.

It all happened so fast, the Gnalish barely knew what he was doing. But somehow, he managed to snatch one of the ropes that attached the span's rail to its floor and hang on for dear life.

For a heartbeat, he couldn't tell if only one end of the bridge had given way or both. Then he realized that it was only one—the one on the far side—and he was swinging back in the direction of the cliff he had left behind.

That was the good news. The bad came when Simenon crashed into the sheer rock surface with bone-crushing force, squeezing the air out of his lungs and awakening a terrible, sharp pain in his side.

Blackness threatened to overwhelm him. It seeped in from the edges of his vision, offering him the warm, welcome balm of oblivion.

But the Gnalish fought it off, pulling in air as hard as he could. His throat burned with the effort—burned horribly as if it were on fire. But he didn't let that stop him. He kept gasping, kept sucking down what little his tortured windpipe would accommodate.

And somehow, he held onto the twisted remains of the bridge. The taste of blood filled his mouth and his ribs throbbed as if someone were taking a hammer to them, but he didn't allow himself to fall to the bottom of the chasm.

"Simenon!" someone cried. "Pug! Are you all right?"

"Yes," said the security officer, who was dangling just above Simenon. "I'm fine."

The engineer couldn't answer. He was too busy trying to fill his lungs with air.

"Simenon!" someone called again.

"Here," he croaked.

"He's below me," Joseph shouted over the wind. "Just a couple of meters."

"Can you reach him?" someone asked. This time, Simenon recognized the voice as the captain's.

The wind keened through the valley as Joseph made his assessment. "I think so," he said.

"I'll go down, too," someone added. *Vigo,* thought Simenon.

"No," the captain told him. "You're too heavy."

"Me, then," suggested Ben Zoma.

A pause. "All right," said Picard. "But first, we'll secure this end of the bridge as best we can."

While they did that, Simenon caught his breath. But the easier it came, the harder his side began to throb. And his right arm—the one that had borne the burden of his weight to that point—was beginning to ache with the effort.

"Take your time," he rasped with false bravado.

Wu regarded Paris across the captain's ready room. The ensign looked surprised by the assignment she had just given him—more so than she might have expected.

"Me, Commander?" he replied after a moment.

"Why not?" said Wu. "You may be young, Mr. Paris, but it's clear to me that you're the best pilot we have—with the exception of Lieutenant Asmund, of course. And we need her to pilot the ship, which won't be any mean feat."

"I suppose not," Paris responded.

Wu briefed the ensign on the particulars of the mission—how far he would have to go and what he would have to look out for, that sort of thing. By the time she finished, he seemed to have gotten past his surprise and was again exuding the confidence that had distinguished him from other young men of Wu's acquaintance.

It was a good thing, she reflected. She would need Paris at his best if they were going to pull this off.

"Then go get ready," the second officer told him. "Mr. Chiang tells me he'll have that shuttle ready in the next twenty minutes."

The ensign lifted his chin. "Acknowledged."

Then he turned and made his way out of the room. As the doors hissed closed behind him, Wu nodded to herself. If anyone could do this, it would be Cole Paris.

Simenon winced as Greyhorse used his fingers to probe the Gnalish's tortured flank. "Careful," Simenon groaned.

"I'm *being* careful," the doctor told him.

"Well?" asked Picard, who was standing over them, a couple of meters back from the crevasse and the dangling bridge.

Greyhorse rolled back onto his haunches and made a face. "You're lucky," he told Simenon. "I don't think those ribs are broken, after all. And your arm's in remarkably good shape considering it could have been torn out of its socket."

Somehow, Simenon didn't feel that fortunate.

After all, his hope of progeny had just been crushed. Unless he could get across the chasm, one of the other teams would claim the eggs waiting for them at the finish line. And without a bridge, the odds of their making it across seemed slim indeed.

Not that it was impossible. The chasm was only six or seven meters from one side to the other. An Aklaash might have had the size and the power to leap across it.

But not a Gnalish of Simenon's stature—especially one who had injured himself the way the engineer had. For someone like that, leaping the gap simply wasn't an option.

"We still need to get across," Ben Zoma said.

"Someone's going to have to jump it," Joseph added.

There was silence for a moment. Then someone said, "I think I can make it."

The Gnalish looked around, eager to see who had spoken. So did everyone else in his party—with one exception.

That of the captain.

Chapter Eighteen

"YOU?" SIMENON SAID.

He had already blurted it out before he realized how derogatory it sounded. But he hadn't intended to disparage the captain. It was just that he hadn't thought of Picard as the most likely candidate to negotiate the chasm.

Vigo, perhaps, with his Aklaash-like strides and his muscular physique. But not a normal-size human with a normal-size human's strength and speed.

"I mean," the engineer added quickly, "are you certain you want to risk it?"

The captain still looked as if his ego had been bruised. "Though you may not be aware of it, Mr. Simenon, I've always been a rather decent track-and-field man. With a little luck, I'll be able to make the jump. Then, if someone can toss me the loose end of the bridge, I can make it fast again on the other side."

Simenon frowned. He had seen Picard engage Captain Ruhalter in some sort of swordplay, even work out a bit on the pommel horse in the ship's gymnasium—and he had certainly seemed proficient in those activities. But he had never seen the man perform a long jump.

And as much as he wanted to win the race, he didn't want to do it at the cost of his captain's life.

"I can't ask you to do that for me," he told Picard.

The captain's eyes crinkled at the corners, as if he had managed to find some humor in their predicament. "I'm not doing it for you," he said evenly. "I'm doing it for generations of brilliant but irascible Gnalish to come."

Simenon looked to his other colleagues. No one was objecting to Picard's proposal—not even Ben Zoma, who was supposed to protect his commanding officer at all times. In fact, the man was smiling as if in appreciation of the captain's quip.

But Simenon didn't find it funny. He didn't find it funny in the least. It was *his* fault they were down here, *his* fault that they were placing life and limb in jeopardy. If Picard came up short in his jump and hurt himself—or worse, *killed* himself—that would be the Gnalish's fault, too.

"Sir," he said, meaning to talk the captain out of it. "If anything happened to you, I'd—"

"It won't," Picard told him unequivocally. He glanced at the chasm, then nodded. "I'll make it."

"But, sir—"

"Belay that," the captain said. His eyes narrowed as he regarded Simenon. "That's an order, Lieutenant."

The engineer scowled. It didn't seem he was being given much of a say in the matter.

"All right," he said, yielding to his superior. "But for the gods' sake, be careful."

"I will be as careful as the situation permits," the captain promised him. Then he turned to the crevasse again and focused his attention on the task ahead of him.

First, he approached the chasm and inspected the turf at its edge. It appeared to be as spongy as the rest of the forest floor, hardly optimum for takeoff. Nor would the spongy surface on the other side lend itself to an easy landing.

Simenon was glad that Picard was taking the time to prepare for his effort. It gave the Gnalish some confidence that his captain might actually survive it.

Next, Picard turned his back on the chasm and walked back into the depths of the forest, brushing aside the odd branch as he retraced the steps their team had taken to get here. By Simenon's reckoning, the man was nearly thirty meters from the group before a tree trunk that had fallen across the trail prevented him from going any farther.

Turning around, the captain regarded the chasm again. He took a breath and let it out slowly. Then he said, "Would someone be so kind as to get those branches out of my way?"

Even with his side aching and his right arm all but useless, Simenon was able to pull a branch back and hold it there. Each of his comrades did the same thing, clearing all obstructions from Picard's path.

Simenon saw the captain's brow furrow. He half-expected Picard to finally yield to reason and admit that the feat was too much for him.

But as he was thinking this, he saw Picard lower his head and launch himself forward. Arms pumping, legs churning, he pelted past the Gnalish a good deal faster than Simenon would have ever predicted, the heels of his heavy-duty boots tearing up the spongy ground and throwing up bits of it in his wake.

The captain gained speed all the way to the near edge of the chasm, then sprang suddenly into the air. For a moment, he rose like a big, dark bird, arms and legs cycling ferociously. Then, as his momentum died, he began to lose altitude.

"Come *on,*" Simenon heard someone say.

Come on, he echoed silently.

For one heart-stopping fraction of a second, the engineer was sure that Picard would fall short of the other side. Then the captain tucked his legs beneath him and threw his arms forward, giving himself the added impetus that he needed.

Simenon cheered inwardly when he saw Picard's heels hit the ground just past the sheer drop of the ravine. The captain had surprised him. He had *done* it.

But as Simenon watched, horrified, it became clear to him that there was something wrong. The captain was still in jeopardy after all.

He seemed to be struggling to keep his weight forward on the spongy, uncertain turf. And little by little, he was losing the battle. Before the Gnalish's disbelieving eyes, Picard staggered back just half a step—but half a step was all it took to send him sliding toward the depths of the crevasse.

"No!" Simenon cried out.

And somehow, as if in response to his anguished cry, the captain stopped falling.

Apparently, he had latched onto something before he could be swallowed by the abyss. As pieces of turf and debris spiraled down into the crevasse and were lost to sight, the Gnalish saw that it was a protruding root that had saved Picard's life.

"Hang on!" Ben Zoma shouted. "I'll be right there!" And he darted back into the depths of the forest to get the same kind of running jump the captain had gotten.

"No, you won't!" Picard bellowed back at his first officer. Then, still dangling from the errant root, he added in a voice full of forced calm, "Stay where you are, Number One. I can do this on my own."

Ben Zoma didn't look happy about it, but he returned to the brink of the crevasse. Then he stood there with Simenon and the others, watching as the captain swung a leg over the edge of the cliff and—finding a dependable handhold hidden under the lip of turf—laboriously wrestled himself to safety.

For several seconds, Picard lay on his back on the spongy ground, breathing deep draughts of air. It occurred to Simenon that he might have injured himself in his climb.

Just what we need, the Gnalish told himself.

"Are you all right, Captain?" Greyhorse called, obviously thinking the same thing.

"I'm . . . fine," Picard called back, gasping between words. "Couldn't . . . be better."

Slowly, he rolled over onto his belly, pushed himself up, and got to his feet. Then he pointed to the loose end of the bridge, which lay in a pile on Simenon's side of the chasm.

"Toss it over," Picard said.

Vigo, the strongest of them, was the one who tossed it. Even so, it took him three tries to reach the captain.

Picard secured the end of the bridge temporarily with a few of the heaviest rocks around. Then he found a big, dead tree trunk in the brush and rolled it on for good measure.

Unfortunately, what was left was no longer something one could walk all the way across. The line of the handrails converged with the bridge's floor by the time they reached the captain's side of the ravine, making it necessary for Simenon and the others to crawl across.

But at least there was something to crawl on. If not for the captain, there wouldn't even have been that.

As before, Simenon figured he would be first to use the bridge.

After all, he was the reason they were all out here. But before he could take a step onto the wooden planks, Ben Zoma stopped him.

"Let *me,*" he said.

The engineer's first impulse was to protest. But when he thought about it, he had to admit that it made sense. If the bridge failed them again, Ben Zoma could save himself. It would be a lot more difficult for a Gnalish with bruised ribs and strained muscles in his arm.

Simenon held his breath as the first officer made his way across the span. But it actually swayed less than when it was whole, and Ben Zoma passed the halfway point without anything catastrophic happening. A couple of moments later, he reached out for Picard's hand and joined the captain on the other side.

"Vigo's next," Picard said.

Again, a rational approach. The weapons officer was heavier than any of them, though Greyhorse ran a close second. If the bridge could hold Vigo's weight, it could hold anyone's.

Picard's construction methods passed that test, too. As Vigo completed the crossing, the captain nodded approvingly. "Now the rest of you. One at a time, of course."

Simenon wouldn't have had it any other way. He went next, using his tail to support and steady himself in place of his right arm. Then came Joseph and a shaky-looking Greyhorse.

Once the doctor was across, Simenon was ready to get going again. But Joseph knelt by the end of the bridge and lingered there.

"What is it?" Picard asked him.

The security officer held up the end of one of the ropes where it stuck out from beneath a rock. "Take a look at this, sir."

The captain came over to inspect the rope-end more closely. So did Simenon, his curiosity aroused.

"It's not frayed," Joseph pointed out to them. "It's been *cut.*"

Simenon could see that the man was right in his assessment. The end of the rope had been neatly sliced.

Greyhorse frowned. "It looks like someone didn't want us crossing this bridge."

"Or winning the race," Vigo added.

Picard turned to Simenon, his expression a stern one. "Who do you think it might have been?"

The Gnalish was at a loss. "I have no idea. "Kasaelek's party, Banyohla's . . . who knows?"

"*These* might tell us something," said Joseph.

He had hunkered down next to a patch of dried mud—a *rare* patch, given the ubiquitousness of the spongy ground cover on which they had made most of their trek.

"What are they?" asked Vigo.

The group gathered around the security officer now. "Footprints," he said. He looked up at Simenon. "And they're recent, by the look of them."

Simenon moved to the spot and placed his foot beside one of the prints. Then he shook his head. "Unfortunately," he told Ben Zoma, "these are my size. They must have been left by the Mazzereht party that came through here last cycle." A cycle was about the length of a Terran week.

"And a party of Mazzereht wouldn't have sabotaged the bridge," Greyhorse noted. He glanced at the engineer. "Would they?"

"Of course not," Simenon said. He stared at the prints for a moment longer, then turned to the bridge and considered that as well. It had to be one of his competitors.

But which one?

"It's a mystery," Ben Zoma said.

Simenon nodded. "A mystery indeed."

He turned to the trail ahead. It led through another dense expanse of crimson forest. And unless his competitors' bridges had been sabotaged as well, they had obtained a healthy lead on him.

"Come on," he said, fighting off his weariness and the ache in his side. "We're losing time."

Wu was about to contact Lt. Chiang and see how things were proceeding down in the shuttlebay when the door chime sounded.

"Come in," she said.

The doors slid aside, revealing Lt. Kastiigan. "I beg your pardon," he said, "but if I could have just a moment?"

Wu shrugged. "Of course."

Kastiigan threw out his chest. "I volunteer to accompany Ensign Paris and Ensign Jiterica on the shuttlecraft."

The offer seemed a little out of place to the second officer. However, she understood the impulse that had spurred it—or thought she did.

"I'm impressed by your scientific curiosity," she told Kastiigan. "But rest assured, the shuttle's sensors will record all we need to know about the phenomenon."

"It's not scientific curiosity that propels me," the Kandilkari explained. "It's a desire to serve my commanding officer, no matter how perilous that service may be."

Wu wondered if she were missing something. "Beyond making scientific observations, what kind of service did you have in mind?"

Kastiigan shrugged. "Nothing specific. But if you should think of some way I can be of assistance on the shuttle, I hope you'll not hesitate to order me aboard."

"Why would I hesitate?" the second officer asked, positive now that she was missing something.

"It has been my experience," Kastiigan said, "that my commanding officers have placed an undue emphasis on my survival. I am only a single cog in a very large and sophisticated machine."

Wu could hardly argue with the metaphor. However, she didn't see what it had to do with the rescue mission.

"I promise I won't place an undue emphasis on your survival," she told the Kandilkari. "However, considering I can't think of any reason to send you on that shuttle . . ."

"I'll stay here," he concluded correctly, though he looked rather grim about it. "I understand."

"Good," said Wu, though she wasn't sure *she* understood.

"Thank you for your time," Kastiigan told her.

"No problem," she said.

And with that, the science officer departed.

Wu expelled a breath. Kastiigan was proving to be a most interesting fellow. She resolved to learn more about him—and she decided it might as well be now, since the only alternative was to sit and wait for Chiang to complete his work.

She had begun calling up Kastiigan's personnel file when the door chime sounded again. *What now?* she wondered. Was Kastiigan going to *insist* that she place him on the shuttle?

"Come in," Wu said.

As it turned out, it wasn't the science officer seeking another audience. It was Ensign Paris. And he looked troubled somehow, distracted—a stark contrast to the confident young man the second officer had seen a few minutes earlier.

"May I speak with you?" the ensign asked.

Wu nodded. "Of course. Have a seat."

Paris sat down in the chair opposite hers and looked at his hands for a moment. Then he met her gaze.

"It's hard to know where to begin," he told her.

The commander knew they didn't have much time—or rather, the people on the *Belladonna* didn't. But she resisted the impulse to rush the ensign, sensing that whatever was bothering him had to come out at its own pace.

"Begin anywhere," she said.

Chapter Nineteen

WU WATCHED THE MUSCLES WORK in Paris's temples.

"Back at the Academy . . ." he said, "my very first semester, I had a class in Particle Physics. One day, our professor decided to spring a surprise test on us. I had barely read the first question on my monitor when my hands began to shake.

"They didn't just tremble a little, Commander. They *shook,* as if I had some terrible neurological disorder." The ensign winced as if in pain. "I was horrified."

Wu had never experienced anything like what Paris was describing. However, she had no trouble imagining how uncomfortable it would have made him feel.

"I tried to hide my hands from the other cadets," Paris continued, "in the hope that no one would see. And to my relief, no one did. But I needed my fingers to tap out answers on my keyboard, so I couldn't keep them hidden forever."

He swallowed. "Taking that test was the worst kind of torture. But I got through it somehow, shakes and all. And I earned a passing grade, while half the other first-year students flunked."

"So you came through," Wu observed.

"Yes," said Paris, "but that's not the point. It was just an exam, and not even a particularly important one. It wasn't as if my whole career was hanging in the balance."

"In other words," the commander translated, "you shouldn't have reacted that way."

"That's right," he said. "And if I were someone else, maybe I wouldn't have. But as I've been reminded all my life, I'm not just anybody." The muscles worked in the ensign's jaw. "I'm a *Paris.*"

Wu was beginning to understand the problem.

"In the years that followed," he went on, "the same problem surfaced over and over again. Most of the time I was fine, as calm and controlled as anybody. But when I was under pressure, when I felt there was a chance I might fail, my hands shook and my stomach clenched and I had to struggle to conceal it."

The ensign paused, his nostrils flaring with emotion. He seemed to be staring not *at* Wu but through her.

"But I *always* found a way to hide it," he said softly, "because I was a *Paris.* Because I had a standard to live up to. Because I had inherited a reputation for courage and dedication and grace under fire."

"Ensign," said Wu, seeing how much it hurt him to talk about it, "you don't have to—"

But Paris was like a dam that had finally burst. Obviously, he felt the need to get this out in the open. And if that's what he needed, she was willing to listen.

"First," he told her, smiling bitterly, "there was my grandfather, Daniel Paris. You may have heard of him at the Academy. He distinguished himself on the *Potemkin* and the *Excalibur* before he came back to Earth, where he was asked to assist Admiral Kirk during the admiral's stint as head of Starfleet operations."

In fact, Wu *had* heard of Daniel Paris—even *before* she had read the ensign's personnel file.

"Then," said Paris, "my grandfather became an admiral himself. His plaque at Starfleet Headquarters says he earned a reputation for wisdom and courage unmatched by any of his peers."

Wu had never seen it. But then, there were lots of plaques at headquarters, lots of officers who had been honored.

"Next came my father, Iron Mike Paris. He was decorated no less than seven times as second officer and then executive officer of the *Agamemnon.*" The ensign's voice dropped. "Unfortunately, his career was

cut short when his ship was obliterated by the Romulans in what's become known as the Tomed Incident."

The run-in with the Romulans that precipitated fifty years of Romulan isolationism. Wu knew it as well as anyone.

"I never knew my father," Paris told her. "I was just an infant when
he died. All I had were holograms and my mother's stories, all of which
made him seem bigger than life."

"I'm sorry," said Wu.

The ensign acknowledged her sympathy with a nod. But there was
more, apparently.

"Then there's my Aunt Patricia, who's five years younger than my
father. She was on the *Maryland* at the Battle of Ankaata, where she
lost an arm saving two of her fellow officers. She retired about the time
I entered the Academy."

The commander grunted. "Quite a pedigree."

"Yes," the ensign confirmed sardonically. "A lot to live up to. But
my brother Owen never seemed to have any trouble with it. He's always
been the brainy type, you know? The type who's going places? People
say he'll be the best Paris of all."

Wu was familiar with Owen Paris. Who wasn't?

In the eleven years he had spent wearing Starfleet crimson, the man
had risen through the ranks like a shooting star. He had impressed commanding officers from one end of Federation space to the other.

And though he had been named first officer on one of the most
prestigious vessels in the fleet, it seemed unlikely that Owen Paris would
stop there. The smart money said he would make captain before the year
was out.

"But I'm not my brother," Ensign Paris insisted, as if someone had
argued to the contrary. "I never have been and I never will be. I'm just
an average guy."

He looked Wu in the eye. "If it had been up to me, I would never
even have applied to the Academy. But when you're a Paris, Starfleet
isn't something you think about. It's your fate, your destiny, your birth-
right. You don't question it, you just go. And later on, when you have
sons and daughters, they will go as well."

The second officer's heart went out to him. Her parents had both
been colony administrators, but they had never tried to sway her choice
of career. It was Wu herself who had opted to join Starfleet.

"I don't belong here," Paris told her. "I'm not captain material. I'm
not even fit to be an ensign."

Wu didn't believe that. She said so. "You like piloting starships. And you're *good* at it, Ensign. You're *damned* good."

Paris shrugged. "I've got an aptitude for it—people have told me that. But how can I man a helm when my hands shake at the slightest hint of pressure?" He shook his head, looking lost and dejected. "The kind of nerves I've got . . . they're better suited to civilian work, and a laid-back kind of civilian work at that."

Wu sighed. "So what you're saying is you don't want to pilot that shuttle for me."

The ensign looked up at her, his eyes full of torment and frustration. "I *want* to, Commander. I want to help in the worst way. But do you want to trust me with people's lives after what I've told you?" He held up his hands, which were trembling a little even now. "Do you want to take that kind of a chance?"

It was a good question.

Did Wu want to wager the lives of Jiterica and maybe a ship full of researchers that Paris would come through for her? Was that the best she could do for them?

The ensign would have to keep the shuttle and its tractor beam steady if Jiterica and the crew of the *Belladonna* were to have a shot at coming out of this alive. But if he gave in to the pressure, if his hands betrayed him as they had in the past . . .

Once, the ensign had seemed like the obvious choice for the job, the most talented helmsman this side of Idun Asmund. But now, knowing what he had told her about his problem, Wu had a problem on her hands.

And it was hers, no one else's.

Picard was on Gnala. Ben Zoma as well. There was no sense in asking herself what they would have done in this instance because she didn't know them well enough to say.

But she knew Captain Rudolfini well enough. Put in Wu's place, forced to make this kind of choice, he hadn't always relied on his head. More often than not, he had relied on his heart.

And not just *his* heart, but the hearts of others.

With that in mind, Wu looked across the table at Cole Paris. Clearly, the young man was scared stiff of bringing disgrace to his family's name, and even more scared of being responsible for Jiterica. He didn't want to let anyone down.

But Wu had seen him working at the *Stargazer*'s helm console. He wasn't just good. He was a rare talent, a prodigy. At his best, Paris was still the number one choice for what she had in mind. In her heart, the commander was sure of it.

She just had to make sure she could get his best out of him.

"I've sat here and listened patiently to what you had to say," Wu told the ensign. "Now you listen to me. Your grandfather, your father, your aunt . . . you may see them as superhuman figures, as gods. But they were people like you and me. And people get scared. I've never met anyone who *didn't,* myself included.

"Ever been in combat?" she asked him.

Paris shook his head. "No."

"You can't imagine how you'll ever get through it. Your knees tremble and your belly clenches like a fist and your heart pounds so hard you think it's going to shatter against your ribs. And it's even worse when other people's lives depend on what you do and say. Then you feel their weight on you, a mountain of it, and you hate to make a move because you're sure it'll be the wrong one.

"But you make it, Ensign. Somehow you make it and you get through to the other side."

Paris looked at her. "But—"

"Your hands shake?" she said, refusing to let him finish, refusing to let him slide back into his morass of self-doubt. "Maybe mine are shaking right now. Maybe I'm wondering if there's a better way to save those scientists—or a way that doesn't involve putting my own people's lives at risk.

"Maybe I'll be wrong. Maybe I'll disgrace myself and my family and have all those deaths on my head, and be haunted by my choice for the rest of my life. But that's the chance I've got to take."

Wu leaned forward in her chair. "I picked you for this job because I thought you were the best, Ensign. I still think it—and not because you're a Paris. Frankly, that couldn't matter less to me. The reason I think you're the best is because you *are*—and I'd be a whopping great fool to send anyone else out on such an important mission."

Paris didn't seem inclined to protest what she was saying any longer. He just sat there, his mouth hanging open.

"Any questions?" the commander asked him.

The ensign didn't say anything. He just shook his head from side to side.

"Then report to the shuttlebay."

Paris nodded, looking as if he had just been slapped across the face.

Then he got up and made his way out of the captain's ready room. As the doors opened, he looked back at her for a moment.

"I'll try not to let you down," he said.

And with that, he went through the open doorway.

Wu slumped back in the captain's chair. Apparently, her words had had the desired effect. Paris would do what she had asked of him.

She could only hope it would be enough.

It was late in the day when Simenon and his companions came to the obstacle he had been dreading the most—a convex wall of coarse, dark rock that rose eighty meters straight into the air and stretched to the horizon on either side.

"Well," Ben Zoma told Simenon as he took the measure of the wall, "you weren't kidding. That *is* a healthy climb."

Picard glanced at the engineer. "Especially when the climber is hampered by injuries."

Simenon imagined that his rivals were climbing the barrier now or had already gotten past it. However, he didn't know for sure because he couldn't see them. Their paths had diverged more and more as time went on, and the corrugated shape of the wall served to conceal the portions of it Kasaelek and Banyohla would be required to climb.

"Fortunately," Picard added knowingly, "your forebears didn't scale this wall. They found an alternative."

Simenon nodded. "Yes." But under the circumstances, he wasn't sure that it was all that fortunate.

The Aklaash and the Fejjimaera were superior to the Mazzereht when it came to climbing, just as they were superior in so many other aspects of the ritual. However, Simenon's subspecies could do *one* thing better than the other subspecies.

They could hold their breath.

And at some point in the history of the ritual, one of Simenon's predecessors had discovered a series of caves that ran beneath the rock wall—a feature still almost completely flooded with water from an underground river.

The engineer had intended all along to swim that river and come up on the other side of the rock wall—a shortcut that had represented an advantage to his ancestors and seemed certain to give him an edge over Kasaelek and Banyohla.

But with his arm hanging limply and painfully at his side, he wouldn't be able to swim the caves. He would instead have to depend on a plan Vigo had come up with a half hour earlier.

The Pandrilite had already found one of the extraordinarily long, flexible vines that grew in such profusion in these woods. Snapping the vine off at the root with his great strength, he tied one end around his waist and made a knot to hold it in place—leaving the last ten meters' worth trailing on the ground.

Tugging on the knot, Vigo made sure it was secure. Then he snapped off another length of vine and added it to the first. And then a third, even longer than the first two.

Finally, the weapons officer turned to Simenon. "Do you think you can hang onto this?"

"I'll have to," said the Gnalish, "won't I?"

The plan was for Vigo to swim through the caves, trailing his chain of vines behind him. When he reached the place where the caves opened up on the opposite side of the rock wall, Simenon would grab the end of Vigo's lifeline and allow Vigo to pull him through. Then the others would follow on their own, one at a time.

"That soreness in your side may make it difficult to hold your breath," Greyhorse pointed out.

"But I won't be exerting myself," Simenon told him. "All I've got to do is hang on and fend off the occasional obstruction."

And with that, he led the way to the cave mouth.

Chapter Twenty

WU ARRIVED IN THE SHUTTLEBAY just as Jiterica was entering the specially rigged shuttle. Paris, it seemed, was already inside the craft. The commander turned to Chiang.

"Everything checks out," he said before she could ask.

She nodded. "Good."

Then she approached the shuttle and watched Jiterica take her place inside it. Ironically, the Nizhrak seemed to have less trouble negotiating the cramped quarters of the auxiliary craft than she'd had taking a seat in the mess hall.

Paris was running a last-minute instrument diagnostic. When he noticed Wu standing at the hatch, he acknowledged her with a nod.

"Commander," he said.

He seemed to have regained his confidence. The second officer certainly hoped that that was the case. There was a lot riding on Paris and his abilities.

"Ensign," she said by way of a reply. Then, after she was certain that Jiterica had taken notice of her as well, she said, "Do either of you have any questions?"

Neither of them seemed to have any. But then, their assignment was a simple one in concept. It was only in its execution that complications seemed likely to set in.

"Then good luck to you," said Wu.

"Thank you, Commander," Paris replied.

"Thank you," Jiterica echoed in her tinny, unnatural-sounding helmet-audio voice.

Then the hatch closed and Wu stood back from the shuttlecraft. She watched as it lifted off the deck and headed for the permeable force field that separated the bay from the airless void.

The shuttle seemed to hesitate for a fraction of a second as it neared the force field. Then it sailed through it with a gentle flash, wheeled to starboard, and was lost to sight.

And Wu, who wished she could have accompanied the ensigns in their shuttlecraft, instead returned to the bridge to direct the rescue effort from the captain's chair.

Ben Zoma considered the triangular cave mouth in front of him, which was little more than a meter high but as many as three meters wide. It was dark inside the opening, but not too dark to catch a glimpse of the water through which they would all soon be swimming.

Joseph turned to Simenon. "How far did you say it would be?"

The Gnalish shrugged. "Not that far. Thirty meters or so. But there's no light and it's not quite a straight path. That's why you've got to hug one of the walls as you go forward."

Ben Zoma filed the information away for when his turn came. But that wouldn't be for a while. Vigo would be the first one in the water, followed by Simenon.

Vigo smiled at the Gnalish, no doubt hoping to inspire confidence in his abilities. "I'm ready to try it if you are," he said.

Simenon frowned as he studied the cave mouth. "All right," he said after a moment. "But now that I think about it, I want someone to tie the end of the vine around my waist. That way I don't have to worry about losing my grip."

"But," Greyhorse protested, "if you get stuck, you won't be able to free yourself. You'll be lost down there."

Simenon looked grim as he glanced at the doctor. "That's a chance I'll have to take."

No one else argued with him. It was, after all, his life at stake. He had a right to do what he thought best.

"Here goes," said Vigo.

He checked the vine wrapped around his middle and pulled the knot that held it a little tighter. Then he hunkered down, made his way into the cave, and took a series of deep breaths. After the last and deepest, he submerged himself and was gone.

The water gurgled and churned as the length of vine broke the surface in the Pandrilite's wake. Like the others, Ben Zoma watched it disappear, meter by meter.

As long as it kept moving it signified that Vigo was moving as well. The last thing any of them wanted to see was slack in the line. And they didn't see anything of the sort—not until half of the last vine had been claimed by the passageway.

Then the safety line stopped flowing into the water. Ben Zoma glanced at his friend Picard. If they were lucky, Vigo had reached the other side. If not . . .

Suddenly, they heard a shout—a booming cry that could only have come from the powerful throat of a Pandrilite, audible despite the soaring wall of rock that stood between them. The first officer breathed a sigh of relief.

Vigo had made it. It was time for step two.

In recognition of the fact, Simenon came forward and wrapped the end of the vine around his waist. Then Picard and Joseph tied a knot in it and pronounced it secure.

The prearranged signal of the Gnalish's readiness was a series of three tugs on the end of the vine. Ben Zoma did the honors. A moment later, he saw the line rise off the ground and go taut.

And a moment after that, it tugged Simenon in the direction of the cave mouth. The engineer looked at each of them in turn, his expression uncomfortably like that of a man condemned to death.

"My turn," he said grimly.

Then, pulled by Vigo, he vanished into the water and left a swirl of current in his wake.

"Leave it to Simenon to get a free ride," said Ben Zoma, hoping to break the tension.

But no one laughed. They would only do that, he suspected, after they knew their colleague had reached the other side.

They waited for a few seconds, then a few more. If all went well, it wouldn't be long before they heard from Vigo.

But after what seemed like enough time, the signal still hadn't come. Ben Zoma and the others looked at each other.

"He's been down there too long," said Greyhorse.

The doctor was right. "Someone's got to go after him," the first officer said.

And without another thought, he scrambled through the cave mouth and hit the water.

It was cold, shockingly so. But then, its source was probably some mountain lake only half-redeemed from the grasp of winter. Ignoring the temperature, Ben Zoma propelled himself through the gloom with his legs, using his hands to feel his way along the wall beside him.

He couldn't see Simenon, but he could hear some kind of bubbling up ahead. It got louder and more insistent as he swam forward, telling Ben Zoma that he wasn't too late.

Simenon was alive. At least, for the moment.

But something had stopped him from getting through the cave chain. And in the now-perfect darkness that surrounded him, Ben Zoma couldn't tell what it was.

There was only one thing he could do—get hold of Simenon and feel around until he found the problem.

With that in mind, he scissored forward until his hand brushed against one of the Gnalish's frantically churning legs. Grasping it, he felt the kicking stop—a sign that his comrade was either acknowledging his presence or had run out of air.

Hoping it was the former, Ben Zoma used Simenon like a ladder and pulled himself up to what he imagined was the Gnalish's face. Then he found Simenon's shoulder and upper arm and felt for the tautness that would suggest his friend's hand was stuck.

As it turned out, it wasn't. In fact, it seized the first officer's wrist and directed it to where Ben Zoma had come from—toward Simenon's feet.

By then, the human was starting to feel light-headed. The impulse to breathe, to replenish the supply of oxygen in his lungs, was becoming almost impossible for him to deny. But he put it aside somehow and focused on the task at hand.

Working his way down Simenon's body again, Ben Zoma felt one leg moving. But not the other one. *Finally,* he thought.

A moment later, he found the problem. Simenon's foot was wedged in a crevice. But as long as the vine rope was pulling on him, he wouldn't be able to get free.

Darting upward, Ben Zoma found the vine and swung his feet in

---

the direction of the cave wall. When they met something solid, he planted his heels there and hauled for all he was worth.

Just as he had hoped, the vine rope relaxed—probably because he had pulled it right out of Vigo's unsuspecting hands. Freed of its pull, Simenon would be able to back his foot out of the crevice.

But just in case, Ben Zoma felt his way down the wall of rock and tried to lend a hand. He arrived just in time to realize that the Gnalish wasn't stuck anymore.

In fact, as the first officer groped for his comrade, he realized that Simenon was gone.

Then he put together what must have happened. Vigo had regained his grip on the rope vine and pulled the Gnalish through.

At least, that's what Ben Zoma hoped. With his lungs screaming for air, he launched himself forward alongside the wall, intent now on only one thing—saving *himself.*

For a single, terrifying heartbeat, it seemed to him that he had waited too long and would drown in the darkness. Then he saw a hint of light up ahead and arrowed through the water with the desperation of a man who knew his life depended on it.

Kick, he thought, a different kind of darkness closing around him. *Kick, dammit!*

He kicked—and broke the surface just in time.

As Ben Zoma dragged in draught after draught of warm, welcome air, he noticed Vigo a couple of meters away on a shelf of flat, dark rock. He was hovering over Simenon, who was gasping even harder than the first officer was, his ruby eyes looking as if they were about to pop out of his head.

"Are you all right, sir?" the Pandrilite asked Ben Zoma.

But the human couldn't speak yet. All he could do was pull in one shuddering breath after another as he joined his companions at the water's edge.

Paris brought his shuttle to a stop as close to the unholy glow of the accretion bridge as he dared, then immediately redirected all available power to his forward thrusters.

As he had anticipated, they held the shuttle in equilibrium. However, it was a rather uneasy equilibrium.

The pull exerted by the sinkhole was so powerful here that he could feel it in his bones. Without some timely assistance, the shuttle would either have to abandon its position or be sucked inside the accretion bridge.

Fortunately, that assistance was just a comm message away. Touching the communications pad on his control console, he said, "Paris to Wu. I've reached the coordinates we talked about."

The return signal was a sloppy one as a result of all the graviton activity, but the ensign was still able to make out the second officer's words. ". . . establishing tractor lock . . . stand by."

"Acknowledged," said Paris.

He glanced at Jiterica, who was sitting quietly in her seat, staring at the accretion bridge through the shuttle's forward observation port. He wondered what she was thinking about.

Him, perhaps? How he and his tractor beam would soon be all that stood between her and the sinkhole?

"Tractor lock . . . established . . ." Wu told him over the comm link.

Paris could see it reflected in his readouts. "Confirmed."

Of course, at the distance the *Stargazer* was compelled to maintain, the beam couldn't do much. But if it cut the stress on the shuttle's thrusters by twenty percent and lent them a little stability, it would be all the help they needed.

Providing I do my job, Paris added silently.

Frowning, he put the thought out of his mind. It wasn't productive for him to try to anticipate how he would perform. He would simply do his best.

Paris turned to Jiterica. "Ready?"

She turned to look at him, the golden glare of the accretion bridge reflected in the face mask of her helmet. He could barely see the spectral features that lurked beneath it.

"Yes, Mr. Paris," the Nizhrak said calmly, almost mechanically. "I am ready."

She got up from her seat and moved aft through the shuttle. With the press of a pad set into the bulkhead, she activated a selectively permeable force field like the one in the *Stargazer*'s shuttlebay—another of the improvements Lt. Chiang had been forced to engineer into the craft on short notice.

Then she opened the hatch.

Thanks to the force field, the atmosphere in the shuttle remained inside instead of rushing to join the vacuum of space. Still, it was disconcerting for Paris to look past Jiterica and see the gleam of naked stars.

Without a second look, the Nizhrak took hold of the hatch frame and swung out into space. The field sizzled around her for a moment, as if nettled at her interrupting its integrity. Then it was intact again—and Jiterica was floating outside the shuttlecraft, her momentum carrying her slowly toward the accretion bridge.

"Ensign Jiterica has exited the shuttle," Paris reported.

"Keep us . . . posted . . . ," Wu instructed him.

"Will do," he said.

Then Paris activated the tractor beam device that Lt. Chiang had installed minutes earlier, trained its shimmering shaft on Jiterica, and established a lock. The procedure went every bit as smoothly as he had hoped.

But the hard part was still ahead.

Keeping an eye on his helm instruments, the ensign ever so carefully used the tractor beam to propel his colleague forward. Unaware that there was any reason not to trust Paris's abilities, Jiterica wafted in the direction of the accretion bridge until Paris had to squint to see her through the viewport.

A little farther, he told himself. Farther still.

And then she was gone from sight, immersed in the furious stream of plasma moving from Alpha Oneo Madrin to Beta Oneo Madrin—her life and those of the *Belladonna*'s surviving scientists dependent on how Paris handled himself.

He told himself that he wouldn't let them down, and he meant it. It's just that he wasn't prepared for what happened next.

Chapter Twenty-one

PARIS CLENCHED HIS JAW as he struggled to reestablish control of the shuttle's tractor beam, which had suddenly begun whipping about as if it had a mind of its own.

With all the graviton flux in the accretion bridge, Commander Wu had anticipated that it would likely affect tractor integrity. She had warned Paris that it might be difficult to keep Jiterica on target.

But she hadn't told the ensign to expect anything like *this*. It was like trying to thread a needle with a strand of overcooked spaghetti.

Frantically, he consulted his monitors. The graviton emitter seemed to be functioning within expected parameters. The same with the subspace field amplifiers.

So it wasn't a malfunction. The graviton storm was just a lot more turbulent than it had a right to be. No doubt, with some careful analysis, Kastiigan and his people would figure out the reason for it after Paris got back.

But that wasn't any help to him right now. And it wasn't any help to Jiterica, either. She was at the mercy of a bizarre and chaotic environment, a small and very fragile leaf in a violent, howling windstorm.

If the graviton flux jerked her around like this much longer, Paris

would lose his tractor lock on her. And if he did, he didn't think he
could catch hold of her again.

Chilled by the prospect of watching Jiterica spiral off into the sinkhole, the ensign expelled a breath. *You can do this,* he told himself,
working his controls. *You're a good helm jockey, as good as any man
or woman in the fleet.*

But try as he might, he couldn't steady the tractor beam. The
forces acting on it were just too fierce, too unpredictable. Every time
Paris tried to compensate, he found himself taking the beam the wrong
way.

Come on, he told himself, a bead of sweat making its way down
his face. *Do it. Do it* now.

But his controls felt funny—as if they were shivering in his hands.
Paris looked down and saw that it wasn't the controls shivering. It was
him. His hands were trembling just as they always did when he found
himself under pressure.

He could feel the weight of his family descending on him, crushing
him, making it impossible for him to function. "No," he groaned out
loud. "Now *now."*

He was a Paris. It was his destiny to succeed. But he wasn't *going*
to succeed. He was going to fail—not just himself and his family, but
all those people on the trapped research ship.

And he was going to fail Jiterica, too. That felt worse to him than
all the rest of it.

No, the ensign heard a voice tell him, a voice that rose from the
depths of his psyche. *You're not going to fail. You're going to straighten
out this beam and complete your mission.*

It took him a moment, but he figured out whose voice it was. It
belonged to the woman who had refused to accept his fear and uncertainty, who had bared her own doubts to free him of his.

You make it, she had said. *Somehow you make it and you get through
to the other side.*

The ensign could see Commander Wu staring at him across the captain's desk, demonstrating a faith that had taken him by surprise. *Not
because you're a Paris. Frankly, that couldn't matter less to me. The
reason I think you're the best is because you are.*

Paris's teeth ground together. If Wu believed in him, who was he
to give up on himself? If he failed in this mission, it sure as hell wouldn't
be for lack of trying.

Shakes or no shakes, he wrestled with the shuttle's tractor controls, doing his best to keep Jiterica on something remotely resembling her intended course.

Picard was the last member of Simenon's party to crawl out of the cave on the far side of the rock wall. As he did so, he saw his comrades shading their eyes and looking back.

"What is it?" the captain asked, using his fingers to comb back an unruly lock of hair plastered to his forehead.

Vigo pointed to the immense, dark gray barrier, first to a spot far on their left and then to another on their right. "We've taken the lead," he said.

As Picard followed his weapons officer's gestures, he saw that Vigo was right. Both of Simenon's rivals and their teams were visible from here, and neither had benefited from the decision to go over the wall instead of under it.

The Aklaash were little more than halfway down, slowly and laboriously using a series of vines to lower each member of their party from ledge to narrow ledge. And the Fejjimaera group hadn't even come that far. They were still in the vicinity of the summit, descending by use of hand- and footholds alone.

The captain nodded his approval. It was the first glimmer of hope they had gotten since the beginning of the contest. And it couldn't have come at a better time.

After all, their underwater ordeal had been a grueling one. They were cold, their legs were rubbery, and their energy was at a decidedly low ebb. But the sight of the other teams' positions was a tonic.

"Let's go," said Simenon, always the driving force behind their efforts. Still breathing heavily, he dragged his battered body away from the cavern mouth. "We've still got seven or eight kilometers to go."

Ben Zoma looked as if he would have liked to rest for a moment. Like the engineer, he hadn't quite caught his breath yet. Nonetheless, he followed Simenon without complaint into the towering woods on the other side of the wall.

Picard could do no less. "Come on," he said to the others. "This lead will evaporate all too quickly if we don't get a move on."

Nor was he offering that simply as a spur. They might be ahead now, but the other teams could do a lot of catching up over the course of seven or eight kilometers.

And no doubt, they *would*.

* * *

Ensign Jiterica had a problem.

She could see the unconsumed portion of the *Belladonna* through the visual-analog apparatus built into her containment suit. It wasn't far away, either—less than a kilometer, perhaps, its gray hull only partially obscured by drifts of fiery golden plasma. But the way she was whipping about on the end of the shuttle's tractor beam made her wonder if she would ever reach the beleaguered vessel, much less get inside it.

The Nizhrak wanted to rescue the research scientists as much as anyone. To accomplish that goal, she would suffer any hardship, assume any risk. However, she couldn't get herself across the space separating her from the *Belladonna*. That was the job of her colleague, Ensign Paris.

Commander Wu had said that Paris was a good pilot. She had told Jiterica that she would be in good hands. But clearly, the rescue effort wasn't going as the commander had hoped.

And the Nizhrak had no illusions about the deadly seriousness of her predicament. If the tractor beam lost its grip on her, if she tore loose from her tether, it wouldn't matter that she could survive the radiation and magnetic forces that seemed to permeate this environment, or that the ebb and flow of the graviton storm couldn't pulp her the way it would pulp a being of greater density.

All that would matter was that she possessed mass, however widely distributed, and that she would be inexorably drawn into the sinkhole like the *Stargazer*'s probe and the *Belladonna* before her. And if the research ship wasn't likely to remain intact through such a passage, there was even less of a chance that she would do so.

Jiterica didn't want to die. But more than that, she didn't want to die for *nothing*.

She had barely completed the thought when she noticed something— that the intensity with which she was being cast about was diminishing. The tractor beam seemed steadier, more resistant to the graviton eddies that assaulted her. A brief respite, she wondered, or the first sign of an actual improvement in her situation?

In the seconds that followed, the beam seemed to assert itself even more. And though the ensign's progress in the direction of the *Belladonna* was a little slower than before, a little more deliberate, it was also markedly less erratic.

Once again, she had reason for hope.

* * *

Simenon was losing his battle.

Despite the terrible urgency that coiled in his belly, despite the dark, looming knowledge of what would happen if he failed, he was slowing down kilometer by kilometer. He couldn't help it. His strides were getting shorter, his legs heavier, his bruised ribs more excrutiatingly painful with each ragged, throat-searing inhalation.

Nor was the Gnalish the only one nearing the limits of his endurance. Greyhorse, who hadn't kept up right from the beginning, had managed to slow down even more. And for that matter, so had Ben Zoma, Vigo, and Joseph.

Of them all, only Picard seemed to have the stamina to maintain their original, ground-eating pace. But it wouldn't do Simenon any good if the captain reached the end ahead of everyone else. After all, it wasn't really a question of who got to the clearing first.

It was a question of who got there last—because none of the teams would be considered to have finished until its last member arrived at the cache of unfertilized eggs.

So if Picard got there in record time and Greyhorse reached the end behind the last Aklaash or Fejjimaera, Simenon would lose. That was why he had gotten so irritated with the doctor in the beginning—because no matter what any of the others did, it was Greyhorse who would most likely determine their fate.

And that of Simenon's bloodline.

As the Gnalish considered that, he stumbled on an exposed root. *Damn,* he thought, sure that he would go sprawling on his face. But almost instantly, a hand reached out and righted him. Glancing at its owner, Simenon saw that it was Picard.

The Gnalish cursed himself out loud and roused a flock of colunnu in the process. *Keep your mind on what you're doing,* he thought. *Concentrate on* that *or nothing else will matter.*

Suddenly, Joseph cried out, "I see a star!"

Simenon cast a glance back over his shoulder at the security chief. What in blazes was the man babbling about?

He was still trying to figure it out when Ben Zoma called out a moment later, "I see it as well!"

It was then that the engineer realized what they were up to—a song sung by cadets back at Starfleet Academy, usually accompanied by copious quantities of alcoholic beverages until it became slurred entirely beyond recognition.

".To reach that star!" Vigo trumpeted.

"I'll go through hell!" Picard barked between breaths.

The second verse was considerably less tasteful than the first, but Simenon's comrades didn't let that stop them. They made the forest ring with that one as well. And then the third verse, which was even bawdier than the second.

Before the Gnalish knew it, he was singing as breathlessly as the rest of them. It wasn't like him to sing at all, much less in front of anyone else, but he was singing nonetheless. And as he sang, his spirits seemed to lift. His legs seemed to churn more easily and his pain seemed to fade into the background.

He looked at Joseph, who saw him looking and winked. Simenon frowned at him. *Singing in the midst of the ritual,* he thought disdainfully. Then he sang some more.

Jiterica knew exactly when she would come in contact with the *Belladonna*'s weakening deflector shields.

After all, her suit's sensor pack had warned her about it soon after she entered the accretion bridge. But she hadn't worried about the research ship's defenses because Commander Wu had conceived a way for her to bypass them.

As Jiterica understood it, ships' deflectors—like other force fields, including the one inside her own containment suit—were emitted at certain frequencies. They were designed to fend off solid objects as well as directed-energy barrages, but not other fields generated at the same frequency.

So if the ensign extended her personal force field outside of her suit, and set it for the frequency most commonly used by Federation vessels, she would be able to penetrate the *Belladonna*'s protective barrier. At least, in theory.

Of course, Commander Wu might have guessed wrong about the frequency of the research ship's shields, in which case the challenge facing Jiterica would suddenly become a good deal more complicated. However, she had decided to—as humans seemed fond of saying—cross that bridge when she came to it.

With the outer surface of the *Belladonna*'s deflector wall getting close enough to reach out and touch with the fingers of her gauntlet, that bridge was now at hand.

As Wu had instructed her, the ensign extended her force field beyond the skin of her suit, instantly placing a much greater burden on herself to maintain an unnaturally dense form. If she had to do this on her own all the time, it wouldn't be possible for her to remain on a ship like the *Stargazer*. But for a short span of time, she could handle the considerable strain of self-containment.

Next, Jiterica matched her field's frequency to the deflector's—or rather, what she expected the deflector's to be. At that point, there was only one thing left for her to do.

She let the shuttle's tractor beam carry her forward.

The ensign's sensors ticked off the distance between her and the *Belladonna*. Twenty-five centimeters. Twenty. Fifteen. Ten. None.

She braced herself for an impact—because if the deflector remained impervious to her, she would bounce off it like any other solid object. But she didn't bounce.

She went right through it.

Wu's theory had proven out. Jiterica had pierced the *Belladonna*'s defenses. And the tractor beam was still carrying her forward.

Once she was certain she was past the deflector barrier, the ensign withdrew her force field into the fabric of her suit again. Then she relaxed, allowing it to reassume the burden of containment.

Better, Jiterica thought with a sense of relief. *Much better.*

The still-visible portion of the research ship was looming in front of her, looking strangely truncated. Also a little curved, an effect of the churning graviton activity in the area.

As luck would have it, one of the vessel's exterior hatches was almost directly ahead. The ensign could make her way toward it as soon as the tractor beam released her—which it would do in a matter of seconds, judging by the rate at which she was approaching the *Belladonna*'s hull.

Again, she braced herself—not for contact with a deflector shield, but with the duranium surface used by the Federation in the construction of spacegoing vessels. But the impact, however gentle, never came. And somehow, though it seemed the research ship was mere centimeters away, Jiterica was still moving forward—propelled dutifully by the shuttle's tractor beam.

At first, she didn't understand. Then she checked her sensors and realized what was happening.

The *Belladonna* wasn't nearly as close as it looked. But then, her suit's visual-analog device was designed to respond to light in the manner of flesh-and-blood optical organs, and lightwaves would be distorted in the presence of all those gravitons. Fortunately for the ensign, her suit's sensor suite responded to other sorts of stimuli, which were more dependable gauges of distance under the circumstances.

Intent on her sensors this time, she tracked her progress toward the research ship's hull. Thirty meters. Twenty. Ten. And then, as if it had been there all the time and had only now decided to take on substance, the hull pressed back against the palms of her gauntlets.

Jiterica had arrived at her destination.

What's more, Ensign Paris must have known it, because she didn't feel any more pressure from the tractor beam. It had carried her as far as it could. She was on her own now.

Activating the magnetic anchors built into her suit, Jiterica latched onto the duranium surface—first with her right palm and then her left, followed by her right foot and finally her left one. Each time she made contact, she felt a reassuring *clunk*.

When she was done, she found herself in a shallow crouch, all four limbs of her suit adhering to the hull. Had she been a human, she would have taken the opportunity to smile. Despite everything, she had reached the *Belladonna*.

Chapter Twenty-two

JITERICA TURNED THE HELMET of her containment suit as she hung onto the *Belladonna*'s outer skin.

The hatch that she had seen was above her and to her left, almost hidden by the curve of the ship. It appeared to be no more than ten meters away, but she had learned better than to trust her visual-analog faculty in this place. Consulting her other sensors, she saw that the actual distance was more like twenty meters.

Detaching her right palm-magnet, the ensign brought it alongside her left and reattached it to the *Belladonna*'s hull. Then she did the same with her right foot. Once her right-side appendages were in place, she detached those on her left, extended them as far as she could in the direction of her goal, and resecured them. And in this manner, she made her way toward the hatch.

She was more than halfway there when she detached her right palm again and realized that something was amiss. Looking down, she saw the feet of her suit drifting away from the hull.

Commander Wu had warned her about this phenomenon as well. The magnetic eddies that existed in the accretion bridge were wreaking havoc with her anchors. If Jiterica wasn't careful, she might go drifting off—and if she did that, it was unlikely that Ensign Paris would be able to reassert his tractor lock on her.

First, she reattached her sole anchors to the hull. Then she moved more slowly and cautiously than before, making sure not to detach any of the magnets until she was certain that the others were secure.

It took a while, but the ensign at last reached the hatch. It was locked, of course—no surprise there. But she had a remedy for that. Removing a hyperspanner from its sheath along the leg of her suit, she went to work on the hatch.

As it turned out, the mechanism was in perfect working order. With the proper tool in hand, it was the work of a minute to swing the hatch door open. Resecuring the hyperspanner, Jiterica maneuvered herself about until she could lower herself into the aperture.

Unfortunately, she still hadn't gotten any better at moving in tight places. However, the hatch was made to accommodate the bulk of a containment suit, so she was able to thrust herself down through the opening without too much trouble. At the last moment she felt one of her hand anchors slip off the hull, the victim of a competing magnetic wave, but by then she was mostly inside the hatch.

Deactivating her magnets, Jiterica pulled the hatch closed. She found herself in a small compartment—an airlock, not unlike those that existed on the *Stargazer*.

It took a moment for air to shoot in and a few more to fill the lock. Though oxygen was of no use to the Nizhrak except as an occasional source of nutrition, she was compelled to wait for the process to run its course. When the readout on the bulkhead indicated that an atmosphere had been established, Jiterica pressed the pad that would give her access to the interior of the ship.

A pair of doors parted, revealing a corridor. Moving out into it, the ensign scanned its length in either direction. There was no evidence of any living humanoids.

But the *Stargazer*'s scan had indicated a number of survivors. Since Jiterica's personal sensors didn't have the range to locate them, she picked a direction at random and set out in search of the *Belladonna*'s crew.

Not much longer now, Simenon thought as he pelted over the dark, spongy ground, barely able to feel his legs.

A couple of kilometers at most, he promised himself. *Just a couple of kilometers. Then the ritual would all be over, one way or the other.*

His friends were all around him, ahead and behind, coping with varying degrees of exhaustion. Their breath rasped in their throats and they grunted every so often, evidence of how hard they were struggling not to let him down.

Simenon hadn't seen any sign of the Aklaash or the Fejjimaera since he left them on the stone wall, but he had a feeling they weren't far behind. If he stopped and listened, he would probably hear them thrashing through the woods on an unseen trail, desperate to close the distance between Simenon's party and their own.

All the more reason to keep going, he told himself. To fend off any thoughts of slowing down for a moment, no matter how tempting they might be. To ignore the savage throbbing in his banged-up ribs and the ache in his damaged arm.

Funny, Simenon thought. In the end, his intellectual superiority over his competitors hadn't made the slightest bit of difference. The only smart thing he had done was refrain from arguing too much when he found Picard and the others standing on that transporter pad. If not for them, he would have lost this race a long time ago.

Suddenly, he felt something sticky on his face. He brushed it aside with his good hand. Then he felt it again. And again.

Sedgmaya, Simenon realized with disgust. Ugly little creatures not much bigger than one of his fingers. They stretched their secretions from tree to tree to catch insects, in the manner of Terran spiders.

Actually, he was lucky. Fully spun sedgmaya webs would have been a lot heavier—heavy enough to wrap themselves around him and slow his progress along the trail. Obviously, it had rained in the last few days, forcing the slimy little beasts to begin spinning new webs.

No, Simenon thought, even in the midst of his exertions. *That can't be right.* If it had rained, he wouldn't have seen those footprints back at the bridge.

Or maybe it *had* rained, he allowed, and the footprints weren't as old as he thought—not even as old as the last ritual. If that were so, someone other than a ritual runner had left them there—having snuck into the forest without anyone noticing and sabotaged the bridge.

But who? Other than one of Simenon's rivals, who would have had something to gain if he fell into the chasm? Who would have benefited if he had died or couldn't finish the race?

And then it came to him, like a bolt of lightning in a vast summer sky.

Anger rose into his throat and threatened to choke him. *No,* he insisted. *I can't afford to think about this now. I need to concentrate on reaching the clearing.*

"Damn!" said Ben Zoma, who was running just ahead of Simenon.

"What is it?" the Gnalish demanded.

The first officer jerked a thumb over his shoulder. "It's the Aklaash," he said with uncharacteristic solemnity. "They're making a race out of it."

Simenon didn't want to look at them. He knew it would only slow him down. But he looked anyway—and his heart sank.

He could see the Aklaash moving through the scarlet trees, showing not the least sign of fatigue, their long strides devouring the ground in gulps. Slowly but surely, they were catching up. And Simenon's party still had at least a kilometer to go before it reached the finish line.

The Gnalish darted a glance back over his shoulder at Greyhorse. As usual, the doctor was bringing up the rear. Simenon swore beneath his breath. What had ever possessed him to let the doctor take part in the ritual?

An inexcusable ignorance of his physical conditioning, the Gnalish thought. A complete and utter failure to question whether Greyhorse would be an asset or a liability.

He knew the answer to that question now, though, didn't he? Unfortunately, it was a bit too late for him to do anything about it.

Just then, Simenon saw Vigo move to the side of the trail and fall behind. *What now?* he thought. Had the weapons officer chosen that moment to pull up lame?

Then he realized that Vigo wasn't hurt, after all. He had just dropped back to join the doctor. Pulling Greyhorse's arm over his right shoulder, the Pandrilite threw his own arm around the doctor's middle and started forward with him.

What's more, Greyhorse didn't utter a protest. He had run out of steam and he knew it. With Vigo helping to support him, the two oversize beings lumbered toward the clearing.

And they still had a lead on the Aklaash. As long as they maintained that, they couldn't lose.

The muscles in Simenon's legs burned like fire. His throat hurt so much he couldn't swallow. But he was close to the end, just a few minutes away from it. He could endure anything—any pain, any suffering.

Especially if it meant avoiding a lifetime of regret.

Then he saw it—the clearing. *The eggs,* he thought, his primal instincts coming to the fore. He could feel them somehow, a presence that drew him on unerringly.

But the Aklaash must have sensed the egg cache, too, because they began to close the gap more quickly. Simenon could hear them cursing each other, taunting each other, inciting their comrades to demand more and more of themselves.

The engineer's heart pounded in his chest, spurred by anxiety as much as by the nearness of the eggs. He would never have believed he could run so far or so fast, especially after the beating he had taken in the crevasse. But he was doing it. He was dredging up every last bit of strength as he closed in on the clearing.

The trail rose, dipped, and rose again. Simenon could hear the Aklaash, their voices cracking like whips. He didn't have to look back again to know that they were gaining ground, driving toward the finish line with all the power they could muster.

But Vigo was a powerhouse, too. And he was using his strength to propel Greyhorse along faster than the doctor could ever have managed on his own.

Come on, Simenon thought. *Come on . . .*

The clearing was right in front of them now. He could see the white robes of the Elders, waiting to proclaim a victor. He could see the black robes of their bodyguards, there to make sure that all transpired in accordance with the law.

The Aklaash started cheering as if they had already won. But Simenon resisted the temptation to cast another glance in their direction. He would see them soon enough.

The trees parted before him and the path widened, giving him a better view of those who awaited him. His breath was coming in sobs now, in strangled groans, his lungs incapable of taking in enough air to meet the demands of his straining body.

A little farther, Simenon told himself, his mouth dry as dust, his eyes starting to lose their focus. *For your brothers. For all those who came before . . .*

And with that thought burning in his brain, the Gnalish burst into the sacred clearing.

He wasn't alone, either. There were bodies plunging past him on either side. Human bodies. Three of them.

Falling to his knees, Simenon turned and looked for his last two comrades. They were close, closer than he had thought they would be,

Greyhorse's arm still slung across Vigo's massive shoulders as they lumbered forward.

But the Aklaash were close, too. They raged toward the clearing down their separate trail, a juggernaut of muscle and bone, the evolutionary apogee of Gnalish strength and endurance.

Run! Simenon thought, urging his comrades on. *For love of the gods, run!*

Wheezing and gasping every bit as badly as Greyhorse, Vigo all but carried the doctor into the clearing. At the last moment, the two of them stumbled and fell in a tangle of long, powerful limbs.

But it didn't matter anymore. They had made it.

Unfortunately, so had the Aklaash. With Kasaelek in the lead, they came pounding into the clearing at what appeared to be the exact same moment as Vigo and Greyhorse.

At least, that was how it appeared to Simenon. But then, his opinion didn't matter. All that mattered was how it looked to the Elders standing in front of the egg cache.

If they thought the engineer's group had come in first, Simenon would be awarded the right to fertilize the eggs. But if they thought Kasaelek's group had beaten them . . .

Simenon didn't even want to think about that.

His comrades gathered around him, their faces flushed and their breath coming fast. "Don't worry," Ben Zoma told him. "We took them, no question about it."

"I think so, too," said Joseph.

But Picard wasn't venturing an opinion. Like his engineer, he seemed to think it was too close to call.

Simenon studied the Elders, waiting for their decision. As wisdom dictated, they turned and consulted with each other. Then, with both parties hanging on their words, one of them stepped forward and rendered their verdict.

"The race has ended in a draw," he said.

"A draw?" Ben Zoma muttered in disgust.

Picard turned to Simenon. "What does that mean?"

The Gnalish sighed. "It means the winner will have to be chosen another way."

The captain's brow creased. *"What* way?"

Simenon regarded Kasaelek, who was grinning and clenching his fists at the news. The engineer wished he felt like grinning, too.

"In single combat," he said softly.

* * *

Commander Wu stared at the blazing section of the accretion bridge on her forward viewscreen as if she could see into it and follow Jiterica's progress.

But of course, she couldn't. All she could see was the tiny speck that represented Ensign Paris's shuttle, its position supported by a tractor beam emanating from the *Stargazer.*

Her officers, on the other hand, could keep track of Jiterica's movements via ship's sensors. And as time went on, they periodically brought the second officer up to speed. But they couldn't say the words she was waiting to hear, the words that would enable her to breathe easily again.

Finally, she heard from the one who *could* say those words. "Paris here," came the transmission from the shuttle.

Wu leaned forward in her seat. "Go ahead."

"She's in," the ensign said.

The commander nodded. "That's good news," she told Paris.

But she knew the Nizhrak's trial wasn't over yet. There was still the small matter of what she had to accomplish on the *Belladonna.*

"Come on home," she instructed the ensign. After all, his shuttle could only get in the way now.

"Aye," Paris said—and cut the comm link.

On the viewscreen, the shuttlecraft could be seen wheeling about, its portion of the mission accomplished. Obviously, Wu had been right to place her faith in Ensign Paris.

"Commander?" said Kastiigan, interrupting Wu's thoughts.

She turned to him. "Lieutenant?"

The science officer didn't look happy. "There's something here I think you should see."

Wu got up and made her way to his side. "What is it?"

Kastiigan pointed a long, wrinkled finger at his central monitor. "I don't know why, but the *Belladonna*'s rate of descent into the sinkhole seems to have accelerated."

"Accelerated . . . ?" Wu echoed, a chill climbing her spine.

She took a look at the Kandilkari's monitor, hoping he had jumped to the wrong conclusion. However, the data bore him out. The scientists' vessel was slipping into the sinkhole faster than before.

Much faster.

No, thought Wu. *She can't do this to us.* She forced herself to ask

Kastiigan the obvious question: "How long before she reaches the point of no return?"

The science officer frowned. "It's difficult to say, Commander. But if she continues at this pace, I would say the *Belladonna* has no more than thirty minutes left."

Thirty minutes, Wu thought. *And Jiterica had gone in thinking she would have a couple of hours.*

If there were a way to contact the ensign and warn her, the commander would have done it in a heartbeat. But had it been possible to communicate with the research vessel, Jiterica wouldn't have had to make the trip in the first place.

Wu would just have to hope that Jiterica noticed the change in the *Belladonna*'s situation and acted accordingly. Otherwise, the ensign and everyone else on that ship were doomed.

Chapter Twenty-three

JITERICA WAS PREPARED to spend whatever time it took to find the crew of the *Belladonna*.

However, she believed she would accomplish her objective more quickly if she headed for a place where survivors were likely to congregate. One such place, she decided, was the bridge.

Following the corridor, she stopped at the first turbolift she came to and summoned a compartment using the pad set into the bulkhead. But she didn't have to take it to the bridge to make contact with the crew of the *Belladonna*. One of them was in the lift when the doors opened, ready to emerge into the hallway.

"Damn!" the scientist cried and took an involuntary step back, obviously surprised to see her there. He was a tall man with deepset eyes and a receding line of dark hair. Recovering, he said, "You're the one who opened the hatch, aren't you?"

"I am," Jiterica confirmed.

He looked at her through the faceplate of her containment suit and his eyes narrowed. Her insubstantial-looking visage must have appeared strange to him. But then, it appeared strange to the ensign as well; she had only created it to make her colleagues feel more comfortable in her presence.

"What—?" the human began. Then he stopped himself. "No. Never mind that. Just tell me . . . are you here to help us? That's what everyone seems to think, and I sure as hell hope they're right."

"I am indeed here to help you," she told him. "My name is Jiterica. I hold the rank of ensign on the Federation starship *Stargazer*."

The man nodded. "I guess that explains the Starfleet insignia on your containment suit."

"How many of you are there?" Jiterica asked.

"Twenty-three," the human told her.

She made a mental note of it. "Casualties?"

"A few injuries, but no deaths," he said. Then he added, "So far."

So far, so good, Jiterica thought, quoting an expression she had heard on the ship.

"My commanding officer has come up with a plan to get you out of here," she said. "However, it will require your cooperation."

Just then, someone rounded a bend in the corridor. It was an Andorian, a female. As she approached Jiterica, her brow creased and her antennae bent all the way forward.

"I guess you got here before I did," the Andorian remarked.

"She's with Starfleet," the human explained before his colleague could ask. "They've come to help us escape this thing." He turned back to the ensign. "What do you need us to do?"

"To begin with," said Jiterica, "I need you to take me to your captain."

Simenon steeled himself for yet another ordeal—one for which he was poorly equipped, to say the least.

"You're sure we can't help?" Joseph asked.

"Surely the Elders can see you're in no shape for this," Vigo pointed out.

Simenon shook his head. "Single combat, to take place immediately after the race. That's the ancient law."

Picard frowned. "Your arm—"

"Has felt better," the engineer agreed. "But I'm going to try not to let Kasaelek know that."

Not that it was likely to matter. In the few times his subspecies had been involved in such combats, they hadn't even come close to winning. And as the captain had noted, Simenon wasn't operating at full strength.

But there was no alternative. He had to face Kasaelek or concede the contest—and the prize.

The Elder who had announced the decision looked to Simenon. "Are you ready, ritual runner?"

"I am," the engineer told him. As if to underline the fact, he moved into the center of the clearing.

The Elder looked to Kasaelek. "And you?"

The Aklaash moved into the center of the clearing as well. "Ready," he said, obviously eager to get the combat over with.

The Elder regarded them. "Let it begin."

Jiterica looked at the captain of the *Belladonna,* a thickset man with close-cropped hair and a full, blond beard, across the confines of his ready room. "That is," she said, finishing her outline of Commander Wu's plan, "if you still *have* impulse power."

"Oh," said the captain, "we've still got it, all right. We just don't know how *much.* After all, we gunned the engines pretty hard trying to get out of this mess on our own."

"I will need to speak to your engineer," the ensign told him.

The captain sighed. "Unfortunately, he was injured early on. His assistant is running things." He leaned forward. "And between you, me, and the bulkhead, he's not the brightest star in the firmament."

The captain of the *Belladonna* was an unusual man, Jiterica observed. Despite the dire nature of his circumstances, he seemed to take it all in stride.

"If you like," the ensign said, "I can offer him assistance. I was trained in engine operations at the Academy."

The captain nodded. "Sounds like a plan. Let's go."

But when the ready room doors opened for them, a human youngling was revealed standing outside them. His mouth fell open as he caught sight of Jiterica.

"My son," the captain explained, throwing his arm around the young man. "Little shy, but he's a whip. Curious about everything. Mind if he tags along?"

The ensign said she didn't mind at all.

* * *

Simenon had expected Kasaelek to try a preemptive strike at the outset of their winner-take-all combat. As it turned out, he was right.

The Aklaash had barely gotten leave to begin before he launched a meaty fist at his opponent. It was only because Simenon was expecting it that he was able to duck and shuffle past the attack.

But Kasaelek wasn't done yet. Not nearly. Unlike the engineer, he seemed to have plenty of energy left in him even after his catch-up sprint through the woods.

As the Aklaash wheeled and came at him again, Simenon had a moment to appreciate how mismatched they were. Kasaelek was proportioned just like him from his scaly head to the tip of his tail, but he towered over the engineer the way an adult might tower over his offspring. And the Aklaash wasn't hurt. It was only a matter of time before he used his superior reach to land a blow from which Simenon couldn't recover.

Unless, of course, Simenon used his vaunted Mazzereht intelligence to even up the contest somehow.

Easier said than done, he told himself, as he ventured to duck Kasaelek's second rush. This time, however, he couldn't avoid it entirely. The Aklaash landed a glancing blow to his right shoulder—the one above his injured ribs.

The resulting wave of pain made Simenon light-headed, but he managed to scurry away. *Damn,* he thought, unable to keep from wincing. He couldn't keep this up much longer. He had to *do* something.

Think, Phigus. Use that nimble brain the gods gave you. If you can fix a warp drive, you can beat a big, dumb Aklaash.

And then it came to him.

Truthfully, he hadn't come up with the idea on his own. *But if you're going to borrow,* he thought, *borrow something you know has worked.*

He waited until Kasaelek came about for another go at him. Then he braced himself, legs apart for balance, knowing he might not get a second chance at this.

The Aklaash bared his teeth and charged—but this time, he wasn't trying to bludgeon Simenon senseless with a single blow. He was coming on with his muscular arms spread wide, hoping to wrap them around his adversary and *then* batter him senseless.

It's now or never, Simenon told himself.

Marshaling what little energy he had left, he scooted between Kasaelek's legs and grabbed his adversary's tail—just as the duwiijuc had done to *him* earlier in the day.

No doubt, it was the last thing Kasaelek had expected of him. With a cry of rage, he whirled about in the clearing, dragging Simenon with him. The engineer felt as if his arm muscles were shredding, as if his ribs on that side were going to crack in half. But he didn't let go of Kasaelek's tail. In fact, he hung on that much harder.

Kasaelek tried to reach behind him, to peel Simenon off. But he couldn't. Even *his* mighty arms didn't reach that far. And the more he tried, the more the effort took its toll on him.

"Coward!" he rasped. "Pile of dung!"

Simenon didn't let the taunts get to him. If anything, they gave him the courage to keep going, to endure the agony in his side—because if Kasaelek was resorting to curses, he had to be faltering.

"I'll rip you apart!" the Aklaash railed at him. "I'll tear out your entrails and feed them to the sanjarra!"

The engineer barely heard what he was saying. He was too busy biting back his pain. But he wouldn't let go.

And Kasaelek, who hadn't shown any signs of fatigue when the combat started, began to show them with increasing rapidity. His breath came harder and harder. He staggered and flailed with arms that looked as if they had weights attached to them. And his fiery insults turned into a long, formless snarl of anger and frustration.

Finally, he couldn't take it anymore. His gigantic frame began to sag. And wracked by exhaustion, he crashed to his knees.

It was exactly the opening Simenon had been waiting for. Thrusting aside his own red storm of pain, he scrambled for a rock at the edge of the clearing.

It wasn't more than a couple of meters away, but it might as well have been a light-year. If the engineer didn't grab it and put it to good use before Kasaelek got to his feet, all the torment he had endured would go for nothing.

As the Aklaash drew in a deep, shuddering breath, Simenon's fingers closed on the rock. Then he changed direction and launched himself at his bigger, stronger adversary.

By then, Kasaelek had planted his right foot on the ground and was preparing to get up. But he hadn't cast a glance in Simenon's direction. At least, not yet.

Calling on his ancestors for strength, the engineer lifted the rock and cracked Kasaelek over the head with it. The Aklaash slumped and grabbed the ground, but didn't fall. Simenon smashed him in the skull a second time, forcing the knee Kasaelek had raised to crumble, but the giant was still fending off unconsciousness.

One last time, Simenon thought.

Clinging to that promise, he raised the rock as high as he could and brought it down on the Aklaash's cranium. And to his relief, it knocked Kasaelek flat, stripping the Aklaash of what little sense still rattled about in his head.

I've won, the engineer told himself.

But it didn't sink in until he looked around and saw his comrades cheering for him at the top of their lungs. Even the captain, who usually kept his emotions to himself. Even *Greyhorse,* for the gods' sake. They were shaking their fists and roaring with triumph as if it were they who had toppled Kasaelek.

I've won, Simenon repeated.

And he had—not only for himself but for his father and his brothers, who would have been celebrating his victory now if they had lived long enough to join him in the ritual.

Someone put a hand on Simenon's shoulder. Looking up, he saw that it was the Elder who had called for the combat.

"Rise," he said.

Simenon heaved the rock away, shuddering at the pain it cost him. Then, ever so slowly and carefully, he stood.

He noticed that the Fejjimaera had entered the clearing. They were standing at its edges, looking downcast at their defeat. Especially Banyohla, who seemed to be injured and was leaning on one of his comrades for support.

Simenon almost felt sorry for Banyohla. *Almost.*

"You have won the running of the ritual as prescribed by law," the Elder told him. "You have triumphed over your rivals."

The engineer liked the sound of that.

"All you need do now," said the Elder, "is produce the insadja'tu and complete the ceremony. Then the nest is yours."

The insadja'tu, Simenon thought, his mind numb and distant in the aftermath of his struggle. It was the stone his father had made for him when he was young, an exact replica of the one the Elder Simenon had carried in his own ritual victory.

The engineer knew what he had to do. He had to present the insadja'tu to the Elder and finish what he had started. With that in mind, he fished in the interior pocket of his garment—a deep, narrow slot into which he had inserted the stone before he left the *Stargazer.*

How proud his father would have been of him, he reflected. How jubilant to see his bloodline go on uninterrupted.

It was then that Simenon's fingers reached the bottom of his pocket—and felt nothing. *Nothing at all.*

"Is something wrong?" the Elder asked.

The engineer felt dizzy all of a sudden. Dizzy and weak in the knees. *It can't be,* he thought wildly.

"Is something wrong?" the Elder asked a little more insistently.

Simenon swallowed and probed his pocket again. It had to be in there somewhere. *Where else could it be?* he asked himself, knowing full well that it could have been *anywhere.*

In the underground waterway. In the crevasse. In the place where they fought off the sanjarra.

Anywhere.

Chapter Twenty-four

JITERICA STUDIED THE MONITOR on the engineering console as she ran yet another diagnostic on the impulse drive. There was still a problem with the driver coil assembly, apparently.

She believed she knew how to fix it. It would take some time, of course, but there was no shortage of that. According to the chronometer in her suit, she still had more than an hour and forty minutes to get the engines ready.

"Ensign Jiterica?" said the captain's son, who had been standing alongside her since she came down to engineering, watching her every move.

"Yes?" Jiterica responded, though her attention remained fixed on the console.

"What kind of being are you?" the human asked.

"I'm a Nizhrak—a low-density being from a gas giant. You've probably never seen one of my people before."

"You're right," he said. "I haven't." A pause. "I hope you don't think I'm being rude but . . . I'm kind of curious about your suit."

"Curious?" Jiterica echoed.

"About what it does for you."

"I see," she said.

She went on to describe how the suit helped her to contain her mass, how it made it possible for her to ambulate throughout a starship, and how it facilitated periodic nourishment. When she was finished, she turned to face him.

"Is that what you wish to know?"

The captain's son nodded, his brow pinched as he absorbed the information. "That's exactly what I wished . . . I mean *wanted* to know."

Assured that she had satisfied his curiosity, Jiterica returned to her work. But a moment later, she heard the human speak up again.

"May I ask you another question?"

She gave him permission to do so.

"How does it feel," he asked, "to be a biological being that has to interface with a mechanical device?"

The ensign considered the question. "To me," she admitted, "it feels awkward. How does it feel to you?"

The captain's son looked confused. "What do you mean?"

"You interface with this ship, do you not?"

"Well," he said, smiling a little, "sure. But not in the same way."

It seemed to Jiterica that he was about to ask her another question about her interaction with the suit—something along more technological lines, perhaps. But before he could do that, she heard his father's voice over the ship's intercom.

"Ensign Jiterica?" the captain said.

"I am here," she responded.

"We've got a problem—or should I say a bigger problem. My sensor officer tells me we're slipping into the sinkhole faster than before. I hope you're almost done down there."

"How much time do we have?" the ensign asked. She didn't think she would like the answer.

"Twenty minutes," the captain told her. "Tops."

Her prediction had been accurate. She didn't like the answer at all.

Picard didn't understand.

What in blazes was an insadja'tu? And why did it have such significance to the elder?

He saw Simenon turn to the Gnalish in the white robe. "I can't find it," the engineer said, his voice uncharacteristically subdued and full of disappointment. "I must have dropped it somewhere along the way."

The elder's brow furrowed above his scaly snout. "Without the insadja'tu, there can be no consummation." He turned to Kasaelak, who was holding his head as he began to regain consciousness. "If the Aklaash has retained his insadja'tu, he may be declared the victor."

Picard frowned. That hardly seemed like an equitable conclusion.

"Kasaelek," said one of his comrades. The Aklaash knelt beside him. "Show the elder your insadja'tu."

Kasaelek was still dazed, but not to the point where he couldn't understand his comrade's instructions. Delving into a pocket of his own, he felt around for a moment. Then he drew his hand out and showed the elders a white stone with black etchings.

The insadja'tu, Picard thought. Little more than a pebble. And this would decide the outcome of the ritual?

They had come so far, gotten through so much. They had won by every reasonable standard. It wasn't fair for Simenon's bloodline to be ended forever on a mere technicality. At least it seemed that way to his Terran mode of thinking.

But they weren't on Earth, the captain had to remind himself. They were on Gnala, and what seemed like a mere technicality to him here may have made perfect sense to Simenon's people.

"I have no choice," the elder said, "but to award Kasaelak the victory. That is, if he can transcribe the glyphs that appear on his insadja'tu without error."

Kasaelak laughed despite the bludegeoning he had endured. Clearly, he didn't believe he would have any trouble doing what the elder had suggested—not when he had his little white stone for reference.

Simenon's head drooped and he looked away. It didn't seem he could bear to watch.

Nonetheless, the Aklaash moved into the center of the clearing, where he found a patch of soft, dark ground unconcealed by the spongy stuff. Then he pulled out his tellek and used it to make a line.

"Wait a minute," said Greyhorse, who was standing next to the crestfallen Simenon. "That's what the insadja'tu is for? So you can draw glyphs in the ground?"

"That's what it's for," the engineer confirmed.

"What if you could draw the glyphs *without* the stone?" asked the medical officer.

"What if I could *fly?*" Simenon rasped bitterly. "Without the stone, I can't do a thing."

For the first time, Picard saw Greyhorse become angry. "Answer me, damn you," said the doctor.

Surprised, the engineer looked up at him. "The law of ritual calls for a drawing. That's it. But—"

Greyhorse didn't let him finish. Limping out into the center of the clearing, he stopped in front of where Kasaelak was kneeling.

"Get out of my way," the Aklaash growled, an unmistakable promise of violence in his voice.

But the chief medical officer didn't answer him. He spoke to the elders instead. "I stand for Simenon," he said.

The foremost elder regarded him. "In what capacity?"

"In *this* capacity," Greyhorse told him.

With difficulty, he lowered himself to his knees alongside another open patch of ground. Then, looking as humble and miserable as Picard had ever seen him, the doctor took out his own tellek and began to draw. And as the captain watched—as they all watched—Greyhorse began to produce a set of glyph-like lines.

Simenon's eyes narrowed as he looked on. "They're the ones on my insadja'tu," he muttered. He turned to Picard. "But how does he—?"

The captain shook his head. "I don't know."

Clearly, however, Greyhorse knew what he was doing. Though he worked intently and exercised great care, he didn't stop even once. He inscribed glyph after intricate glyph as if he had known them from the moment of his birth.

Ben Zoma chuckled. "Amazing."

"It is indeed," Picard agreed.

"This is an outrage!" Kasaelak growled, his ruby eyes full of fury. He got up and charged the elders, stopping just in time to keep from bowling them over. "You gave *me* the victory!"

"We gave you the opportunity to inscribe the glyphs," said one of the elders, unruffled by the Aklaash's display. "But only because Simenon could not. Now, it seems, he *can.*"

"But that's not Simenon!" Kasaelak snarled, pointing a thick, long-nailed finger at Greyhorse. "That's an offworlder! Bad enough he was allowed to accompany the Mazzereht on his journey. But to let him inscribe glyphs in our sacred ground . . . that is beyond reason!"

The elder shook his head from side to side. "We have already determined that the offworlder may stand for Simenon—not just in one aspect of the ritual, but in all of them."

Kasaelak sputtered with anger, but he had to see that he wasn't going to make any headway with the elders. Which was, no doubt, why he whirled and faced Greyhorse instead.

Too late, Picard saw the Aklaash lower his head and go after the doctor. All he could do was cry out a warning. But Joseph wasn't too late. He bolted for Greyhorse as well, embarking on an intercept course with the powerful Kasaelak.

For a moment, Picard wasn't sure which of them would reach the doctor first. Then, with a desperate burst of speed that surprised the captain, the security officer interposed himself between Greyhorse and Kasaelek and took the brunt of the attack.

Aklaash and human rolled across the clearing in a tangle of arms and legs. Predictably, the larger and stronger Kasaelek got to his feet first, intent on doing further damage to Joseph.

But someone intervened. Not Vigo, who was best equipped to have done so. Not Picard or Ben Zoma or Simenon or any of the black-robed Aklaash who stood at the edges of the clearing.

Someone else got to Kasaelek first, tackling him at the knees and toppling him, and then leaping on top of him to deliver a crude but enthusiastic right to the Gnalish's jaw.

It was Greyhorse.

Before Kasaelek could shrug off the blow, the Aklaash guards surrounded him and pulled him to his feet. And Greyhorse backed off, holding his right hand with his left.

"Are you all right?" Picard asked as he joined him there.

The doctor frowned as he inspected his hand. "As if tracing those glyphs wasn't *already* difficult. Now I'll be doing it one-handed."

The captain glanced at the elders, who didn't look very happy with Kasaelek's behavior. "I think you'll be granted a certain amount of leeway," he said.

It turned out that Picard was right. Greyhorse was given all the time he needed to complete the glyphs on Simenon's insadja'tu—time enough to describe where he had seen them before and how they came to be planted so firmly in his mind.

For all the captain knew, they might all have been perfectly accurate. Or then again, they might not have been. All that was important was that the elders accepted them.

Maybe by then, they had recognized that Simenon had earned his posterity many times over.

Finally, the engineer was officially declared the victor. But he didn't celebrate. More than anything, he looked relieved.

"As my teammates," he told Picard and the others, "you can stay and watch me inseminate the eggs." But his tone and his expression indicated that he would rather they didn't.

"I don't think so," the captain said.

Ben Zoma smiled. "Maybe some other time."

So Picard and his officers left the clearing, walked back into the scarlet woods and waited. And when Simenon came to get them a short time later, it was after he had done his part—injuries and all—to add to the longevity of his bloodline.

Wu couldn't wait any longer.

According to Kastiigan's sensors, the *Belladonna* had slipped into the sinkhole almost to the point where it would be futile to try to drag her out again. If they were going to try to stage a rescue, they would have to do it *now.*

But the *Stargazer* couldn't do it alone. As long as the scientists on the research ship had recognized the urgency of their situation and gotten their engines ready, they had a chance. If they had failed in that regard, perhaps because the impulse drive was just unsalvageable at this point, the *Belladonna* and all hands would be lost.

It was that simple.

Wu turned to Idun. "Helm, take us within a hundred kilometers of the accretion bridge."

The helm officer did as she was told, her fingers moving nimbly over her controls. Almost instantly, the plasma stream began to loom larger on the forward viewer. After a while, all Wu could see from one side of the screen to the other was brilliant, red-gold turbulence.

Paris had returned from the brink of that chaos with his shuttle safe and sound. But Jiterica was still trapped inside the accretion bridge along with the people she had tried to save. Wu prayed that the ensign's efforts there had paid off.

Finally, Idun turned to her. "One hundred kilometers," she reported, though from the look in her eyes she would have liked to dare more.

Wu glanced at Gerda. "Give me a tractor lock."

The navigator carried out the order. "Got it," she said a few moments later.

The second officer frowned. This was it. If Jiterica had succeeded, they would know it soon enough. "Reverse engines and proceed at one-quarter-impulse. Let's get them out of there."

"Reversing engines," Idun told her.

"Come on," Wu breathed, staring at the screen as if that could make a difference. "Give us a hand."

"I'm reading engine activity in the *Belladonna,*" Kastiigan announced from his science station. He looked up. "They appear to be operating at rated power."

Wu nodded. Jiterica had done it. She had gotten the impulse drive ready in time. But would it be enough?

She felt a shudder in the deckplates. The *Stargazer* was straining to carry out her part of the bargain. But if the research ship was emerging from her trap, Wu couldn't tell from the image on the viewscreen.

Needing to see what was going on, she got up and joined Kastiigan. "Progress?" she asked hopefully.

"None to speak of," he said, intent on his monitors.

Wu bit her lip. The longer this went on, straining both their engines and the *Belladonna*'s, the less likely they were to pull the research ship out of there.

"All available power to the engines!" she snapped. "Shields, life support . . . everything but the tractor feed!"

The lights dimmed on the bridge and she felt another tremor run through the deck. Then she turned to Kastiigan's monitors, which seemed brighter in the relative darkness, defying them to tell her that her order hadn't helped.

In fact, it *had.* More of the research ship had crept out of the sinkhole. But she still wasn't free. Wu needed to do more for her.

"We need more power," she said out loud.

But there *wasn't* any more power. They had already tapped all their vessel's resources. Or had they?

They were still pumping incredible amounts of energy into their tractor beam—enough to maintain its integrity in this titanic tug-of-war across a hundred kilometers of graviton-riddled space.

They didn't dare compromise the strength of the beam. But if they cut down its length, even by thirty kilometers, and shuttled that suddenly-available power to the engines . . .

"Take us in closer," Wu told her helm officer. "Within seventy kilometers of the accretion bridge."

Idun looked at her. "Aye, Commander."

And she brought them in closer.

Of course, there was a problem with Wu's idea—a flaw of which she was well aware. At some point, the sinkhole would begin to exert a pull on the *Stargazer* again as well. Then they would be trying to drag two ships at the same time—the scientists' and their own.

Wu could only hope that flaw wouldn't become a fatal one.

"Seventy kilometers," Idun told her. She studied her instruments and frowned. "We're being drawn in."

Wu's heart sank. "What about the *Belladonna?*" she asked Kastiigan, too discouraged to look for herself.

A pause. "She's moving," the science officer replied, a note of surprise in his voice. "Yes . . . she is definitely moving."

But so was Wu's ship—and in the wrong direction. If she allowed that to go on much longer, the *Belladonna* wouldn't be the only victim of the rift. The *Stargazer* would be sucked in along with her.

The only prudent course of action was to deactivate the tractor beam and retreat while they still could. After all, Wu had the lives of her crew to consider. But she couldn't do it. Not with all those scientists depending on them, clinging to the slender thread of hope only Wu and her officers could offer them.

And it wasn't just the *Belladonna*'s crew she was thinking about. Jiterica had trusted her, risked her life at Wu's request.

How could Wu fail to return the favor?

Pull, she urged the *Stargazer,* intent on the yellow blip that represented the research ship on Kastiigan's monitor. *Pull with everything you've got.*

And as if her invocation had given the *Belladonna* the courage she needed, the vessel surged free of her prison, a flying thing too long denied flight.

Gerda turned to Wu, her eyes alight with triumph. "She's escaped the sinkhole!"

"So she has!" the commander returned.

But it wasn't over yet. The *Belladonna* still had to escape the sinkhole's *pull.*

"Her impulse drive is giving out," Kastiigan said, putting a damper on his colleagues' enthusiasm. He pointed to the monitor that showed him the other ship's energy levels. "Another few seconds and she will be without propulsion."

But in the meantime, she was getting closer to the *Stargazer.* And the closer she got, the less energy it took to maintain the tractor beam that held her in tow.

Wu felt a muscle in her jaw begin to spasm. *Wait,* she told herself. *Just a little longer . . .*

To their credit, none of her bridge officers questioned her judgement. Paxton, Dubinski, Kastiigan . . . they remained silent and uncomplaining, watching along with Wu as the *Belladonna* slowly climbed out of the swirling plasma of the accretion bridge.

And just as the commander had hoped, the *Stargazer* began to win *her* battle as well. Even without any help from the research vessel's impulse drive, the starship pulled away from the sinkhole—further and further, giving her crew more reason for optimism with each passing moment.

Then something strange happened, something Wu had never experienced in all the time she had spent on the *Crazy Horse*. Someone on the bridge began to *cheer.* And someone else joined him. And before the second officer knew it, everyone around her was cheering or applauding or grinning at her with unmitigated pride.

Part of her noted that it was very much against regulations to cheer on the bridge of a starship. But it was a very small part. The rest of her enjoyed every second of it.

Chapter Twenty-five

JITERICA FELT A WAVE of relief as she studied the readout on her console in the *Belladonna*'s small but efficient engineering facility.

Despite her best efforts, the ship's impulse drive had failed. But it had held out long enough to do what was required of it.

The *Belladonna* was out of danger, the sinkhole falling farther and farther behind her with each passing moment. Her crew was safe. The ensign took pride in that outcome.

Abruptly, she realized that there was a hand on the shoulder of her containment suit. Turning her helmet, she saw that the appendage belonged to the *Belladonna*'s captain. He and his son had come down to engineering without her realizing it.

The captain smiled in the depths of his beard. "Thank you," he said, "from the bottom of my old, black heart." Then he held out his hand.

Jiterica knew what she had to do with it. After all, she had seen humans do it often enough on the ship. Exerting the requisite control over her containment suit, she placed her gauntlet in the man's hand.

His smile widened as he clasped it. "Ever have a yen to visit the colony on New Stockholm, Ensign?"

"No," Jiterica had to confess. She didn't even know what system New Stockholm was in.

"Well," the captain said, "you should. It's a beautiful place. If you ever feel like seeing it, look me up. I'll be happy to show you around." As he looked around the engineering facility, his face finally showed the stress he had been under. "I think after this, I'll be content to stay at home for a while."

It occurred to Jiterica that she *couldn't* "look him up." She lacked an important piece of information.

"What is your name?" she asked.

The captain's eyes opened wide as he realized his omission. "Hansen," he said. "Erik Hansen." He put his arm around his son's shoulder. "And this is Magnus. I'm sure he'll be happy to show you around as well. But you'd better visit soon, or he'll be off on a voyage of his own."

Magnus rolled his eyes. "I'm only thirteen, Dad."

"In years," said his father, who was obviously proud of him. "But you've already got more smarts than most grown men."

The boy looked at Jiterica and shrugged. *Parents,* he seemed to say. *They'll embarrass you every chance they get.*

The ensign knew the feeling. Hers were the same way.

Simenon stopped pacing the small meeting room when he heard its only door open.

"Phigus?" said his cousin Ornitharen as he poked his scaly head in.

"Yes," Simenon said, "I'm in here." He gestured for Ornitharen to come in and join him.

Ornitharen took a deep breath. "I wasn't sure which room it was. Those Aklaash in the black suits don't give very good directions. If I hadn't been here in the Northern Sanctum just the other day, I never would have found you."

"I'm glad you did," said Simenon.

His cousin frowned at him as if realizing something for the first time. "You look terrible, Phigus."

The engineer grunted. "I *feel* terrible."

Ornitharen looked sympathetic. "You lost the race, didn't you?"

Simenon shook his head. "Actually, I won."

"You *won?*" his cousin echoed wonderingly.

"Yes. Fertilized the eggs and everything. Our bloodline will go on at least another generation."

Ornitharen grinned. "That's . . . that's incredible. I'm so happy for you. For us, I mean."

"I knew you would be."

His cousin looked at him askance. "Something's wrong."

"What makes you say that?" Simenon asked.

"You should be happier about this. What's going on?"

Simenon frowned. "Someone sabotaged the vine bridge at the crevasse."

Ornitharen gazed at him wide-eyed. "Are you sure?"

"Quite sure."

"But who—" Ornitharen thought about it for a moment. "You mean Banyohla? Or Kasaelek?"

"Neither of them."

"Then who, Phigus?"

Simenon looked at him. *"You,* Ornitharen."

His cousin looked hurt. "You must be insane. What would make you say such a spiteful thing?"

The engineer's frown deepened. "There's no longer any point in feigning innocence, Ornitharen. I found Mazzereht-sized footprints near the bridge and had them compared with yours on a hunch. They turned out to be a match."

"Then the records people made a mistake," Ornitharen insisted.

Simenon shook his head. "There's no mistake. It was you who was trying to kill me. And the more I think about it, the more I believe you had a hand in my brothers' deaths as well."

"But why would I do that?" asked his cousin.

"That's what I asked myself," said Simenon. "Why would Ornitharen try to kill me? What could he gain by spilling my blood? And then I came up with the answer."

Ornitharen remained silent.

"I was the progenitor," the engineer told him, "the one whose seed would carry on our line. But you didn't like that situation, did you? You wanted it to be *your* seed. And if I were dead, it would be *you* running in the ritual instead."

Again, his cousin failed to respond to the accusation.

"You can save us all some trouble," said Simenon, "and admit what you've done. You're going to be found guilty in any case."

Ornitharen glowered at him for a moment. Then he made his reply, his voice dripping with resentment.

"Do you have any idea what it's like to be second-best, Cousin—to know you'll *always* be second-best? Do you know what it's like to have to kowtow to a *sedgmaya* who doesn't give a *colunnu* feather about your family's affairs?"

Simenon shook his head. "If you weren't happy with me, you should have brought it up a long time ago. We might have been able to work something out. As it is . . ." He shrugged. "It's a bit too late for that."

Ornitharen spat at his feet. "Had I been born a week earlier, it would have been *me* racing Kasaelek and Banyohla."

"I might have been content with that," said Simenon, "if it meant my brothers would still be alive."

His cousin didn't say anything more. He just glared at the engineer one last time and left the room for the corridor outside, where the black-garbed Aklaash were waiting to take him into custody.

For a little while, Simenon remained alone, contemplating the lengths to which people will go when they're thwarted in their ambitions. Then there was a knock at the still-open door.

"Come in," he said.

Picard led Simenon's other colleagues into the room. All five of them.

"You and your cousin appear to have completed your business," the captain observed.

"They're taking him away?" Simenon asked.

"Yes," Picard confirmed.

The Gnalish heaved a sigh. "Families can be a great responsibility." Picard nodded sympathetically. "They can indeed."

Simenon looked around at his comrades, who—until his progeny hatched—were the only *real* family he had. "And once in a while," he found himself adding in a wildly uncharacteristic display of generosity, "something of a comfort."

Ben Zoma looked at him as if he had grown another head. "I must be dreaming. Was that an expression of *gratitude* I heard? From our chief engineer?"

"I believe it was," said Greyhorse, joining in.

The Gnalish made a sound of dismissal. "Don't get too accustomed to it, either of you. You're not likely to hear it again."

"Now that," said Ben Zoma, feigning relief, "is the Phigus Simenon we've come to know and love. For a minute there, I thought you'd been exchanged for your evil twin."

That drew a few chuckles from the others.

Enough banter, Simenon thought. And enough time spent risking his skin in primitive forests. He longed for the civilized simplicity of his life back on the *Stargazer.*

Not that he would give his colleagues the additional satisfaction of hearing him say that. He was grateful, yes—but he had already expressed his gratitude far too extravagantly.

Assuming his trademark scowl, he said, "Shouldn't someone be contacting the ship for a transport about now? Or would you like to run that course again just for the hell of it?"

As no one seemed eager to do so, Picard agreed to make the call.

Commander Wu arrived in the transporter room just in time to see Ensign Jiterica materialize on the hexagonal platform.

She turned to the operator on duty, and said, "Good work, Mr. Refsland."

He wiped a bead of sweat from his brow. "Thank you, Commander."

Wu knew it wasn't easy to transport a Nizhrak—particularly one in a force field-reinforced Starfleet containment suit. However, Refsland and the other transporter operators would have to get used to it.

Jiterica had proved for the second time in as many months how valuable she was to this ship and crew. Captain Picard would be a fool to let her get away, even if he had to build a special chair for her so she could join her fellow crewmen in the mess hall.

"Commander," said the ensign as she stepped down from the platform. The visage behind her faceplate looked surprised.

Wu smiled at her. "I wanted to congratulate you as soon as I could. What you did out there was . . ." She couldn't find the words. "You should be proud of yourself, Ensign. I know I am."

Something amazing happened then. Jiterica *smiled.*

"Thank you," she said in her tinny, mechanical voice. "I am pleased to hear you say that."

Wu was about to tell her that she hoped to say it a lot. Then she remembered that that wouldn't be the case—not with her rejoining Captain Rudolfini on the *Crazy Horse.*

Just then, the doors to the transporter room opened again and someone else came in. Glancing over her shoulder, the commander saw that it was Ensign Paris.

He was grinning like a hyena, looking nothing like the doubt-ravaged young man who had poured his heart out to Wu in Picard's ready room. It was only after he saw the second officer standing there that he assumed a more professional demeanor.

"Commander Wu," he said. "I hope you don't mind my coming here. I just wanted to make sure Ensign Jiterica got back all right."

Wu understood. She would have given into the same impulse if she had just risked her life with someone.

"Actually," she said, "I'm glad you're here, Ensign."

Paris became concerned. "You are?"

"Yes. I was just telling Ensign Jiterica what a wonderful job she did—and the same goes for you."

He seemed to take the praise in stride. "I appreciate that, Commander. But . . ." He shrugged. "I would never have had the chance if someone hadn't had more confidence in me than I had in myself."

Wu felt a lump grow in her throat. She shook her head until it went away. "Don't flatter me, Mr. Paris. Any commanding officer worth her salt would have had confidence in you." She turned to Jiterica and added, "In both of you."

It was a pity that she was leaving, the commander reflected. It would have been fun to watch these ensigns grow—both as people and as professionals.

"See you on the bridge," she told them, and left them to each other's company.

Chapter Twenty-six

PICARD EMERGED from the turbolift and took in his bridge at a glance. The Asmunds were at their usual posts. Paxton was at communications. And Dubinski appeared to be instructing Ensign Nikolas in the proper use of an engineering console.

It was good to be home, the captain thought.

Nikolas was the first to glance his way. "Captain on the bridge," he announced dutifully.

Picard saw everyone present come to attention, the ensign included. "As you were," he told them.

As his officers resumed their duties, he turned to Kastiigan, who was working at the science console. "Do you know where I can find Commander Wu?"

The Kandilkari jerked his head in the direction of the captain's ready room. "I believe she's in *there,* sir."

"I see," said Picard. "Thank you, Mr. Kastiigan."

"I'm glad to be of service, sir," the science officer told him, and returned to his work.

Crossing the bridge, the captain waited outside his ready room doors for a moment—as a courtesy to Wu. When they slid aside, he walked in and saw his second officer standing behind his desk.

"Welcome back," she said.

He smiled. "It's good to *be* back. I understand you had a little excitement in my absence."

"A little," Wu told him. "But nothing we couldn't handle, thanks to the crew. And in particular, thanks to Ensigns Jiterica and Paris."

The captain was pleased to hear it.

"They demonstrated valor and resourcefulness," his second officer continued. "I couldn't have been prouder of them."

It was high praise. "I look forward," he said, "to reading about it your report."

"Which will be available for your inspection first thing in the morning," she assured him.

If Picard had been the second officer, he would have taken the opportunity to leave the room at that juncture. However, Wu didn't show any intention of leaving.

He was about to ask why when she said, "I have a request, sir."

He shrugged. "What is it, Commander?"

Wu hesitated. "If it's all right with you, I would like to rescind my request for a transfer to the *Crazy Horse.*"

At first, the captain thought he had heard incorrectly. "You want to *stay?*" he asked, just to make sure.

"That's correct, sir."

Without question, he was pleased with the decision. But he had to admit to a certain curiosity. "If you don't mind my asking," he said, "what made you change your mind?"

Wu smiled. "I've given it some thought—and I've concluded that I can do more good *here* than on the *Crazy Horse.* With certain crewmen in particular, you understand."

Picard looked at her. Given the way she had talked about Paris and Jiterica, he had a feeling he knew who those crewmen might be. But he was a bit puzzled.

Do more *good?*

The Nizhrak had been disoriented and isolated from the rest of the crew from the moment she had come aboard. It was clear that she had needed a helping hand from someone. But Paris didn't seem to have needed any such help. He had appeared comfortable on the *Stargazer* from the beginning.

No doubt, Picard would gain a better understanding of the situation once he read his second officer's report. "Have you apprised Captain Rudolfini of your desire to stay with us?"

"Not yet," said his second officer. "I'd like to do that now, if it's all right with you."

"It is," Picard told her.

After Wu left his ready room, he sat down in his chair and leaned back contentedly. Not only did he get to keep a good officer, he wouldn't have to pore through personnel files searching for her replacement.

It was shaping up to be a very pleasant homecoming. Very pleasant indeed.

Ulelo was sitting in the mess hall, eating by himself because he couldn't see any opportunities for intelligence-gathering among the junior-grade crewmen seated around him, when a tray full of food landed next to his own.

He looked up and saw that the tray belonged to Emily Bender. "Fancy meeting you here," she said.

The comm officer didn't know what to make of her joining him. Stalling for time to think, he glanced at her plate. "What's that?"

Emily Bender smiled accusingly. "Chicken and rice. I'm sure you've seen it before."

He had, in fact. "It just looked different," he explained—rather lamely, he thought.

She didn't respond to his excuse. Instead, she dug her fork into her chicken and rice and said, "When we spoke in my quarters, I turned down your offer of friendship. But I've had some time to think about it."

Ulelo didn't know what to say. The best he could do was "Oh?"

"And I think I'd like to be your friend after all."

"My . . . friend."

"Yes." She looked up at him. "If that's what you want, of course."

Ulelo frowned. He didn't know the answer to that question.

It was critical that he put his mission above all else—and without question, a friend could complicate that mission. That was why he had been careful to keep all his acquaintances on the ship at arm's length.

But mere acquaintances left his need for companionship unfulfilled—and mission or no mission, a man still craved companionship. Emily Bender would fill that need if he let her—if he could cope with the idea of her getting closer to him but not *too* close.

"Yes," Ulelo found himself saying. "It's what I want."

He only hoped he wouldn't come to regret it.

Vigo found Kastiigan in the science section, where he was running a diagnostic on a sensor bank.

"Ah," said the Kandilkari, favoring him with a glance. "I see you're back from your away mission. I heard it went well—though regrettably, no one got the opportunity to perish for his comrades."

"Er . . . that's right," Vigo agreed. But he hadn't come here to speak of his adventures on Gnala or how close they had come to perishing. "I was hoping we could talk for a moment."

"Of course," said Kastiigan. He gave the weapons officer his full attention. "What about?"

"It's . . . about your talk of dying." Vigo searched for some diplomatic way to make his point, but finally had to settle for the direct approach. "I find it disturbing."

Kastiigan looked surprised. "Disturbing . . . ?"

Vigo nodded. "You have to understand . . . we Pandrilites never speak of such things."

The Kandilkari's brow furrowed. Clearly, he was making an attempt to understand his colleague's feelings in the matter. Finally, his purple eyes brightened.

"I see what you mean," he said.

Vigo smiled. "You do?"

"Of course. Talk is of no value. All that matters is what one does— and to this point, I have not been aggressive enough in my struggle to perish for the good of my comrades."

The Pandrilite shook his head, horrified. "That's not—"

"No," said Kastiigan, holding up a hand for silence, "there's no need to elaborate. You have made your point most eloquently. When I perish, it will be with your friendship and kindness foremost in my mind."

"You don't understand," Vigo started to tell him.

But before he could get all the words out, he was interrupted by the captain's voice coming over the intercom system. "Picard to Lieutenant Kastiigan."

The science officer looked up. "Aye, sir?"

"These readings you took of the sinkhole are quite remarkable. I'd like to discuss them with you in my ready room."

"Of course, sir. Kastiigan out."

"Listen," said Vigo, still intent on clearing up the Kandilkari's misapprehension, "I didn't—"

"Sorry," Kastiigan told him, "duty calls."

And before the weapons officer knew it, his colleague was on his way out of the science section. It occurred to Vigo that he could go with him, explain the matter en route.

But by the time he decided to do that, it was too late. Kastiigan was out the door, down the corridor and out of sight, headed for the nearest turbolift.

Vigo frowned. Perhaps he would get through to the science officer another time. But somehow, he had his doubts.

Carter Greyhorse was lying in bed, trying to endure the assorted aches and pains he had accumulated on Gnala without the benefit of medication, when his door chimed.

He swore beneath his breath. Swinging his legs over the side of the bed, he sat up and steeled himself. Then he got up, defying cramps in his quadriceps, his calves, and his lower back.

"Be right there," the doctor muttered, and began making his way from bedroom to the anteroom that stood outside it.

The door chimed again.

"For the love of heaven," he sighed, "what is so urgent? I *said* I'd be right there."

The door had chimed a third time before Greyhorse made it to the center of the anteroom. Taking a deep breath, he gritted his teeth and stood up straight.

Then he said, "Come in."

That's when the doors parted and revealed the last person Greyhorse had expected to see there.

"I heard about your adventure on Gnala," Gerda said. She walked in and the doors hissed closed behind her. "It appears you acquitted yourself rather well."

Greyhorse had a feeling the navigator had only heard part of the story. Quite clearly, his comrades hadn't told her how he held the team back by lagging behind.

"I made a contribution or two," he allowed modestly.

Gerda didn't respond. She just stood there, eyeing him with an intensity he had never seen in her before.

"So . . . you've come to congratulate me?" he asked, feeling increasingly uncomfortable with the way she was looking at him.

The navigator's lip curled. "More than that, Carter Greyhorse. Judging by what you accomplished on Simenon's behalf, I believe you're ready to attempt a new level of confrontation."

Greyhorse swallowed back his nervousness and looked at her askance. "I beg your pardon?"

Gerda came closer. And as she did so, she raised her hands in a kave'ragh posture, elbows up and knuckles extended, her right hand coiled and poised to strike.

"A warrior does not beg," she told him, her voice suddenly seething with emotion. "A warrior *takes.*"

"This is going to be good," said Nikolas as he made his way to the ship's gym.

"Are you certain that you wish to go ahead with this?" asked Obal, who was doing his best to keep up with the human's longer strides.

Nikolas grinned incredulously at his friend. "Am I certain? Do Vulcans have pointed ears?"

The Binderian made a face as he bounded along. "It is only that I am concerned about the possibility of injuries."

The ensign waved away the idea. "I'll take it easy on her, I promise. Believe me, the last thing I want to do is *hurt* her."

Then they had arrived at the gym. Nikolas pressed the pad set into the bulkhead and watched the doors slide apart in front of him, revealing a single figure waiting for him in the gym.

A single, very *lovely* figure.

"Ensign Nikolas," said Idun, by way of acknowledgement. She glanced at his companion. "Lieutenant Obal."

"Lieutenant Asmund," the Binderian said, though it sounded to Nikolas more like a sigh.

Nikolas's original date with the curvaceous helm officer had been postponed because of the *Belladonna* crisis, which had required her continual presence on the bridge. But Idun hadn't been the least bit reluctant to reschedule.

"Thanks for walking me over," the ensign told his friend, keeping his gaze locked on his sparring partner. "I can take it from here."

"You're absolutely sure?" Obal asked.

Nikolas nodded. "Never been more sure in my life."

"All right," the Binderian told him. "I will see you . . ." He hesitated for a moment. "Later."

"Later," the ensign agreed.

He waited until Obal had departed and the doors to the gym had slid together again. Then he rubbed his hands together in friendly anticipation and approached his partner.

"Have you had a chance to warm up?" Nikolas asked.

"I have," Idun acknowledged. "You?"

"It'll take just a moment," he said.

Usually, the ensign warmed up slowly, not wanting to invite injury. But this time, he rushed it a bit. After all, he didn't want Idun to change her mind.

"All right," he said. "Ready."

Idun nodded. "Good."

She began to circle him, her hands curled like claws. She held her left hand forward and the right back near her chin.

"Interesting stance," Nikolas observed.

"It's Klingon," she told him.

He smiled. "Really."

"Really," said Idun.

Then she came at him, shooting her right hand at his face. Nikolas moved his head to one side and avoided the blow without any trouble. Then he returned it with one of his own.

It wasn't anything like his best shot, of course. He had meant it when he told Obal that he didn't want anyone getting hurt.

As it turned out, the ensign's attack missed by more than he expected. Idun was fast. Almost as fast as he was, it seemed.

Abruptly, she changed her stance. Turning her palms inward, she held her hands in front of her chest.

"Don't tell me that's Klingon too," he said.

"As a matter of fact," she returned, "it is."

Idun came at him again, but this time she didn't use her hands. Her body rolled gracefully and her right foot lashed out, her heel headed for his mouth.

As before, Nikolas avoided the maneuver without too much trouble. And this time, he put a little more mustard on his counterpunch.

His opponent handled it flawlessly, showing him that her earlier move was no fluke. She really *was* fast.

"Nicely done," he said.

Idun didn't answer him. Instead, she changed her stance again, reverting to the one with the clawlike fists. And she continued to circle him, her eyes as hard and blue as sapphires.

"You know," Nikolas said, "I have a confession to make."

"What's that?" she asked.

He smiled. "I only staged this match because I wanted us to become better acquainted."

"Really," she responded.

"That's right," he confirmed.

"I assume," said the helm officer, "that you want to become acquainted with *all* of me."

Nikolas felt himself blush. He had hoped this little "date" of theirs might eventually lead to something amorous, but he hadn't expected Idun to be so blunt about it.

"Well, yes," he replied. "Yes, I do."

"With every facet of me?" she asked.

Nikolas couldn't believe it. "Every facet," he assured her. "Every last bit of you."

"Thank you. I wanted to make certain," Idun told him.

Then she came at him in a blur of motion.

Admiral McAteer looked out his office window at the San Francisco Bay and the island of Alcatraz that sat in the center of it, and decided that it was officially a beautiful day.

Not that he cared all that much about the view. It only mattered to him as a symbol of how far he had come and how much he had achieved to get there.

What made the day so beautiful was the prospect of having Lt. Shalay on the *Stargazer.*

Picard might very well recognize the Bolian for what he was—McAteer's spy. But even if he did, he couldn't keep Shalay from observing what went on there. And with a 28-year-old in charge of the ship, a *lot* had to be going on. The admiral was confident of that.

Once he got his hands on the right information, Picard would be cannon fodder. Likewise, his first officer. And next to fall would be the esteemed Admiral Mehdi, who had made the rash decision to promote those two in the first place.

As McAteer was thinking that, his intercom came alive with the voice of his assistant. "Admiral?"

"Yes, Mr. Merriweather?"

"Sir, I have a communication from Captain Picard on the *Stargazer.* I believe it's a response to the orders you sent."

McAteer smiled to himself. He had looked forward to seeing Picard's face when he learned that yet *another* second officer was being foisted on him. Now was his chance.

"Thank you," he told Merriweather.

Then he tapped out a command on his keyboard, brought up a list of messages that had been sent to him, and noted the one that was labeled

"Picard." With a deep feeling of satisfaction, he opened the message and saw the captain's face appear on the monitor screen.

McAteer leaned back in his chair. *I've got you now,* he thought.

Picard looked nettled, even a little annoyed. However, the admiral didn't sympathize in the least. There was no room for 28-year-old captains in Starfleet, nor was there room for men like Mehdi who tried to put them there. If Picard thought he was discomfited now, he would absolutely *hate* what was in store for him.

"I must say, sir," the captain of the *Stargazer* began, "I'm at a bit of a loss. You seem to think Commander Wu is inclined to transfer off this vessel. In fact, nothing could be further from the truth. Wu tells me she has every intention of staying right here."

McAteer felt his face go hot. "What?" he said out loud.

"It's true," said Picard, "that she spoke with Captain Rudolfini and discussed the openings that have occurred on the *Crazy Horse.* But she wanted me to emphasize that she is not going to fill *either* of those openings." He smiled. "I repeat, Admiral, so there will be no further confusion—Commander Wu isn't going *anywhere."*

McAteer cursed long and volubly. Either his source on the *Crazy Horse* had been lying to him—which he sincerely doubted—or Picard had somehow gotten Wu to change her mind.

But why would in heaven's name she do that? Wu prided herself on her efficiency, sometimes to a fault. What could possibly keep her shackled to a captain several years her junior, a man as raw as one of the oysters the admiral had eaten at lunch?

And what was he going to tell Shalay? That Wu had decided to stay on the *Stargazer* after all? That he had resigned his position on the *New Orleans* for nothing?

Maybe, the admiral told himself, he could come up with a reason to relieve Wu of her duties on Picard's ship. Then he could insert Shalay as he had planned.

No, he argued inwardly. *You can't.*

It was *his* order that had placed Wu on the *Stargazer* in the first place. If he got rid of her now, it would look like he had made a bad choice, and he hadn't gotten to be an admiral in Starfleet by making himself look bad.

McAteer pounded his fist on his wooden desk, shivering everything on it. Damn Picard, he thought. Damn Wu. And damn Mehdi for putting him in this position in the first place.

But the war wasn't over. Eventually, Picard would make a mistake. And when he did, McAteer would be there to capitalize on it.

Nikolas opened his eyes and found himself in sickbay.

"What am I—?"

"Doing here?" Greyhorse said, finishing the question for him. The doctor was standing to one side of the ensign's biobed, checking its readouts. "You had a little accident."

"Accident . . . ?" Nikolas muttered.

"That's correct. In the ship's gymnasium."

It started to come back to him. He was sparring with Idun. She had asked some pretty startling questions. And then . . .

"She hit me," the ensign realized.

"Several times in succession," said Greyhorse, "if the bruises you sustained were any indication."

Nikolas shook his head. "Amazing."

"I agree," said the doctor.

He wasn't speaking to the ensign when he said it. He was gazing in another direction, as if lost in thought.

"Doctor Greyhorse?" said Nikolas.

Greyhorse turned to him, his eyes still a little out of focus. "Sorry. I was just thinking of . . . another patient."

He didn't mention who it might be. But then, Nikolas didn't really care. He had other fish to fry.

Swinging his legs aside, he sat up and said, "I think I'm okay now. Mind if I go?"

Greyhorse gave him a disparaging look. "What sort of physician would I be if I released someone who had just been worked over by one of the Asmund sisters?"

The ensign frowned. "Just how long do you think it'll be before I can get out of here?"

The doctor shrugged. "That's hard to say. Mr. Nikolas. In the meantime, just out of curiosity . . . what did Lieutenant Asmund do to catch you at such a disadvantage?"

Nikolas described the maneuver to Greyhorse—at least, to the extent that he could remember it. Then, a little curious himself, he said, "Why do you ask?"

To the ensign's surprise, Greyhorse went red in the face. "I'm your doctor," he said, a note of annoyance in his voice. "If I'm to treat you, I need to know how you were injured."

It made sense, Nikolas thought. But for just a moment there . . .

No, he told himself. Not again. He had gotten into enough trouble lately by misinterpeting what someone was thinking.

From now on, the ensign resolved, he would stay out of people's heads—especially when they fought like a Klingon.